Chapter 1

The patter of velvet rain on the moss-covered slates nudged Dr. Dell from his slumber. As he became self-aware, he smiled.

He could hear his beloved pair of German shorthaired pointers clanking dishes in the kitchen below, lapping water, letting him know they had survived the night. As he eased his small frame off the tiny fold-out cot, the flooring creaked like an old oak in a windstorm. Looking out over the knotted pole railing, Dr. Dell couldn't help but admire the immensity of Mount St. Helens. The lopsided peak, still smoldering three decades after its cataclysmic explosions, filled the loft's triangular windows. A million visitors each year came to take photographs from the base of the monster volcano, blithely assuming it was finished killing. As a scientist, Dr. Dell knew better. Humans were so stupid.

A glance down from the bedroom loft revealed a scene of far less majesty than the snow-capped peak outside. The interior looked like the aftermath of a rave party. Pills and bone-white powder covered the small room's cheap mirrored tabletops. Clear bottles with liquid remnants lay interspersed with funnels, latex tubing, and scales. The room had a cold, clinical feel even though the Franklin stove quietly crackled with the last of a quartered fir stump. Two young women lay intertwined, unmoving, on the pillow-top couch.

Dr. Dell padded down the stairs and into the rustic kitchen, where his eager pets mobbed him, licking his face. He rubbed them vigorously behind the ears before gently shooing them away. Pulling open the refrigerator door, he saw the disgusting contents. *Milk.*

He grabbed both jugs, twisted off the caps, and glugged both gallons down the drain. He fought the urge to vomit, almost succumbing when a tiny spatter of white foam hit one lens of his glasses. The collection of milk represented all he hated. *Dairy farmers were no better than*

1

thieves, kidnappers, and murderers. Their product was often filled with fake growth hormones and force fed to children under the guise of government lunch programs. Dr. Dell had had enough. His animal rights army would right all those wrongs.

Moving with determination, Dr. Dell picked up two tins of lantern kerosene and refilled the milk jugs. The unpleasant smell obliged him to breathe through his mouth. He let some of the fuel slosh onto a pile of dish sponges and watched the light pink, blue, and yellow turn dark. With the point of a steak knife, he punched a hole in the middle of each sponge, just big enough to admit the delicate wooden stem of a vanilla incense stick. The crude ignition-delay devices would smolder like wet cedar cones for at least an hour. He would be fifty miles away before the punks burned their way down to start the inferno.

Dr. Dell stood still for a moment, imagining the hiss of flame penetrating the containers, then the ensuing lake of fire spreading across the spruce floor, to the curtains and the old couch. No matter, the women were already dead. Grabbing his duffel bag, he stuffed his notebooks into a zippered pocket, pushed open the screen door, and threw down the tailgate of the SUV hybrid backed up by the front porch.

Both dogs, Speedy and Mango, sprang up and over both rows of seats, tumbling and fighting like schoolchildren for a coveted spot next to the driver. As Dr. Dell pulled away, he said a prayer for the two girls, whom he knew only by their nicknames. Certainly, some god of something could find a place in heaven for their devoted souls. The day to eliminate the white noise of human existence had finally dawned.

Chapter 2

Investigative Reporter Colton Wiley normally hated attending political press conferences, but he had a smug notion today was going to feel different.

Pink tents adorned a slim stretch of lawn in front of Seattle City Hall as Cole nestled into the throng of other reporters. He noticed right away he was the only guy not wearing a tie. An "End Homelessness" banner hung behind a podium as the mayor began to speak. Flashing still-camera lights created a slow-motion strobe effect on the dreary midday canvas. Television live trucks hummed with activity from a side street.

"It's the compassionate thing to do," boomed the mayor's voice over a pair of speakers. "Beginning immediately, the new law allows these tents in Seattle parks and on any sidewalk between midnight and six A.M."

Cole half listened as he read a media release passed down through the crowd like a collection plate during church. It stated in bold print that the city was going to pay half the three hundred thousand dollars needed to provide these *"innovative, low-cost shelters,"* while a federal grant took care of the rest. *"To help those in need stay out of the rain,"* Cole read in silence, thinking, *if that's the goal, move the hell out of Seattle.*

Everyone who met Cole told him he looked like he was supposed to be on television. At 30 years old, his Midwestern looks weren't striking, but his broad shoulders and steady gaze gave him a certain air of authority with an audience. His resume brought him respect from rival reporters and a sense of dread from the subjects of his reports. It was never a good day if Colton Wiley showed up at your doorstep asking questions.

Cole zipped up his leather jacket and motioned for his videographer to stop recording the mayor and start following him.

3

"Urban camping. Sounds fun," Cole whispered beneath his colleagues' headphones just before he stepped forward and struck a match. He gently flicked the small flame onto the closest neon tent. *Poof!* It erupted into a flash of orange flames and quickly melted into a glob of evil-smelling black goo. Cole had recognized the flammable, recalled material half a block away.

As a stunned cadre of officials and media stood openmouthed, Cole's understated comment won the day for KZPR-TV: "I'm not sure your program is such a good idea Mr. Mayor."

Cole sauntered away, pretending not to see the angry press aide weaving her way through the crowd toward him. His cell phone vibrated before he had to stop and listen to her complaints. An image of a raging forest fire on his screen let him know who was calling.

"What's up, Nolan? I swear I didn't post that undercover video of your ex-girlfriend on YouTube."

Nolan Burke was about the coolest, most laid-back guy Cole had ever met. He wasn't in the "sources" file hidden inside Cole's electronic contact list, but in the "friends" file (though untitled—as an arson investigator for the United States Forest Service, Burke could get in serious hot water for palling around with the likes of Colton Wiley).

"You should take a drive. Right now. It involves dead bodies, so don't dick around," Nolan said, uncharacteristically ignoring Cole's gibe, which cried out for a comeback line or two.

Nolan Burke's tone of voice set Cole's heart going half a beat faster, though not out of fear for himself or his friend—those emotions weren't naturally part of his repertoire. The adrenaline was seeping into his veins because he could already taste a great story.

Cole knew whatever adventure was about to come next, he didn't need permission to pursue it. KZPR-TV's management gave its best reporter a very wide berth when tracking down leads for new investigations. Cole had won that trust by proving that a state legislator was paying high-dollar prostitutes for S-and-M sex while his taxpayer-hired security guards waited outside, and by videotaping the Russian mob buying automatic weapons on the Seattle docks. He repeatedly found stories that drew large audiences to the nightly newscast which in turn filled the KZPR coffers with advertising cash.

"Give me an address and I'm there," Cole shot back to his buddy.

Nolan's voice was partially washed out by the loud crackle of spotty reception. Cole pressed the receiver tight against his ear and jotted down shorthand notes on the back of a manila folder.

"South through Chehalis. Hang a left down Highway Twelve toward the Gifford Pinchot National Forest. A few pastures after Morton, hang a right and follow the river about ten miles. You'll see my truck off to the right. I put up some caution tape to block the access road. Obviously, cell coverage sucks, so hit your horn when you get there. I'm sending my tech back to the office with some lab samples in a couple of hours. I'll make sure it's just you and me here. Move it, dude!" Nolan warned.

He paused a second, then added, "And, Cole, no photographer. You're going to have shoot this yourself. No quick turn for tonight's newscast. Don't tell your bosses where you're going."

Perfect. Because Seattle ranked as the thirteenth-largest TV market in America, seasoned reporters had long ago lost interest in going solo—they were above working without a producer, photographer, and editor. This was perfect! To Cole, the one-man-band or "backpack journalist" arrangement meant he didn't have to count on anyone else. He'd learned long-ago the ability to pre-focus a camera on a light stand, extended to six feet, three inches, before he stepped into the frame to record himself solo.

Cole hung up the phone and resisted the urge to snag a high-dollar HD camera out of the news van. Keeping this self-assignment secret was more important than annoying the videographer's union. His personal camera equipment was mostly set up for undercover surveillance, but a change of lenses would more than suffice. He jumped into his navy-blue truck, sped past the Pike Place Market, and swung wide around the skateboarder with a full-sleeve tattoo slaloming down the street in his Death Cab for Cutie T-shirt.

For an investigative reporter, driving anywhere was perhaps the sickest, most twisted trip down memory lane imaginable. Most travelers looking off Interstate 5 in South Seattle would see the colorful art adorning the Vietnamese restaurants in the International district. Not Cole—he thought about videotaping rats in the kitchens there. Normal people saw Seahawks Stadium and pictured the lime-green sea of fans cheering inside; Cole saw it and thought about which professional football players got drunk and beat their wives. A triple murder at a house up on Beacon Hill . . . a corrupt politician who stole tax money in Tacoma . . . a registered sex offender living next to an elementary school in Olympia. Those were the associations that popped into Cole's head as he drove through the heart of the state.

After several hours of driving, Cole spotted some crime-scene tape strung between hemlock boughs. He pulled onto the soggy shoulder of the rural road. There was no smell of freshness in the damp air. When rain fell anywhere else on earth, that sweet aroma of clean chlorophyll Febrezed the landscape, but not in coastal Washington. The constant showers in the long, dark months between October and April created a terrarium of sorts, permeating the air

6

with the faint odor of dead worms left over from a slow fishing day. Getting out of his truck, Cole grabbed two mainstays of his work: a digital video camera and a loaded Kahr PM9 handgun. He strapped the gun to his left ankle, and the camera to his right hand, then tapped the truck's horn but didn't wait for a response. He slipped under the roped-off area. The 350-year-old cedar beasts here were at least a meter thick and towered higher than many of the buildings in downtown Seattle. Rain didn't fall on Cole under the umbrella of its canopy. The trail ahead was squishy, but there was no mud—a foot-deep cushion of lichens, fungi, and bright green moss made dirt a foreign concept. It was like walking on thick carpet in a flooded basement. Cole could see his pal in the distance slowly sweeping the ground with a paint brush.

Nolan Burke was a towering African American former firefighter from Eastern Washington. Growing up the son of a fruit farmer, Nolan loved working outdoors: rain or shine. The government-issued badge hanging from his sleeve said he was 32 years old, but the last time Cole went with Nolan to the county fair, the age-guessing carnival worker had to give up a stuffed lion after saying she believed Nolan was 22.

When Cole first met Nolan, six years prior, it was also in the middle of nowhere, surrounded by ashes and death. Nolan had started his Forest Service career as a gung-ho smoke jumper, routinely plunging from airplanes into blazing hell worlds.

Once the smoke jumpers hit the ground with a shovel, a chain saw, and a few days' drinking water, they would start slicing away mountainside vegetation in hopes of starving the fire of fuel. If it worked, they were heroes to a few remote cabin owners. If their attempt failed, the firefighters dropped their tools in a footrace for their lives. That happened at the Black Canyon fire. Seasonal firefighters were mostly college kids and convicts. Anyone who wanted a bit of adventure and some pocket change could spend the summer mostly mopping up smoldering grass with buckets of water or throwing spadefuls of dirt on long-gone brush fires.

But at Black Canyon, things went very wrong. An inexperienced cleanup crew strayed down a dead-end road with no radios. There was no way they could have known what was closing in on them. Cole heard it from Nolan a million times; how he wished with all his heart he could have been a hero that day, but six dead kids said otherwise. They had tried to hide in a shallow creek, with paper-thin pop-up heat shields as the only protection against a 1,500-degree flash fire. But the heat wasn't what killed them. The fire sucked every drop of oxygen out of the air to feed its furious need to grow, and they suffocated. Lying outdoors, in thousands of acres of National Forest, they died for lack of air. Cole could never reconcile that in his head.

Cole was roaming the woods in search of new clues that might lead to a story about homicidal arson when he ran across Nolan. Neither needed a friend, but both needed a beer. Over the years, the converse became more often the case.

Refocused on the burned cabin in front of him, Cole watched Nolan squatting amid the smoking embers. Cole's normally perfect sandy hair was matted flat from the moisture in the air. Droplets of rain sizzled into steam in a couple of hotspots left from what had been hot fire the day before. Cole imagined the satellite image: a canvas of jade and lime and emerald hues in a peaceful patch of the Gifford Pinchot National Forest. If anyone could then zoom in, they'd see a darkened square, black in the center and brown at the edges, where the burned cabin used to sit. Zoom in closer, and you could see two small rectangles of yellow: body bags filled with charred torsos, skulls, teeth, and bones.

"Holy crap!" Cole gasped to his soot-covered friend. "You're the expert, but I'm guessing you won't find the frazzled cord of an old space heater to blame here."

"Not likely." Nolan stood and stepped over a thousand tiny particles of blackened glass. "I can still smell the accelerant."

"It looks like a meth lab to me, Nolan. Piles of jars and beakers. An off-the-grid cabin. Come on, man! Don't you think this is a case of divine justice? A set of cranked-up tweakers blow themselves to bits trying to make ice! Whatever happened here saved the taxpayers a million bucks in dental care and prison food," shouted Cole.

Nolan pulled some latex gloves from his pocket, threw them to Cole, and motioned for him to slip them on.

"Look, pretty boy, when I tell you my suspicions you won't have to pull out your pencil and notebook. You'll get it as soon as the words leave my mouth. I called you not just because I trust you—I'm going to need *your* help. You, Mr. Investigative Reporter, are going to have better sources than I do on this deal. Animal rights groups have been committing acts of non-violent domestic terrorism for three decades . . ." Nolan paused. "How about if I told you this is the first time, they killed somebody?"

Every major animal rights group on the west coast considered Colton Wiley one of its own. It was not only a strange pairing of personalities, but proof that God had a sense of humor. Members and sympathizers of dozens of groups spent their nights clad in black masks and armed with bolt cutters, freeing minks from fur farms. They sneaked into university research labs and stole detailed research out of locked cabinets. Some fringe members might even toss a Molotov cocktail or two through the window of a newly constructed mega home, built on the edge of a pristine spotted-owl infested forest preserve. Animal-rights groups historically had only one ironclad rule: do no harm to animal or human. Not an especially original motto, but one that all believers steadfastly lived by. They spent countless hours on stakeouts to make sure whatever facility they were targeting was empty. Members were free-spirited ideologues, not killers. Yes, arson and theft and trespassing were crimes, but the committed activist believed that twisting a screw into the head of a cynomolgus monkey, to study the effects of brain injuries in humans, was far more egregious. They hated animal-killers but were not killers themselves.

When the Department of Homeland Security was created after 9-11, for reasons more political than anything else, a dozen left-leaning animal and environmental rights groups were labeled domestic terrorist organizations. Given that their activities to aid animals and protect nature had never harmed a fly, Cole considered it a strange decision. For years, federal prosecutors had said, "*What if* they threw a fire bomb through a lab and the janitor was sleeping inside?" Or "*What if* a firefighter who arrived to put out the blaze had a roof fall on him?"

Cole loved animal rights for reasons that any activist would find revolting. He knew that stories about abused animals scored huge ratings with viewers. There was no better TV than videotape of a choking kitten with a tube down its throat being used to teach ambulance techs how to incubate an infant, or of a starving dog chained in the middle of a snowy yard. In simple terms, Cole exposed many horrible abuses and held the abusers up to public ridicule (and sometimes sent them to jail) because it was *popular*. Animal-rights leaders mistook his efforts for activism, and members flooded the investigative unit with tips, so Cole could help animals. And help them he did—because it helped his career. In turn, there wasn't a reporter in the country who knew more about the inner workings of their very secret societies. He knew members' real names. He was on their covert operations e-mail list and, at times included as a viewer on their live video streams during illegal field operations. Agents from the Seattle FBI office were so peeved about his connections, they successfully petitioned bosses in D.C. to place Cole on their terror watch list, just to let him know he was mixing with the wrong crowd.

Nolan motioned his friend to his side.

"I'm guessing this fire occurred last evening, but the medical examiner hasn't had time to get here yet to give me an exact time of death for these two females. I think his day job is selling used cars."

"Figures," Cole said without a hint of surprise. "Females? How do you know? Yeesh."

"Basic anatomy. Fire didn't burn hot enough to completely wipe out their forms. They had on matching necklaces. Mean anything to you?"

Cole tried to ignore the horrifying stench of the burnt flesh by breathing through his mouth as he reached out to rub the soot from a blackened silver medallion. The pendant looked like a farrier-hammered coin from the era of the Roman Empire, but it was clearly an artist's rendition, not an expensive artifact. The metal was rough, like a nugget, but with a smooth sliver of crescent moon jutting out of the center. On the back, someone had used a dull knife or nail to gouge out an alphanumeric code: "N5G." Ignoring his friend's suggestion that taking notes wasn't necessary, Cole jotted down the digits on the inside of his arm with a black marker.

"You're right, Nolan," he said. "That crescent moon symbol screams, 'Hey! We're with the Animal Liberation Brigade.' It's a relatively new group. Small. Tight knit. Super mysterious. These animal-rights fanatics have their own symbols—not that different from gangs that craft an identity by repeatedly tagging train cars. I've seen the groups use dolphins, fake dog tags, burning towers—even tiny snail shells filled with sand—as symbols. That 'N5G' notation in addition to the crescent moon is new to me. Could be a subgroup or a project. Hell, it might not mean anything more than 'that lump of flesh is Nikki, and this pile of ash is Gigi, and they've been sleeping together five years.' Give me a few days. If it's relevant, it won't take me too long to figure it out."

11

"I know it won't. You've got more contacts inside that animal-rights culture than anyone on the planet. The Animal Liberation Brigade left its signature at four different unsolved arsons this month . . ." Nolan paused and carefully slipped a small shovel under one of the dead girls' shoulder to look for more clues. "They burned down a sheepskin factory, a dog track, and a couple of restaurants that served foie gras. They spray-painted that moon at every scene to take credit and get their name in the paper. Nobody gets hurt except some insurance company. That game just changed." Nolan looked up to the misty sky. "It's time to start tapping your critter-loving friends. I need a solid lead. This is a double-murder that officially ends the days of 'do no harm.'"

Chapter 3

The snaking path of the yellow line in the Highlander's headlights put Dr. Dell's brain on autopilot as the miles ticked by. There had been no time to sleep. Honing the final elements of his research was more important. Disappointment crept into his mind, and he wished he had stuck around to see the cabin erupt into a billowing mass of smoke and ash.

Dr. Dell had grown up in the shadows of the University of Washington campus. His mother, a plant biologist who came to the States from the Soviet Union, had adopted him before his first birthday. She named him Hadar. Tired of hiding her Jewish roots from her Communist bosses, she had slipped away to an Israeli-run safe house while in Venice for a conference. She couldn't have kids of her own but was lucky enough to find a partner who enjoyed the idea of adopting. His father was an architect with a degree from the University of Mumbai, then Oxford. He had an office right up the hall from his mother's laboratory. Their household was in a constant state of loud, educated debate. Especially when the discussion ran to religion, Middle Eastern politics, modern art, or astronomy, things could get a little heated.

Both parents had also shared a passion for the outdoors, and they took their only child camping nearly every weekend. In summer, they slept in a tent, snuggling and laughing while their sleeping bags, piled like cotton bales, kept them from the night chill. In spring and fall, they would rent a yurt or a teepee. There was always a fire burning. Little Hadar would dry out his eyes staring at a slow-burning log, waiting for it to collapse on itself.

Driving south approaching Oregon, Dr. Dell could still smell that campfire. He wondered aloud if that pleasant scent was from his daydreaming, or cigarette smoke that had soaked into his Argyll sweater vest.

The blur of brown in the middle of the road appeared so suddenly, Dr. Dell thought at first, he had nodded off. Reality set in with the shattering of glass and the screech of his tires, punctuated by the horrid thump of a carcass slamming into the hood. The dogs howled in pain and alarm as thick antlers exploded through the windshield and into the front seat. Dr. Dell also felt his shoulder momentarily dislocate, then slam back into place, while his long, curly dark hair flew forward, wrapping around the edges of the inflated airbag. After veering and spinning down a shallow ravine, the entire mass of metal, flesh, bone, and blood jolted to a stop. Sprawled across the dashboard and hood lay most of an eight-point buck. Through the blown windshield, Dr. Dell watched two does bound into the forest, abandoning their leader and mate. He draped his injured arm around the deer's neck while running his other hand over the warm fur of the beautiful, dying creature's chest. He could feel the heart thumping slower and slower, until the tense neck muscles went limp. He began to sob uncontrollably.

"Forgive me, beautiful friend!"

As the adrenaline of the moment wore off, he fell into a quiet state of tears. The devastating impact of the event went beyond what most people could comprehend. Dr. Dell felt like a father who had just accidently shot his child dead while cleaning his gun.

As a boy, he had spent many of those nights in camp with his parents, dreaming what it would be like to be an animal. In the tent, he listened to the sounds of wolves fighting for dominance at the edge of the tree line. He was never scared. He would envision himself as one of the fighters: fangs bared, lips curled back, only partially seeing his competition through amber eyes narrowed to slits. As he drifted off to sleep, curled up next to his mother, he could feel himself running on all fours. The movement across the ground was cold and furious. His heart pounded, but he never got tired.

A heavy thud snapped Dr. Dell out of his dreamy reverie.

"Hey, buddy!" shouted the state trooper, banging his long metal flashlight on the roof of the SUV. "There's blood everywhere. How much of this is yours? Are you with me? Can you tell me what day it is? You been drinking, sir?"

The officer's voice droned on and on. Dr. Dell could hear the questions but answering was not on his mind. The front end of his car was destroyed, but the driver's door remained unscathed. He stepped out of the smashed SUV, ignoring the officer's instructions to stay put.

With two quick motions, Dr. Dell was the wolf. He drew the serrated section of his knife blade against the officer's left jugular vein, pulling hard from back to front, toward himself. With surgical precision, he rolled his wrist and slit the other side of the throat. For good measure, he sank the blade straight through the larynx. A high, wheezing rush of breath seeped out. *Odd,* he thought. It sounded much like when, as a lad, he used to wedge a nice, wide piece of green grass between his thumbs and forefinger to make a whistle. Sort of funny, given the circumstances.

"How does that feel, Officer? You don't really have to answer, of course—it's rhetorical."

As the trooper lay dying in the ditch, Dr. Dell stepped over the body and sat back down inside his SUV. He leaned over and kissed the deer on the lips.

"Puppies, time to go! We have work to do."

The dogs, Mango and Speedy, had names though Dr. Dell never uttered them out loud. He wanted them to love him and him only and allowing another human to speak to them in such a personal manner might taint that very special relationship.

Dr. Dell quickly stripped the uniform off his victim, leaving him there in T-shirt and boxers. One of the dogs was limping badly, encouraged by the other to keep moving until they got to the trooper's black and white Taurus. After turning off the overhead emergency lights, Dr.

Dell used the turn signal and got back onto the quiet highway. He was guessing he might have a

good half hour before anyone figured out that the dead man in the ditch wasn't the driver of the

deer-damaged SUV. By then, the cop car would be at the bottom of a fast-flowing river, and he

would be far outside the initial search grid for suspects. Killing one person was exhilarating.

Killing millions was going to feel damn near orgasmic!

Chapter 4

The chaos of a newsroom made the center of a three-ring circus feel like a funeral parlor. The scanners thumped a mix of blaring sirens and the panting voices of cops chasing low-life criminals twenty-four hours a day. The assignment desk fielded hundreds of calls from tipsters each hour. Every citizen who saw black helicopters above their home at night, and every mental patient who called to complain about the creepy-crawlies in their padded room wanted to talk to a warm body. Crazy people hated voice mail.

Assistant news director Chuck Reynolds knew how to filter out the clutter and focus on what mattered most.

"Call that lying-sack-of-shit public relations lady at home!" Reynolds growled. "The union rep just told me the garbage strike is a go!" He had moved well beyond fuming and punctuated the order by kicking the newsroom's recycling bin.

The man had a face for radio, which perhaps made him the most valuable asset behind the scenes in the entire television newsroom. At 59, he still had most of his hair, and not quite all of it silver. He hadn't changed its style since the 1960s. Fat, with black glasses perched over puffy red cheeks, he well knew that if he had chosen to be an on-air reporter earlier in life, they would have fired him long before now.

"She interviewed with us a couple of hours ago and said the city had worked out a deal to avoid it. I swear if she doesn't get out of bed and come down here for a live apology during the eleven-o'clock news, I will post her damn social security number and home address on our Web site! I might find a few college spring break photos of her, too!"

He had seen many pretty faces, fake boobs, and chiseled anchorman chins over the years. Few of them could look credible without Reynolds's help and guidance. Whether it was

17

researching the latest interstate expansion proposal, dialing a video uplinked from Yakima, or motivating photographers to skip lunch to shoot video of a boat on fire, this self-professed news junkie always figured out how to get the job done. Reynolds figured out ways to force or cajole unmotivated reporters to do their best on the treadmill of yearly stories. Getting talent excited about covering the murder trial of a heroin-addicted mother who had cooked her baby in the oven wasn't too hard. Having a reporter volunteer to drive up to Snoqualmie Pass and tell viewers, for fifteen days running, that it was indeed *still* snowing on the mountain, took a Swiss-army-knife of personal skills.

Reynolds owed his career to perfecting the daily grind of news, but he loved investigative journalism more than he loved his own children (who dutifully called on Father's Day and Christmas.) Build a bond with your family or build a bond with the newsroom—you couldn't have it both ways. Peeking into the black-ops lives of the investigative team, provided Reynolds the elixir he needed to survive the mundane. And Chuck's favorite high came in the person of Colton Wiley. The pair trusted each other; something that took years to accomplish, especially since Cole hated authority, resented structure, and never believed anything anybody told him. Reynolds gave Cole great leeway and although technically his boss, always treated Cole as a peer.

Reynolds continued to rant while pacing around the newsroom's worn carpet.

"Better yet, tell that PR garbage bitch I'll send Colton Wiley to unravel her life if she does not come clean with us on this goddamned strike!"

Reynolds's vacant threat reminded him that he had not seen his star reporter all day. He slipped into his office and punched in a quick text message.

"You alive?"

"Alive and not carrying a gun, per station policy," came the immediate response from Cole.

"Call. Heard scanner traffic about missing state trooper near OR border. Can U check?"

"Already found him. Standing over his body right now. Very dead. No photographer. Send satellite truck to milepost 30. I'll bail U out for 11 news.

* * *

Cole and Nolan stood shoulder to shoulder peering into a ditch, both using a cupped hand to shield their eyes from the glare of passing headlights. They looked like conjoined twins in the rapidly flashing ambulance lights. While following the medical examiner's van, carrying the two burned bodies from the cabin fire, the pair diverted to the fatal trooper's crime scene using a combination of luck and instinct.

The weight of a large corpse matted down three-foot-high weeds. The lack of structure at the scene let Cole know the real commanders had not yet arrived. He used the opening to get closer. He moved boldly down the embankment straight at the dead trooper, hoping Nolan's presence and badge would make it appear they were law enforcement partners. Nobody stopped them. *Gun missing from his tossed aside holster . . . blood around his neck not coagulated yet.* The name "Fitzgerald" stamped on a lapel pin, caked in dirt, lay unnoticed a few feet from the underwear clad body.

Cole turned his attention to the SUV. It would be mere moments before someone threw up a rope between squad cars to prevent contamination of the scene. He memorized every detail that might help describe the crime for his viewers during his upcoming live shot. Cole also noticed something that he knew he would not share with the public. Ripped to shreds by the windshield wipers and the broken glass, clumps of fur which stuck up in every direction smeared with blood and flaked with tinted glass. Cole could see five thin fingerlike lines running lightly over a small section of the dead deer's chest. Someone – a human – had stroked all the hair in the same direction. *Creepy.* He slid his Sony digital camera from his pocket and banged off thirty seconds of video inside the SUV, then eight seconds on a wide shot of the entire interior.

Hold still. He counted in his head. Any less than eight seconds, and editing was difficult. Cole panned another shot from the police lights on the highway, through the windshield, and onto a tighter shot of the deer's head. For good measure, he recorded several very tight cutaways: one of spattered blood on the door, another of a hoof propped up on the steering wheel. He moved away and recorded a final short segment of the exterior of the SUV, making sure not to get any footage of the state trooper's partially naked body. The station's producers would certainly use that most gruesome footage for the headline tease, so Cole took the high road and conducted some self-editing until the trooper's family could be notified.

As hard as he pushed, and as big a jerk as the world saw him to be, Cole held high ethical standards. He had them not because of his upbringing, but despite it. With the click of a mouse, the public could view Cole's work history, but he preferred to keep his personal life story, before he became a journalist, a bit murky. Slimy defense attorneys were always looking for a reason to turn a jury against him. His stories were always accurate, but the days of "as long as the facts are right you can't get sued" were long over. Slander cases were now all about "tone" and "context"—buzzwords for lawyers looking to score some big money from the bank known as a TV station. If they could get a jury to believe that Cole represented sloppy journalists over the years, it meant free money. A jury certainly didn't need to hear about his mentally ill mother and murderer father.

"Can I see some ID?" came a commanding voice from behind Cole.

Cole pretended to dig for his wallet. "Sorry, Officer. I was simply curious about what happened. My friend and I heard a commotion on the police scanner. I'll get out of your way. Again, really sorry, Man."

Cole kept moving up ditch, without looking the cop in the eye. He could tell that the guy didn't think he seemed suspicious. In a few steps, Cole disappeared into the blinding emergency lights and to freedom, with both his video clips and his anonymity intact. His smart phone buzzed with a dozen messages, many marked urgent. He called Chuck Reynolds.

"Jesus Christ Superstar! I'm going to have a heart attack! We have a newscast in twenty minutes. Where do we stand?" Reynolds barked into the phone.

Cole's relaxed demeanor oozed confidence even over a phone line.

"Relax, boss. I told you I'd get this done. I have exclusive video and enough details to make your ratings spike tonight. Don't give away the whole story in the anchor lead. How about leading off with something like; "A state trooper dies in the line of duty near the Oregon border. Police aren't talking, but our investigative reporter is live on the scene and is certain this was no accident."

"Perfect!" Reynolds shouted as Cole could hear him tapping the words into the computer, which, at the stroke of a key, put them up directly on the anchor's teleprompter. "The feed truck is a quarter mile up the road. Get there and give me some tape ASAP."

"We don't use tape anymore old man, but gotcha," Cole replied.

Cole jogged up to the KZPR-TV truck, which already had its massive dish locked on to an orbiting satellite.

The grisly videotape of the deer-versus-SUV crash was sent 22,000 miles up into space, and 22,000 miles back down to the station receiver in Seattle. Back when Cole started his career, that kind of instant image access was expensive and difficult to implement cleanly. Now it was cheaper, and perfect with the push of a button. Dishes whirred, buttons beeped, and—*bam!*—the complicated connection locked in between a satellite moving at ten times the speed of sound, and a parked truck. And he had no doubt that in another few years, even the operator pushing that button would be out of a job. Cell phone video and Skype were a much cheaper substitute.

"Cole? Come on, Cole. Can you hear me? Three minutes to the top of the show. Give me a thumbs-up. *Something.* You hear me? We need get an audio check now, or we have to bump the piece down the show."

Cole heard only the tail end of the director's chatter as he was putting in his custom earpiece. He waved at the camera.

"Ready to roll whenever you say 'go.'"

But instead of hearing "go," Cole heard the off-air audio feed of an anchor reading word for word the introduction he had thrown out to Reynolds. Cole had no notes, but he didn't need any. His style had always been simply to converse with the half-million viewers watching him on TV at home, as if he were telling his buddies a story at the bar. Cole knew his opening line would get everyone to stop brushing their teeth or finishing the dishes or checking their e-mail and pay attention to *him.*

"We have a cop killer on the loose," flowed from Cole's mouth with a hint of drama.

At that very second, Cole could envision employees at three other television newsrooms, and a few local newspaper editorial staffs, throwing up. They had just had their asses handed to them. Not only was Cole the only reporter on scene in time to go on TV live, but he had already confirmed that the death was no accident. That meant that every family in western Washington was flipping over to KZPR-TV along with most of the households on the Pacific coast of Canada.

"The body of a Washington state trooper is, at this moment, on its way to the Clark County Medical Examiner's Office. Stab wounds were apparent to me, but exactly what occurred here isn't going to be easy to figure out unless some unknown witness steps forward."

Cole wanted the video images to start running, but he had not given anyone the "roll" cue, so he started casually twirling his finger in a helicopter pattern. He'd worked with Chuck Reynolds so often, Cole could picture what was occurring in real time back inside the TV control room. The tiny space was filled with audio technicians, producers, directors, graphics creators, and wide-eyed interns hoping someday to be stars. Inside the low-lit room, a half second was eons, so when it took a full second for someone to punch the yellow button to put video on the air, Reynolds was always ready to erupt. Luckily for the crew, he rarely got his mouth open before images appeared. This time, a screen full of dead deer and a crushed SUV produced the kind of memorable TV where no one could avert their eyes. The story was flat-out mesmerizing. Cole paused and let the shocking footage sink in, then intentionally picked up his verbal pacing to add some excitement to his voice.

"I took these images of the interior of a sport-utility vehicle that had clearly been involved in an accident with a deer. The driver is nowhere to be found. First responders thought the dead man in the ditch nearby was that driver, then, after some time elapsed, realized it was, instead, a Washington State Patrolman. Police scanners are chattering with alerts to be on the lookout for someone with unexplained cuts, injuries, or blood on their clothes. The mystery person also likely stole the trooper's vehicle to escape . . ."

23

Cole spent a few minutes describing the scene and promising that KZPR-TV would stay on the story until this horrendous crime was solved. He wrapped it up with a serious look on his face, because it was now the right time to act the part of a concerned citizen. Inside, Cole smiled from ear to ear with glee over his exclusive. *Dead cop or not, this was amazing shit.*

****

Chuck Reynolds didn't have to fake it, because he wasn't on camera. He was elated. He ran to the newsroom and started shooing reporters and videographers out the door on side assignments.

He roared into the air, pointing at every employee in sight, "Cancel whatever plans you had for the night—or, for that matter, the weekend. *You* head south and take over at the scene. *You* head to the coroner's office. *You* find this trooper's family. *You* get a picture of the cop in uniform. I'm sure Cole has the name already; I'll text it to you all. Let's get a jump! Roll. Go. Go! Jesus! Don't trot—*run*! Go!"

Reynolds had had a few chances to move up the corporate ladder early in his career. He hesitated, though, after seeing *his* news director called into a meeting with bean counter accountants because they thought the newsroom's toilet paper budget was too high. Reynolds had always figured the adrenaline of chasing fires and windstorms would wear off and he'd grab that next rung. He seemed unaware that his drunken blackouts kept the title "assistant" permanently in front of "news director" on his business card. He had a messed-up personal life, but he was far from alone in that regard. To a newsman, it seemed almost like a badge of honor to commit fully to work and let one's home life go into the crapper. The vast majority of TV personalities had some form of extreme outlet to forget the blue-faced bodies of children they saw pulled from a local creek, or the bullet-riddled corpse of a south-side hooker. Reynolds often

24

wondered about Cole's coping mechanisms, but given his star reporter's expertise at keeping secrets, he figured it was a lost cause.

Chapter 5

It was hard to be silent with two cans of spray paint shoved into the pockets of a hooded sweatshirt. The metal ball inside for agitating the colorful chemical mix plunked against the concave bottom with each step. The group of five moved quickly down a narrow path a few clicks outside the town of Snohomish. Just before midnight, the stars were buried under a thin layer of clouds, making even the shadows invisible.

Wendell Canyon could see the barn lights at the Lukashenko farm, three-quarters of a mile to the left. He slid his tall, lanky body between the slats of a wooden fence and slunk toward the target. A light breeze brought the pungent stink of mink excrement. Apparently, cleaning out cages was a waste of time. This wasn't the Ritz, not by a long mile. It was more like a hospice that accepted Medicaid patients only—a filthy, squalid sty to spend your dying days.

The Lukashenkos were Washington's second-largest fur pelt producer, and animal rights activists regularly picketed the dirt road that led to their grimy kill operation. That didn't do much to scare this tight-knit clan, who earned upward of a million dollars a year stripping the skins from still-live mink. The industry always said they used humane slaughter methods, like dropping the furry creatures into a carbon dioxide-filled tank to knock them out before slitting them open.

Canyon wondered if the people lining up for the "showers" at Auschwitz had thought the Nazis humane.

A dog barked in the distance, but none of the warriors with Canyon was worried. After weeks of surveillance by other Animal Liberation Brigade volunteers, the team knew that the Lukashenkos didn't have a dog. In fact, the entire family would be far away for at least another twenty-four hours. It so happened that the Lukashenko boys were excellent wrestlers—their

26

names were in all the papers yesterday as they advanced to the state meet at the Tacoma Dome. The boys would likely win their weight divisions, get some medals draped around their thick necks, and stop at Dick's for greasy burgers and fries to celebrate. The smiles on their faces would evaporate the moment their car headlights shone on the open Morton-building doors.

The ALB raiders moved slowly but with purpose, alert lest some unforeseen uncle or nephew should be keeping tabs on the mink operation. Canyon walked to the center of the yard. Man-purse draped over his shoulder, he stood there in the open for a good five minutes, listening while the others hid behind a tall hedge separating the barns from a cedar grove. He was baiting anyone who might be near enough to see him, shout, or throw a light on inside. As expected, the only sound was the racket of the tree frogs.

Canyon understood that ALB's leader cared deeply about the animal rights cause, but there was a more sinister side as well. ALB had put the word out it was seeking a new breed of recruit: one not adverse to committing crimes which included violence. All the animal rights groups Canyon previously tried to join wanted eager, young activists who would hand out brochures on college campuses and help raise awareness of monkey smugglers, scientists who performed brutal vivisections on rabbits, and chicken producers who might be spreading salmonella in their packing plants. The volunteers were more like flower children. *Speak softly. Protest like Gandhi. Hold a sign at a rally.* But the public wasn't paying enough attention, so the Animal Liberation Brigade was preparing to up the ante. Nobody asked Canyon for his resume'. If they had, all they would have found out is that at 12-years-old he was technically "born" on a piece of paper in the fifteenth-floor lobby of the U.S. Citizenship and Immigration Services Building in Los Angeles. If asked, Canyon's father told strangers the family's heritage was Persian. It sounded so nice, so exotic.

He grew up as American as any kid on his street but decided long ago that eating meat was cruel. He never considered himself a common criminal, but more a Robin Hood for both animals and underachievers. He was the kind of guy who considered trespassing signs optional reading and who saw the person he stole a necklace from as merely the temporary vehicle for a more equitable distribution of the world's wealth. Wendell Canyon also happened to believe that the Lukashenkos didn't need ten-thousand mink.

After five full minutes of silent watch, he threw up the all-clear sign. The others appeared like ghosts at his side. Canyon popped a slipknot on his backpack, releasing a small pair of bolt cutters. Sprinting to the sliding metal doors, he bore down with all his strength, snapping the only barrier between the team and a successful mission. He pulled hard on the cold metal handle, and four human bodies breezed past him in a rush to enter.

The tinny clink of wire doors swinging open soon filled the vast barn as the group fanned out and started flipping open the tiers of cages. Some mink leaped from their kennels and bounded for the door; others, scared and confused, froze in place.

Canyon shouted encouragement to the timid ones, louder than he should have. "Head for the woods! Be free! Get your furry little butts outta here! Scram! Stay and you die!"

Reaching a thick-gloved hand inside a cage, he scooped the terrified, biting, clawing creature out onto the floor. Another member recorded with a digital, action-helmet camera, and hoped to post the illicit mission on the Web before sunrise.

Canyon started in one corner of the football-field-size barn and began herding a sea of hopping, darting dark blurs toward the dirt driveway. After ten minutes, only a few hundred mink were still in sight, many sitting in the piles of sewage that had accumulated under the bottom tier of cages. The rest were fleeing into the night, for the first time feeling the soft, mushy ground under their pads.

Free at last, Canyon rejoiced. *Thank God Almighty, they're free at last.*

He and his animal-loving crew all felt that same emotional surge, which felt not so different from the high of tooting a line of cocaine. Still, Canyon had no illusions about what was happening just past the farm lights. Great horned owls could hear the creatures tumbling across the forest floor, and their large pupils could gather enough starlight to pick up the fleeing shapes. Dozens of mink were surely already prey. And if they did elude the airborne raptors, there was always Highway 2. Big rigs, carrying logs down from the Cascades, ran fast and late, and they didn't brake for anything less consequential than a human. The stream of trucks, along with drivers who had had a few beers at the Pissing Well Ale House, were soon strewing the rural road with a slick coating of mink.

Canyon gave the paint can a quick shake and hit the farm building wall with a message: "*Mink Murderers Are Terrorists Too! ALB!*"

"Let's find those breeding logs!" he hissed to the rest of the team as soon as the laggards had hied off into the woods.

Canyon smashed the small padlock off a storage locker in the corner. Inside was a pair of three-ring binders. He flipped them open to make sure.

"Jackpot!" he crowed.

Canyon knew that the detailed notes on when and where each mink was bred, born, and sold were the real key to destroying a mink farmer's worth. It was a felony to catch wild mink and then sell their fur, and the U.S. Department of Agriculture eagerly enforced the law. To get around it, pelt farmers inbred purchased stock. When the feds came to do an inspection, the logs were proof they could do business. Without them, the Luskashenkos couldn't even recapture their own mink that were hiding in the nearby woods after the raid. The farm would go out of business permanently.

Canyon hit the edges of them with a butane cigar blowtorch and dropped them into a metal feed can pretending to warm up his hands over the flames.

"Now, tell me that doesn't make you feel all warm and fuzzy inside," Canyon said, laughing as the other ALB members momentarily huddled around.

As the last pages turned black, they all left without a word, disappearing back down the river trail. Following procedure from the unwritten ALB code of conduct, each ran in opposite directions, careful to avoid stepping on anything with shiny eyes that might happen to be slinking through the darkness. By the time the expanse of woods began to lighten Canyon knew he'd be sound asleep. He hoped Dr. Dell would at least hear about his efforts but suspected such a brilliant visionary had little time for such mundane missions. Canyon knew he'd have to do far more to compete with Dr. Dell's visions for a new world order.

Chapter 6

Without even opening the tent flap, Montana Harms could tell it was going to be another perfect day for climbing. The early morning sun was already warming up the granite wall that pressed against her hip. Fifteen hundred feet straight up Goat Canyon, she carefully unzipped the top of the down bag. A neoprene skin, two fiberglass rods, and four titanium-alloy bolts were all that held her to the side of the cliff. Montana was in no hurry to find flat ground. She peered out over the Cascade Mountains. A thick fog enveloped the lowlands, but sun shone brightly on the higher elevations, highlighting fresh pockets of last night's snow.

"Global warming, my ass," she said aloud, pulling a sweatshirt over her thick black braids, now streaked with white climbing chalk. Yesterday, that chalk had started on her hands, helping keep them dry. Every hand and foot placement, while creeping up the sheer rock face, had to be perfect. Even though he had proper gear, a mistake while alone meant a long, bumpy fall and possible death. Not that death was such a big deal to Montana—her grandfather had taught her there were far worse fates.

Growing up on Cherokee tribal land, she had sat for hours, listening to her grandfather console grieving families. Though he ran a small general store, he was the most powerful elder in the tribe. Two centuries ago, he would have been a medicine man, a mystic with the ability to see straight into somebody's soul. Tribal members from all over the country stopped there for advice, confessions, fortune telling, blessing of their children, and always when a particularly devastating or tragic death snatched another Native American's life. Montana remembered how her grandfather, with his soothing, gravelly voice, would tell the story of the beginning of Earth: how Earth was all water until a Cherokee boy met a duck. Grandfather always drew attention away from their sadness and filled them with hope.

31

"Yes," he would whisper. "There is an afterlife. An afterlife that is not heaven, not hell. It is where all warrior began and where they will return. A place of unimaginable natural beauty where all creatures are forbidden to suffer."

Montana didn't need to lift her face to the heavens to ask Grandfather for safety on her ascent up the cliff that loomed above her. She saw him peeking around every arete and in each small flower growing out of a crevice in the rock.

With that thought, Montana flexed her sinewy thighs, slid out from under the flimsy cover of her tent, and put on her rock shoes. Then she pressed her foot onto a cherry-size nub. In one rapid motion, she clipped her harness into a rusty piton pounded into the rock by some climber decades ago. *Good enough.* Easing all her weight onto the hardware, she felt the straps pull tight across her 122-pound frame. It reminded her how sore her muscles were from yesterday's long haul. She rolled up her tent and stuffed it into the haul bag, clipped the portaledge below the bag, snarfed down some Electro-Bites, and headed toward the top. Her First Nation instincts did not alert her that a pair of eyes was watching her from far below.

She climbed with precision and speed, having mastered the route long ago. *Gaston. Crimp. Crimp. Crimp. Latch. Dyno! Yeah, baby. Teach that at Harvard!* Montana chattered away as if she were with a partner. Her voice echoed off the wall and back into the valley.

An hour later, she was standing on a flat rock painted with the initials of hundreds of climbers. Hers were in fluorescent pink. She stayed only long enough to rig a rappel from the summit anchors. As with everything else in her life, the series of rappels back down was fast but measured.

32

As soon as she was down, Montana cleaned off two days' worth of crud with a half box of baby wipes, then headed back toward civilization in her beat up 4Runner. She could afford something much nicer, but expensive cars and the climbing culture just didn't mix.

* * *

The diner door dinged just loud enough to momentarily mute the sizzle of frying potatoes in the tiny kitchen.

"Good evening, honey. I see you're in one piece. I'll get that lemonade started. You go to the back and wash those hands with real soap."

Every time Montana Harms stopped into the Route 20 Café, Cheryl, the waitress, wished aloud she were twenty years younger and slightly more adventurous. Montana had been coming in for a decade, eating pasta on her way out to a climb, then loading up on steak afterward. She used the café staff as a buddy system. Before a climb, she wrote with a gel pen where she was headed and when she planned to be back, on the bottom of a place mat. If she wasn't back within a day of that date, the Route 20 Café called the sheriff. Like protective parents, the cooks and waitresses fretted over each hour Montana was late returning. Few of them had any family that gave a damn about them, or they wouldn't be out in the middle of nowhere serving coffee and eggs to the passersby of life. Although the Cascades beckoned peaceful, nature-loving people to hike, cross-country ski, and fish for lake trout, none of these people lived in the area. The sense of community was no larger than the diner itself.

As she partially shut the thin particle board bathroom door, Montana could hear Cheryl rip her latest note off the wall by the register and tossed it into the trash. She also heard the ding of the diner door and rough voices. Montana peeked around the corner.

"Can I help you fellas with directions? Pie for the road?"

Cheryl stepped between the counter and the booths near the door to slow the rapid entry of three burly men in open-collared starched shirts and sport jackets. Montana was unsure if the waitress noticed the slight bulge of what was surely a holstered weapon under each left arm. Robbery around these parts was usually no more than a drug addict wanting a few bucks for his next fix, but wild-eyed addicts, these guys were not.

"We need a word with Hiawatha! Get her out here pronto or I will knock the fucking dentures out of your mouth, Grandma."

A pair of diner guests at the corner table quietly put their forks down and hurried outside, leaving their stack of waffles and whipped cream untouched, and a twenty under the saucer. Cheryl kept eye contact and appeared to want to hold her ground, but before she had to make any potentially dangerous decisions, Montana stepped into the florescent lights. The back door was only a few feet behind her, but she didn't even think about sneaking out.

"Me-um right here, beefcakes."

She had no fear of slipping off a moss-covered vertical rock. She had no fear of a rattlesnake biting her when she stepped over a down log. This bunch of goofs didn't even make her list of top fifty scariest things. The leader of the pack took two strides, grabbed Montana by the throat, and scooped her high into the air. She landed on the relative softness of a booth seat, wedged between the wall and a guy who smelled like Aqua Velva.

"We weren't sure if you've been getting our messages. Didn't try smoke signals, but just about everything else. It's time we partner up, Miss Oklahoma. Your options are limited," growled one of the faux triplets.

Montana Harms had grown up in Tahlequah, Oklahoma, heart of the Cherokee nation. She was lucky to come from a bloodline of native royalty. Her father had started a bingo hall when she was eight, and by the time she was in high school the Bureau of Indian Affairs in D.C. had granted the Cherokees the authority to expand into the full gaming industry. As Montana headed off to the University of Oklahoma, she took with her the title of "Casino Baby." The misery, alcoholism, and unemployment still lingered for her people, but Montana now had more money than she could ever spend. The addiction gene bypassed her immediate family, which only enhanced the mystique of power and influence. Until recently, she had been blissfully unaware of how her father kept control of such a vast empire. An MBA wasn't necessary if you had enough muscle and political juice.

The Russian mob had asked, rather nicely at first, if it could diversify its business ventures by helping the Cherokees manage their money. Their plan was to increase the house take slightly in every game and keep part of the difference. In return, the Russians would provide security, liquor, and an allotment from their off-shore and Internet poker sites in the Bahamas. The Cherokee Nation would make millions from the deal, but they knew that the Russians only wanted to use the cash created at the casino to launder much dirtier money. Negotiations never really got off the ground. The tribal elders were a greedy enough bunch, but they weren't about to vote themselves into a relationship that could draw the scrutiny of the FBI. Besides, if they were going to increase the house take, they could do that alone and keep it all to themselves. The Cherokee people felt that the government's approval of their casino was a wink-wink form of restitution for the enormous suffering that had begun long before the Trail of Tears 180 years earlier. If the U.S. government didn't feel guilty about it, the Cherokees didn't, either. Still, getting in bed with stone-cold killers like the Russian mob seemed a major risk.

"Your dad has hired a small army to keep us away from Tahlequah. Gave shoot-on-sight orders if we showed our faces near his casinos again. That's not very friendly. He must not give a shit about you to let you hang out here all alone . . . I'll let you deal with that in family therapy."

His Russian accent was so subtle, Montana figured he was as American as she. *A mob baby.*

"I'm like bait in a muskrat trap," Montana replied with a disarming grin. "You come swimming up, think you're going to get an easy meal, then—*snap*—you're dead. It's not even an 'Oh, I see the warm, soft light' kind of death. You start chewing off your leg, but you can't quite get it done before you drown."

Cheryl stood silently watching, her hand wrapped around a cast-iron skillet handle.

"I'm in Washington all alone because the depth of vengeance among my family is such that Putin and the whole FSB itself couldn't keep you alive for a week if you screw with me. If you think you can arrange a deal with my father and his casino clan, knock yourself out. Me, I don't know the difference between roulette and slots. I'm not a pawn, and I am certainly not your ticket to the bargaining table. So why don't you *boys* just go back outside and get in the blingmobile and have yourselves a little circle jerk behind those tinted windows."

The mobster flexed his jaw and slammed down a ceramic coffee mug on Montana's hand. Hot coffee sprayed onto the other two goons, but they didn't blink an eye.

"Now, smile."

Montana looked away from the blood oozing out of the dent in her hand and stared blankly into the flash of a smartphone camera.

The Russian rat pack all stood up at the same time and started for the door as the leader growled one last message.

"I don't expect you to cower in fear. I don't even think you'll tell your dad about our friendly encounter. Don't worry, though, I will make sure he gets the message: his little girl is in our sights."

Montana was the only customer left in the diner as the rented Escalade with spinning rims screeched west on the highway, back toward Seattle.

"Come on, Chef! That steak should be charcoal by now," Montana yelled toward the kitchen as she dabbed her hand with a wet napkin.

Cheryl came over to the table. "We need to call the sheriff and report this as an assault."

Montana flipped her wrist dismissively.

"Nah. Off concrete, they're out of their element. They'd be screwed on our mountain in those New and Lingwood shoes. If I need to get away, they won't be able to follow. I promise."

Montana could hire an entire squad of bodyguards, but what fun would that be?

Chapter 7

Dr. Dell watched a battered van pull up in front of the office at the Motel 4. He had chosen this fleabag for its averageness. The owner must have been a real chiseler. What kind of businessman avoided paying a small franchising fee to Hotel 6 by subtracting two from the name? The faded blue sign needed painting, but that was fine—an innkeeper who cared so little about his property would not take much interest in his guests, either. No questions. No eye contact. Cash only. It really was the perfect situation.

A poor, scruffy family man, got out of the van and lugged a thin stack of the *Seattle Times* toward the coin-operated rack.

Pathetic, worthless existence, playing out right before my eyes. Pity, the days of the freckle-faced paperboy are apparently long gone, Dr. Dell ranted to himself.

After being up a good portion of the night watching Colton Wiley on television and attending to his injured dog, Dr. Dell yearned for a mug of freshly ground Herkimer coffee. At one point, he had filled the bathtub with water and ice, got naked, and eased into the tub with the male German shorthair, holding the animal and telling him it would be all right. The cold helped reduce the swelling along the dog's ribs. The third rib down on the right appeared to be broken near the sternum. He wrapped the dog's midsection in cut-up sheets to ease its labored breathing, then gave it a small dose of Previcox. Visiting a veterinarian so close to the murder scene wasn't wise, but he knew he'd take that risk if his furry companion's health didn't improve soon.

Although a collision with a deer was impossible to plan for, Dr. Dell was not stupid enough to use a traceable vehicle. He could see the two-inch-high headline through the chicken wire of the newspaper's cage: "TROOPER SLASHED. MANHUNT UNDER WAY."

Dr. Dell fished a pair of quarters out of his pocket. Inside the pages, the reporters blathered on and on in their columns, about the cop's grieving wife and kids. There was also a bloated article about how his outraged colleagues planned to catch the killer. Detectives were running blood samples from the crime scene. They were theorizing that Trooper Thomas Fitzgerald pulled over to investigate a car crash and was attacked by the driver, one or more passengers. Dr. Dell thought it disgraceful that there was no mention of the buck's tragic death. Happily, he didn't have a criminal record—there would be no DNA on file to match his blood profile. Whatever database they tapped would come up empty. Dr. Dell wasn't even sure his blood could be so easily isolated. He smiled at how they could be thrown off the trail for months looking for a couple of German shorthairs.

As he thumbed through the rest of the paper, another article caught his attention. Dr. Dell was delighted to see that ALB was getting credit for dismantling a mink farm operation. He had no idea exactly who was behind the raid and that was the way it was supposed to be.

Each ALB cell worked in isolation. The FBI liked to study patterns and probabilities to catch organized criminals, but animal rights groups were so seemingly disorganized, the feds struggled to work their way up the criminal food chain. Informants couldn't get inside the operations. It was like trying to slip an undercover agent inside a high school—the other high schoolers rarely bought the fact that some adult was really a new kid who wanted to deal drugs. If you didn't eat right, talk right, regularly attend all the weird functions, and routinely engage in degenerate or antisocial behavior, nobody trusted you. Getting into al-Qaeda would be easier.

The FBI once got lucky enough to capture an 18-year-old arsonist setting some high-dollar beachfront condos on fire. The dummy wanted to punish the landowner, whose parking lot lights flared brightly toward the ocean. The arsonist figured the hatchling sea turtles, having dug out of their sandy pods, would confuse the lights for the glow of the moon and migrate in the wrong direction, to their deaths. A cheap security camera had ID'd the kid, but it didn't help that he had left his backpack, with his name inside it, next to a nearby fence. The U.S. Attorney's Office threatened him with twenty years in prison for criminal conspiracy unless he started naming the real players. They pressed hard, but the poor college kid was clueless about the ALB hierarchy. He'd met a cute girl and a couple of guys getting high out back of a party. They were bitching about some rich developer and a lawsuit against the city to keep his lights blazing over the parking lot. That conversation led to his giving the girl his cell phone number. Next thing he knew, he was getting regular text messages called "ALB Action Alerts." He acted just to impress a piece of ass and to back up his Save the Planet bumper sticker.

Good luck, Ms. U.S. Attorney. Throw the book at 'em. Waste two years and millions in tax money to prosecute a "terrorist."

In the end, somebody on that jury took a stand: twenty years for trying to keep baby turtles from dying? *Not guilty*. It drove the Justice Department crazy.

Dr. Dell punched the top recent call tab in his cell phone.

"Oz? I need you to pick me up. Head toward Kalama. I'll text you the address. Get me some fresh clothes, dog food, and a cheap medical kit. If you're still snarfing down those Oxycodone pills, bring me some of those, too."

Dr. Dell hung up and wandered down to the office to pay for his seedy room and pick up a free toothbrush and razor.

* * *

Former Army explosives expert, Sergeant Oscar "Oz" McKinsey, was already driving south in his beat-up Saturn.

Oz pulled off at the next exit and parked illegally in the handicap spot closest to the Walmart's front door, mentally adding a 5-hour Energy drink to his list. He lit a cigarette and took three long drags before tossing the lit butt out his window into the gutter. A woman yanking her three brats into the store gave him a nasty look.

Inside, Oz suffered through Walmart's barrage of smiley faces and offers of "Can I help you, sir?" The only thing the place had going for it was that it sold guns and ammo. He piled his cart full of supplies as fast as he could, paid cash, and hit the road again. Dr. Dell didn't seem to be the kind of man who liked waiting.

Oz believed in Dr. Dell. If the visionary behind the Animal Liberation Brigade wanted supplies, okay with him. If he wanted someone shot point-blank in the head, that was okay too. Dr. Dell had made Oz a promise of revenge in return for his loyalty. Oz felt it was more than a fair trade. He seethed with anger every single day thinking about his dead dog, Sparks.

The Kansas native had trained at Redstone Arsenal in Alabama to be an explosive ordnance disposal specialist. He was never very good at school. The Army liked that. When he volunteered to fight in Iraq, they gave him two options: he could learn to fix trucks or learn to blow stuff up. The latter sounded fun.

Oscar McKinsey's buddies in the Second Stryker Cavalry Regiment started calling him "Oz" when he decided to grow a mustache and beard without command permission. The whiskers grew for months, hidden from scrutiny behind a bandanna, ostensibly there to block the ever-present windblown sand. Once revealed, the long, thin hairs gave him the look of a Hells Angel wizard. His commander laughed so hard when he saw it, he let Oz keep it.

Oz saved countless lives in his first six months around Al Doura, spotting and disarming improvised explosive devices. His fearlessness gained him not only near-celebrity status, but also a unique opportunity—one that would change the course of many lives. The Army provided EOD Specialist McKinsey a German shepherd puppy. Oz held it up by the scruff, looked into its dark eyes, and told it, "Don't you ever piss on my boots and we'll get along fine."

Oz named the scrawny pup "Sparks" shortly after he started training it to sniff out explosive devices. The skinny critter naturally loved to chase the fast-moving burning orange hue of dynamite detonating cord. Oz had to break him of that, since the dog wouldn't understand the end of that chase until it was too late.

Oz read everything he could find on training dogs. Dogs had been used in war for centuries. The Egyptians and Romans loved their mastiffs, Irish wolfhounds pulled armored soldiers from their horses during the English conquest of Ireland, and the U.S. military dabbled in using dogs to detect land mines during both World Wars. Training included forcing the animals to walk around a yard where bare electrical wires shocked them repeatedly until they figured out how to avoid touching the metal. It was a horribly stressful exercise and one that didn't work all that well. After a half hour of gingerly walking around a mine field, looking for tiny metal nubs sticking out from the ground, the dogs stopped. It was safest to give up. When bullets were flying, the time they spent finding land mines dropped to even less. A child's thirty-five-dollar metal detector of the sort used to find coins at the beach worked a lot better anyway. Finding modern explosives, however, was a much different scenario. Make a mistake getting too close to the source, and you lived just long enough to see the flash of light, but not to hear the boom.

On hot days, Oz initially let Sparks ride on his lap in the advance Humvee. As the puppy grew, it learned to curl up between Oz's feet on the heavily plated floor. At night, Sparks lay sentry near the inside flap of the unit's tent, protecting them all with the sharp crack of a bark if anything sounded out of the ordinary. Training consisted of getting exposed to explosives at least a hundred times a day.

There were two opposing camps when it came to how best to train explosive-sniffing dogs. Experts on one side demanded that the dogs never receive any praise when they identified their target—just food. That way, anyone could handle the dog, since it would work for food regardless of who was holding the leash. Oz chose the other camp's philosophy. Each time Sparks hit on an explosive smell and sat down during training, not only would Oz praise him, but they would run off and play. They'd yip and whoop and tumble and "good boy" it until the rest of the unit couldn't help but smile. A man and his dog. Sparks' favorite toy was a pair of Arab kaffiyeh-and-agal headdresses, tied in a huge knot and stuffed with two pairs of Oz's old socks. This training method meant Sparks would hit on explosives only for Oz. The technique bonded the pair as mates, like gander and goose, for life. C-4 plastic explosive was the easiest for Sparks to find. It emitted a strong odor like oily asphalt. He had a knack for quickly picking up the more difficult materials, too. Sticks of buried dynamite, backpacks full of TNT, jars of potassium chlorate, grenades hidden under stinking dead bodies—nothing got by Sparks. Sitting down when he located Tovex was the hardest chore. The ammonium nitrate and PR-M had such a faint smell, Sparks had to really focus. He wanted to please Oz, so he sniffed tirelessly. At times, the dog would guess, just to see if he was right. When he guessed wrong Oz would turn his back to his pal. It was devastating to both. The team of Oz and Sparks saved so many soldiers, brass stopped counting. Their pictures were a mainstay in the *Stars and Stripes* newspaper.

January 13 was a Wednesday. Oz would never forget. The blast furnace of heated sand was starting to ease up slightly as a hazy moon crept over the horizon. Oz was showering off under a cut-off section of garden hose strung up to a broken-down water truck tank. The soldiers had to suck on the end of the hose to get it running, just as some of them had done siphoning gas from a neighbor's car as cash-strapped teenagers. Sparks was soaked, too, frolicking in the water splashing up off the ground, when Oz heard a new voice approaching. The voice was speaking not to him but rather *about* him, in a group of tanned men in camouflage fatigues. He heard the phrases "fucking dog" and "I don't much give a shit." Oz stepped out from behind the blankets on the makeshift shower, and quickly tied a towel around his waist. He stood straight and threw up a bare-chested salute the moment he saw the colonel's eagle pin. The ranking officer didn't mince words—something that nobody thought particularly strange.

"Soldier, these men around me are arguing, at their own great peril, that you're the only goddamn person in the whole goddamned world who can use that scraggly fucking mutt."

Sparks sat quietly but glanced up at his master. "I'm telling them that the United States fucking military owns you. The United States fucking military owns *him*. The United States fucking military giveth and it taketh away at my fucking command. Unless you have some general's stars hidden under your ball sack, boy, hand over that dog. I have a different job for him!"

Though Oz was panicking on the inside, he kept his composure.

"With all due respect, sir, the United States military does own me, and I'm willing to die for my country at your command. But, sir, that dog only responds to commands from me. He will not provide you the needed services unless I command him. If you'd like me to do that for you, sir, we'd be honored."

This was not the answer the colonel wanted. "The next word you speak gets you tossed in the brig. Hand over the dog."

Oz didn't move. Sparks inched closer to his master's feet, taking a defensive posture. When the colonel reached for Sparks' collar, Oz smashed his right fist into the colonel's left cheekbone. Sparks wasn't really trained to fight, so he mostly jumped up and down and barked furiously, cheering like a front-row fan at a mixed martial arts match. Oz dropped his shoulder back and threw a devastating kick to the colonel's nearest bodyguard, catching him in the ribs. The second bodyguard chose not to pull his sidearm, instead wrapping a beefy arm around Oz's neck from behind. The choke hold had Oz seeing bees swarming in the blazing desert sun. As the bees swarmed thicker he kicked and swung for another second, then passed out.

The colonel's boys worked him over even though he was unconscious, and when he woke up in a makeshift jail cell he was missing a tooth and his ear was full of blood. On the floor was a two-day supply of dehydrated food and several canteens of water. On the third day, Oz got a visit from the unit chaplain.

"Oz, I'm so sorry. There is no way I can soften the words. Sparks is dead. I hope you believe in heaven and hell. I believe strongly that God will let that dog of yours run straight through the Pearly Gates. I also believe that Lucifer himself will be shuttling Colonel Granderson to a very different sort of place. After I tell you unofficially what happened, I pray you will not be the man who sends the colonel to hell before his time."

Oz sat down, teared up with rage and sorrow, and listened silently. He had seen the chaplain at a few holiday church services, but he was by no means a regular.

"I'm here to tell you unofficially what happened. None of it will ever end up in a report. Colonel Granderson needed your dog for a contest he was having with several other brigades and battalions. Kind of a Hunger Games for dogs. There were a bunch of lieutenant colonels, a couple of full colonels, and a brigadier general all laying big-money bets on a dozen explosive-

45

sniffing dogs. They set up a timed scavenger hunt, burying grenades, hiding C-four under broken-down cars, dropping packs of Tovex into barrels of gasoline along this short course they created. None of the stuff was rigged to explode. The first few dogs went through. Everyone cheered. The odds board changed a couple of times. When it was Sparks' turn, he seemed a little confused. Instead of heading out into the course, he slipped under the fence and ran the opposite direction. The other brass was laughing so hard at Granderson, they almost wet themselves. Sparks sprinted to an outdoor market across the road. Granderson goes ballistic when he sees your dog is transfixed on a little kid eating a lamb kabob. Sparks is whining, licking his chops, scooting on his belly behind the boy as he walks along in the crowd. Granderson caught up and grabbed Sparks by the scruff. He was screaming stuff like, 'You have a job to do! And, you screw me because you're hungry!? Unacceptable soldier!'

Granderson kicked Sparks really hard, than drew his pistol and unloaded his magazine into Spark's head. A minute later, an explosion ripped through market, killing ten people. The boy had a bomb strapped under his karta. Your dog tried to save all those people with his warning."

Oz wished with all his heart that he could have been there to comfort his dog in those final moments. He vowed the U.S. Army, *hell the entire human race*, was going to pay.

Chapter 8

Coverage of the murdered trooper's funeral and burial was spectacular. The final live video clip looked like a Steven Spielberg production. Assistant news director Chuck Reynolds was beside himself with joy. KZPR's helicopter, its nose-mounted camera steadied by a gyroscope, hovered over the top of the coffin, sending video back to the station. A videographer slowly zoomed the shot tighter and tighter toward the hole in the ground. Moments before the casket was fully lowered, the camera panned to a gorgeous close-up image of the dead cop's wife. Viewers at home could see the tears streaming down her face, while the young daughter stood stoically holding her mother's hand. Chuck had the graphics department create a special banner that ran across the lower third of the screen. It was a waving ribbon of steely blue, with Trooper Fitzgerald's badge number in the corner. The title touted "live coverage" in the other corner. Beveled boldfaced words told anyone close to a TV what was going on: *Trooper laid to rest. Killer still on loose.*

Five reporters on the ground went round-robin on their assigned topics for the day: street closures and traffic concerns for the funeral procession; "where does the murder investigation stand?"; reactions from sad friends, family, and fellow officers; basic funeral coverage; and a final story about politicians' hand-wringing over the lackluster State Patrol Crime Lab's budget, which meant a backlog slowing the speed of DNA matching. The male anchor in the studio wore his darkest gray suit and his brightest jewel-colored tie. The female anchor wore all black except for a pearl necklace and an emerald pocket flower. They skipped sports coverage but let the perky weather announcer get in on the action. Sunny conditions for the funeral, but it had rained earlier, during the wake.

While doing day-to-day operations of television newsrooms his entire life, Chuck Reynolds had probably orchestrated more than a hundred high-profile funerals. Dead politicians. Dead celebrities. Dead kids caught in the crossfire of a drive-by shootout. Once, he even covered the funeral of a dead orca whale. The public loved these things. The surviving family put up with the media intrusions partly out of shell shock and partly because they wanted to honor their loved one in a very public way. The bigger the funeral, the more important the person's life seemed to be. Reynolds knew that it was a historical tradition started by America's earliest newspapers in their obituary columns. If some low-class horse-stable owner in Muskegon, Michigan, died, the local newspaper would put his death notice in the smallest print possible, usually on the back page, his long life boiled down to a couple of paragraphs. But when a mighty lumber-baron worth a million 1870 dollars croaked, the newspaper put out a special-edition front-page photo, combined with story after story about the robber baron's golden heart and philanthropic soul. Your life's worth truly was decided by a newspaper editor after you kicked the bucket.

Reynolds was proud to keep that tradition alive. He personally wrote the close to the show. He avoided using Bible passages. He once chose a Psalm, and the next day a loud horde of Wiccans and atheists picketed the station. For this day, he selected a poem by Mary Frye:

> *Do not stand at my grave and weep,*
>
> *I am not there, I do not sleep.*
>
> *I am a thousand winds that blow.*
>
> *I am the diamond glint on snow.*
>
> *I am the sunlight on ripened grain.*
>
> *I am gentle autumn rain.*

Do not stand at my grave and cry.

I am not there, I did not die.

As the anchor read the passage, a photo of Trooper Fitzgerald in uniform filled the screen, then faded to black. Before a commercial for a furniture store started at full volume, Reynolds let a few moments of dead-air silence pass. He felt like running around the newsroom giving high fives, but that would look tacky and could be risky. He didn't have many enemies in the newsroom, but someone could easily take cell phone video of him whooping it up and royally screw him in the court of public opinion. Instead, he gave the board operators a pat on the back, and the director a "nice job," and slipped out a back door into the alley. A neon bar sign was calling his name.

The first glass of Crown and Coke was always his favorite. The bartender drew a chilled tumbler from the cooler, topped it with ice, then filled it with whiskey. The soda on top was only to give it a tiny aesthetic fizz. Chuck Reynolds loved the way that dry cold felt in his hand. The glass had not yet started sweating. He was never very good at science, but the fact that somehow a wonderful alcoholic mixture could pull moisture from the air and form flowing rivulets of water was like magic. By the third round, his napkin was soaked. He shook a little salt on top, clinked the ice cubes, and gave the nod for another.

"Now looks like a good time to renegotiate my contract," Colton Wiley teased as he plunked down next to the only boss he had ever really understood. "Solid coverage today! I think I saw the news director from the Fox affiliate outside weeping. You kicked the hell out of everyone else on the funeral."

Reynolds grinned widely, tossing his glasses down on the bar. "Well, it's about time you came in from the cold! Great to see you! The news director keeps asking me, 'Where's Cole? Where's Cole?' in that whiney Kinko salesman voice. 'On assignment,' I say. 'A super-secret assignment. You're going to be glad in the end that you left him alone. An Emmy-winning assignment.'"

The bartender slid a pint of Guinness in Cole's direction.

"He wants to see you on TV more often. Says you're an expensive toy and he wants more of a return on his investment."

Cole had heard that plenty of times in his career.

"Just tell me when you want me to start turning a story every day. I have a treasure trove of fantastic ideas that'll wow the audience and take mere minutes to put together. Let's see . . . Oh, here's a good one. An undercover investigation: What your dog does when you're away. Or how about a consumer warning on recalled baby strollers? No, wait. Better yet, which teeth whitener makes your smile shine! Now we're cooking. I see the Nielsen meters peaking off the charts. Give me the word and I'm all over it."

"You wouldn't show up for work ever again, would you?"

"Not a chance."

Reynolds knew that wasn't an idle threat. Cole didn't care about money or fame. He didn't even *like* being on television. All he wanted to do was discover what was supposed to stay secret.

Cole jumped up. "Let's head to that back table for some privacy. I'll bring you up to speed."

Reynolds gathered up his fourth drink, walked past the table, and slid the glass across the lacquered top.

"Gotta piss. Be right back," he shouted as he made a beeline for the bathroom.

Cole sat down, eyes toward the door. Corporate security had stopped counting the number of death threats he had received. Al Capone had made it a policy to always have his back to the wall while eating. Since Capone had died of heart failure instead of a bullet from his enemies, Cole figured it was a pretty good policy. He automatically scanned the room for escape routes: an exit sign to the right and another to the far left, near the kitchen. There were ten people in sight. None looked familiar. A woman near the dartboard was glancing over the top of her boyfriend's head at Cole. She wasn't hitting on him, just trying to figure out where she had seen him before. That meant Cole could have, at most, only one more beer. The last thing he needed was to have some loudmouth tell the bitchy newspaper media critic that he was drunk. Colton Wiley was the favorite whipping boy of other reporters and journalism watchdog groups alike. It was an "attack, tear down, and destroy" mentality that would make Saul Alinsky proud.

The bar across the room was solid maple. When he first came in, Cole had knocked on it with his knuckles and decided it would be a safe place to take cover, especially considering that the bartender very likely had a handgun of some sort near his cash register. State law didn't allow Cole to bring his Kahr pistol inside anyplace that served liquor. He hated that law, but he followed it. There were no security cameras inside, but two in the parking lot.

"Brought you a Coors Light. I'd hate to drink alone," Chuck Reynolds called out a little too loudly as he returned.

"Yeah, right. That'd never happen," Cole retorted as he sipped the ring of foam off his still-full glass and let the bottle sit.

"Well, come on. I'm dying to hear what's going on. Start with how you *just happened* to be in the neighborhood while a state trooper lay bleeding to death in a mud-soaked ditch."

If Cole had been called into the newsroom by managers to explain his convenient whereabouts, he would have laid out a very simple summary. He always downplayed the significance of his stories, in order to lower expectations. Former New York mayor Rudy Giuliani had under promised and overdelivered, which made a heck of a lot of sense to Cole. However, this was one of those rare, special circumstances in which Cole needed to reveal his cards. It was a calculated move that, he believed, would lead to a month of freedom from the newsroom to pursue what was potentially the biggest story of his life. He needed to be given permission to disappear, not check in, and not be expected to turn a single story. Even for Cole, it was a lot to ask.

"I have reason to believe someone connected to the Animal Liberation Brigade is on a murdering rampage."

Like the lead line in a story, it was sure to get his boss's attention, even as blurry eyed as he was starting to appear.

"God. Sounds dangerous and very sexy. Those are your kind of people. Take whatever time you need. I'll cover for you. I'm handing you that up front so you don't have to sit here and beg and lie and manipulate me to get that permission at the end of this conversation. Now, give me the sweet details. I'm dying to know everything."

Cole showed every tooth in his mouth, enjoyed his freedom-from-oversight victory for a millisecond, then started weaving a tale worthy of a crime novel.

"I saw a pair of young women, burned up, both wearing necklaces with the same coding. I hit up my sources in PETA, the Humane Society, Friends of Animals, and at the Abolitionists of Vivisection. None had a clue. I must have rattled enough cages because my cell phone rings out of the blue, and this guy goes all Deep Throat on me—Nixon's Watergate, not the porn flick. He says, 'Oz knows.' I say 'Ozzy Osborne? Crazy Train was kick ass.' I'm only messing with the guy, trying to get a feel if he's a prank caller or one of the many people in my world who need serious medication. There's this long pause. I figure he's going to hang up. 'The dead girls are guinea pigs. Oz knows.' *Bingo!* Eight little words that lead me down another rabbit hole. And, Chuck, this is a very dark hole."

Cole eyed the room, especially the pair of 20-somethings in the booth nearest his table. They were yakking on and on about coffee-bean roasting—no interest in eavesdropping.

"I do some checking, and "Oz" is a seriously deranged activist named Oscar McKinsey. He attended the University of Washington after getting out of the Army a few years back. He's an anarchist who might love animals, but he's also using that as an excuse to create chaos. He's a loner and a firebug, but no master of the universe. The dude's not a leader. The tip said he 'knows,' which makes me think he didn't actually do the killing. I figured it was safer to ask questions about Oz to my tightlipped pack of critter protectors, rather than asking about a double murder. I spread the word that our investigative unit needed some background on the UW monkey lab and that I heard a guy called Oz might be able to get me inside. Everyone said the same thing: 'Oh, you mean Oscar McKinsey.' I play like I'm an absolute moron. I then go on and on about how I think putting needles in monkey's eyes and pins in their heads needs to be exposed. The ophthalmology program needs to be shut down. The whole bit."

"Does it?" Chuck jumped in, compulsively finding the need to throw a question at any reporter speaking with him.

"Focus, boss," Cole chided with his world-class smirk. "One investigation at a time. Oz keeps his personal life off the radar, but several of my sources told me he hangs around with some girl called Jelly Bell. She turns out to be an activist named April Slade. I visited her mom."

Cole slipped a folded letter from the inside pocket of his charcoal Valentino suit and flipped it open on the table for them to view together.

"Mom tells me April recently pens home a cult-inspired, weird but revealing letter: *'Love you . . . good parents . . . store my stuff . . . can't come home . . . feds might be watching . . . changing the world.'* Okay, to the good part."

Cole read it verbatim: *" 'Rain is our savior, for it replenishes the earth. In the coming weeks, remember these words. You are the ark. Do not drink from the Well. It is poisoned with truth.' "*

Eyes squinting, Chuck Reynolds's journalist's brain had no trouble editing out all the crap in the letter. He read hundreds of crazy letters written to the station every week. He could scan the page and find the thesis in less than five seconds. If he saw the words "trailer park" or "discrimination" or "state took my kids," it went straight into the trash. Sadly, that took care of the bulk of the "help me!" correspondence.

In the coming weeks. The words lingered over the table in the small space between their faces.

"Could be the ramblings of yet another nut," Reynolds added. "But given that you think the nut is probably one of the dead girls from the cabin arson, it makes it a bit more intriguing."

"A *bit?*" Cole raised the pitch of his voice. "April was only 21-years-old. She is assuredly one of the crispy corpses in the forest. I figure she got in way over her head. This letter tells me *almost* everything. The Animal Liberation Brigade is already making plans for a major event—

one so dangerous that April figured she'd better say good-bye to her folks. It's also a warning, but for her parents only. They live a few miles inside the Oregon border, and I assume this terror outfit wouldn't target only April's hometown. So we're looking at action in a broad area, like an entire state or the West Coast. Maybe they're going after the food or water supply or some kind of an attack on the government or the monetary system. April loves animal rights activism enough to die for it, but doesn't love it enough to keep her mouth shut if her own parents are at risk. She's also worried about the FBI or Homeland Security. I don't think she cares about jail, so that means she thinks the feds might already have a hint as to what is going on. I've already started reaching out to every spook I've ever met, to see if there are any rumors. That rain-and-ark riddle sounds a lot like David Koresh. Religious references are apocalyptic, so she believes, at least in her head, that something of biblical proportions is about to go down. My anonymous caller said the dead girls were guinea pigs, which probably means they volunteered for something that went wrong—a practice round, so to speak. That means April had direct contact with someone much higher up the chain of command. Someone smarter, someone more manipulative. And from what I know about Oz , it isn't him."

"Reality check, Cole. You need to tell the cops. I know they might jack up your story, but this is serious."

"I've covered my ass with law enforcement, so if things go bad, it won't be a public relations nightmare for KZPR-TV. Trust me." Cole hoped that "telling" Nolan counted as "law enforcement."

"Get on it then! Don't forget to roll the camera once in a while. When this is all done, I expect a wall full of journalism awards. Big 'J,' not little."

Cole strolled out the bar doors, into the relative silence of a side street. He could hear a bit of gravel embedded in the leather sole of his shoe tap the sidewalk with each step. Out of the corner of his eye, he noticed the soft light of a cell phone glowing up from the console in a dark-green van parked along the near curb. He could spot a surveillance setup a mile away. Maybe it was some private investigator, hired to record video of a cheating boyfriend. Maybe it was the Seattle PD's vice squad, trying to sweep up a few teachers and ministers picking up hookers along First Avenue. Maybe it was the FBI, wondering what color tie Colton Wiley was wearing tonight. Cole didn't care. Nothing was going to stop him from figuring out what kind of animal rights mission was so damn important that it required murder to keep the bigger secret.

Chapter 9

The Lewis County Medical Examiner's work space was not the high-tech Hollywood version of *CSI*. It fell on the scale somewhere between the garage of a funeral parlor embalmer and the infirmary of the state prison up the road. Two stainless steel tables, filled with the two girls' charred remains, stood over a large drain on the floor. A small microphone, which reminded Nolan of one he had seen used by the ring announcer at a Vegas title fight, hung on a cord above the bodies. This was the arson investigator's second homicide update of the day. The first had been a straightforward account of Trooper Fitzgerald's slashing. Nolan didn't ask any questions of the Clark County coroner about the cop, because technically it wasn't his investigation. His buddy, Cole, thought there might be a connection between the cop's murder and the two young women found dead in the woods. It was a wild theory, based on nothing but Cole's instincts. And that, to be honest, was good enough for Nolan.

The small circular saw in the coroner's hand began to whir. It sounded like the muffled chainsaw of a logger working deep in the woods, but the smell was nothing like a freshly cut grove of cedar trees.

"Hey, Doc," Nolan said, pulling his sweatshirt up over his lower face, "dead *before* the fire or *because* of it?"

"It's tough to tell given the condition of the bodies, but I analyzed a small section of lung tissue that survived the fire. I see no signs of smoke inhalation. I'd say with ninety-five percent certainty that they had already stopped breathing when the smoke enveloped them."

Nolan towered over the medical examiner. At six feet-five, he had the same view as someone in a soap opera who died on the operating table, left their body, flew into the corner to watch, then survived to tell everyone about their death experience.

His résumé as an arson investigator was unmatched. Nolan could take one look at a fire and visually extrapolate a full-color image of the location and direction of flames long extinguished. This case, however, was his first murder investigation. The U.S. Forest Service frowned on getting involved in homicide cases and usually nudged them over to the FBI. Not wanting that to happen, Nolan had let his regional manager in San Francisco assume that the girls died accidently. Nolan convinced him that the key to the case was catching an arsonist. Catching a murderer was just a side benefit.

"So how did they die?" Nolan motioned for the sawing to stop.

"I can't say for sure, but I ran a chemical broadband to see if I could trace any foreign substances in their systems. The initial scan only matches the most basic chemicals. The detailed results take forever to get back. They go to a fancy lab in North Carolina. Fire does amazing and unnatural things to the structure of blood and cells. That said, I don't see any evidence of drug use, except a little pot. There is one strange spike on the charting. Both their blood sugars were *way off*. I'll e-mail you the report when it's done."

"Thanks, Doc," Nolan said while heading to the door, hoping to get out of the room as fast as possible. He didn't quite get clear before the medical examiner restarted his bone saw, and shouted a question his direction.

"Hey, Nolan! Any luck identifying either of them? As long as the toe tags say 'Jane Doe One' and 'Jane Doe Two' I have to store this meat in the freezer. I'm limited on space in there."

"Your compassion for human suffering is overwhelming," Nolan replied, and spun for the exit again. "When I do confirm the identities, I'll tell their families; then I'll make sure you're next on the list."

Nolan smiled and winked at the secretary covering the phones in the office on his way out. She melted, as had many others before her. Nolan couldn't remember having only one girlfriend at a time since eighth grade.

Growing up near Yakima, Nolan Burke was always the star athlete, and that came with certain perks. His father owned an apple orchard and trucking company, running fruit over Blewett Pass and up to a Canadian processing plant. He grew especially close to his dad while spending countless hours in the metal shed, learning how to rebuild a Cummins diesel engine and replace a transmission. His mom did the books from a home office so she could keep an eye on Nolan and his four brothers and sisters. Not until he traveled outside Yakima for a basketball tournament in Seattle, his sophomore year in high school, did he realize that outside his rural bubble, there were some bigger, badder kids looking to knock his confidence. The experience made him work harder to compete, but "big fish in a small pond" best fit Nolan's personality. When he applied to the National Fire Academy, his test scores made him the perfect candidate. He averaged 87 percent. Academy statistics found that recruits with test scores exceeding that number typically left the fire service and changed careers within five years. Simply put, the really smart wannabe firefighters soon got bored with the work. After the high up-front costs of training a firefighter, the academy wanted to shoot a little lower. Nolan fit the mold. His reputation as a big, strong, fearless leader quickly grew, but it was his easy-natured country-bumpkin attitude that ultimately vaulted him to class favorite. He would still be jumping out of airplanes as a hotshot firefighter, but the pay stub at the end of the month was lousy. As an arson investigator II, he had a real chance at retiring in ten more years with eighty-five percent pay on a government pension plan.

Nolan ran his hand over the thick scar on his stomach as he realized he hadn't eaten since yesterday. His pocket started to vibrate. The phone's screen said "Annoying Reporter" in case the brass in either Portland or Washington, D.C., ever snooped through his phone records.

"Cole, my man! You should have been with me at the ME's office. It was ghoulish, but I did see a superhot chick that works in the office."

"Good thing you're alone, then. If I'd been with you, she would have thought you were gay. How close to Oregon are you? A friend of mine who works for a bill-collections agency found an address for an ALB member named Oscar "Oz" McKinsey outside Portland. He could be a fun-loving rabbit-whisperer, but just in case, bring all that official looking cop stuff you carry around."

"I'll meet you at that diner off I-Five, north of the Columbia River. I'll ditch my government car. I'll be the guy at the table by the kitchen, wolfing down Grand Slams."

"So much for 'your body is a temple.' See you in two hours."

* * *

By the time they teamed back up and then reached Portland the late-afternoon rush-hour traffic was a nightmare.

"Should have kept that government car," Cole wished aloud. "A siren would be awesome right now." Nolan ignored him, digging curiously through Cole's glove box as if it were a box of Crackerjack. Mint gum. Bullets. An insurance card. Extra video cards. Two BAND-AID wrappers. Nothing fun.

A water-logged, faded Initiative 28 sign, with a big vote checkmark next to a marijuana leaf, was propped up next to the alleyway garage at the address Cole's source had provided. Cole pulled over and popped the hood of his truck in case a neighbor should glance out the window

60

after hearing an engine turn off. Nolan got out, and the pair leaned over the motor, pulled the dipstick, and waited to see if anyone came outside to help. After a few minutes of being ignored, they felt anonymous enough to make a beeline for the back door. Cole had a small black bag with an undercover camera rolling inside. He stood back while Nolan knocked.

The screen rattled in its frame. They listened intently for any sounds inside. A cat meowed.

"Did you hear that?" Cole asked.

"Yeah. I think I did. It was someone saying, 'Come on in.' It was kind of weak, though—maybe they're in trouble." Nolan held a straight face, knowing full well the house was empty. "Which exception to the Fourth Amendment do you want to put in my report: consent or exigent circumstances?"

"Consent, for sure. You have a witness."

Nolan didn't wait to see if the door was locked. He wedged his full weight against his hand on the knob and popped loose the sliver of wood that held the deadbolt to the rotted frame. Cole made sure the camera was momentarily pointed in the opposite direction. There was no sense in having to explain felony breaking and entering if they had the wrong house.

The skinny cat escaped outside to forage for dinner near the garbage cans. The kitchen was drab and all but barren. A crossword puzzle from the prior week lay on the counter. Nolan pulled gloves and an evidence bag from his pocket and placed a used orange juice glass inside, hoping to get a decent fingerprint. He also bagged a slick flyer from Evergreen State University. Cole stood motionless with the bag-camera so he could get usable snippets of video. Both suddenly became aware of what sounded like running water on the floor above them. They froze. Was someone in the shower and hadn't heard them come in? A small, clear puddle began to form

61

on the kitchen floor, flowing from beneath the wooden trim. A dripping sound came from inside the wall as the smell of gasoline hit their nostrils.

A snapping noise that sounded like a downed power line began echoing above their heads. Like Butch Cassidy and the Sundance Kid, the pair of investigators instinctively lurched back toward the open door, then jumped out and off the tiny porch just before a deafening roar shook the house. A rush of flames, glass, and insulation blew Cole and Nolan down the weed-choked sidewalk. Cole could feel his hair singe and curl up along the back of his neck. Nolan rolled in the grass while tearing off his sweatshirt. The burning nylon cord on his hood momentarily bonded with his skin. There was no need to call 9-1-1: the billowing dark cloud sent its own beacon.

"Holy shit, Arson Boy! I guess we found the right house!"

"Apparently," Nolan deadpanned, rolling over to sit up and stare at the disaster, "At least we saved the cat."

"That is truly finding the silver lining—thanks for that."

Within a minute, the entire structure was engulfed. Within two, the sound of sirens marked the arrival of Portland's finest. Nolan stopped the first engine lieutenant as soon as he came scrambling off the truck, to make sure the firefighters knew the home was likely empty. He didn't want anyone risking their lives on a sweep inside.

* * *

Water poured through hoses onto the roof for several hours. Cole stood in the back of his truck and shot images with his good camera, but even at that distance, the heat nearly melted the plastic off the lens shield. As other TV stations from Portland arrived, Cole slid into the crowd so they wouldn't notice him. So much for keeping their visit to Oz's place a secret.

Cole watched as Nolan pulled the "I'm a federal agent" trump card and put a clamp on what the public information officer could say. At Cole's urging, he thought it best to keep the story as local as possible. A nonstory would be even better. Nolan knew the flames made for fantastic visual effects, but as long as reporters moved on to another topic tomorrow, it would barely cause a blip in the news world. It would be much safer if Oz and any other Animal Liberation Brigade members were left in the dark.

The press release read, "*A three-alarm fire erupted today at an unoccupied house. Arson investigators are on the scene, but initial indications are that a natural gas line on a water heater malfunctioned, causing an explosion. The rental home was a total loss. Media inquiries should be directed to the PIO on call.*"

Cole watched as reporters did their live shots for the eleven o'clock news. Neighbors gave quick ten- and twelve-second sound bites. They all used the word "boom." Nobody knew who lived there. *Some brooding guy with a tattoo of a dog snaking up the side of his neck.* They knew that the home's owner lived in Hawaii but the renter kept to himself. Everyone was glad the cat that lived there was found in the alleyway, alive and well. Several reporters thought that was the best angle on the story. By 11:05 p.m., live-truck engineers were wrapping up their cables and downing the masts. By 11:15, the neighborhood was quiet except for the hum of fire department generators running klieg lights. A small contingent of firefighters from Station 14 was hanging out playing cards on the power-hose platform. They were ordered to keep an eye out for hotspots overnight.

Nolan saw Cole in the shadows and stepped across the line of light. Cole had changed into a T-shirt, jeans, and a green Dekalb seed-corn cap. His buddy handed him a badge to wear around his neck so he could move around the scene without being noticed.

"Your happy-go-lucky buddy Oz didn't just want to burn the house down, he was trying to trap and kill whoever entered. I'd like to find his ignition source. Grab your handheld video camera and pretend you're documenting my investigation. It'll look official. Besides, I really could use the tape later to help analyze the scene."

"What the hell happened here?" came an angry voice from behind them. "And why are the Feds pushing my guys out?" Portland's fire chief approached, decked out in a white uniform and hard hat. Cole could tell he was more than a little annoyed and a lot curious.

Nolan took command of the conversation. "Chief Wallingford! Nolan Burke, U.S. Forest Service arson investigator. Glad you stopped by: we need to speak off the record, but if you're cool with that, I'm glad to fill you in."

Bill Wallingford was a legend. A former Oregon State linebacker, he came out of the Portland Fire Department training camp as its top recruit back in 1990. His career was filled with heroic events, which included charging up a burning staircase to save two kids and their dog. A taut scar on his neck from skin-graft surgery was his telltale badge of valor.

"One hell of a fire for a natural gas leak. Such horse pucky! I hate lying to the media. I'll give you a very short leash. Start talking."

Nolan took a deep breath. He had to play this just right.

"The cause of this house fire was definitely arson, but you don't have a firebug on the loose that is going to torch more houses here in Portland."

Chief Wallingford cut Nolan off before he could explain further. "A punk-ass federal psychic—wow, that's great! I'll go home and sleep like a baby now. When the mayor calls, I'll tell him I met this guy who reads the future."

"I know it was arson, because I was inside before it started to burn. I guess that also makes it an attempted homicide on me and Sherlock Holmes here."

The chief cocked his head and sent a bushy pair of eyebrows scrunching away from his receding hairline. Cole looked familiar to him, but he couldn't quite put his finger on the face.

Nolan continued. "This Oscar McKinsey guy, who was living here, is some fringe environmental or animal extremist wack job. Most of these animal coddlers are pretty laid back—they trespass on a Kentucky Fried Chicken sidewalk or bang pans in the woods on the first day of deer season."

"I hate that. Makes me want to shoot 'em," the chief had to add.

"Me, too. So, I come here to see if he knows a college-aged girl that's missing. Well, we think dead, but that's why I came to talk to him. See what he might know. Turns out he's a lot bigger nut than I imagined. I didn't notice until it was way too late, but the door was holding a wire drilled up through the ceiling. We didn't hear any noise at first, then the distinctive sound of liquid pouring like rain on the room above us. It was intentionally set up so the outer wall holding the door would be full of fuel, then ignite before any trespasser could get out. The trap was well executed not only to take out all the evidence that might be in the house, but to incinerate the intruders. I didn't get a chance to go upstairs, but I can guess you'll find some remnants of burned plastic under a heavy couch."

Cole kept his eyes down, with the brim of his hat covering part of his face, hoping he could get out of this conversation before anyone put a name to it.

"I've seen this setup before," Nolan said, grabbing a pen and clipboard from the chief's assistant and drawing a quick diagram. "You tie a wire to the front leg of a heavy piece of furniture and run it up through a hook, like the kind that holds plants from the ceiling. You pull the couch a couple feet or so off the floor, so it's propped up on just two legs, kind of balanced. It doesn't put that much weight on the hook. It's easy to stick into a door jam. The arsonist fills five or six of those plastic camping water carriers with gasoline, stacks them under the couch, and leaves the caps off. When the door opens, the string lets the furniture drop and the weight of it forces the accelerant to ooze out the open filler hole. Pop some holes in the drywall at the floor level so the liquid fuel gets into the walls and, presto, you get accelerant right where you want it. Getting it lit isn't nearly as simple, but it can be done. Leaving a cut-up electrical cord plugged in might do the trick. The answer is in those ashes, Chief. Let me at it."

"I can't keep this from the police, and I certainly can't keep it out of my report," Chief Wallingford said with a note of genuine sympathy, "but I can work really slowly. That would be no surprise to anyone working in this screwed-up town. Citizens are more worried about my hoses over there blocking a bike path than the cause of this fire."

Cole's cell phone rang quietly from his pocket. Nolan thought the distraction was perfectly timed for their exit.

"Thanks, Chief. And no need to call in the cops. My buddies at the FBI are on the way. Let them deal with the local jurisdictional fight. And, uh, Go Beavers!"

Nolan headed toward the smoldering ruble while Cole slunk back into the shadows of the alley. It seemed like a black hole after the bright artificial lights blazing down on the arson scene. Water from a nearby hydrant ran down the cracked asphalt, flowing up against Cole's shoes before sluicing off into a muddy hole.

"Yep." Cole kept his introduction simple as he answered. He instantly recognized the cold monotone voice.

"You should have been more careful. Oz knows. You're dead. We're all dead if you don't expose N5G."

Cole ignored the gravity of the message.

"You seem to know a lot. Why not tell me what the fuck is going on? Pampering a tattletale isn't my style."

There was a long pause. Cole knew from interviewing thousands of people that shutting up during a long pause made the subject uncomfortable. People felt the need to fill the void with the noise of their own voice. This was usually when the best sound bite came out of their mouths. Words at that breaking-point moment were unguarded and not normally part of the script.

"I only hear rumors: snippets from hushed voices. Evergreen State. A secret lab. A guy they call H_2O. I didn't sign up to do a Jim Jones. I only wanted to help animals! That's it. I've already said way too much."

Before Cole could say a word, the call went dead.

Chapter 10

Dr. Dell stood barefoot outside his door, smoking a clove cigarette. His dogs sat sphinxlike, flanking him: ears raised, eyes darting from the approaching headlights to their master and back. Their ears perked at the soft crunch of Oz's decelerating car tires digging into the soft gravel parking lot behind the motel.

Oz stepped out of the car and peeled the tops off half a dozen tin cups of pate dog food. The sound of the empty containers being pushed about on the sidewalk by canine noses soon followed as they tried to lick out the final scraps.

"That's a nasty cut on your forehead. You okay?" Oz said, hoping to elicit more information without asking anything too stupid.

Dr. Dell had made a couple of stitches in his eyebrow using the button-replacement travel kit that came with his free toothbrush at the front desk.

"This is a small reminder that we are in a life-and-death struggle to save the planet. My suffering is nothing compared to the suffering of a parakeet forced to sing inside a cage, or an elephant beaten with a nail-embedded club so it will stand on one leg in the circus. It's time to call everyone together. I have finally perfected the key part of our plan."

Oz looked surprised but nodded like a good soldier. He had met many smart activists like Dr. Dell, who talked a big game and always acted as if they were the world's savior. In the end, none of them had the intestinal fortitude it took to get dirty and win the war. Dressing up in turtle suits or standing naked in a chicken cage outside Chick-fil-A drew attention to the cause, but it would never stop the big corporations from stomping their massive carbon footprints all over the world. Oz was one of the few activists who wanted to go the whole way and be a terrorist. He dreamed that someday he could be the Timothy McVeigh of animal rights.

It suddenly dawned on him that Dr. Dell might actually be the architect of incredible destruction. His loyalty tripled.

Dr. Dell slipped the still-lit butt into a faded beer bottle, converted by transients into the motel ashtray.

"Strip the room. Steal some new sheets and towels from the maid closet and do a swap. Burn what you need to, but not here and certainly not this whole damn building. Don't leave any evidence that I was here. I don't want to draw attention—or, I should say, any *more* attention. That fireball at your house today may have been necessary, but I'm not a big fan of federal agents descending on the Pacific Northwest."

Oz had been listening to radio snippets on the fire, and it seemed that the reporters were downplaying the importance. A friend had sent him some cell phone stills of the flames within minutes of the explosion. Oz wished mightily that his arson trick had killed whoever was snooping around his rental house. The pixel settings blurred the details, but there were definitely two men standing in his front yard. One of them looked a lot like a reporter who was always hanging around, pretending to be down with the cause. Oz was elated, however, with reports that his cat had escaped unharmed.

"Don't lose focus," Dr. Dell cautioned. "We're too close to screw this up now. ALB might seem like society's enemy to those who don't understand, but history will mark this moment with a greatness on a par with the resurrection of Christ."

Oz hated church. *If God's power couldn't help poor Sparks, then the hell with him.* Oz gravitated toward reading Revelations and left the rest of the Bible to others. He doubted that the man before him cared much about established religion, either, given that he kept saying he dreamed of killing every human on the planet.

"And hurry up! I need to get back to my research."

After gathering all the evidence from the hotel, Oz drove to a nearby state park, nearly filled to capacity with families enjoying a night's camping. He pulled into an empty site and started a fire in the pit. While others nearby toasted marshmallows to make s'mores, Oz toasted a pile of bloody towels and clothes.

Dr. Dell waited in the car, preparing e-mails to two member of his entourage on his laptop. He saved the drafts until he could get into Evergreen State College servers. Once inside, he could bounce the e-mails off hundreds of other college computer systems, resending his secret communications along a path so complicated as to make it untraceable. He made sure not to use any words that might trigger the NSA's Echelon spy system. He knew that America's top spooks routinely ran software on cell phone text messages and Web-based e-mail. They hoped to catch al-Qaeda terrorists relaying information electronically about future targets. It was relatively easy to avoid using words like "explosive" and "White House" in the same correspondence. It wasn't quite as simple to get meaningful messages to his core group without using the words "mercury fulminate" and "toxin" and "mass casualties".

> **To Chi**: Eyes on the prize. Scan all frequencies for animal chatter . Willow house in 3 days. We'll have a jam session.
>
> **To Spirit:** Can use help. Gnomes a tricky bunch. You stabilize me. Willow house workshop now.

Chapter 11

Pulling onto the Evergreen State College campus, Dr. Dell thought this could never be mistaken

for a place of fun. Students dressed mostly in black. An activist's base paid in full by

Washington taxpayers. Walking slowly up Geoduck Lane, Dr. Dell wished he ran the local tattoo

and piercing shop. He'd be set. Campuses were typically full of youthful exuberance, whereas

Evergreen State looked more like a funeral parlor parking lot. The college had a national

reputation as the place where students chose their own grades. Scholastic emphasis centered on

environmental causes such as sustainability and public service. It was perhaps the most

politically liberal ten acres on the West Coast. Courses of study included 500 Years of

Globalization; Native American Ceremony: Relating Hospitably to the Land; and Dance of

Consciousness. If any protest needed some sign-carrying beatniks or a few sullen anarchists, this

was the place to draw from.

Even though the administration and professors preached the evils of capitalism, they were

secretly money-grubbing whores. Evergreen State collected millions of dollars a year from tax

coffers and kept millions more of its own alumni contributions in reserve. If they had to raise

tuition 7 to 10 percent a year on students to keep profits high, so be it.

The college loved Dr. Dell and had him on the staff even though he taught no classes. An

expert at writing government grants, he had earned his freedom from scrutiny and oversight by

getting the Department of Agriculture to hand the college twelve million dollars to study the

dangers of bioengineered vegetables. Then he skillfully manipulated the disbursement so that it

all went to other professors and programs. The Evergreen State president personally thanked

him, throwing a wine-and-cheese soiree. Dr. Dell also wrote a grant for himself, telling the

administration it was a top-secret Interior Department project. Although that made the board of regents uneasy, approving the use of several million more dollars in free funding was a no-brainer. Only Dr. Dell knew the true source of funding and for what purpose his research might serve.

Once to the center of campus, Dr. Dell motioned for Oz to slip into the shadows along Red Square to keep vigil while he swiped his key card at the door of an uninspired building known simply as Lab One.

Dr. Dell's motion activated the light switch, and the concrete basement hallway inside Lab One took on a feeble glow. The eco-friendly bulbs would take ten minutes to warm up to full power. He keyed open a metal box that, to a casual observer, looked like an electric fuse panel. He punched "893," the radio frequency of the small independent radio station on campus, into the keypad, then put his eye to a retinal scanner. An unmarked steel door chirped open.

Inside the lab was an array of electronics the Pentagon would be proud to call its own. Some large monitors ran software programs of DNA manipulations. AGGGCATACCAATTGTCCCGTATGGTTAAC ran in endless loops and formations across a large screen. Hydrogen, oxygen, and carbon atoms spun around, transforming themselves, then reattaching in vast, colorful arrays of random order. They merged in endlessly changing sequences, like a hacker trying to break the combination of a bank's financial firewall. Red, blue, green, and yellow dots created a whir of 3-D animations. The Tinker Toys of life. Other monitors showed satellite weather models: rivers, oceans, and dammed-up reservoirs started as aqua dots from space, then grew as if the camera were on a bullet shot toward Earth. Several smaller screens were also tapped into security and traffic cameras up and down the West Coast. A crude clay model of a volcano sat pushed into the corner of a table. Lying on the desk were some trade magazines: *Proceedings of the National Academy of Sciences* and the *American Journal of*

72

Physical Anthropology. A long row of cages filled the back wall. A pair of gibbons swung casually between tire swings. The glowing eyes of rabbits, rats, raccoons, and cats lit up as they rushed to the front of their boxes. Dr. Dell spent a few minutes feeding each one by hand. He spoke softly to them, as if he were praising children for eating their creamed spinach. As a scientist, it gave him a little tingle to realize that the many hours of failures, adjustments, and new trials conducted painstakingly in this lab had finally come to fruition. The very character of life on earth was about to change forever.

* * *

Oz picked the girl because she was so stupidly alone. He could hear her iPod playing Nirvana before she even came into view. He swung the lead-shot-filled blackjack, landing a solid blow to the back of her head. He caught her by the backpack before she hit the ground. Moving quickly, Oz dragged her to the edge of some shrubbery. Outside the library loading dock sat several large recycling bins. He rolled the blue plastic container to his attack point and, with a heave, pitched the unconscious student inside. Oz strolled across the red brick pathway with his prize in tow. Dr. Dell would be pleased. The main entrance to the Lab One building was supposed to be locked at this time of night, but chemistry students fiddling with formulas for a test tomorrow had shoved a block of wood into the doorway. Oz headed for the elevator and hit P2. He left the cart in front of Dr. Dell's lab door, rapped hard once on the metal, and then kept walking. With all the fanfare of an ore car heading to a coal mine, the girl disappeared into the doorway.

* * *

The next twenty-four hours felt like a dream to freshman Anna Dipler. She kept thinking she needed to wake up, that she was late for a test but couldn't figure out how to get to the door of her dorm room.

The steel cage was cold on Anna's butt. She shivered uncontrollably. Her shoes squeaked when she moved, like a basketball player cutting to the lane. She still believed she had fallen asleep at the library, studying for her trig exam. Her jeweled belly button ached in the crease of her stomach. Fear filled her veins as a hand violently rattled the door of the cage. It brought her from near comatose to half aware. A middle-aged man in a lab coat laid a handful of saltine crackers on a tiny drawer that slid into a drop box inside the cage.

"Hey, Bunny. Eat something; you'll feel better."

Anna snapped off tiny pieces like the unleavened bread at communion. She hoped the wine was on its way. Her throat was so dry.

* * *

Dr. Dell toiled through the night with no sleep. He readied a dozen Dixie cups around midnight. He wasn't sure what day it was. His subject was breathing lightly, sitting with her head squeezed between her knees, when he finally decided it was time.

He pushed a small cup of water through the animal feed door and watched with great anticipation as the young woman gulped down the liquid.

Dr. Dell glanced at his watch's second hand. Nothing at first. No sign that his perfected juice was working. Then, at thirty-two seconds, small beads of sweat began to form on the young student's forehead. Her eyes shot open. Tiny capillaries in her cheeks started to burst under the skin. The girl's mouth suddenly clenched so tightly that Dr. Dell could hear teeth breaking. She was limp and dead in fifty-six seconds. He smiled. Moving with purpose, he took the remaining paper cups to each cage and emptied their contents into the bowls of his animals. They drank with abandon, little pink tongues lapping in unison. The parrots squawked; the mice chittered; the monkeys slurped. Dr. Dell fidgeted and paced, but an hour later, all the creatures were happy, relaxed, and drifting back into the corners of their cages.

Dr. Dell scribbled furiously into his dark leather notebook. He wanted to make sure history gave him his due. On page one, the idea was born: for decades, scientists had known that nearly 99 percent of human DNA is identical to that of chimpanzees. While researching how great apes adapted to drought conditions in the Democratic Republic of Congo, he had read a paper by researchers at the Tokyo Metropolitan Institute. Three glycobiologists there discovered that humans were missing the ninety-two-base-pair section of the genetic line that coded a hydroxylase enzyme in other apes. Master's-level biology students knew that humans were missing a particular form of sialic acid found in all other mammals. The sialic acid molecule, a harmless sugar, sat on the surface of every cell in the body. It could act as a receptor for messages from other cells. Dr. Dell spent a year trying to get different toxins and pathogens to dock on to the sugars. Cholera and influenza used it to gain a foothold on the cell, but those simply weren't deadly enough for his plan. Flipping through his workbook, he reviewed his drawings of sequence after sequence. Sialic acid in humans was N-acetylneuraminic acid. The form in other mammals was N-glycolylneuraminic acid. The only difference was that humans didn't have an additional oxygen atom. With each successive page, Dr. Dell's scribbling became more and more frenetic. He wanted to know how to make humans sick while allowing animals to live normally. After years of manipulating every variation of adenine, cytosine, thymine, and guanine, he had finally succeeded beyond his most fevered dreams. He was not only going to make people sick, he was going to devastate the populations of two continents. The world would

be a utopia not seen since a naked Adam and Eve gazed up at the Heavens.

Chapter 12

Colton Wiley beamed as he listened to the playful, sultry voice mail of the most non-pressuring girlfriend a guy could dream of.

"Hello, handsome. I'm back to civilization and could use your body in my soft bed. Call me."

He hadn't heard from Montana Harms in weeks, but her stash of underwear in the back of his sock drawer was a sign things were going in a positive direction. She had also left her cappuccino machine sitting on his small breakfast bar during her last visit. As long as those two items were left behind, Cole knew she would return, and that was good enough for him. Without exception, when she came around, it was fun and interesting and relaxing. Lots of beautiful women took shots at catching Cole's attention. Tall, single, on TV, and making a boatload of money—Jesus, he would want to date *himself* if he could. Being an investigative reporter came with a curse, however. Every day at work was such a wild adventure that ordinary people—even model-gorgeous ones—grew dull quickly. Cole's dates sucked the life out of him, absorbing the gritty details from his dangerous encounters and feeding off his fearless assault on society's most powerful institutions and people. If he wanted to be worshipped, keeping a girlfriend around would be easy. But most hours of the day, he insisted on being the center of attention, so when he had time to pair off, sitting across from someone at a quiet corner table over a glass of Barolo Bricco Rocche, the last thing he wanted to do was to perform.

When Montana Harms met Cole at a Woodland Park Zoo fund-raiser, she had no idea he was a local TV celebrity. Cole didn't know she was filthy rich. They ended up at the same table because they were the only two at the event who hadn't brought a date or a spouse. Cole had shown up to please a nagging animal rights source of his, Montana to make a secret auction bid on an eagle sculpture. She planned on bidding $100,000 whether she really wanted the iron bird or not since all the money went to charity.

Cole liked her so much, he ran a full background check on her as soon as he got home. Date of birth: 8/08/1980. Two parking tickets in the past five years. One arrest for trespassing after she got caught climbing up Snoqualmie Falls. Never married. No IRS tax liens. Ownership of a nice condo overlooking Puget Sound. Political donations to both Republicans and Democrats, all of them incumbents. And he didn't need his special databases to tell him how stunning she looked. Her high cheekbones and jet-black hair set her apart in a crowd, coming or going.

Cole hit return. Montana picked up on the second ring.

"Cole! Climbing was so awesome. You really should have come with me. My muscles are so frickin' sore, I'm begging for a massage. Tell me you're in town."

"I'm not, but I can be in three hours. I met the chef at Canlis the other day, and he says the Copper River salmon and porcini mushrooms entrée is damn near an aphrodisiac. How about a private kitchen tour and a quiet table for a late dinner?"

"Sounds luscious. Gives me time to unpack my gear. Three hours it is."

"Perfect," Cole said as he glanced down at his smoke drenched T-shirt, along with the blood caked on his knee. "Gives me time to run home and change - again."

He knew he couldn't get back to Seattle in time in his own truck.

"Jess, my man!" Cole shouted into his phone over what sounded like the static of an old UHF channel going off the air. "I need a ride ASAP from the Portland station back to Seattle. How far out are you?"

Jess Teeter was one of the few men left in this world who wished the Vietnam War still raged on. Flying news helicopters held tiny moments of excitement, but nothing could top the rush of whirring up the Mekong Delta in a Huey Cobra. Jess often still heard the roar of his 7.62 Miniguns tearing through four thousand rounds a minute. He often day dreamed green tracers zinging past his open cockpit door while his crew laid down rocket fire into a jungle line filled with Viet Cong. Those were some good days. Now a good day was chasing a teenage car thief as he slammed a stolen Porsche turbo into parked cars trying to outrun police. A horrible day was hovering over a jammed freeway with a traffic reporter. So goddamn boring he practically fell asleep at the sticks. Colton Wiley and Jess had been in their share of trouble together. Jess was an adrenaline junkie who broke FAA safety rules whenever it suited his fancy. It was a good match of personalities. The two of them plucked flood victims off rooftops live during the 6 p.m. news, chased an tornado across the Eastern plains, and crash-landed in a marijuana field after drug runners shot out the helicopter's hydraulics.

They both came close to getting fired after a high-profile stunt on Mount Rainier. Cole thought it would be amusing to have Jess fly him to the top and drop him off with a camera a few minutes before a former Vice President reached the summit. The VP's entourage had spent three days roped up, in crampons, hoofing it over deep crevasses and slick ice. When Al Gore finally got to the top, Cole's "Good morning, Mr. Vice President" was met with Secret Service machine pistols. Cole still had some numbness in one slightly frostbitten earlobe after being left handcuffed face down in the snow.

In less than an hour, Jess eased his newly painted slate gray Robinson Eurocopter-350 onto a faded rooftop cross on the outskirts of Portland. He lowered the engine's revs long enough for Cole to step up on the skid, climb aboard, and shut the flimsy aluminum-and-Plexiglas passenger door. Cole donned headphones, clicked the double-cross harness into place, and gave a big thumbs-up.

He kept relatively quiet, clearing messages from his cell, until Jess had crossed the Columbia River and dealt with the various flight control towers along the path back to Seattle. *Delete. Delete. Delete. Don't Care. Moron. Don't Care. Delete. Delete.*

Jess flipped a switch on his helmet microphone, so the rest of the trip's conversation stayed inside the chopper's bubble, and spoke his first words to Cole. "What am I supposed to put in the flight log for this trip, my oh-so-close-to-being-a-federal-felon son?"

This was always a fun game. The last time they went up together, Cole had Jess position the helicopter about even with the forty-fifth floor of the Columbia Tower during a wild party thrown by a couple of Seattle Mariner baseball players. Video of naked underage girls and starting pitchers taking hits out of a giant bong were quite a highlight reel. When Jess turned in six flight hours at a thousand dollars a pop to the station accountants, the invoice read simply "SKYLINE VIDEO AT NIGHT."

"Let's put down 'alternative energy research.' I can't think of anyone at the station who wouldn't approve that expense."

Jess smiled, thinking how many gallons of aviation fuel he was burning per minute.

"So, what are we *really* up to?"

"Just saving the world. But first, I have to get to a meeting with a certain female source of mine."

Jess pushed the throttle open. "If that means Miss Harms, I'm more than happy to play taxi."

80

Cole filled his pilot friend in on the arsonist's attempt to kill him, and the bizarre state trooper murder. Zero real evidence connected the two cases, but Cole never ignored his gut feelings. He didn't believe in extrasensory abilities or any other such garbage. He did listen for nuances in people's speech, watched for slight movements in their faces, and looked for clues that Scotland Yard's best might miss. Cole was a truth detector who wasted no time chasing stories that, after months of research and surveillance, would never work out. He could sit at his desk and ignore blaring police scanner traffic day after day, then sit bolt upright the moment his previously muted ears heard thinly veiled panic in the breath of a beat cop calling in a routine suspicious-persons report.

Jess rounded the Space Needle and eased down on a floating helipad tied to a dock on Lake Union.

"Be careful, Cole. I know a thing or two about dangerous situations, and you're chest deep in shit on this one. Don't forget, your mission is to uncover a hellacious investigative story. Let Nolan do his job. Document it. Blow open the scoop of the century, but don't miss history because you're ducking bullets."

"That's the best advice I've heard in years. Thanks, Jess."

* * *

As soon as his feet hit the shore, Cole dialed up a town car service. Drivers wasting time by the Experience Music Project a few blocks away peeled U-turns in the middle of Broadway and battled bumpers to see who could reach the dock first. Cole got into the winning car and had the uniformed driver wait while he ran up to his apartment, showered, and changed into black jeans, a fresh T-shirt, and suit jacket. His cat, Mario, was miffed at having to drink out of the toilet for the past few days, but his round midsection showed no sign of missing meals from the heap of dry food in his bowl. Cole hardly noticed the weather: "fifty-one degrees and misting rain" applied to half of any given year. He grabbed two Red Hooks from the fridge and was in front of Montana's spacious condo well before the local affiliate started its nine o'clock news. She leaned into the limo and gave Cole a short kiss and a long giggle.

Dinner was glorious. A sommelier wandered in and out of their conversation. An amuse-bouche of parsnip soup, a couple of creamy crab risottos, and warm fudge brownie topped with homemade caramel sauce obliged both of them to talk and laugh with their mouths full. Time evaporated. Cole paid the bill in crisp hundred-dollar bills, no change, so they could talk without even breaking eye contact. He had noticed Montana's swollen hand and avoided asking about its color until they slipped back into the limo.

"Angry rock or hornet sting?" Cole asked as he gently touched the swelling.

"I'll tell you all about it, but first you promised me a massage. I really hope you plan on using that request as a lead-in to some tantalizing foreplay."

Montana's condo was warm, her body warmer. For the first time in months, Cole was disconnected from the ongoing turbulent, awful world outside. After a passionate but quiet hour of lovemaking, he slept without nightmares.

Predictably, Cole didn't have to shield his eyes from any sun when he awoke. Panoramic windows provided a spectacular view of Puget Sound. He pulled on his jeans and wandered into the next room, where the smell of chocolate and espresso drew him to a kitchen island bar stool. The *Seattle Times* sat unopened in a wet plastic bag. Montana blew him a kiss as he rounded the corner.

"I already watched your morning newscast, and I promise you're not missing anything too exciting. Top story was a logging truck rollover accident. Nobody killed, but the freeway's a

82

mess. It went downhill fast from there. Some Bandido biker got stabbed in a fight near Belltown; then I got ten minutes of weather from that cute Hispanic boy you hired. I like how he says 'La Niña.' Makes me want to take a vacation in Mexico."

"I'm working on getting off the Department of Homeland Security's watch list first. I guess I ruffled some feathers with that story I did about the director slapping his wife around. Too bad they didn't erase the nine-one-one recording—seems pretty inept. I'm not sure they'd let me back in the States after we've been lying in the sun for a week. For you, though, I'm willing to take the chance of spending the night in a Third World jail."

Montana slid Cole a giant ceramic mug. "Thank you for last night. You bring me these little emotional surprises every time we meet. You pretend not to notice my injured hand when you pick me up, so I feel beautiful all night. Then, when you do ask about it, it's out of genuine concern and interest. I give you a 'no comment,' which I know you reporter types abhor, and you just move on to rock my world."

Cole didn't know what to say, so he gave Montana a powerful hug. He could see her face flush with emotion.

"Sit down and drink some coffee. I have a story to tell you. After I got done climbing, some Russian thugs showed up at my favorite diner. They want to scare Dad into letting them run his casinos. My problem really isn't the mob—I can muster a security detail that would obliterate their pathetic scare-the-little-Indian-girl operation. The problem is my dad. Some wife-beating Igor smashes my hand, takes a Kodak moment, and zips it to Cherokee HQ. Old Chief Harms went ballistic. Wants me to come back to Tahlequah or Norman. *Orders* me back. He wants to kill Vasily Anchov."

Cole knew more about Anchov's operations on the West Coast than any civilian should dare. Big Vasil's enterprises included smuggling automatic weapons into the Port of Seattle, running a massive car theft ring from British Columbia to Los Angeles, and stealing millions of dollars a year using a variety of food stamp and welfare fraud schemes. For several years, Cole had been picking away at an investigative piece about Anchov. Late one-night last month, Cole was sitting in an undercover van, secretly videotaping a midlevel crime lieutenant and his minions outside a storage facility chop shop. He watched as a stolen Mercedes was dismantled and stowed in a shipping container. To his left, Cole had seen another van up the street, and by zooming in with his night scope, he could see an FBI agent struggling to set up a mini tripod behind the driver's seat. The Russians closed the shop door, shielding the operation from the outside, as a light rain swept in. The FBI missed all the action and, alas, never spotted Cole.

"You know I've been working on a series of stories about Anchov forever, but I haven't aired anything yet. He's an unpleasant, overfed troll. I have enough evidence on his operations now to really throw a crimp in them, but not enough to lop the head off the snake. He's really careful to play the 'businessman' role and not get caught doing any of the criminal dirty work. I'm with your dad on this one. Don't mess with this guy. I don't want you stuffed in an oil drum and dumped at sea." Cole left out the "set on fire" part—though true enough, it seemed too much like a movie actor's line.

"Oh, Colton Wiley, you always say the *sweetest* things!" Montana gushed in a breathy voice, batting her eyelids like a vaudeville hooker. "I figure we can hatch a plan that sends Big Vasil to prison or back to the old country. You in?"

Cole smirked and stared and smirked some more, silently processing ideas that could earn him another national journalism award, create a huge public stir, put him on a mob hit list (again), please his girlfriend, and, undoubtedly, save some lives. He almost waited too long to open his mouth—he could see her starting to think he was mentally processing ways to get out of saying yes.

"You just handed me the final nail in Big Vasil's coffin," Cole said.

He spent the next hour laying out his plan. Montana was blown away by both its complexity and its assured effectiveness.

Chapter 13

It was the only house on the block that didn't have an illegal grow operation going. Two stories

with a cellar, the rental went for eight hundred dollars a month. The rotting wooden porch steps

made an inviting home for carpenter ants. Each window and doorjamb held a thick, uneven bead

of ugly white caulking, hastily applied. The yellow paint was basically intact, and an "I [heart]

my dog" sticker added a noticeable splash of red to an upstairs window. The furnace hadn't

worked since the Carter administration. A faint layer of soot covered the windows inside—

someone had forgotten to open the flue on the fireplace one evening. Nobody cared enough to

wipe the smoky film off anything. Small cat paw patterns weaved a visible path from windowsill

to food bowl and back. In the middle of the backyard stood an old weeping willow—old at least

by weeping willow standards. Thirty-five years of watching families and college frat boys play

beneath its draping wands. The shortened late October days had turned its lanceolate leaves buff.

Its long silken hairs floated on the breeze and stuck fast in the mud patch that stretched from

fence to gate.

The landlord, who lived twenty-two blocks away, hadn't visited in nearly a year. He got

his money in cash, two months in advance. It was always dropped off by an older teenage girl

who never spoke. She rode a child's bike up his sidewalk on Hazelton Drive to make the

delivery. Rainbow tassels hung from each handlebar. But folks around Keizer, Oregon, didn't

like to judge. That meant nobody stared. Nobody lingered long on even the oddest of

circumstances. *To each his own.* The ALB had chosen Willow House's specific location because

it sat adjacent to a crescent-moon-shaped lake just north of town. Artemis, the Hellenic goddess

of wild animals, used the crescent moon as her symbol after having a lesbian love affair with

Selene, the moon goddess. It was the perfect place to hide in plain sight. As a bonus, it was illegal to fish in the lake—the retirement center that owned the lake said so.

At three p.m., guests started to arrive. Wendell Canyon had been at the flop house for several hours, spinning a fresh blob of clay into a flower vase. A hired mercenary named Brian Zander casually wheeled up on a unicycle, softly whistling the Pixies' "La La Love You." Chivas Riviera stepped off the bus at the corner, pulled his wool scarf tight around his mouth, and jogged inside. Wynona Wanagi stopped near the curb, picked up a cigarette butt, and fired it up for its final two puffs. Her face was covered with lines of henna. The reddish-brown brushstrokes resembled a forest of bare branches in the dead of winter. Oz and Dr. Dell were the only two to arrive in a car.

The living room of Willow House looked better suited for a PTA meeting than a terrorist espionage planning session. Cheese and crackers sat on an IKEA table. The bottles of cream soda and beer looked so similar that everyone had to pause and read the label before choosing. The only thing out of the ordinary was a large wand that Chivas Riviera was sweeping over the light sockets, walls, and floors. Chivas occasionally froze in his footsteps, tuning his audio electronics packet and listening intently into a pair of expensive headphones plugged into a thick jack. The words that were about to be spoken were for a select, thoroughly vetted team of animal rights fanatics. FBI bugs inside, and inferred voice-recognition lasers outside, had to be eliminated as a possibility.

Chivas had an engineering degree from the Federal University of Amazonas in Manaus, Brazil. The city sat at the confluence of the Rio Negro and the Amazon. Raised by his uncle, Chivas had learned early in life that if he wanted to eat, he'd better bring the food home himself. The Amazon rain forest provided all he needed: 1.7 billion acres full of palm hearts, acaí berries, avocados, figs, plums, and nuts. He became an expert fisher at five years old, able to straddle a floating plastic bucket and harpoon the fat, ten-kilo Tambaqui rising to the surface to feed on rubber tree seeds. He walked past the centuries-old church on his way to his favorite watering hole each morning. He never went inside, but did say a prayer in Portuguese every time he passed, thanking God for the *floresta amazônica*. When his uncle had a heart attack and died Chivas felt like the luckiest teenager on Earth. He buried him in the home's tiny backyard, using a rusty shovel borrowed from a construction site. Nobody ever came by to ask where the old man went, so Chivas inherited whatever meager things his uncle possessed. He fixed up an old generator stuffed under the porch, and sold it so he could buy some new clothes. From that clothing store in downtown Manaus, he walked straight to the Nokia cell phone factory at the edge of town and applied for a job. They needed smelters to make tiny wires. It wasn't long before Chivas could not only build the entire cell phone but also manipulate the electronics board inside to ramp up connection speeds.

The company bosses hailed Chivas as a bright young *indígena* prodigy and created a scholarship for him to attend UFAM. Chivas realized quickly that he was the only one at the school who wasn't from the upper class of society, but it suited him well.

When Chivas indicated that the room was clean Brian Zander playfully muscled his arm around Wendell Canyon.

"Time for you to take a walk, my friend," he said. "Dr. Dell doesn't quite trust you yet."

With a look of mock indignation, Canyon replied, "I free a million mink, burn down a couple of sawmills, and shoplift all the batteries you need, but you're still not convinced, eh?"

"Look, man, you're a supercool activist, but you don't want any of this big-league stuff. I'm doing you a favor. Here's fifty bucks. Go find pizza, lots of beer, and a good football game. Sayonara."

The group watched as Canyon skipped out the door, flipping his hoodie up against the spitting rain. Zander knew he'd kill Canyon a bit later. *Drunks fell off the dangerous cliffs all the time.*

Despite being the most brilliant chemist since Dmitri Medeleyev, Wynona Wanagi was best known at Willow House for starting their meetings off with a cleansing. Growing up in Tobolsk, Siberia, she had learned the ways of the Chukchi from her mother. Using a feather and a small rattle from a diamondback, Wynona hummed a song from deep within her throat. She blessed the Willow House room by room, blocking energies from the outside world. She touched Dr. Dell's solar plexus, the life force center, and prayed to her spirit world for a full fifteen minutes. When Wynona fell silent, Dr. Dell began. The final meeting of the Animal Liberation Brigade's carefully selected army was about to get under way.

Standing in front of his hand-chosen followers, Dr. Dell felt like a god, and in a sense, he was about to become one: a megalomaniac with an advanced degree. The others in the room saw nothing delusional in him as they awaited his words. Hard-line Islamist militants didn't think a Hamas terrorist crazy for exploding a hunting vest full of C4 at a bar mitzvah. Why would this group of animal rights fanatics think anything strange about a thoughtful plan to kill a few billion humans when it meant that animals would rightfully inherit the earth? To regular folks who simply loved their dogs and despised dogfight arrangers such as Michael Vick, ALB's plans were so grandiose, so far beyond comprehension, that even if they were physically in the room and listening to Dr. Dell explain the plan, they wouldn't believe him. They'd just think he was another nut job in need of meds.

"When I first took over the Animal Liberation Brigade, I felt a special calling to help relieve the suffering of animals at the hands of humans," Dr Dell started. "We never wanted to be PETA or the Humane Society. ALB was meant to be different. I wanted to find that balance between activism and creating fear in those who oppose us. I fondly remember dipping hypodermic needles in HIV virus and mailing them to a professor who burned pigs with a blowtorch—he wanted to research a new, soothing aloe salve. Lord, the satisfaction I felt when I read online that he'd stabbed himself opening the box. I also enjoyed setting a bear trap near the president of Buckmasters' back door. I called to let him know someone was in his yard, stealing his ATVs at two in the morning. He ran outside, shotgun shouldered, ready to kill, and, *crunch*. Now he wears prosthesis."

Zander and Oz snickered and gave a little fist bump.

Dr. Dell continued, "Over the past year, I've watched hundreds of dedicated young ALB enthusiasts come and go. Most did our work out of the goodness of their hearts. But I was not really looking for animal lovers. I was looking for human haters. I was auditioning activists, trying to find the special few who felt the urge to literally tear the lips off a fisherman. Activists who were willing to slice the balls off a wool producer. Activists who could take pliers and yank all the teeth out of a zoo veterinarian and not lose a minute of sleep. You, my lieutenants, are that chosen few. Too many animal lovers fall apart when the FBI starts asking questions. I know that the people in this room would rather die than betray our cause. We've been doing good work. Hanging that pharmacy company vivisector in his closet to make it look like a suicide was excellent, Wynona. Pulling his pants down was a nice touch."

Dr. Dell reached down and deftly traced the hand-drawn spiderweb of henna crisscrossing Wynona's forehead. She kissed the tops of his fingers.

"I was looking for human haters like my friend Sgt. McKinsey. You see, Oz is a patient man. He never said a word about his treatment in the Army," Dr. Dell continued. "He never filed a complaint against the colonel who shot and killed his beloved dog. Oz even received an honorable discharge. What nobody knows is that about six months after that asshole Colonel Granderson retired to the posh Virginia suburbs of D.C., he burned to death in an "accidental fire", officially caused by a space heater malfunction, while Oz watched and listened to his screams from the woods nearby.

Oz kept his head down, fighting back tears of rage. Chi set his jaw muscles tight with renewed determination, now fully understanding he was in a room with people who would never yield or conform.

Dr. Dell let silence fill the room before revealing his world altering secret.

"The time has finally come for us to make history—make the ultimate difference and remake this world. Wynona and I have perfected a formula which, once ingested by humans, kills them in less than a minute. But then, cyanide does that, too, doesn't it, my love?"

Chivas raised his finger for Dr. Dell to pause, pulled his headphones back onto his ears, then flashed the all clear to continue.

"For simplicity's sake, I call it 'the Sugar.' '*El azúcar*' for my dear friend Chivas. We didn't develop a poison that some frail old lady could use to off her deadbeat husband of thirty-two years for his life insurance policy. The glory of this substance is that it won't harm a single animal. Not one. Death to man. *Eternal salvation for all animals.*" Dr. Dell overemphasized every word in the last sentence.

"Animals can drink it with no ill effects. The Sugar looks like water. Has no taste, no smell. It's not detectable by any standard. One drop could theoretically contaminate tens of millions of gallons of water. It's a living thing, seeking out flaws in the cells of humans . . . multiplying . . . The key to this creation was our discovery of how to manipulate a virus that binds with sialic acid, or N-glycolylneuraminic acid. It's known by scientists as Neu-five-Gc, hence the code name of our mission. N-5-G is a basic sugar that, in mammals, has an extra oxygen atom. That atom fills a perfect odd-shaped hole in the surface cells of monkeys, chimps, dogs, cats, mountain beavers—you name it. Humans have a void in that place. Maybe we humans don't have the right enzymes required to break that molecule down. Who knows? Maybe God thought such an infinitesimal imperfection in our cells didn't matter. Well, it does today. I am filling that hole. I am filling that hole with a type of highly charged, genetically corrupt glycoprotein that binds with the sialic acid. It will suck water into cells like a pool drain or a sump pump. The human cells fill with water, with no way to turn off the flow. Within seconds, the membranes burst water balloons. Cramping starts immediately. The lungs go next. People will feel like they are drowning."

Wynona giggled. Her empathy for human suffering fell below the zero mark—she actually enjoyed witnessing it. When she was 14, the family doctor labeled her bipolar, but that was being overly conservative and naive. Wynona was a full-blown schizophrenic, with an overlying multiple-personality disorder. She actually had three beings inside her head. The dominant personality was that of a geeky, eccentric college student whose brilliance in molecular science and engineering attracted the Glavnoye Razvedyvatel'noye Upravleniye, a Soviet army spy group known and feared as GRU. More secretive than the KGB, GRU had unlimited funding to research ways to kill people. If plutonium 210 ended up in the mayor of Moscow's glass of wine, the KGB got blamed, but it was GRU that made that kind of stealth murder possible. Wynona seemed a perfect fit for them. Loner. Slightly if not fully crazy. Whatever came out of her mouth, nobody believed, which made for solid deniability. But GRU didn't do a good job of factoring in Wynona's second personality: that of a vengeful rape victim. When she was twenty-four, a fellow scientist startled her one afternoon, jokingly tickling her ribs from behind while she was staring into a microscope. Wynona jabbed both his eyes out with a ballpoint pen, then strangled him with an electrical cord. The rush of adrenaline sent her into the rare third personality: the Condor. GRU staff ran into the lab and saw Wynona circling the bloody face of her colleague, arms wide, preparing to scavenge his body. They grabbed her a fraction of a second before she could begin chewing off his fingers. GRU had her tossed into a local psych ward, where the proper mix of medications had her writing new chemical formulas in no time. On a particularly clear-headed day, she sneaked out of the ward under a pile of dirty linens. She showed up in Geneva a week later, asking for political asylum.

Dr. Dell continued his sermon. "The chemistry works. We are sure of that. The problem that has kept me up night after night is how to deliver the virus to massive numbers of people without being detected. I, at first, filled three notebook tablets with potential targets: The New Croton Reservoir, the Yellow River, Lake Okeechobee, the Amazon. The list of rivers, lakes, streams, and watersheds went on and on. I realized that even the most successful plan required an army of people—and in people, I do not trust. Someone would chicken out, thinking there had to be some other, less violent, way. Fools. Maybe one of our animal-saving troops loves their parents or sister or grandma more than they love our cause. A word of warning to any person who doesn't fully understand what we're doing, and all our work will be ruined. I have found a way for a handful of us to potentially kill a quarter of the human beings on Earth, while preserving the lives of all Mother Nature's other creatures. The Animal Liberation Brigade will be known for saving this planet by rebooting populations back to the beginnings of history. And God said, 'Let the water teem with living creatures, and let the birds fly above the earth across the vault of sky.' Amen."

Chapter 14

Nolan Burke always made it a point to stand up when his boss approached his desk. It was a dick move, but a simple way to remind the smaller guy that power as a government bureaucrat and the power of physical dominance were quite different.

"I asked for a written update two days ago on that cabin fire and that debacle in Portland. I've got Homeland Security and Quantico both breathing down my ass and my boss's ass and her boss's ass. Come on, Burke! I can buy you more time, but only by bogging this case down in meetings and brainstorming sessions. Write the damn report and get back into the woods."

Nolan smiled that kind of smile that had allowed him to get away with so many things in life.

"You got it, boss. Believe me, I wouldn't be in this fluorescent-glowing, carpet-covered government building for any other purpose. I'm almost done. Five minutes, and your e-mail will ding."

"You have a regular old garden-variety pyromaniac in mind, or is this really a terrorist operation, like DHS so badly wants it to be?"

Nolan grimaced and cocked his head to the side before answering.

"Hard to say just yet. The fires I'm investigating were set to cover up other crimes. Those crimes probably have something to do with the Animal Liberation Brigade. ALB is listed on the terror watch list. It's a fringe group with, at most, a couple dozen people involved. Homeland Security says they don't even know who actually leads the merry little band. I question that. It feels like America's watchdogs in Washington D.C. are keeping a few secrets of their own. ALB picks up recruits who usually get kicked out of some other animal rights group for being too violent or extreme. The FBI has never figured out how they coordinate activities, either. ALB crows about their accomplishments via blogs, texts, and through a Web site that runs off a server in Denmark."

Nolan spun his computer screen toward his pencil-pushing boss.

"The front page of the ALB site right now touts an eyewitness account of how one of its members drove steel railroad spikes into a dozen century-old Douglas firs near Mount Baker. The protester was angry about some court ruling that failed to protect a rare butterfly. The metal was high enough on the trees that the loggers didn't even notice. When the logs finally found their way to the mill, the spikes did a real number on the ripping blades, tearing them to shreds. Some poor schlep pushing the timber into the chute caught a piece of diamond blade in the shoulder—damn near tore the arm off, but he lived. The ALB-loving writer took great joy in the maiming of some guy with three kids whose wife had died of cancer earlier in the year. The last line of the story says it all: 'I hope his kids will someday realize that Daddy is murdering the planet and leave him to rot in some one-star nursing home.'"

"Despite what you think," Nolan continued while punching the send button on his e-mail, "I'm not demanding the U.S. Forest Service keep an exclusive on this case. We really could use the FBI and a few spooks with underworld connections to dig around. This N5G insignia must mean something to someone. I just don't want to get sidelined. We need more time to secure the motive for killing those two young women near St. Helens. Have those agencies put some heat on known ALB members for new leads. That should be distracting enough to keep them from seizing control of our investigation."

Nolan emphasized the *our* so his boss would feel as if he were involved in the exciting twists and turns of the case and had something to gain from his continued involvement. He knew that the midlevel forestry division manager who stood slightly below his chin would take the bait. A murder investigation was sure to add spice to the day of a guy who was normally in charge of overseeing budgets for salmon restoration projects.

A low rattling sound filled the cubicle. Both men grabbed for their pockets. Nolan saw it was Cole, and headed toward the door, hoping reception would improve rapidly as he jogged toward the parking lot. He punched return on his cell.

"Dude, where you been? I left, like, ten messages!" Nolan chided his friend.

"I knew you had a good time on our three-day man date, but you really will never get me into bed sounding so desperate," Cole zinged.

"Bite me," Nolan shot back. "I put a trace on Oscar McKinsey's bank cards and got a hit in the Olympia area. Wanna make a run on a few businesses? You know how your pretty mug makes people want to spill their guts."

* * *

Cole was pulling back into his Seattle TV station parking spot after Jess had dropped him back off in Portland to pick up his truck. Most of the anchors and reporters had name tags posted at the front of their spots. Cole's space, however, was a nondescript spot at the edge of the lot next to the storage shed. The last thing he needed was a name placard. As it was, he figured dying from old age was a long shot—he didn't need a monogrammed parking space announcing to every pissed-off subject of one of his investigations just where to plant a car bomb or sight in a sniper rifle. Cole wanted a fighting chance—at least make them work for their revenge.

"That's nice police work, Nolan. A little basic for my taste, but high-five anyway. I have something we also need to check out. Get to get that blood rushing again. I've been bored since we nearly got blown to bits. I held out on you in Portland. I was worried you might put it in some report.

"What's the 'it,'" Nolan asked.

"A guy—I can't really call him a source—called and whispered a few rumors in my ear. Whoever it is knows I've been asking around about ALB and the arsons, so I know he's at least in the animal rights arena. My gut tells me the information is legit. I'll meet you at Evergreen State near the Daniel J. Evans Library in a few hours. That's where we're supposed to dig around. Then we'll check out the financial transactions. Later."

Cole hung up, threw open his door, then lipped the lid on the locked tool box in the back of the truck. He wondered if he needed to replenish his supply of camera batteries. Hearing a faint shuffle of boots on the sidewalk which ran outside the station parking lot wall, he reached down and unsnapped the holster on his Kahr PM9. When Chuck Reynolds rounded the corner, he loosened his grip, stood up, and leaned back against the fender well.

"I thought I heard your truck engine! I was up the street getting some pizza for lunch," Chuck shouted a bit too loudly from several car lengths away.

Cole suspected he'd had a few brews with that pizza. The assistant news director longed for the good old days when everyone in the newsroom had a bottle of their favorite booze and a Dixie cup in the bottom desk drawer. Chuck spoke quickly.

"November ratings are coming up. The promotions department's going crazy because they don't have a clue what you're up to. They have a hundred and eighty thousand slotted for radio ads alone. I need to give them a summary of a sure-thing investigative series in less than two weeks. I didn't breathe a word about arson or animal rights or terrorism, but I did promise a roomful of people who write our paychecks that you will blow away all expectations. Have you shot anything yet? Edited something?"

"Relax, Chuck. You haven't overpromised. I already have enough material to destroy the competition. It doesn't take much to fake out the suits upstairs. They think investigative journalism is testing which fast food French fry is lowest in calories. I have a long, long way to go before I nail down the specifics on this arson, but I'll give you permission to throw the general manager and promotions director a bone. Here's what you do: Tell 'em you need to meet. Really secret. Nothing can be put in writing. Say I'm under deep cover working to get inside an animal terrorism group. Ask them to increase security around the station. Scare 'em a bit. Casually sift the words "bomb," "revenge," and "target" into the conversation. Tell them Cole has already written the anchor lead-in. Then—and this is the most important part—recite it using your best anchor voice. Have some fun. Mess with 'em. You ready? Here's the lead line: *'ARSON HAS ALWAYS BEEN A TOOL OF TERROR FOR THE ANIMAL LIBERATION BRIGADE, BUT TONIGHT KZPR-TV INVESTIGATIVE REPORTER COLTON WILEY LINKS THE GROUP TO MURDER AND ATTEMPTED MURDER. IN FACT, WILEY WAS ONE OF THE PEOPLE THEY TRIED TO KILL.'*"

Reynolds stood with his mouth slightly agape. "You are a goddamn poet. A sick, twisted, cold-blooded liability nightmare of a news poet."

"I know. Keep up the good fight, boss. I won't let you down," Cole said as he was pulling away, heading toward Olympia.

He wasn't even close to getting a full investigative piece together for sweeps, but he was a realist. There was already a story developing in his head. It played out like a movie or a dream and was often accompanied by the sound of an old Olivetti 33 manual typewriter. The words flowed to him with ease. Cole figured he'd start by relaying to viewers a firsthand account of what happened to him—and what nearly happened—at the Portland house. How someone tried to kill him and a federal agent. He could do a live shot surrounded by the blackened debris of the burned house. It wouldn't be a crime scene for much longer, so he would have free access to the property by then. He made a mental note to call Portland's demolition contractor and see what it would take for the crew to leave a room-size area of rubble where the kitchen used to be. Cole would walk viewers through each move that led him closer to danger and near death. Up the still-standing concrete steps, pretending to open the bent screen door, describing the sights and smells of the room, then he would pretend to hear the sound of leaking fuel. He didn't have to lie to recreate the excitement and danger, which was all still very real to him. A wireless microphone hidden beneath the knot in his tie would give him full range of motion. The videographer could light the entire lot using filters to give it a spooky red glow. A small battery-powered light on top of the camera, in a bluer hue, would then make Cole pop out to viewers as if he were standing inside their living room. Just that live portion could be an outstanding lead story that would make the bosses spew in their pants, and once the tape started to roll, no one in three states and lower Canada watching a TV would move a muscle.

He rewound his hidden camera footage from the day of the explosion and was pleasantly surprised at what he had captured. While he was diving onto the lawn, the camera bag happened to be pointing back toward the erupting fire. Cole figured that with minimal effort, he could also interview April Slade's mom. He had set the stage of trust with her early on. Of course, he would be the first person to tell her that her daughter was dead, the victim of murder. He even practiced: *She didn't feel any pain—the fire was set to cover up her death.*

He was experienced at delivering such news while cameras rolled. It was one of the few unplanned, unscripted moments left on TV. What viewers got was a gut-wrenching sneak peek into a grieving person's heart. Cole watched night after night as people faked their emotions on the local news. Pretend anger from a fist banger at a city council meeting. Pretend sadness from a missing girl's mom when the kid had, in fact, been beaten to death by the mom and buried in the backyard. Pretend happiness from an overstressed dad taking his five kids sledding at first snow. His fellow reporters gladly put all that bullshit, untrue, made-up crap on the air every day, and nobody criticized them. However, anytime Cole made a subject of one of his stories uncomfortable, the newspaper editors and bloggers came unglued. They wrote column after column about shoddy yellow journalism and pointed at Colton Wiley as the Antichrist of the Fourth Estate.

Cole planned to do a short profile of April and her animal-loving ways. He had exclusive video of the cabin arson scene. He'd get Nolan to give him a quick, official-sounding fifteen-second sound bite: "... *under investigation, following leads, horrific sight to see,*" and so on. When the cameras came back to him live at the house, he'd be holding that Animal Liberation Brigade necklace with the N5G etching on back while delivering a final line that cops always appreciated: a plea for tips.

"This was around the neck of each dead girl. Officials don't know exactly what it means. If you do, call the FBI, the Forest Service Arson Hotline, or, if you want to remain anonymous, call me directly and I'll pass along the information."

That last part was most important of all. Cole knew there was a bigger story, but he had to be conservative on what he reported until more of it was confirmed. Plenty of loons would call him with junk, but in all that dirty river gravel, there would be a gleaming nugget or two. He couldn't, in good conscience, report his suspicions about the trooper's death being linked. Putting Oscar McKinsey's name out there didn't seem wise, either. If he confirmed those elements before the story aired, great, but he didn't have to push the envelope to win his slot or

101

attract a boatload of advertisers. Cole's favorite part of this half-baked plan was that all those reporters who actually covered the explosion of Oz's house in Portland would get bitched out by their news directors for not unearthing the real story.

He again punched up talk radio and enjoyed the drive back down I-5. When he pulled into the Evergreen State parking lot near Longhouse, Nolan was sitting on a low rock wall, his long legs dangling within an inch of the ground, drinking a grande caramel macchiato.

* * *

Nolan felt as if he could sit here all day. Some of his earliest memories were of sitting in the cool morning darkness with his father, hunkered down under a small camouflaged canopy. They would listen for the wild turkeys to drop with a thud from the trees at dawn. They gabbled and cackled at one another while they gathered for breakfast in the center of the grove. Nolan's dad had taught him how to slowly tap and grind a pair of hand-smoothed wooden blocks together to sound like a female turkey looking for a mate. The short, high-pitched chirps usually brought a big tom within seventy feet of their gun

Cole slid next to his friend on the wall and looked up into the gray sky: water droplets lofting down like mist from a Disneyworld cooling rack. He eased his camera bag down the few inches to the concrete.

"How long you been sitting in this soup?" Cole inquired, truly trying to understand why his partner in crime wasn't drinking that unmanly coffee inside the cab of his truck.

Nolan grinned and took one last lukewarm sip before free-throwing it into a nearby trash can.

"A half hour or so. What? That weird to you?"

"Sitting still. Contemplating life. Enjoying the rain. Not talking. Studying nature's beauty. I don't get it. Just like I don't get people watching commercials instead of fast-forwarding through them when you DVR a TV show. I will admit I enjoyed sitting relatively still on a beach in St. Martin for a few days, but I was drunk the entire time. I'm not good at pause."

"Then let's roll—find ourselves a killer. Where to, Nancy Drew?" Nolan jumped up, brushing water off the top of his shoulders.

"This anonymous guy has reached out to me a couple of times about our murder victims at the cabin. I can't get him to talk in real sentences. Might be dealing with borderline mental issues or incredible guilt. Either way, lead me here. This caller mentioned Evergreen State, the nickname H_2O and a lab. That can't be that hard to figure out, can it?"

Cole led the way across Red Square to a map painted on an Evergreen State information kiosk. Nolan looked up at the clock tower that loomed over an open space filled with students zipping between classes like ants. He couldn't help but notice how unsettled it made him feel.

It reminded him of the college tower that rose high above the University of Texas, where, on August 1, 1966, a former Marine named Charles Whitman killed fourteen people for the fun of it. Unimpeded for 96 minutes, he sat there with his sniper rifle and picked off kids and teachers one by one. Textbooks and backpacks and girls' shoes lay strewn over the cobblestones, mixed with gallons of blood, by the time someone finally kicked in the tower door and shot Whitman. Nolan sort of kept Cole between him and the tower, just in case. After all, what were friends for?

They stopped to study the map, and Cole wrote down the locations of every lab on the back of a business card. A pair of teenagers stood nearby, hawking flyers to anyone who came within ten feet of their spot.

"Hey, mister," one of the kids called out to Nolan.

Nolan almost didn't look up, because it didn't dawn on him that he was a mister. He still felt as though he could walk into a dorm kegger and fit right in.

"We're looking for our friend Anna. She disappeared sometime earlier this week. Her parents are worried sick. Not like her to skip class and tests and run off."

He handed Nolan a color picture of a girl with a pixie haircut and a beaming smile. He was folding it, ready to stuff it in his pocket, when Cole grabbed it out of his hand and stepped toward the hawker.

"She probably ran off with her boyfriend to a concert or to drive to a warm, sunny, not-so-godforsaken place for a break. You sure she wouldn't do that?"

"A teenager missing for a few days. Who the hell cares?" thought Nolan as he studied Colton's face.

"You're that reporter. Take a flyer and put it on the news, man. Maybe the cops will take it seriously."

"The cops never take this shit seriously unless you get kidnapped by a known sex offender and five people witness you getting dragged into a windowless van. They let this kind of disappearance work itself out. If something turns up really ugly, they jump in. Sorry. That's the realities of life, kid."

The young man paused, looked around, and then lowered his voice.

"She's not the first freshman who's fallen off the face of the earth this semester. The chicks are on edge. Sororities have been ramping up their buddy program after dark. Campus mall cops found Anna's cell phone right over there, but the provost quashed a real investigation. He doesn't want to panic parents."

Cole shook his head in disgust, and Nolan saw his friend's mental wheels turning.

"Hold on, man. We don't have time to investigate a missing kid," Nolan warned.

"The story isn't about a missing college kid. It's about a cover-up at the highest levels of a government-run institution. Butt-covering by bureaucrats, at the expense of a scared and worried family. Typical bullshit. Makes me mad," Cole said with finality of a set mind.

He turned back to the student. "Provost should worry more about me. I'll see what I can do," he said before whipping out his camera. He shot five or six video clips of Anna's friends distributing flyers.

Wide angle . . . medium shot . . . tight framing of flyer . . . wide pan, then push. Cole did an informal shot sheet in his head. He made Nolan monitor the camera on an extending tripod while he did a five-minute interview with a pair of the missing girl's friends. Cole was thinking the quality of both audio and video were way below his standards, but the news managers had no such standards—they would take anything that filled a black hole.

"Come on, Cole. I know *you* don't work for the U.S. Forest Service, but these animal rights murders are a really big deal. It's the most important case either of us will work on, maybe ever in our careers. You can't take time out to screw around with a runaway college student!"

"I know, you're right. But there's something about this tickling my sixth sense. When we're done today, I'll do a backpack journalist thing. I don't sleep much anyway. My bosses have long loved the concept of firing all the photographers and editors and only having a few cheap, star-struck reporter types do entire news segments on their laptops. I'll pretend I'm embracing the idea. The news director will piss himself with delight."

Cole and Nolan slipped into the library and wandered over to a series of narrow marble stair steps until they found the resources room. A few taps on a computer sitting in the corner sent them to a shin-level shelf along a center wall. A cracked, crisscrossed-pattern light cover full of dead bugs hung overhead. Nolan knelt down to look at a series of numbers stamped out on a twirl-wheel labeler stuck to a metal brace. *EVERGREEN STUDENT AND STAFF DIRECTORY* was the fifteenth book from the end. Nolan turned to sit awkwardly on the floor—more leg than the aisle could handle. Cole sat next to him. Inside the book were 294 faculty names, 294 pictures of smiling professors, lab assistants, secretaries, and coaches. No middle names and nobody with the initials "H. O." There was a Stella Creek and a Greg Puddles, but nothing in either name cried out as obviously water related. Neither worked in a lab. In the student section, two others had the initials "H. O.": Hector Ortiz and a person who appeared to be his identical twin brother, Horacio Ortiz. Cole pulled out his smart phone, signed into Facebook under the name "Ed Murrow," and did a quick search for the keywords "Ortiz," "Olympia," and "Evergreen." "Likes" included girls with tattoos, reruns of *Law and Order,* and *chorizo con huevos.* Unlikely to be vegetarian-arsonist-killers.

Cole was frustrated. "Maybe the fucking mastermind of animal terror just sweats a lot. Kids make up names in middle school and they stick with you for years. You know, 'Look at Timmy's gross pits. Let's call him H_2O.' I still can't shake my nickname, Donkey Dick."

Nolan laughed loud and smacked the book shut, drawing the ire of a homeless man trying to sleep at a table. This was the best shelter around: quiet, warm, dry. And even if you stank like garbage, nobody dared say anything, for fear they would be seen as uncompassionate. Nolan reached into his pocket and pulled out a ten-dollar bill for the man and laid it on the table on his way by. Cole scooped it up right behind him, shaking his head in disgust at his friend's weakness.

106

They headed across campus, following their lame map drawn on the back of the card. It was forty-eight degrees and spitting rain. Weathercasters in Seattle had the easiest jobs on the planet. Nolan held the door open for a young female student as they entered the Lab Two building. He felt vaguely pedophilic for staring at her 18-year-old bum as she scooted past with a thank-you. They headed to the top floor, opening doors and staring into room after room for anything that might be related to the tipster's clues. They paused at a class for Environmental Engineering and watched for a few moments through the glass door. The professor looked disheveled while he worked through a PowerPoint presentation on how river erosion affected steelhead spawning. When class was over, Nolan walked in, flashing his badge.

"I'm with the U.S. Forest Service, Arson division. Can I speak with you for a moment?"

Cole stuck his head into the hallway with a vastly different approach, half-jokingly shouting "Yo, H2O. You here?" He disappeared.

The engineering professor seemed irritated by the commotion, but Nolan saw no hint of recognition stemming from Cole's shenanigans.

"I'm sure I put out my campfire the last time I went to the forest, so yes, how can I help?" the professor said with an appropriately fake smile staring at Nolan's shirt patch.

"Does the nickname H2O ring a bell with you?" Nolan asked

The professor appeared to be doing his best to dig deep into his memory, running through a mental list of all his students and colleagues. He walked over to his desk and slid a long list of names out from his desk drawer and glanced over it, finger tracing from top to bottom.

"Sorry. I've never heard anyone called that. I can give you directions to the human and student resources office. Maybe they can help. What's this about?"

Cole came back in the room, interrupting Nolan in mid-response.

107

"Come on! Come *on*! We gotta go. Leave him to his duties of brainwashing young minds into believing evil cars are killing polar bears."

Out in the hall, Cole led the way down the stairs, outside, and to the front of an adjacent building. He eyeballed Lab One while Nolan waited patiently for some sort of explanation. He had learned long ago that it did no good to ask or try to rush the process along. Cole's brain needed time to run through every single scenario, just like the Navy's twenty-seven-ton ENIAC computer from 1944. The end results were impressive, but it was brutal waiting for the calculations to ramp up and spit out an answer.

Cole finally spoke. "While you were quizzing that wild-haired liberal I was goofing off in the hall. Obvious, I know. I'm loud and attracting attention, and this janitor gives me a dirty look and one of those big, dramatic finger-pressed-to-the-lips *Shhhh*'s. I'm sure Evergreen State doesn't actually call him a janitor—probably a 'maintenance technician.' Makes more money than you do. No wonder the kids' tuition rates get hiked twenty percent every year. Anyway, I pretend I'm really sorry and apologize. Then it dawns on me that janitors know everything. They wander around night and day, standing in the shadows like vampires with a mop and a rag. They hear kids spreading rumors. They know where TAs sneak off to smoke pot. They know who keeps weird hours and who screws who in the cold parking lot after work. For Christ's sake, the janitors dig through the trash of this place and see what kind of *gum* you chew! So, I introduce myself and he gets all impressed and tells me he watches me on the news all the time. Big fan. South-of-Seattle viewers are definitely my peeps. Anyway, I ask one brilliant question: is there any place on campus that he's been told *not* to clean? His eyebrows ruffle. He frowns. He gives me that lean, like he's not supposed to tell me what he's about to deliver. I never understood why anyone in their right mind would tell a television reporter something and expect it to remain a

108

secret without some kind of express verbal contract. Does that make sense to you?" Cole took a breath.

Nolan shook his head and, with the patience of Job, let the diatribe flow.

"The janitor says his crew received notice about a year ago to stop cleaning in the basement of Lab One. Contractors spent a few months remodeling. He wandered down there to see what all the fuss was about and says the basement hallway looked the same as it had for thirty years. The only noticeable change was a high-tech door and a bunch of new electrical panels and heating/cooling ducts. As I stand here and look at Lab One, I wonder why there is a shiny exhaust pipe winding up the side all the way to the roof. Can you say 'incinerator'? I'm not saying it's a sure thing, but you must admit, if anything is going to carry the label of 'secret lab' in this enclave, this tops the list."

"Let's go see the provost." Nolan spun forty-five degrees toward the administration building.

"I would normally pan that idea as having a fatal lack of imagination and adventure, but actually, I'd love the see him," Cole smirked. "I have a few questions." He was on his cell texting the news desk:

> *"Need a shooter asap. contact govt beat guy. I can almost see the capitol*
>
> *building downtown from here. need him at Evergreen State. get him here in 15*
>
> *min & I can guarantee you a lead story at 5.*

He hit Send.

"Cole, there's no time for that missing girl," Nolan grumped, then gave an exhausted sigh.

"Sorry to say, buddy, it's going to be a very inefficient day, but not because of me," Cole shot back. "Here's how the next few hours are going to go: You wander in and speak with the provost's secretary without an appointment. She is pleasant but makes you wait for frickin' ever listening to elevator music in the lobby. Maybe you'll get to thumb through a couple of *Multiculture Review* magazines on the glass table. Then the provost will meet you with a big grin and welcome you into his humble twenty-four-hundred-square-foot office. He will listen and smile and nod. You want him to let you into the lab to see if it might be anything important to your investigation. He says sure, no problem, but it's college policy to have a search warrant before that occurs. 'Teachers' rights are über important.' More smiling. Believe me, when I ambush that rat bastard with a hot TV light, asking about a missing girl, you're going to enjoy it as much as my viewers."

Chapter 15

Vasily Anchov loved having his fat fingers massaged and pampered by the manicurist. He refused to remove his diamond-and-platinum pinky ring, so it sat partly submerged in a small glass bowl with warm, sudsy water as he soaked his cuticles. The young blonde woman doing his nails had once dreamed of becoming a mail-order bride for any red-blooded American man who could figure out the visa paperwork out of Minsk. Instead, her role until death would be to do whatever Big Vasil wanted. She quietly ran a soft-bristle brush over his nails while, in the far corner of the room, a man screamed for mercy.

"Too loud for my sensitive ears," Anchov said. "Mute him."

A wiry man with small glasses took a three-inch deck screw from his tool bag and slipped it through a quarter-size metal washer, then used a cordless drill to drive the screw up through the soft tissue of the man's mouth. The screw spun up through the skin and muscle between the jawbone and the trachea and spiraled through the tongue, meeting scant resistance until it met the bony plate on the roof of his mouth, where it bit in and cranked to a stop. The screams turned to a muffled cry, at a tenth the earlier volume, as blood trickled down onto the captive's stomach and then to the stainless steel drain pan on the floor.

"Much better!" Big Vasil said as the two men who had been causing the earlier screams slipped a plastic bag over the man's head. "Complaining about very fair interest rates I give you on loan for family restaurant was mistake. Thirty-eight percent a month is capitalism at its finest. You need; I lend. Supply and demand. A perfect marriage. Now, I suppose, Vasil Enterprises owns another food establishment. What kind food?"

"It's an Italian place, sir," said one of the goons, looking up from suffocating the borrower.

111

"How ironic! Who would think la Cosa Nostra get so weak that they let a peasant like me stomp on their turf and own Italian eatery? I *love* America!"

Vasil's phone chirped. Soft, sudsy water dripped from his hands as he reached for his cloned cell. He smiled broadly as Montana Harms' picture popped up on his screen. It was the same picture his associates had taken at the diner and that he had e-mailed to her father in Oklahoma.

"The lovely Miss Harms. To what do I owe this exquisite pleasure?"

"My father, brothers, and the entire Cherokee nation police force, which happens to be on my father's payroll, are hatching up a seriously violent plan to make sure you don't threaten me again. It seems a little over the top. They actually brainstormed ideas on a dry-erase board. I had two favorites, both old-school: stake you to the middle of a brush pile and slow-roast you; OR cut your ears off, bury you up to your neck in red clay, and let the vultures and coyotes eat your face. I understand turkey buzzards like to go for the eyes first."

Big Vasil laughed, and the deep rolls of belly fat rippled and shook like quicksand in an earthquake. "I can only assume you are concerned for my personal well-being, or you wouldn't be so kind as to warn me."

Montana Harms had spent much of her thirty-three years as a mediator between her not-so-politically-correct father and the rest of the world. She carefully crafted the Harms family's reputation by volunteering on the right nonprofit boards, donating money to the right causes, and manipulating the media into doing fluff feature stories on the casino empire. Montana had orchestrated a Food Channel special featuring some four-star chefs who worked in the casino's restaurants, and she had even managed to get a front-page *Wall Street Journal* featurette on how gambling profits were successfully being used to reduce domestic violence and child abuse on nation lands.

"Can we meet this weekend? Leave that meathead Dolph Lundgren lookalike who smashed my metacarpal at home. I assume you aren't in the mother country?" Montana probed.

"I don't like questions, my dear, but am happy to entertain the idea of what I hope is sound business proposal. I love money. I love gambling. If you're offering to help me invest in these things, I will clear the schedule. Yes."

"Great. I'll be in Vancouver, B.C., for a charity event this weekend. How about Stanley Park before sunset Saturday? In the open. Nothing weird. If we can have a reasonable chat, I think you'll be happy with the financial results. I can be very persuasive with my father. Let me be clear, though: he doesn't know a thing about this. He wants you tortured and dead. If that happens, there's a chance the chief spends the rest of his life in prison or on the run. I'm sure you have plenty of other enemies, but I don't want to chance that. Plus, I don't think this war is good for business or my inheritance. This will be a peaceful, productive meeting *if* you let it."

Big Vasil huffed, "I will be there, but I need a few men with me nearby. As you said, "'I have enemies.'"

"Relax. You'll be glad to know that I chose to meet with you in Canada because the FBI here in the United States is starting to unravel some of your misdeeds. You and I both know it wouldn't take much to issue warrants for your arrest. Fraud. Extortion. And my favorite catchall crime: conspiracy. And I bet you haven't been paying taxes to Uncle Sam on all that drug and gunrunning money. On the other hand, the Royal Mounties are way behind. They know your organization runs stolen car parts up and down the coast, but they're having a hard time getting any of your runners or moneymen to flip."

Big Vasil looked around nervously. He didn't appreciate Montana airing dirty laundry on an unsecured line. She could read his mind.

"Don't worry, though. Vancouver police aren't anywhere near. Why would I set you up? The last thing I need is to get arrested with you and get my picture on the front of the *Sun*. We'd look like Jabba the Hut and Princess Leia.

The goons, listening in with one ear on each side of their boss chuckled, then stopped short when Big Vasil did not crack a smile.

"Want some final advice?" Montana didn't wait for the answer. "Get back to Seattle and try to clean up your act. Gambling regulators are a pain in the ass. If they smell a rat like you anywhere near a casino, nobody cashes in. By the way, you know not to cross back into the U.S. at the main gate in Blaine, right? Skip over east of Lynden and do the self-serve border crossing at two in the morning. Border Patrol's soft over there. Cameras are always down."

"I don't need lesson sliding into and out of countries, my dear. Borders are like sieve," Big Vasil bragged. He sucked a deep breath past his three chins. "You have done your homework. I like you, my bold Indian princess. Feisty, like my first wife, God rest her soul. Terrible accident with cinder block falling on head. Pity. I do not like being disappointed, Ms. Harms. Bring your best and only offer. I will take or leave. Negotiations not my strong suit. Good day."

Chapter 16

Cole guessed Evergreen State College Provost Albert Russell morning went something like this:
He woke up early, walked his dogs, had a cup of coffee, and kissed his wife of twenty-something
years good-bye before heading to his luxurious office near the heart of campus. When he got to
work, he banged his twenty-something secretary on the Turkish rug near his desk. Yes, it was a
perfect start, but Colton Wiley had a way of changing anybody's day, and rarely for the better.

Cole was forced to give a quick pep talk to the videographer, who arrived on campus
after getting pulled out of a Senate hearing on ferry fee increases. The shooter was nervous. He
had little experience at confrontation. Cole understood that most of the camera guys were used to
taking an hour to set up an interview, dicking with ten lights on special-colored filters, set at
perfect angles to avoid throwing shadows. They rearranged furniture, so the shot had depth. They
tried different microphones, listened to repeated audio tests in headphones. *Ten . . . nine . . . eight
. . .* Jesus! It drove Cole crazy. Today he needed less Steven Spielberg and more Quentin
Tarantino.

"Do not turn off the camera, no matter what. I don't care if the guy we're going after
tells you to. I don't care if the campus cops come racing across the parking lot and order you to
'put it down.' Punch that record button and leave it rolling. Keep the lens focal point fairly wide.
I'm going to talk with the provost. I want us both to be in your frame. You're recording a
conversation, not just his answers. I doubt he will stop and talk, so we're going to be on the
move. Get to the side. Keep one eye in the viewfinder, but keep the other one scanning for curbs,
sprinkler heads in the grass, signposts, et cetera. Got it? If you get caught running backwards,
pull out even wider on the shot, point the camera in the right direction, and don't fall on your
keister. That's an eighty-thousand-dollar camera you're trying to protect."

Cole saw a nod but didn't see any heart. *Oh, well, at least the poor nervous bastard hadn't pulled out his union card and recited the "I don't feel safe" clause.*

Several best-in-show pussies had done that to Cole in the past. One particular videographer only agreed to do interviews wearing a bulletproof vest. Cole was mystified by the lack of adventure. Perhaps all the real men in the world were getting selected out of the gene pool by their dangerous lifestyles.

"Here's the plan," Cole continued. "Go hang out by that box van parked a few spaces up. Either leave your camera on the ground on the back side of the tire or hold it low. Watch me through the windows. Don't worry if someone thinks you're casing the cars. This won't take long. When you see a balding man with glasses approach this Jaguar right here," Cole said, tapping the top of the racing-green beauty, "hit the red record button, slide around the van, and, *bingo,* our interview is under way."

Cole dialed Provost Russell's secretary. Raising the pitch of his voice, he sped up the delivery of his words.

"Gosh, I'm really, really sorry, but I'm pretty sure I dented the provost's car. I always see him driving around campus in it. My dad will pay for the damage, I promise! I don't know what to do."

The secretary said something reassuring, then put him on hold. Cole pulled up his coat collar, turned his back to the administration building, and pretended to pace nervously near the Jaguar. He could feel the eyes of the administration building burning a hole in his back, but he resisted the overwhelming urge to glance toward the windows. After less than five minutes, Cole could see his videographer perk up. He gauged Provost Russell's distance by watching his cameraman's eyes through the van windows. Cole flipped on the wireless microphone module snapped to his belt. Even after Cole spun around, the provost had no idea what was coming. One of the most powerful men in the state was about to learn a lesson in humility.

"Good morning, sir. Colton Wiley, KZPR-TV. I'm told you quashed the idea of contacting the Thurston County Sheriff's Department when a freshman girl suddenly disappeared from campus this week. If you aren't requesting police help, may I then ask what you are personally doing to make sure she is found safe?"

As the question flowed from the newsman's lips, Cole could tell Provost Russell was processing the train wreck unfolding in front of him as fast as he could. He probably wanted to start out his response with "You little fuck," but he wasn't willing to throw away a lifetime of portraying the coolheaded academic snob. He couldn't will away the sweat already beading on his forehead, though. Cole suspected his prey was about to puke. For a moment, Provost Russell looked away from Cole and into his own reflection, beaming back at him from the camera lens.

Cole had done hundreds of these ambush interviews. The subjects responded in one of three distinct ways. A select few were calm enough to pretend they were expecting a reporter and camera to show up. Those rare subjects smiled and showed the audience an immediate willingness to answer every question. Cole loved it when this happened. It balanced his story by giving his prey a fighting chance in the public arena to salvage reputation and honor. The second method for dealing with Cole's ambushes was simply to silently bolt and run. Crooked roofing contractors, a government worker caught gambling in the middle of the workday, a registered sex-offender pedophile standing on a kiddie playground—these folks knew they were screwed the instant they saw a camera. Perhaps it was just basic survival instinct kicking in—something like a Pleistocene human running away from a saber-toothed cat. When you ran, viewers knew instantly that you were guilty of everything Cole was reporting and more. There was no salvation for a runner. But Provost Russell appeared as if he was about to join the third and final group of subjects: the "I'm really busy, can't talk right now, but would love to answer your questions if you'd be so kind as to set up an appointment" crowd. This was the toughest group to crack, because viewers saw such a request as reasonable. Thus, Cole could easily look like a badgering jerk instead of a hard-nosed reporter. Such a fine line. Audiences were a fickle bunch, and Cole had never had a single subject who, after saying "Let's talk later," actually sat down and did an interview. It was a terrific way to blow off a reporter's probing questions forever. The very best players in this group would wait until the day the investigation was set to air, then send a well-crafted written statement to Cole addressing the general situation under investigation. This forced Cole to edit out the "no comment" part of his story while still denying him the opportunity to unravel all the false statements in the press release. Provost Russell had been coached and trained in this third method of avoidance, but unfortunately for him, he froze. He didn't freeze for long, but four seconds of silence between Cole's question and his first word felt like an eternity. Provost Russell had no choice but to start spinning half lies on the spot to salvage his immense salary, job, and prestige. He spun about and headed back toward his office, but at a casual pace. It was a good forty yards, so the conversation was on the go.

"I'm, uh, I'm glad you asked that, Mr. Wiley," the administrator stammered while trying to recover. "Our campus security has been doing a terrific job in tracking down possible leads, but we haven't found Anna. I don't believe she's in any danger, but I've decided, just today, that it's time to ask for help from the sheriff's department. That's all I can say for now. Due to federal education privacy laws, any more detail would get me into trouble."

Cole had a half-dozen questions that would make the provost look like a buffoon, but gauging the distance to the administration building glass door, he knew he had time for only one.

He already had a sound bite for the missing-girl story, so he decided to switch gears. This was a moment when words were banal but reaction meant everything.

Cole pressed. "Provost Russell, what can you tell me about the purpose of a secret lab in the basement of that building right there?"

Despite being only a few feet from the sanctuary of the administration building, the provost stopped cold and looked at Cole. His mind was obviously twirling, panicked.

Cole had asked the question, not because he had made any connection, but because he thought it might help Nolan get a search warrant. To Cole, the two questions were completely unrelated. But in the next instant, he knew.

"You think the two are related?" Cole followed up.

Provost Russell turned gray, pursed his lips, and slipped away behind the door without a word.

Cole stood there, stunned. Then, looked over his shoulder to his shaking photo journalist, "How'd you do, man? Get some pictures and sound?"

"I totally nailed it, Cole. No problems. That was awesome!" The photog couldn't hide the powerfully addictive rush he felt inside.

"Great. Then I'll make sure we get to do this again someday. For now, get back to your news van and start loading that *first* statement from the provost into the portable editor. Do *not* load that second part of the interview. Oh, and here. Take this video-card of stuff I shot earlier today. It has some B-roll of the missing girl's picture, flyers being handed out, and a couple of interviews with worried students. I'll whip a script together in the next half hour and voice it. I'm sure this will lead the five P.M. news, so get crackin'."

The videographer jogged off back toward the parking lot while Cole whipped out his phone. Nolan picked up almost before it rang.

"That looked fun! I've been watching you harass that poor provost from the coffee shop next door. All the students were pressed up against the window yelling, 'What the fuck! TV man is chasing him! Not cool; media's a tool.' Stuff like that. It's fun to sit back and listen to what people really think about you. I will say one super-smokin'-hot goth chick in the corner defended your honor, saying you do lots of stories that help animals. I almost told her I knew you and we were best friends so I could score her phone number."

The tension in Cole's neck disappeared as he laughed out loud. He hadn't realized how stressful the encounter had been.

"Age of consent is eighteen, but as always, work comes first, buddy. Any progress on getting into that locked lab?" Cole faked sounding hopeful, knowing the answer.

"Come on, it's only been a few minutes, dude. My buddy at the electric company is writing up a report right now that shows the Lab One building, on the whole, dramatically increased its kilowatt usage about six months ago. You and I know it's probably the incinerator and a bunch of computers sucking up all that power, but I'm going to try to convince a judge that it could be a grow operation. It's a serious stretch, but I can honestly testify that Evergreen State College is Weed Central. I called a narcotics agent I went through training with, and he said they had made numerous dime-bag buys from a dealer in the area. A snitch of his said someone on campus grows the stuff. Good enough story for me."

"No way a judge is going to go for that. They probably smoke more dope in their garages after work each night than the students do in a month. I'm not knocking the idea too hard, because until a few moments ago, we had no other plan. That's changed, my friend." Cole stopped to let the mini drama build. He loved pauses. He loved knowing things that others didn't.

"Okay, I'll bite. What happened a few moments ago?" Nolan was an expert at playing this stupid game with his pal.

"Provost Russell believes our missing freshman, Anna Dipler, and that lab have something in common."

Nolan Burke shot out of the coffee booth, unfolding his entire doorframe-size person with such ease that the saucer didn't even rattle.

"Holy shit, Superman! I take back everything I ever said about your hair, your breath, and that ugly beast of a girlfriend you shacked up with three years ago. I know you don't think she had a lazy eye, but seriously, man, she looked like a retarded pit bull, only not as cute. Operation Lie to the Judge about a Weed Grow is out. Operation Find Anna is in!"

"I thought you'd enjoy that. Call your buddies over at the Sheriff's Department. Or is it 'Sheriff's Office'? They always get pissed when I screw that up on the air. Anyway, a locked room a few feet from the last known location of a missing college student is certainly the first place I'd look if I were a detective. It's a slam-dunk search warrant. If you can, make it a midnight raid or later. The other media are going to come storming in here to play catch-up on the missing-girl story this evening after I break it. Let's make sure none of them find out about that lab. Don't know about finding this Anna chick, but I'm positive there are clues inside that will help solve the mystery surrounding what the Animal Liberation Brigade is really up to. I want my competitors to do the Anna story so it gets as much publicity as possible, but this arson-murder animal rights investigation is mine . . . I mean, *ours*."

Inside the live truck, Cole slammed together a two-minute story, jotting scripting notes onto the back of the missing college student's flyer. That way he could hold the picture up to the camera and still have a cheat sheet, with perfectly scripted text hidden on the back of the photo, away from the audience. The art of credibility on TV was giving the impression you weren't reading but, rather, chatting with several hundred thousand people in a way that made each feel that you were connecting with them individually. Cole hit the air at 4:58:35. The investigation started with the word "exclusive" and got better every second he was on the air. The ambush interview with the clearly flustered provost would be replayed at five thirty, six, and eleven. Cole masterfully wasted four seconds of valuable TV time in each show by leaving in the hesitation between his question and the college administrator's answer. Too many reporters would have edited that out to save more face time for themselves. Cole made sure the last portion of the interview did not air.

As soon as the live shot ended, Cole asked the truck operator to tear down and get the hell out of Dodge. When shamefaced reporters from other stations began slinking in to scavenge the leavings, he wanted them to walk onto a dark, empty campus. It gave the feeling that they were so late to the story, it had already passed them by. This kind of psychological warfare helped strip innovation and enthusiasm out of normally inquisitive reporters. They'd do the story, but with no video of students handing out flyers and no interview with the provost, the best they could hope for was to score a picture of the missing girl from the cops. Some reporters might physically leave Evergreen State College to find Anna's family, but Cole already knew they weren't home. How did he know? Easy: he had called the house and told them a crush of media would soon be at their door and that if they wanted to avoid that, they should find a hotel for the night.

Anna's mom thought Cole was a hero, and promised to speak only with him when the time was right. Such a sensitive reporter, to warn the family! Cole called that kind of smooth manipulation "pissing in the well." Like a Wild West gunslinger, he got the sweetest drink of water after a long, hot ride in the desert because he was first into town. But when the posse of other reporters chasing him got to the well later in the day, they must swallow the bitter, tainted piss water that he left them. They would survive, but there was nothing pleasant about trying to catch up to Colton Wiley. He lived to break investigations, then move on. Regular beat reporters could do the pedestrian follow-up work. At KZPR-TV, that sloppy-seconds job often fell to Rachael Fredette.

***

Before Chuck Reynolds went off to quench his thirst with a half-dozen tumblers of rum, he assigned her to progress Colton's story.

"Why doesn't *he* do it?" she grumped. "He's so godlike that you don't want him to work overtime and stand in what's sure to be an effing rainy parking lot at eleven? I don't get it. You want me to drive two hours to front a story that isn't mine and that I have zero chance to progress? I'm not an intern. I have a degree from Northwestern! I'm so sick of this shit."

Chuck wanted to slap her. Tell her to cover those acres of tits with a tweed jacket. Tell her that if she wore any more makeup, the Transgender Foundation of America would make her president. Tell her that if she disliked KZPR-TV in Seattle, there was a nice station in Grand Junction, Colorado, that would be thrilled to take her. But, since Chuck knew she was "dating" the general manager, he had nothing to add except "You're our best nightside reporter. This is a lead story, and that's where you belong." Rachael seemed mollified with that false compliment and grabbed a female videographer. While heading south to Olympia, she no doubt was thinking of ways to knock the Great One off his pedestal.

Chapter 17

Building any bomb was a tricky business but assembling bunker busters in a non-climate-controlled warehouse outside Keizer, Oregon, was just plain stupid. Oz knew that but didn't care—didn't care about his own life, let alone the lives of the 150 people who worked in the Four Corners Business Park. The explosive-making materials had taken nearly a year to gather. Oz used creativity to avoid the trip wires set by the vast sub-departments within the Department of Homeland Security to flag terrorist activities.

Although he considered himself in no way a terrorist, Oz understood how creating three two-ton guided-bomb units might make him look like one. He made sure he didn't order a single item over the Internet or have anything delivered by the U.S. Postal Service. Dr. Dell seemed to have an endless supply of money, so conducting this kind of illegal enterprise in secret had been a breeze so far. Using skills learned on Uncle Sam's dime, Oz had stolen some of the most sensitive, difficult-to-obtain materials from the Army munitions depot at Fort Lewis, and the Navy base in Bremerton. He had few options for creating hardened steel without drawing undue attention, so he pilfered a half-dozen used torpedo shells. To make sure the Navy didn't launch an all-out investigation to find them again, Oz planted evidence to make it look as though meth heads were stealing scrap metal for quick cash. He placed a sign on the door of his business park storefront that read "Jimmy J's World Class Racing Cars," so when he ordered lead-acid batteries for their sulfuric acid, shippers didn't bat an eye. It also made sense when he ordered crude oil and paint thinner, materials from which he could cull toluene. Oz spent countless hours at local libraries, collecting phone numbers the old-fashioned way: thumbing through fat phone books. Using throwaway cell phones he bought under false names from big box stores, he called dozens of mom-and-pop photo shops and art suppliers. To make TNT from scratch, he had to get his hands on a large quantity of nitric acid. Although it was legal to use in small quantities to produce a negative-effect picture on metal, the feds perked right up anytime someone tried to buy more than a quart or two.

Oz tried to break into glass master Dale Chihuly's Tacoma studio to steal a barrelful, but a battery of security alarms that would rival any top-shelf bank setup scared him off. Who would have thought that hunks of colored glass shaped like clams would be so important? Oz later saw where one Chihuly flower arrangement had commanded a million dollars at auction. None of that wealth would matter once Oz cooked up gorgeous amounts of TNT with the nitric acid, sulfuric acid, and Toluene. Combine that with wax, aluminum, and some corn starch, and the N5G project was ready to rock and roll. Oz got his deliveries by using trucks driven only by nonunion independents. The Teamsters were in bed with so many politicians, handing out campaign contributions like candy, that Oz had to wonder whether their delivery rosters were open game for eyes at NSA and the FBI. The possibility of quid pro quo was too great. He instructed his cash-only drivers to arrive right before closing time. It cost three times the normal rates, but that bought loyalty and no questions.

The warehouse loading dock faced what was labeled an environmentally sensitive area at the back of the park. There was even a tiny sign that read "Wetland Watch," stuck in the ground between the asphalt parking lot and the unkempt grass. Oz chuckled when he first saw it, because to build the two-hundred-thousand-square-foot warehouse buildings and massive tar-drenched parking lot, city developers had to fill in the wetlands. Before they started, that same sign had been posted as protection next to what was then a quiet rural road. They had simply moved the sign after destroying the ecosystem in the way of a profitable real estate deal.

126

Oz made sure he never physically met the truck drivers. He left written instructions that they were to place the shrink-wrapped wooden-boxed pallets on the outside of the concrete and rubber dock. Even though some of the supplies, like boat propellers, would never raise attention, Oz didn't take chances. Every morning, he would glide a small aluminum johnboat into the far side of the swamp behind the warehouse and paddle softly in the dark through the cattails until he could see the pallets. He would watch quietly with his night scope, making certain no one else was conducting surveillance on his fake race car operation. At dawn, he would jump on an old propane powered forklift and run the pallets inside. As supplies arrived he checked off his very long to-do list. The top of one notebook read *"Bunker Buster GBU 37."* Another read *"Cloudmaker T-12."* While he worked on such destruction, Oz spent hours also wondering if what he was doing was the right thing. He didn't care much for his ex-wife, who simply could not understand his inconsolable sorrow over the loss of a dog. *"He was only a dog,"* she'd say. His three-year-old boy didn't judge.

From the middle of a pile of used cell phones came a small tinging sound.

"Yep," Oz answered because the caller ID said "Private number."

Dr. Dell's distinctive countertenor sliced a high pitch through the ear hole's cheap electronics. "Specialist McKinsey, I'm two minutes from the warehouse. I assume you're there?"

"Yes sir. The wet bangs are almost ready. I'd love to show them off."

Moments later, Dr. Dell let the pair of shorthairs out of the backseat, and they rolled head over heels through the warehouse door, playing a sort of docked-tail tag. They loved the gigantic open space inside. As they ran headlong through the maze of equipment and electronic testing stations, it crossed Oz's mind that it was possible the pair of mutts could actually set off 8,340 pounds of freshly engineered explosives.

"Halt!" shouted Dr. Dell, realizing the same thing. The dogs stopped instantly and sat down, awaiting their next command. Dr. Dell hated to yell, and used a loud voice on his dogs only in the most extreme circumstances.

Oz was not a hugger, but Dr. Dell insisted, calling him a "brother in the fight to save the planet." To make himself feel less uncomfortable with the hug, Oz thought of it as a kind of chest bump with the much smaller scientist.

Dr. Dell could see sixteen-foot torpedo housings lying together, strapped in twos, residing snugly inside sturdy crates. Custom-cut wooden V's cupped them to keep them from jostling. Open hinged metal flaps allowed Dr. Dell to see the array of wires and computer components inside the steel tubes. The smell of tritonal explosive hung thick in the air.

Oz felt like a proud eighth-grade science fair student, giving his best pitch to a judge stopping by to score the project.

"They weigh about twenty-four hundred pounds each. I formed an eighty-twenty mixture of homemade TNT and aluminum powder. That should greatly improve the brisance of the TNT. I rigged up a propelling mechanism and timer out of a diver's watch and a charter boat prop. I can either program them to explode at a certain depth or set them to explode when the heavy tip stops moving downward and levels out. Cool, huh?"

Oz stroked his beard. He enjoyed impressing his leader. He continued.

"They're essentially like the earthquake bombs from the Korean War, but with a hundred times the punch. One of these will create a fifty- to a hundred-foot cavern, but the most beautiful part is, that's only a fraction of the true destruction. The shock wave created by the initial boom uses the weight of the material blown from the hole as a kind of battering ram to collapse back into itself. The pressure redoubles every tenth of a second. It's like a hurricane, swirling toward

128

the low-pressure eye of the storm. In theory, I could make the Sears Tower fall straight down into a hole, then have the Earth cover it back up, like nothing was ever there. Like Atlantis. I could do more with a nuclear tip, but I got the impression you didn't want to take the risks of acquiring one. You can never trust the damn Russians, anyway. They have more yellow cake and old nukes than they do bread on the shelves of an Omsk grocery store. But as soon as you get into the market for something that might start a war, they'll take your money, provide the nukes, then call the government and see if there's a big cash reward for catching someone with nuclear material. Double-dipping motherfuckers . . . Sorry, none of that last bit is relevant."

Dr. Dell nodded quietly, staring at the rather simple weapons lying nearly complete in front of him. Oz continued to hold forth, sounding uncharacteristically more like a professor giving a lecture than a crazy killer in the making.

"These bombs were originally invented to kill a small group of specifically targeted people. Army Rangers usually sneak within about five hundred yards of a building where some militia powwow is going on. They paint the side with a laser; then, way up in the sky, a stealth three-person crew in a B-12 drop the smart bombs from the relative quiet of fifteen thousand feet. They even install microphones on the exterior of the shell and tell the computer to count the number of floors it crashes through on its way down. Top floor, fourteen, thirteen, twelve, eleven, ten, nine, and *bam!* Everybody at the meeting on the ninth floor turns into pink mist. When the enemy got smart and went underground into heavily fortified concrete bunkers, it took Boeing engineers, like, two seconds to recalculate. A smidge of $C_6H_5CH_3$, a glug of H_2SO_4, toss in a splash of HNO_3, and cram it so fucking far down a hole in the ground that even if the structure below survived, the people's brains in the protected room would be puddled by the shock waves. I trust you, Dr. Dell. I trust when you tell me to build three sets of these that they

129

won't be wasted killing a few dozen people. I trust that when you say my work here can save this planet, these weapons can somehow accomplish that. I believe in your Armageddon. I don't care if I live or die. I'd like to see ol' Sparks again, anyway. Tell me what to do next."

"They are beautiful, my devoted friend. Seal them up. Go buy three grocery delivery trucks. Make sure they have freezer units to properly store our capsules until the time is right to release them. Bring the trucks here. Gas them up. Wait for my call. Wynona and I still have a lot of preparation to do, but she needs to take our first package out of here in two or three days."

Before he could call the dogs out of their positions, an alarm pinged from a small metal ball hanging from a chain around Dr. Dell's neck. It flashed from orange to green and back. He frowned and grasped the orb like a cross.

"Forgive us our trespasses, as we forgive those who trespass against us. Amen. I will be back to help you load materials tomorrow. The restoration of purity is upon us."

The dogs matched Dr. Dell's brisk pace out the warehouse door.

Chapter 18

The door of the Lab One building may have been built for Fort Knox, but the exterior wall was just a stack of bricks. Thurston County SWAT team lieutenant Al O'Brien spent the evening studying the retinal scanning device, pin code electronics, the strange blinking light sequences, and steel locks attached to the room he wanted to enter. It was mostly a show for the rest of the team because using his higher processes to solve problems was not his strength. The former NCAA wrestling champion's bulging musculature, nonexistent neck, and high pain tolerance made him a perfect fit for either police work or professional boxing. He would just as soon keep his teeth, so policeman it was.

Lieutenant O'Brien had knocked down plenty of doors while serving search warrants. The procedure usually included a flash bang through a side window, followed by an eighty-pound hand-swung battering ram. If the drug dealers wanted to buy some time to flush as much contraband down the toilet as possible, they would weld steel bars on the outside of the door, in which case the SWAT team would trot out its giant armored vehicle. Two guys would rush up and snake a cable with a U-bolt through the bars, and the truck would yank the bars—and maybe some of the wall—into the street.

A quiet college hallway outside a science lab, on the other hand, actually put O'Brien at a disadvantage since surprise and brute force were not a tactical advantage in this situation. O'Brien had never met Nolan Burke, but it didn't matter—*everyone* loved Burke. He was one of those guys who became your best buddy inside the first minute.

"The security setup's impressive," O'Brien said, stating the obvious in the hope that Nolan could at least give him some affirmation. "Expensive and out of place." He verbalized his checklist of attempted entries to date. "We've tried to blowtorch the hinges. We got our best computer tech down here in an attempt to try to hack the password. We tried crushing the door frame with the fire department's jaws of life. Unless you have another idea, I say we start blasting."

Nolan stood shoulder to shoulder with the beefier SWAT member, staring at the unmarked door. "I like blasting!" he said, all boyish enthusiasm. "You know us arson guys are one match strike away from becoming pyros."

The two men peeked outside. It was dark and quiet. All the media who had illuminated the campus main square as a backdrop for the eleven o'clock news were gone.

"What are the chances that missing girl might be inside?" O'Brien asked.

Nolan didn't hesitate. "Alive? Near zero."

O'Brien yelled down the hall. "Clear!"

The SWAT team jogged outside single file, and he shouted a dozen orders in fifteen seconds. Breaching the military-grade security measures on the interior wall of the lab was no doubt going to cause significant secondary destruction. O'Brien could see the headline in tomorrow morning's edition of the *Olympian:* EVERGREEN BLDG. COLLAPSES, with the subtitle SWAT DECISION QUESTIONED. Not really the résumé builder the sergeant preferred.

The hole cut for the new incinerator chimney, which wound its way up the outside of Lab One, was clearly the weakest point of the room. O'Brien asked his team to start by pulling the sheet metal out of the wall. This revealed a rough hole. The incinerator was not in full operational mode, but it was on, and the residual heat from the gas burners put a long delay in the operation. Using explosives to breach the wall, only to have a natural-gas main ignite under the campus, would, at a minimum, bring back a horde of television reporters. Worst-case scenarios included students being burned alive in a massive government blunder. Sometime around one a.m., the gas company electronically closed a valve that stopped gas flow to campus. Nolan was impressed with the SWAT team's patience—he was chomping at the bit himself. The SWAT boys were milling around, arguing over whether Boise State had a tough enough football schedule to be considered for a major bowl bid, and which Hollywood starlet would be their dream date. However, when the Lieutenant clapped and rotated his finger in a circle, eight grown men mentally said, "*How high should I jump?*"

Nolan expected a plan involving blasting caps and dynamite. He got sledgehammers and crowbars instead. The SWAT team looked like a whole crew of John Henrys, slamming away at the steel bit. Chips of brick and mortar flew in every direction. In less than a minute, they had knocked a hole in the lab wall. Nolan could hear the sound of crumbling rock turn into the sounds of a sheet-metal shop. As Lieutenant O'Brien had predicted, the elaborate security system constructed to scare off any attempt at forced entry had a flaw: the interior wall reinforcements were installed after the incinerator. The SWAT team's plan was to uninstall it in the messiest fashion possible. They pried and pushed the Inciner8 A2600 toward the center of the room until there was barely enough room to slip between the still warm animal waste disposal unit and what remained of the building's brick wall. Nolan watched as a lanky Asian policeman wriggled inside, mindful of possible booby traps. A minute later, he gave the all clear, and with a whir and a *ker-lunk,* the secret door opened. O'Brien gave a hoo-rah and stormed inside looking for clues to a missing freshman. Tiny twenty-watt pin lights in tracks flickered alive along the top of the back wall. Each light was spun to throw a pattern of warm, bluish color into specific sections of cage floors. The doors on the kennels were open and empty. Each was so clean, Nolan wondered if they were new. Kneeling down, he stuck his head inside one of the medium-sized cages and caught a slight whiff of bleach. A dozen canister lights, snaking down on black cords from the

133

beige-tiled ceiling, created harsh spotlights in the middle of the same number of tables. The dark cedar-topped desks held wide-screen computer monitors. The power cords were unplugged, and the computer connectors cut in two with a sharp knife. The metal shells of computer mainframes were toppled over on their sides. It didn't take a Steve Jobs to see that someone had removed all the hard drives.

Nolan pulled a small video camera out of his coat pocket. An hour ago, it had been in the hands of Colton Wiley. Neither thought it would be a good idea for the sheriff's department to see the pair of them working together. Nolan needed the SWAT team to trust him, and vouching for an investigative reporter who wanted to wander about a potential crime scene wasn't the way to go about it. Cole had attached a small wireless transmitter to the back of the camera so he could see what was going on inside in real time. Although the recording going on inside the camera itself captured perfect high-definition video, the transmitter gave blurrier, snow-filled images sent directly to Cole's phone.

Nolan shot video for ten minutes, documenting the raid, the property left inside the lab, the empty cages. Playing director in his head, he called *wide shot, medium shot, tight shot, cutaway.* Maybe when at last they fired him from the Arson Squad for leaking classified government materials to a reporter, the TV station would take pity on him and let him be a photog. Chicks loved photographers—*The Bridges of Madison County* proved that. He was about to shut the video transmission down and head back outside to collaborate with Cole when he heard a softly uttered "Holy shit" behind him. He let the camera fall to his side and turned to see a cluster of Thurston County's finest standing around the open door of the now smashed-up incinerator. Nolan walked over, and the group parted to let him up front.

One of the SWAT team members held up a ladybug-size crimson jewel, intertwined with blackened metal wire. Nolan's heart sank. He peered into the darkened hole. The knotty end of a human femur stuck out the top of a massive pile of gray-white ash the size of a beer keg. Lieutenant O'Brien used a gloved hand to gently shake the bone free of its dusty matrix.

"You're the arson expert—is that what it looks like?"

"Thighbones and teeth are about all that survives high temperatures. There's no doubt that's human," Nolan said as he raised the camera, doubting that he would ever again see four murder victims in the same month.

At seventy-five yards, he couldn't hear Cole yelling, "Eight seconds. Come on, man, eight fucking seconds!"

The SWAT team, circling around Nolan, stood quiet for a few moments, sad that their smashing and pounding hadn't turned into any kind of positive ending for the college girl. Then, like army ants, they all launched off in different directions to secure the perimeter. Lieutenant O'Brien dropped his camouflaged helmet onto a cold metal table, where it wobbled like a helpless turtle before falling still.

"Damn. I hate it when rescue operations turn into recovery."

Nolan nodded a little, gritting his teeth. "Get your homicide detectives, crime lab, and medical examiner out of bed and have them hump it down here ASAP. I want a DNA profile of the marrow inside this bone before we lose jurisdiction. Once the FBI gets here they operate in a blackout—that poor girl's family will be left wondering about their missing kid for an extra three or four days. I'd rather they learned the hard truth before they waste a lot of energy praying for a miracle. At least this way, the Almighty gets to keep a little of his credibility."

Nolan walked down the basement hallway and stepped out into the night air—damp with a freezing light fog. He stood in the well of the stairway and looked for stars. When he was growing up in the Yakima Valley, even on a new moon, Orion, Cassiopeia, and Scorpius lit the fields so brightly, he could pick strawberries at two in the morning. But in Olympia, the clouds were perpetually caught low between the Pacific Ocean and the Cascade Range. The city lights bounced up off a high bank of fog, to give the swirling sky the same look as a smoke-filled ceiling in a mobile home right before it burns to the ground. He stared at the mesmerizing nothingness.

"I do love your Zen-like stance, but maybe we should get a little jump on solving not only four murders but a clear case of burning on U.S. Forest Service lands without a permit. Those crackpot critter lovers aren't going to get out of that without paying a pretty stiff fine," Cole whispered from above, ending his friend's brief reverie.

"I'm standing here trying to piece together a motive or pattern, and it's just not there, Cole. Maybe the first case, where the two young women got toasted in the woods, was a simple, accidental house-fire. Maybe the trooper happened to stop a Mexican drug cartel fugitive for a broken taillight. Maybe we almost got blown to bits because the renter was trying to protect his weight in dope in the upstairs bedroom. Maybe that leg inside the incinerator is part of an old cadaver from Human Anatomy class last semester. Am I chasing a pattern where there isn't one?"

Cole dropped a fir cone onto the top of Nolan's head.

"Pull up your skirt, Nancy. I've been doing real investigative work while you played brick breaker with your Chippendale chums. I downloaded the Evergreen State College staff directory into a database, then cross-matched it with *another* database that lists government science grants. This place is lame. The University of Washington has, like, a thousand hits, but Evergreen has only thirty-four. The richest government grant went to a professor by the name of Dr. Dell. He got millions of dollars from the Interior Department with no strings attached. That's fishy as hell, but I digress. He doesn't teach any classes. He's not a social guy. No Facebook account. I ran utilities and rent checks, and the latest address I have for the guy is from 2001. He has no known relatives, no bankruptcy filing, no tax liens, no house, a juvenile criminal record (which is sealed, naturally), but—and I say 'BUT' in a huge, sweeping *Let's Make a Deal* kind of way . . . pause, pause, pause—he has a traffic ticket! The address on the ticket comes back to Evergreen State College, so he didn't give away where he lived to the cops. They did, however, pen in his date of birth. I pumped that baby into my backgrounder databases and found a few aliases for Dr. Dell. His real name is Hadar Orin O'Dell. H_2O, baby. H-two-muv-fucking-O!"

Cole held his arms wide, like Jesus on the cross, and put on a cheesy fake smile usually seen in local car-dealer commercials.

"Nice. Very nice." Nolan relaxed and used the "nice" comment as time filler, the way others used "uh" and "um." He mind was firing on all cylinders now. "So your anonymous caller-slash-stalker knows something more than he's saying. He sent us here. Scared or not, he needs to come out to play. Can you make that happen?"

"You suck at jubilant celebrations," Cole muttered. He reached into a pocket of his Gore-Tex shell and unlocked his cell phone. "When he calls I get the word 'private' on the screen, but I know someone who might be able to help."

Cole spun through his contacts until he got to the "T's," for "Tracer." The tracer had a name, but he wasn't entirely sure that what she did was legal, so he left the name blank. Cole had never met the tracer. She was supposedly a former T-Mobile cell phone collections specialist.

The tracer claimed that cell phone companies hired her to track down freeloaders who had large unpaid cell bills. In return, she had access to every user's billing information. The database contained millions of names. She could take a cell phone number and match it up with an address where the bills were mailed. For a small cash gratuity, the tracer might also get her hands on the actual bills. They showed details such as the exact time of calls and the specific number the call was made to. For a larger monetary show of appreciation, Cole's cell phone hookup would actually dial a cell number and pretend to be from the phone company. She would imply service was about to get canceled. Even the smartest criminals never caught on that the tracer was picking them clean for personal information. She was an expert at gleaning a physical location for them, even though they might have put a P.O. box down for a mailing address, or getting them to tell her where they were standing at that precise second. She'd ask them to stand still for a signal strength test. Crooks always had their cell phones. It was their lifeline to making money and trouble.

Cole's dial didn't make it one ring before the tracer picked up.

"Hey, cutie pie," she said with a pleasant, faintly sexy Southern drawl. "How can Mama help?"

"Sorry for calling so late. Or early? I don't know which coast you're on. I figured you'd be asleep—I was going to leave a message. But since I got you live and in person, here goes. I've gotten a few calls from a private number. Can you detail the source and get me that person's information?"

"Honey, if they used a land line, I can't help. If they used a cell phone, it's possible. I have some ideas. Tell me the exact time and duration of your last encounter, and where you were

138

standing at the time the call came in." She sounded eager to try something that pushed her skills to the limit.

Cole spun through his history. "Twelve-o-three a.m., October fourth. I was on the south end of Portland, Oregon. We talked less than a minute."

"Two calls would make this much easier."

"Oh, right. He did call me another time in Seattle. Less than a minute that time, too. I deleted the history in this phone, but I've got it in my notes somewhere. It was within a day or two before the specific call time I gave you."

"I'm going to run a computer query, searching for any one phone making a call to Seattle Oct 2 or 3, then to Portland on October 4, concentrating on that last minute as a reference point. I'll create a program to look for a person who blocked their identity by programming in 'Private.' I should have a short list in an hour or two. I'll text you. In lieu of cash payment this time, how about you score me a pair of tickets to a Sounders soccer game?"

"You get me this info, and I'll make 'em box seats."

Cole hung up, feeling guilty about breaking the trust of an anonymous source. Whoever was feeding him the tips obviously didn't want to be part of any news story. But this wasn't simply about journalism any longer. Something ominous was taking shape—something that, if he didn't help stop it, would make him regret it the rest of his life.

Nolan was pacing impatiently under a dim streetlight. "Sounds like we have to wait for an answer. Come on, I have an idea."

Nolan led the way past the Daniel Evans Library to a small computer science building at the edge of campus. As expected, the lights were on. Three computer geeks and a grunge girl wearing thick black eyeliner were enjoying the speed at which they could work in the early-morning hours, when server traffic was at a low ebb. Nolan flashed his badge as the four students glanced up from their glowing screens.

"Nolan Burke, arson investigator, U.S. Forest Service. I could really use some help. Anyone interested in being a conscientious citizen today?"

One of the young men, who had rigged his laptop to the hard drive of several other computers with a series of homemade connections, unplugged the tangle of wires in seconds and brushed past Nolan out the door. Another grumbled a quiet profanity-laced tirade that started with "po-po" and ended with a barely audible "no fucking way, Jackson."

The girl, who wore a long ponytail intertwined with a blue ribbon, studied Cole, then looked at Nolan. Her accent was a subtle combination of California surfer and Canadian.

"I'm not a lawyer yet, Smoky Bear, but I'm certain you don't have the legal authority to ask me to do squat."

Nolan was such a Boy Scout, he readied the kind of speech that a dad might give to his disobedient teenager. Cole stepped in before he embarrassed himself.

"Look, bitch, why don't you and your metrosexual buddy there slink back to your dorm rooms or your broken-down Microbus or wherever you hang out? My friend asked if you wanted to help, that's all. He's not here for your abuse, so save the ration of righteous shit for someone more deserving. Oh, and as you leave, don't go to the right—there are about thirty-five steroid-fueled hippie-hating cops, still looking for payback after your WTO riot shenanigans."

Despite her initial tough talk, like most Washingtonians, she folded under true confrontation. In a matter of moments, the room was empty and quiet but for the hum of cooling fans.

Nolan stood there amused, then quickly realized that his plan was now shot to shit.

"Why'd you chase them off? Inside that horror of a science lab, there were a bunch of chopped fiber-optic lines. I was hoping to get a peek into what the now missing computers were researching. What the hell is wrong with kids these days, anyway?"

Cole shrugged and sat down at the nearest computer station.

"Dude, I snoop for a living. I can't write Java or FORTRAN, but chasing droplets of information back to a source isn't that hard."

Cole spent the next few hours familiarizing himself with the setup, clicking through applications, and studying properties. By sunrise, Nolan was dozing in the corner.

"Enough rest, Z-man! Here we go. I found a list of college-owned servers. There's about a hundred. I ranked them according to the date they went online. That secret lab went hot about, what, six months ago? A lot of the servers are older than that, a few newer. The H, I, and X drives are in the ballpark. History of the amount of CPU and Internet activity shows all three were used to their peak capabilities all summer long. Two of them are still being heavily used. One, the X drive, hasn't been used at all in the past day. Voila! We've isolated the server. Slick, huh, country boy?"

"Pretty slick. What are you doing with computer skills?" Nolan asked innocently, not that he worried about offending Cole.

"It's simple. I don't trust anyone to do anything for me and get it right. There's tons of information on the server. I have a pretty easy way to alphabetize the files, but I have to go back to the station. Hopefully, I'll see some sort of pattern."

Cole highlighted the menu and dragged it over to his laptop about the same time his phone chirped once with a new e-mail message.

"Good news, I hope?" Nolan asked, half asleep.

"She says to call. Too sensitive to put in writing."

"'Sensitive' in the sense of 'illegal'?" Nolan asked.

Cole ignored him and called the tracer back.

"You had some success?"

"Of course," came the honeysuckle drawl. "Nationwide, I found fourteen cell phone owners who called first Seattle and then Portland at the exact same minute your mystery man rang. All but three spent more than one minute in talk time. I thought getting it down to three was pretty good, but, honey, I want those soccer tickets. One of the phones belongs to a big trucking company. Their bill shows they make one-minute calls nonstop to every corner of the States. I suspect they're pinging the location of their drivers. So that leaves two possibilities. I'll text you both numbers and you can do your investigative-reporter thang. If you want my opinion, I'd bet my money on the 202-654-0995 number. It's a Blue Tech mobile—a supercheap throwaway. They call them 'prison phones.' Girl goes to see her cocaine-dealing convict boyfriend with one of these up her hoochee so he can do business on the outside. There is no way to trace it back to the name of a person. Triangulation of the phone's location isn't easy, either, because Blue Tech piggybacks onto other companies' cell towers. The big boys sell extra space for an extraordinary fee. Criminals don't care. Poor people and illegal immigrants don't know the difference."

"Two Club One seats for the next game will be at will call in my name. Enjoy a cold microbrew for me."

Cole hung up, took a deep breath, then stepped outside, under the shield of a small concrete overhang, and punched in the magic phone number.

Chapter 19

After getting kicked out of the latest Animal Liberation Brigade meeting, Wendell Canyon spent the night a few miles away at the McNary Golf Club, sleeping on a cot typically used by the head groundskeeper for his afternoon nap. Canyon often used the quiet closet, tucked behind the men's locker room, to get away from the constant noise and activity at Willow House. He had been mowing greens, laying sod, and moving flag placements for years at the redwood-lined course. The owners of the club even trusted him with a key. He pulled on a hooded sweatshirt and set out across the tenth fairway, leaving size 14 tennis shoe imprints on top of the dewy zoysia. He could see a few eager golfers sitting in their cars in the parking lot, waiting for the first tee time. He enjoyed the burning in his calf muscles as climbed the crooked path to a gorgeous overlook above. He never understood why anyone would get on an indoor treadmill for exercise. Canyon stood at the top, only slightly out of breath, among the old graves of the Claggett Cemetery and watched the sunrise. A weathered bronze plaque, put up by a now defunct historical society, lay embedded in a low rock wall that separated him from the rugged bluff. It read *"Here lies the Pugh twins. God rest their souls. 1862-1863."*

A loud series of bird chirps from his pocket let him know he had a call coming in. He didn't recognize the number at first, but on chirp three, he broke into vulgar rant. It was Colton Wiley.

"Fuck, fuck, *fuck*! Are you kidding me?" He started pacing furiously from side to side like a caged bear at a carnival. Before it could go to voice mail, Canyon answered with a furious hiss, "You had no right to track me down. Do you know my name?"

"Not a clue, but if I did, I'd take it to my grave. I figured out your number. That's it. Don't hang up. I'm calling to thank you for your tip about the Evergreen State lab. You've given great peace of mind to the family of a missing young lady. They can bury her soon."

"I don't know what you're talking about, but you're missing the big picture. ALB wants mass casualties. Think terrorism, not murder," Canyon fired back. He paused, then felt compelled to ask, "What was inside the lab?"

"Nothing except an incinerator full of ashes. And, of course, the bones of a dead English major," Cole said laying on the sarcasm with a trowel.

"I doubt that's all that's there. H_2O is some sort of mad scientist. Hunt for trace materials. And for God's sake, don't call me again!"

He punched "end" and disengaged the battery, tossing it in one direction, the cell phone in another. On the follow-through, he felt a sharp, deep pain in his side. He looked down to see the short feathers of a crossbow arrow sticking out of his sweatshirt, blood oozing up into the knit.

Instantly in full survival mode, Canyon sprinted for the rugged trail leading down the cliff, back toward the golf course. All he could think about was maximizing his running form to increase speed. *Heel to toe, heel to toe . . .* He heard whistles zip past his head, and the clank of arrows caroming off the rock walls. Swarming, darting black bees started filling his vision. Then he felt the sting of gravel on his face, which brought him back to reality.

He crawled behind a large boulder and picked up a sharp stone, ready to fight. He was furious with himself for getting so distracted with the reporter's call that he didn't sense an ambush. Canyon's long neck was an advantage as he peeked over the sagebrush growing through a crack in the wall. He could see Oz and a much beefier tattooed man fiddling with the crossbow and discussing options near the cemetery ridge. *Those dirty bastards!* Just as Canyon's first thought was survival, his second was revenge.

* * *

Nolan stood at the other end of Cole's abruptly ended conversation, waiting to hear whether the mysterious caller had provided any new tidbits of intelligence.

"That went about as I expected—you get anything new from the guy?" Nolan finally asked.

As usual, Cole stood silently thinking, waiting an uncomfortable length of time before answering. "He said 'hunt for trace materials' and 'mass casualties' in the same ten-second time frame. Maybe we're talking about some sort of radioactive material. Poison? Virus? Until we figure it out, it might be best to have the SWAT boys—and you—get nekkid and wash off in that cheap decontamination shower stall the drug lab cleanup crews use."

Nolan was a bit alarmed and started off toward the Lab One building, then stopped in mid stride.

"Do you smell that?"

The unmistakable odor of rotten eggs, added to unscented natural gas by companies trying to avoid silent-killer lawsuits, was prevalent in the air. Almost instantaneously, Thurston County's finest came running around the corner, grabbed the pair, and spun them around, forcing them back toward the student commissary. Lieutenant O'Brien shouted as Nolan and Cole were forced to shuffle backward, lifted and towed by the entire SWAT team scrum.

"Gas line for the incinerator opened up full throttle! Run! Move it!"

And Cole thought he just might do that if they would only let his feet touch the ground.

A microsecond before the actual explosion, Cole felt the air around him turn cold and press hard against his flesh. The concussion force rattled his eardrums and took his breath away, but the brick building between him and the fireball prevented any real trauma. A blue, then orange, then red flash of light expanded into a brilliant, pupil-contracting aurora, then back to blackness in the next blink of the eye. As the flash fell back toward its source, the Lab One building was instantly engulfed in flames, fueled directly by a four-inch gas line.

"What the fuck happened?" Cole yelled as the group stopped and dropped him out of the danger zone. "I thought the utility company shut down all the juice!"

Lieutenant O'Brien was not happy about having to retreat, but he seemed thankful his men appeared unscathed.

"I don't know! We were about to collect some evidence swabs after we finished taking crime scene pictures. I heard this click and hiss; then natural gas began pouring into the room. It was so thick, you could see that heavy wave of rainbow colors from your knees down, like a desert mirage."

"Please tell me you got that bone," Nolan moaned.

"I got it, but that's about it."

* * *

From the edge of the parking lot, Dr. Dell never saw Colton Wiley, though he did his best to kill every SWAT team member who had violated his beloved research facility. It took him some time to get back to Evergreen State from the warehouse. He was disappointed he couldn't get his iPad to remotely control both the natural gas flow and the pilot light on his incinerator at the same time. It wasn't that hard to hack into the campus natural-gas grid and turn the flow back to full, then cripple the choke stop on the appropriate pipe. It was a shame he had to log out before slipping back into the system to restart the tiny pilot flame inside his incinerator. The time lag had allowed the cops to flee. Sitting there behind the steering column of his car, he seethed with anger for a few moments, but his mood instantly changed when his pups leaned forward, looking for a quick stroke on their furry heads.

"Let's get out of here, my precious love-dolls. Those bad siren sounds from those fire trucks are going to hurt your beautiful ears. Yah. Love you, baby. Kisses all around!" he cooed, licking their tongues.

* * *

Nolan ran into an open space next to the computer lab and spun around in every direction, looking at the perimeter of the campus. He could see the faces of dozens of gawking students, all still as scarecrows, looking directly at the fire. He spotted vehicles spinning around to come back toward the action likely curiosity getting the better of them. People were running. Buses stopped in the middle of campus streets. Professors stuck their heads out doors and windows. Every single eye was focused directly on Lab One. Who wouldn't be drawn to this inferno?

Then Nolan saw what he was looking for. A dark green sedan easing out of parking lot C. One dark-haired male, two dogs, and a tattered powder-blue peace symbol bumper sticker stuck to the back window. The driver never glanced back.

Cole recorded some unbelievable fire video, then hit Lieutenant O'Brien with a couple of softball questions about the missing girl and a possible connection to the fire. He said his team was on campus following leads about the missing girl, when a gas line nearby started leaking and caught fire. He was glad nobody was hurt, and they were continuing to investigate. They had recovered a human bone from an incinerator and were rushing it to forensics to see if it was related to the case. Lots of unknowns. Very factual. No speculation.

Cole texted the morning show producer and briefly filled her in on his story. He fired up his laptop and used Skype to go live from the scene.

"A missing freshman, a human bone, an explosion, and the near incineration of an entire SWAT team—that's what's topping the news on KZPR at this hour," the segment began. "I have confirmed that very early this morning, the Thurston County SWAT team executed a search warrant here on the Evergreen State College campus . . . then this." Cole stepped aside and used the motion eye camera on the computer to show the fire. He walked right up to the yellow tape separating him from the crime scene. As he hit his roll cue, the grainy live pictures from Skype were replaced by the prerecorded video of higher quality that he had shot with his handheld camera earlier.

***

Rachelle Fredette was having eggs in her bathrobe, watching for the next traffic update, when Cole's face filled the screen.

"This is not possible!" she screamed into the next room. "I was standing there six hours ago. No SWAT team. No fire. Nobody actively hunting for a missing girl. He says he happened to be on campus doing 'research' and stumbled into the biggest story of the month! Seriously? He's a liar—*nobody's* that lucky. He's hiding something. Honey, you don't want liars working for you. Do something about this prick before he ruins the station's reputation!"

KZPR's general manager, Alan Eaton, nodded in agreement and lowered his eyes from the TV to Rachelle's shiny, long legs.

"Oh, I couldn't agree more" Alan moved in close, sliding his hands around her back and onto her naked butt. The GM had a broad notion that his star reporter was working on some animal rights story that included arson. He figured it was related, but if pretending—at least for the next hour or two—that he was going to crack down on Cole made Rachelle happy, that was a game he was happy to play.

"I'll haul him into my office as soon as I get in today. I'll make sure I reel in his rogue, cowboy ways and get to the bottom of it."

Alan was a tough, seasoned veteran in the industry, having fired dozens of journalists over the past two decades. He especially despised highly paid, egocentric anchors and other big stars who believed the TV station couldn't survive without them. "Untouchable ratings machines," some considered themselves. Although advertisers and, at times, the viewing public ranted when a popular on-air talent was shown the door, Alan found it exceedingly useful that the staff at the station fear his power. He wanted all to know that he held their professional lives in his hands. It motivated people to work extra hours for free and forced them to smile at him as they passed in the halls. Colton Wiley, however, had a different vibe. Money didn't seem to drive him at all. Neither did stardom. He was the only employee Alan had ever been around who made him feel nervous. There was something dangerous about Colton—not the disgruntled-postal-worker-who's-into-guns kind of dangerous, but dangerous none the less.

* * *

After Cole finished a series of live shots in front of the burning lab building, Chuck Reynolds pleaded, wheedled, threatened, and finally tried to bribe him to stay and keep providing on-the-scene news content, but it wasn't going to happen.

"Boss, anyone can pick this up and make a great résumé tape out of it. Send your prettiest reporter to bat her eyes and speak breathlessly about 'a big, scary fire' and the bravery of muscular men in uniforms who put it out. The cops aren't going to talk until they know what happened, so there's not a new angle to get from here. And believe me, they don't have a frickin' clue. In fact, the FBI's on its way, so media silence is guaranteed the second they high-step onto campus. Send two reporters: one to stand at the charred ruins of the lab and talk to students, blah blah, then another to cuddle up to the poor missing girl's parents and wait it out. Use my name. That will get them in the door. In a few days, the medical examiner will confirm our suspicions. Anna Dipler is dead. I'm heading back to Seattle to find out *why* she's dead and who killed her. We'll kick the shit out of the other stations *again* in two days, I promise. We're already winners, already own this. Now let's stay ahead. I'll see you in an hour or so."

Cole noticed Nolan across the student walkway, being debriefed by the feds, so he decided to leave without a word or a wave. By the time he got to his computer at KZPR, the news coverage of the fire was on every station. He noticed that all the reporters were now standing blocks away from the barely smoldering building. As he expected, the FBI had pushed the crime scene a hundred yards farther out than was remotely necessary. Nobody would get any new information standing that far from ground zero.

In every other newsroom in the country, if a reporter nailed such a huge exclusive story, when they returned to their desk they'd get swamped with "Nice job" and "Let's go for a beer after work—I want to hear all about it!" Like a fisherman, the reporter at the center of attention would banter back some exaggerated tale of adventure. Although there were plenty of people in the newsroom who would have loved to do that with Cole—those who really appreciated his street smarts—nobody was dumb enough to approach. He had made it crystal clear long ago that when he was working, chitchat was not welcome or tolerated. His face read like a "No soliciting" sign.

The bright green bar rose steadily as Cole dragged and dropped the server history from Evergreen State onto his own C drive. He wished the information were in pretty files all labeled

150

with names like "Top Secret Killing Research" or "Dead College Girls," but as expected, the stream of information was all mashed together in a nonsensical mess. He tried importing the data by merging functions. No good. He tried guessing the numbers of a possible fixed-width format. No way. He tried writing a simply SQL program. Nope. He finally pulled out his rarely-used pattern ID software program and played with the parameters, letting his computer figure out the alpha-numeric similarities.

After several hours of hit and miss, the Evergreen server information was mostly in columns and rows that made sense: date, time, length of visit, Web site visited, pass code user ID, download (Y or N), and programs accessed. Cole converted the data again into a spreadsheet so he could manipulate it.

Coverage of the explosion had been blaring on the newsroom TVs for hours, but the afternoon talk shows were finally bringing relative quiet. Cranky old ladies at the nursing home would flood the switchboard with a thousand complaints if the station broke away from its afternoon programming. A big fire, where a dozen cops were nearly killed, wasn't as important as watching Judge Judy tongue whip a landlord.

Producers filed past Cole on their way to the afternoon meeting. When Chuck Reynolds walked by, he pounded Cole on the shoulders and jokingly whispered, "I live through you. If I had to go to all these news planning sessions without some real news, I'd have blown my brains out years ago." Reynold put an imaginary finger gun in his mouth and pulled the trigger.

Cole continued simple alphabetical reordering of the server information. He hit "page down" over and over to get a sense of what information might be there. For the time being, he focused on cache Web searches. Topics filled the screen: *Triple-A road service, BRE proteins, ESPN football scores, goldenbuckyballs, Karst aquifers, NCBI, transgenetic, veganrecipes,*

151

Zionism. He didn't see anything out of the ordinary for a science lab on a college campus. He reordered the history by date and scrolled straight to the end. The last recorded piece of data was for Olympia-based moving companies. The next ten Web sites were news searches that included the words "missing" and "student" and "evergreen." The pattern was far clearer using the "by date and time" ordering. He could see where the user of the computer started on a main Web page, then whether they progressed deeper into the Web site, into detail pages. It helped Cole start gauging the searcher's level of interest on each subject. Someone had typed "green energy," clicked twice on the Siemens Energy Web site, then moved on. Cole assumed the user wasn't that interested. On the other hand, when the user surfed fifteen subpages deep into research at a German University, something there had to be more interesting or important. He wrote a short query to have the computer rank the length of time spent on each site. As it cranked away he realized that he hadn't eaten anything in a very long time, and slipped off to the wheel-of-death vending machine. He pushed the button and watched doughnuts, cheese-topped southern-style chicken sandwiches, and milk go around in their tight little slots. He was thankful when his phone rang before he could stick his money in the horrid device. He was even more thankful when a picture of Montana, sliding like a spider up a rock wall, popped up on the screen.

"Saw you on the news this morning. Kick-ass story. You can fake it for the rest of the world, but I'm guessing you haven't slept since you were in my bed a couple nights ago."

Cole could hear concern in her voice.

"I'm okay, but you're right. I need sleep and some food. I can't think any more. Would you suggest I buy tuna-fish snack pack with crackers or the microwavable Pasta Roni tubes?"

"Christ, Colton, you are *not* putting that crap in your body! Get over here. I'll have the chef at the restaurant downstairs make you something with actual vegetables in it. Do you have a vague idea where your truck is, or should I send a car?"

"Good question. I'll drive myself. See you in a half hour."

Cole walked upstairs and, with a few keystrokes, made sure the results of the query would automatically get forwarded to him when it finished. He brushed his teeth in the water fountain, used a steakhouse wet-nap to wipe off what was left of the hated on-air TV makeup, jumped in the truck, and roared down a back alley near the station.

He felt like a slob standing at Montana's door with his tie half undone. She had eaten a late lunch, so as Cole ate a gorgeous pea risotto she sipped wine from a giant Merlot glass. She sat close, leg draped over his lap, eyes fixed on his. After eating, he slipped off his shoes, socks, and shirt, then dropped his head onto a pillow. He never slept more than four or five hours, so Montana decided to nap with him. She knew they had work to do before dawn.

Chapter 20

Brian Zander watched as the mustachioed Oz stared at his heavily pierced, tattooed body. An armed mercenary, Zander enjoyed his status as a dangerous thug. The young radical had been exceedingly loyal to Dr. Dell. He knew the rest of the group suspected it had more to do with money than heartfelt animal rights convictions. Maybe they were right. Zander tossed his green hockey-gear bag full of outdoor clothing and ammunition into the warehouse corner and then flopped down on an old couch next to Dr. Wanagi. She was doing some sort of weird meditation, but Zander was getting pretty used to weird. Chivas was studying a topographical map whose far edge was held up with nails stuck into some wooden stairs.

Dr. Dell was uncharacteristically nervous, pacing back and forth cradling a house cat in his arms. He started another one of his speeches, enunciating like a New Orleans street preacher.

"The human race will never realize that its very existence threatens all of God's other creatures," he said with eyes closed. "Our species learned nothing when they wiped out the Carolina parakeet, killing it for feathers to make rich ladies' hats. We learned nothing wiping the quagga off the plains of South Africa so farmers could raise sheep where they were never intended to be. They learned nothing killing off the pallid beach mouse or the spectacled cormorant or the Caspian tiger. Those wonderful creatures are extinct because of human greed and thoughtlessness. I want to make sure no other species falls victim to *Homo sapiens'* arrogance. My friends, they will call us murderers, even though a rabbi who slits the throat of a mother cow is fondly called 'tzaddik'—'righteous.' They will call us terrorists, even though the doctor who cured polio was called a saint for dismembering rhesus monkeys by the thousands. They will call us criminals, even though the president of the United States is called a patriot when he authorizes the death of hundreds of dolphins while the Navy trained them to detect

154

underwater explosives. Our small army is going to level the playing field. Specialist McKinsey, are the trucks loaded?"

Oz nodded an affirmation, the scowl never leaving his face.

"I have written instructions for each of you inside our electronic trap door. You all know how to find it. Coded decipher is 'Lima Golf twenty-two.' We have some long days ahead of us, but I know the world will thank us in the end. This is not a suicide mission. I have set up hidden camps for each of you to survive for at least two years. Locations are part of your packets. Food, drink, ammunition, shelter—it's all there. Stay alive. Enjoy our new earth. You will be the leaders of the future. Oz, you're with me. Wynona, my darling spirit, take Mr. Zander with you. His mission is to keep you, um, on task. And Chivas. I love you like a brother. I have faith you can succeed alone."

"Keys are in 'em!" Oz shouted as he jumped up. "They have insurance. Temporary registration's in the glove box. Don't fucking speed! If anyone asks about the cargo, you're hauling frozen fish and blocks of ice. And what*ever* you do, keep the cooling units on!"

Wynona appeared in a giddy mood. As Dr. Dell's close confidante, Zander assumed she didn't need any instructions. He felt honored to watch over Dr. Wanagi as her carefully-chosen bodyguard.

He drove toward the Boeing Field airport on Seattle's south end. Wynona rapidly clapped her hands and repeatedly sang something that sounded like "gee soo moo su, you so amazing, ga ta vaz coo, you so amazing." Zander pursed his lips and kept quiet as the lyrics wandered back and forth between Russian and English.

"On the bench a cat is sleeping. Hush, you mice, don't make such noise. Or you'll wake up Vaska Cat!" Wynona sang over and over.

Zander thought of the other members of the Animal Liberation Brigade gang as his family. Nobody else ever gave him a chance to do anything with his life. *Now all those teachers and cops and social workers would pay for their indifference.*

He'd met Dr. Dell at a "Don't Eat Meat" rally in downtown Seattle. Zander was having fun smashing storefront windows with a parking meter he'd torn from its concrete casing. Dr. Dell helped him escape down a back alley just as riot police started tossing tear gas into the crowd of protestors. Over time, Dr. Dell helped him understand the true meaning of anarchy.

Zander put in his ear buds and listened to music, hoping to avoid any direct conversations with "Spirit" Wynona. He knew she had a loose screw rattling around in that pretty head. He snapped open a Red Bull and sucked it down as he steered the former Igloo ice delivery truck onto East Marginal Way. Wynona motioned for him to go left, then right. She guided him into the back lot of Big Air Cargo. A line of modified 747s sat behind a razor wire-topped gate. He watched for a short while and determined security was a joke. Vendors wandered in and out of the unlocked gate, and the guard at the vehicle entrance was dead asleep. By the looks of their tattoos, Zander figured most of the cargo-loading crew were Samoan gangbangers. The other few were a mix of illegal Hondurans and Uzbekistanis. The only Caucasian within half a mile was a manager in a teal-colored golf shirt, wildly waving a clipboard. He was orchestrating the movements of five forklifts loading shrink-wrapped engine parts on pallets. Wynona jumped out of the truck and went inside the small office with a black gym bag and returned with only a yellow sheet of paper.

"We're cleared. Time to go home!" she crowed, jumping back into the passenger seat.

That was easy, Zander thought. "Are we unloading the cooler?" he asked, expecting some simple instructions. Dr. Dell had told him virtually nothing except to guard the contents of the truck with his life.

"No. No. No, my brawny Brian with the oh-so-serious face. Head through gate B and drive straight into the belly of that Seven-forty-seven," Wynona laughed hysterically. "I love it when my darling keeps secrets! H_2O is such a naughty boy. It's so much more fun this way. An adventure. An adventure. An adventure. Just you and me! Irkutsk is so beautiful in the fall!"

Zander knew only that Irkutsk was somewhere in Russia, because he had grown up playing Risk with his brothers. He loved it when he had three dice in his hands and lots of horses and cannons in Kamchatka, Yakutsk, and Mongolia. It sometimes took a hundred rolls, but by the end of the hour, he would invade and own Irkutsk. Zander was upset that nobody had told him, but he showed no emotion. At 25 years old, his only role in life was now to be a mercenary for a cause, with a side benefit of staying alive through whatever apocalypse this group had planned.

"You got it," was all he said as he shifted into first gear. Until this moment, he had thought that somehow, he would be able to ride out the end of the world comfortably from a rented condo.

Once the jet had them and the truck airborne, Wynona curled into a tiny ball and slept, pulling her faux-fur parka hood tight around her face. Zander wandered around the back of the cargo bay with a crowbar. Thick nylon straps cinched the containers tight to the floor, leaving narrow aisles between the towering stacks. Zander looked for any kind of label that appeared to be food related. The only pile that looked promising was labeled "U.S. Mail." He began shaking boxes and tearing them open until he found an Alaska Smokehouse snack pack being shipped to

Moscow. Herb-crusted salmon, rye crackers, and a chocolate truffle for dessert were way better than the military MREs that Oz had stuffed into his coat pocket on the way out of the warehouse. Even with a quick fuel stop in Hong Kong, the jet was wheels down in Irkutsk in less than twenty-four hours.

"Now what, O Spirit of the Weird?" Zander jabbed toward Wynona, then paused with his finger inches from her ribs, suddenly remembering the stories he had heard about her violent proclivities when spooked. Wynona had already dropped a large box-cutter down her coat sleeve and into her hand. She fought to regain control over her rage before speaking.

"You will soon see where our war begins and ends."

Wynona spent the next hour wildly waving her entry papers on the airport tarmac and yakking in fluent rapid-fire Russian. The handover of a sizeable amount of cash to port authority officers led them both to wander away from the back of a loading bay.

"What a turd cluster!" Zander grumped. "I thought they'd never leave. Greedy bastards." He couldn't wait to get out of the cramped, dark quarters.

Wynona held out her palms. "Not yet. Wait. You don't understand the Russian way. Those two cops don't really have the authority to let us go. They just want me to think that, so I pay them off. Their boss will stop us as soon as we hit the next gate. That's where we get fucked, because there are cameras at the exit and that guy's boss is watching him. He won't take a bribe at that location."

Because the 747 couldn't be unloaded until the ice truck came off the back, it wasn't long before a squat, square-headed crew boss started yelling. Wynona ignored him. A minute later, a ghostly-pale manager walked into the cargo hold. Zander stayed seated behind the wheel, with a ball cap pulled low over his face. No one needed to notice that he was American. He could feel the truck rock back and forth as someone yanked open the cooler door. The refrigeration unit generator on top of the box kicked on with a loud sputter. Zander could see Wynona in the side mirror, motioning for the Russian to have a look the inside. She had an ominous grin.

Speaking Russian, her voice was easy-going, almost hypnotic.

Zander didn't know the language well but could pick up the words salmon and gift.

Even in the fish-eye lens, the manager looked very interested. He stepped up into the back of the truck. Zander got out and went to the back, expecting to use his considerable size and fighting skills. As the manager peered into the darkness, waiting for his pupils to adjust, Wynona stepped past Zander. She moved close behind the man, pressing her body into his back and whispering something quietly into his ear. He started to turn his head toward her face but got only a quarter of the way around before she tightened the Catalan garrote. One turn, two, and the carotid artery bulged into a fat bluish slug. Three turns, and Wynona gritted her molars together, as the garrote slowly dug through the layers of the epidermis, crushing the neck muscles. Five turns. Six. The manager had lost consciousness in the first three seconds, and since he was getting too heavy to hold up, Wynona let him drop face-first onto the freezing metal floor of the truck bed. Straddling his back, on the seventh turn, Zander heard the man's head pop free—still connected by ligaments and soft tissue, but free.

Wynona told Zander to head west as she wiped her hands on a roll of paper towels that had been jammed behind the bench seat. She stuffed the blood-soaked remnants in the glove box. Zander wasn't big on asking questions, and he had none about what had just happened in the back of the truck. Still, he could no longer hide his curiosity regarding the final plans of Dr. Hadar O'Dell.

"I believe animals are the root of this earth," he said. "And I fulfil orders without question or fail. But if you could shed light on why the fuck we are in *Russia*, maybe, just maybe I could do my job without getting us both killed," Zander began probing with an angry intensity. "This is obviously something a lot more messed up than releasing a few thousand chickens from their shitty, cramped laying cages."

Wynona stared at Zander for a long time. He stared back at her calculating, cold-blooded killer eyes wondering if he'd made a mistake accepting only fifty-thousand dollars for this mission. She suddenly erupted into gales of laughter.

"I like you my buzzy bee! I tell you what. Tomorrow, we are heading to Olkhon Island on Lake Baikal, to set up camp and wait for further instructions. Very serious. But tonight, I have special plan—one that I've been dreaming about since I was a young girl. You will be happy. We're almost to town. Turn right on Dekabrskih; then weave your way down to the Angara River. We wait until nightfall in the Listvyanka neighborhood."

Zander followed the speed limit signs carefully, keeping one eye on the neon-painted kilometers per hour on the inside of the dial. He drove past ornate, dilapidated wooden houses. A few structures had sunk into the ground up to their first-floor windows as the repetition of freezing and thawing gobbled them up little by little, year to year. He parked along a wide boulevard.

Zander wondered if Dr. Wanagi had permission, or the proper cognitive wiring, to take on whatever personal quest she had set in motion. He hoped it would not put the larger mission at risk. And although he still didn't know the specifics, the bombs in the back of the truck were not in Russia for entertainment.

***

Within the next two days, Dr. Wynona Wanagi hoped to start the process of killing nearly every human within a thousand miles. And if she succeeded tonight, Svelta and Meeska might be saved.

She recalled sitting next to her father when she was twelve as the rail car thumped gently along beneath her new red shoes. It was her first trip on the Trans-Siberian Railway, and the last with her loving father. She didn't find out until years later that he had known even then that he had cancer—his early-retirement gift from the government-run copper mine. She remembered walking hand-in-hand with him down a small wooden boardwalk to the Nerpinary. Gazing at the beautiful pool, she was awestruck when a pair of Baikal seals swam into view. It was the purest, most exciting moment of her life. Svelta and Meeska spent the next hour dancing on their tails, playing catch with a multicolored beach ball, counting the number of fish laid out on a board, and "talking" back to the trainers. For the big finale, Wynona was chosen out of the audience to help the two seals paint a picture. Her love of all nonhuman creatures began that day.

Her understanding of how the proud, barrel-chested seals were trained to perform such magical feats came much later. She learned that the trainers thumped their sensitive noses with a wooden club for failing to respond. They were held captive in small pens and deprived of food for long periods so that when showtime came they wouldn't defecate in the pool. Tonight, Wynona would make sure the two Baikal seals got to feast on omul salmon and frolic, free at last, in the deep, cold waters of Lake Baikal.

There were plenty of local animal-rights activists from eastern Siberia who would be investigated for the theft of the seals, giving Wynona and Zander ample time to carry out their primary mission without police scrutiny. Irkutsk was a proud haven for all sorts of rebels. The population of the town had exploded during the Decemberist Cultural Revolution under Czar

Nicolas. Artists, politicians, nobles, and some of the county's top scientists had been exiled here, where they thrived in their own system of individualism. The Communist plot to make them all disappear, along with their inconvenient ideas, failed miserably.

The lights inside the Nerpinary seal aquarium went out as the cleaning staff headed home around eight p.m. The doors remained untouched for the next three hours, and the entire neighborhood was asleep before midnight. Zander was an expert at cutting locks and breaking into buildings. He clipped a large padlock on the back-delivery gate, smashed a tiny side window in what appeared to be a toy storage room, then slipped back to the safety of the truck. Not seeing any security response, he waited another hour before deciding it was time to make a move. Silent as her shadow, Wynona swung open the fence on the driveway. Zander pulled close to the door and opened the back of the ice truck. The airport cargo manager still lay in the middle of the floor. After a few minutes, Wynona raised a garage door and disappeared inside. Within a few moments, Zander could see her waving a couple of fish at two seals in the dark. The pair shuffled water along the concrete floor, eagerly following. She threw the fish inside the truck, and the seals galumphed up the metal ramp. Ignoring the frozen body in their path, they sat down right on top of it to eat their late-night snack. Zander left the lights of the city, ready for a six-hour drive in the blackness along the shores of Lake Baikal.

Chapter 21

Chivas Riviera hated driving a truck that got only six miles a gallon, but then again, in a matter of weeks, the world consumption of gasoline could drop from 900 million gallons a day to a trickle. Driving west along the interstate, he decided it was time to know his final destination.

He pulled over behind a Starbucks and fired up his laptop. He didn't have any trouble finding the electronic portal, because he was the one who created it. It was an ingenious way to use a regular Web site for subversive activities. Big companies that ran free e-mail were always breaking customer confidentiality rules and couldn't be trusted. They all caved into pressure from the Justice Department when it came to any allegation of terrorism. *So much for the First, Fourth, and Fifth Amendments.*

Keeping that in mind, Chivas created a Web site called FlowersoftheForest. He filled thirty-plus pages with photos of red heather, Indian paintbrush, Tolmie's saxifrage, Cascade blueberries, and glacier lilies. He got a kick out of creating beautiful images while cloaking what just about anyone would consider the most repugnant material ever created: plans to threaten half the world's human population. The page dedicated to the Columbian tiger lily was special. ALB members knew that if they held their mouse exactly over the third anther on the twelfth lily, a small colored window would appear. To anyone who just happened to stumble onto it, it would look like a teensy, inconsequential glitch.

Chivas typed in the code "LG22," and a bulletin board appeared. His name blinked in the corner, telling him he had a new message. Dr. Dell had posted only three words: "Keith County Nebraska."

Chapter 22

For a moment, Cole actually thought he could feel the softness of Montana's stare caressing the day-old stubble on his face. His eyes still closed, he could smell her sweet, light breath a few inches away. His internal clock was always right on the money. He didn't need to ask the time: 3:30 a.m.

After giving her a smile to let her know he was awake, he said, "Let's make a couple of margaritas and I'll tell you what we're going to do with Big Vasil."

Montana smiled back. Minutes later, he set their drinks—one on the rocks and one blended—with their rims touching on a high little nook table. The lights along Lake Union bled through the window, making wide rainbow circles in the thin fog.

Montana started. "I set up a meeting per your instructions. He was weird about it, but he's going to show up. He's a greedy pig. If he thinks there's a one-percent chance I can guide a dollar's worth of casino business his direction, he can't stop himself."

"You're awesome. I know you trust me, so I won't even ask such a stupid question. We can't risk putting an undercover camera or microphone on you. I'm sure his goons will feel you up. When they do, spit on them or kick them in the nuts—whatever you feel like doing. Enjoy whatever punishment you dish out. Big Vasil won't let them hurt you as long as he can smell money. I'm going to set up an ice-cream cart about thirty-five yards away. I'm never going to look your way. I'll have a parabolic mike tucked high under the top of a big red umbrella; it'll record every word in perfect clarity. Not legal in the U.S., but the Canadians don't give a shit."

Cole wondered what kind of stories normal people told about their days at work.

"I'll also be recording video from two angles. I have a wireless camera about the size of a quarter that will be in a tree right over your head, shooting down. It'll throw the signal to the ice-cream cart. I'm also going to have a serious telephoto lens on a video camera in a parking lot van. I've got a buddy up there who'll run it. I don't need to coach you on the conversation. Simply have Big Vasil tell you what he wants. You're a businesswoman who has access to your dad and millions of dollars. See where it goes. The only acting you have to do is to pretend you might actually consider going into business with him."

"He's such a gross dirtbag, I would *relish* ending his career," Montana said with a fierce light in her eyes. "What do we do with the video?"

"Do you love me?" Cole asked out of the blue.

Montana paused a beat.

"I promise I will answer completely and honestly, but first tell me why that's important in the middle of a conversation about a mob boss trying to extort money out of an Indian casino empire."

"It's simple. My plan is to air a heavily promoted investigation into Big Vasil's empire. It will be complete with video of his desperate, highly illegal plot to shake down a young millionairess casino baby from Seattle. I ask if you love me, because the only way I can do this story with any journalistic integrity is to tell my viewers that you're my girlfriend. I feel like I have to let everyone know I have an emotional conflict of interest. Full disclosure is important to me. In the eighties, *a major network* was trying to air an investigation into faulty pickup truck gas tanks. The tanks supposedly exploded during certain kinds of crashes. The news crew destroyed a couple of trucks, but no bang, no fire. Nothing. So the team of producers and reporters and photographer decided lighting a flare under the truck before they rolled it over was a great idea. Not much of a surprise that on the next take, the truck erupted into flames. Well, they didn't tell viewers—kept that scrap of important information secret. Of course, eventually, everyone found out they rigged the tests for better TV. Mind you, the truck gas tanks were almost certainly defective, and in exposing the problem, the consumer investigative team was doing the public a great service. But nobody believed any of the rest of the story, because they faked one part. The reporter was hung out to dry and demoted to some local station near a sandy beach, and the show slowly lost ratings shares and drifted off the air.

Montana looked pensive, side eyeing Cole as if she hoped he'd tell her how he felt first.

"So how does any of this affect you, me, and Big Vasil? 'Do you love me?' isn't a trick question. I plan on telling a million people about that fat Russian prick's many misdeeds while, at the same time, telling them that my point of view could be colored because I am in love with the main subject of my report. If you don't want that information debated on radio talk shows and at the next Investigative Reporters and Editors conference in Phoenix, then I need to know now."

Montana rose from her chair and slid outside onto the chilly deck. The mist in the air cooled her off. Cole followed in his bare feet. She had no trouble answering the question.

"I didn't think it was possible for me to still get butterflies like an adolescent girl at the ninth-grade dance, but you make me feel special every single moment I am in the room. If you want to tell the world I'm off the market, that's more than fine by me."

"Cool. Then let's go put the hurt on that sleazy ex-commie." Cole smiled and moved in for a quick kiss, which turned into a passionate kiss, which nearly derailed their departure.

"You better stop using those Indian life-force spells on me or we'll never make your meeting," he teased.

Montana laughed. "I wish that hokum really worked. I expect you're not that easily hypnotized, Colton Wiley." She bit her lower lip, flushed in the cheeks.

166

They stood up at the same time and headed to the bedroom closet, holding hands part of the way. Cole grabbed a backpack of extra clothes while Montana shut off the lights in the condo.

They were at the TV station five minutes later. Nobody looked up when the pair of them darted through the newsroom, gathering undercover cameras, batteries, computers, and sophisticated listening devices. The overnight producers were used to Cole's sudden appearances and departures at odd hours and had long ago stopped asking what he was up to. The answer was always the same: "catching bad guys being bad."

The undercover van wasn't the most comfortable ride for the three-hour trip to Vancouver, B.C. Cole didn't care, because it had just the right exterior—the dented fender well, bland color, and smoky-tinted back window helped it blend into any neighborhood.

Ninety-nine percent of Americans breezed right through the Canadian border crossing near Blaine, but never Colton Wiley. Montana waited inside the comfortable immigration center, reading the *Vancouver Sun*, while agents outside did everything short of a body-cavity search on Cole. Border agents unpacked camera gear onto a wheeled, portable surgical table while others pulled the seats out of the van. Cole had irritated them last year by exposing how their multibillion-dollar ground-penetrating radar was throwing off false readings when grazing cattle kept tripping it. Whatever delay the border agents could legally inflict on him, that was what they were going to do. They asked him if he had liquor or potatoes. And pressed him relentlessly about owning a gun.

After several hours, Cole emerged in good spirits. "I shouldn't have joked about the Canucks choking in the first round of the NHL playoffs last year," he said as they jumped back in the van. "I'm sure that added a half-hour to this little payback affair. I couldn't resist."

167

"I just realized you had to leave your trusty sidearm at home?" Montana blurted with a look of concern.

"Not much of a choice, but I promise, I got you covered," Cole said with an assuring grin. "The Canadians walk around like drunk cowboys, with six-shooters on their hips, firing away at moose and trespassers and anything else that moves, but the border patrol wants to make sure Americans don't stray into their pure, maple-leaf-embossed land with a firearm. Ridiculous, but you know I'm a law-abiding guy. They say no guns, I don't bring a gun. However, the freelance videographer I hired to run the camera from the van also happens to be a former Navy SEAL. By the way, if you hear me yell 'You scream, I scream, we all scream for ice cream!' Move to your right and stay low."

"No killing, please," Montana chided even though it sounded so unreal when she said it.

Stanley Park was always a funny place to be in the morning. Well-heeled waterfront condo owners came to the rolling hills for their three-mile jogs, decked out in five-hundred-dollar jackets and expensive trail-running shoes. At the same time, Vancouver's homeless, decked out in their trash bags and filthy army coats, were just rising from their benches and bushes.

Cole took a tiny undercover camera and transmitter from the jumbled glove box and headed straight to a large tree several hundred feet into the park. Taking a short run, he sprang up to the first branch and shinnied up into the tree. He positioned it to a clear, wide-angle focal length, then secured the setup with a dab of glue, sure to cover the power indicator light with a dab of black marker. The batteries would last twelve hours, so he left it on. His ice-cream cart was already in place, padlocked to a sturdy, yellow pole. He had paid a local private investigator a thousand dollars for the creation and drop-off. It was full of frozen Fudgsicles, Bomb Pops, and Drumsticks. Maybe he could hawk a hundred dollars in sales to recoup some of station's costs.

Turning in investigative expenses was always a sensitive task—so much so that he ended up paying for a lot of the odder items himself. The accountant always wanted so many explanations. There wasn't really a category or column for the daily rental of a refrigerated food cart. Chuck often stepped in to help, but some expenses never got past the bean counters: a hundred dollars' worth of Cuba Libres his photographer bought at a strip club while filming a sex-industry king pen, a clown outfit, delivery of a potted cactus, and an electric wheelchair were a few Cole recalled as walked back to the undercover van.

He double-checked the video monitor and recorder. The tree shot was perfect. Donning headphones, he nodded in satisfaction at hearing two squirrels chattering on the parabolic microphone tucked into the ice-cream umbrella.

Cole gave Montana a final assurance that all systems were in place.

"We're set. We have a few hours, so let's get out of here and go rent you a new Mercedes. You need a show-stopping arrival!"

Big Vasil's advance team arrived an hour early. Cole was already in place. He could tell they were staring at him, seeing if he would look at them and then glance away—a sure sign of surveillance. Cole resisted and focused instead on hawking ice-cream bars to a group of kids, secure in the knowledge that his hired hand was in the van hunkered down, watching, and recording the entire scene.

Big Vasil arrived in a limo, apparently not concerned in the least bit about drawing attention to himself. Instead of wearing a well-tailored suit, he had on green velour pajama pants and a zip-up sweatshirt. His goons didn't give Montana an airport pat-down. Instead, they held out an inexpensive metal detector, which went off on her belt buckle. The guy pulled up her shirt to find an elaborate silver design of the sun and crescent moon.

"You want us to wash your dirty money, Vasil?" Montana started. "It's that simple?"

"I have much income I cannot send overseas. It will trigger IRS or bank audit. I want to be investor in your casino. Build hotel or something. And my money is no dirtier than Chief Harms' profits."

Cole's parabolic microphone was catching every word in crisp stereo sound.

"The best part of dealing with us, Vasil, is that Natives don't pay any taxes. We don't get audited by regulators—only the Bureau of Indian Affairs, and they're almost as corrupt as you. But enough chitchat. What's in this for me?"

"I am sure your father takes good care of you financially. But he is not a young warrior anymore. When he dies, your brothers take over business. I see a big family fight. I can offer you ten percent of profit on my investment. Millions of dollars a year. Yours. No more asking Daddy. When brothers try to cut you out later, you have me in your corner. I can be very persuasive."

Montana fired back, "And if I'd like a bigger cut than that?"

"No negotiation. You take it or leave it. Of course, we're then back to square one. I will kill your father, let you sit through his funeral, then come and kill you," Big Vasil replied without a hint of emotion. "Your brothers inherit the casinos. My intel says they are less . . . how you say? . . . high and mighty. I believe they play ball with me if chief is not telling them what to do."

Montana knew those were the homerun words for Cole's investigative story. She so badly wanted to look around to the van or over to the ice cream cart, as if to say with her eyes, "You got that? Please tell me you got that." But she merely lowered her voice to just above a whisper.

170

"I've been in your presence for, what, three minutes, and you're already threatening to kill me? You clearly have mommy anger issues.. I need to discuss our conversation with some people I trust. Give me a week. I'll have some sort of answer. Love the PJs by the way. Very slimming."

Montana left the Russian goon squad standing in their semi-circle and walked briskly back to her three-hundred-dollar-an-hour rented car. As she drove away, the adrenaline rush from such a dangerous encounter made her hands tremble. She had never felt so alive! No wonder Cole loved his job.

Chapter 23

Dr. Dell was glad it had been a relatively warm fall. As he drove down Highway 62 into Crater

Lake National Park, he could see a scurf of snow sticking to the mountain hemlocks ringing the

upper reaches of Garfield Peak. His app said forty-eight degrees and sunny—the kind of forecast

that brought Oregonians out in shorts and T-shirts while, elsewhere in the country, people would

be digging sweatshirts and mittens out of their winter drawers. The road around the rim of Crater

Lake was designed for jaw-dropping views of the clearest deep-blue water in the world. No

rivers or tributaries flowed into the lake. It stayed full and vibrant by the constant absorption of

melting glaciers and almost daily rain or snow. It was so pure that according to the Secchi test,

human eyes could see objects 142 feet straight down into its depths.

Dr. Dell pulled into a small asphalt parking lot next to the Steel Information Center at the

National Park headquarters. He left the ice truck idling, took a spare key, locked the door with a

beep-beep, and pulled a baseball cap down to his eyebrows as he went inside. After all this

effort, it would be stupid to get identified by a cheap gift-shop security camera. Still, incognito

didn't have to mean bland. The logo on the cap held the image of a blood-spattered golden arch,

reminding passersby that the restaurant slaughtered more cows and chickens for its fast-food

franchises than any other company in the world. He pretended to look at postcards for a good

fifteen minutes, waiting for the small shop to be vacant of tourists, before he approached the

desk.

"I'd like to buy a scuba diving pass," Dr. Dell said to the federal employee in olive-green

fatigues who stood grinning behind the counter. "How much?"

The woman reached for a drawer to her right. "It's awfully chilly in the lake this time of

year! You have a dry suit and a NAUI certificate?"

"You betcha. Both." Dr. Dell faked an East Coast accent as he laid a fake scuba instructor's license on the lacquered log counter. "Are the boats down at the Cleetwood Cove still operating?"

The government employee didn't even look at Dr. Dell's face. She picked up the certificate, headed to the copy machine, and stuffed the paperwork into a drawer.

"The boats are still down there, but the captains are finished taking sightseers to Wizard Island this season. You might get lucky and catch one of them doing some repairs. No guarantees. You still want the permit?"

"Absolutely." Dr. Dell wanted to sound as sure as possible without coming across as too enthusiastic. "I have a friend who's a researcher. He wants to see if we can find the hydrothermal holes and do some testing of the bacteria near the warmer water. Is there a way I can get permission to use one of the boats for research? He's a college professor, working on a grant from the National Science Foundation. It's not essential, but if you aren't too busy, I'd sure like to see if we could make sure a boat is available."

"All the tourists are gone for the year. I don't think that's a problem. I can't make it happen today or tomorrow. We're short-staffed, but how about the day after that?"

"Perfect. And thank you." Leaving the run-down building, Dr. Dell shook his head a little and laughed softly to think that that smiling face was going to be filled with terror very soon, dead in the first wave. He turned to stare at Crater Lake. He had camped here ever so long ago. He couldn't help thinking of his father, sitting by a campfire, telling story after story to his young son. Dr. Dell tried to push the memories aside, but they kept playing in his mind as he drove back toward Medford, eighty-four miles away.

Always the curious child, little Hadar had wanted to know how such a lake got stuck in a hole so high in the mountains. His father at first told him of an old Makalak tribe legend involving Llao, the spirit of the underworld. Dr. Dell could still see his father's closed eyes in the low light of the campfire embers as he told the story.

Llao came up to Earth and stood on Mount Mazama one day and spotted the Makalak chief's beautiful daughter. He promised her eternal life if she would just marry him and return with him to the dark underworld. She snubbed his advances, and in a moment, his anger erupted into fire and ash and boulders, flung for miles in every direction. The god of the sky, Skell, heard the commotion from Mount Shasta and entered the fray, trying to protect the tribespeople from Llao's fury. In the ensuing battle, Mount Mazama was destroyed. After both Gods returned to their homes, a soothing rain came for many days and nights. It extinguished the fires and pooled as one droplet into the hole left behind as Llao made his hasty retreat back beneath the soil.

When he got a little older, Dr. Dell looked up what really happened, and was equally fascinated with the geological truth. Nearly eight thousand years ago, lava formed a giant dome under Mount Mazama. One of a chain of violent volcanoes in the Cascade Range, Mount Mazama percolated and boiled and steamed for hundreds of years and then went off like a nuclear bomb, launching debris right up into the stratosphere. Parts of the mountain ended up in British Columbia, Canada. North of the mountain, a desert formed with ash fifty feet deep. The lava dome emptied so quickly that the thin layer of crust between it and the air outside collapsed,

174

creating a caldera. After many more years, the volcanic activity subsided. And as that empty

bowl on top of the old mountain cooled, water stopped evaporating as steam. Crater Lake

naturally filled up. By the 1970s, its natural beauty began drawing a million gawking tourists a

year. The almost perfectly circular lake held some 4.6 trillion gallons of water, but the only boats

allowed on it were either research craft or excursion boats to Wizard Island. There was really

nothing to do inside the national park but sit and stare at its beauty. Two thousand feet of solid

rock wall rimmed the water, but climbing was discouraged—for liability reasons, Dr. Dell

supposed.

Any hint of happy childhood thoughts at Crater Lake suddenly vanished as Dr. Dell had a

vivid flashback that reminded him why he had never come back here as an adult. He was asleep

in his pup tent when he heard quiet noises outside. His father was sitting on a stump in the

predawn light, tying a treble-hooked fishing lure to an all but invisible monofilament line. All

decked out in a broad-brimmed hat and waders, he was whistling as he looked up to see young

Hadar.

"Wanna go fishing, my boy?"

Up for doing anything outdoors with his father, Hadar was ready to go in under a minute,

although he didn't know exactly what he was volunteering for. They walked down to a quiet

shore, along the way spotting a Cassin's finch, a Cascades frog, and a quick glimpse of a

badger's tail scuttling into a thicket of quaking aspen. They picked up a few massive sugar-pine

cones for his mother, who liked to decorate the foot-long cones as snowmen around

Christmastime.

The very first cast caught the attention of a three-pound rainbow trout hiding under a fallen black cottonwood. His dad yanked the tip of his old Zebco rod, set up with a spin-cast reel, and started whooping it up.

"How 'bout that, Hadar, my boy! First cast of the day!" his dad crowed.

The trout fought hard, tearing a hole through the side of its mouth, but the hook held against the hard lower lip. Dr. Dell remembered sobbing as he watched the trout gasp for breath, its eyes seeming to follow the young boy, pleading for help. Hadar ran as fast as he could back to camp and into his confused mother's arms. That evening, he heard his dad telling her he was sorry that he took Hadar fishing, not realizing the boy had such a soft spot for animals. By the time he was in college, Dr. Dell learned that the trout and kokanee salmon that flourished in Crater Lake weren't supposed to be there in the first place. Humans had determined that the "dead" lake needed to have fish, so they stocked it with millions of fingerlings.

Dr. Dell fumed at the idea that humans had to have fish in the lake just so they could pierce their guts with hooks, then slit their bellies open and dump their entrails on a shiny shoreline rock. The woods surrounding the lake provided ample nutrition already. Their huckleberries, gooseberries, Virginia strawberries, wild celery, and comfrey had kept the Klamath Indians well fed for centuries as they came to this spiritual oasis to pray.

Dr. Dell jumped back in the ice truck and texted Oz: *"Meet at Medford Jill Mart. One hour. Chopper rental better be a go. Park empty. Time to honor Sparks. You ready?"*

The reply came in seconds: *"You lead. I follow. Sort the rest out in hell."*

Chapter 24

"Call me! Call me! Call me, call me, call me anytime, call me!" Nolan belted out his best Blondie impression onto Cole's voice mail. "Seriously, dude, I have a clue we need to track down. You doinking that beautiful Indian? Come on, man. Back to work."

Cole played his best friend's message out loud on the speaker of his phone as Montana laughed until she cried. "We're *doinking*? Is that what we're doing?"

"Apparently—which, by the way, is more than fine by me—but you're an *Indian*? I'm not sure my mother would approve." Cole gave a look of mock concern. "Sorry Nolan is such a Neanderthal. It makes him lovable, like a big, dumb St. Bernard puppy."

Cole waited until he got back across the U.S. border to return Nolan's call. He wasn't about to give the Canadians the dollar-fifteen foreign service fee for roaming. The station paid the bill, but Cole stood on principle. He punched "call back."

"I decided to skip sleeping and run out a different investigation this morning. I figured you'd be stuck with the FBI terrorism task force for a few days on the Evergreen State fire. How'd you get free so fast?"

"It wasn't easy," Nolan answered. "An assistant director of Homeland Security showed up and had a thousand questions—good ones, actually. She's starting to think something is up. I was like 'Oh, wow! Really? You must be a *genius*.' They've been hearing smatterings of intel about something big about to happen. I tossed out a couple of our paper-thin theories, which seemed to set off a flurry of calls and e-mails and shouting."

Cole smirked that smirk that was forever getting him into so much trouble. "You mean the theory that the Animal Liberation Brigade is killing college girls and state troopers in the name of saving wild burros and snail darters?"

"Kind of. Her task force hadn't made many connections directly related to the crimes we've been chasing. Instead, they'd been working on a bunch of other rumors, most of which she didn't share with me. But when I gave her my theory on the Animal Liberation Brigade's new violent army and mentioned N-5-G she jumped out of her skin. Grabbed me by the arm. Told me to 'lower my voice.' She let me know something we didn't. About five years ago, they first heard about the formation of a radical wing of ALB. Super mysterious. Membership was small. At first, they never appeared to commit any crimes—only went around convincing other groups to. They would anonymously send communiqués to other idealists, then—*Bam!*—some Humvee dealership would go up in flames. Or some botanist's office, involved in grafting orange tree saplings, sizzled into ash. The college professor who was running the lab at Evergreen is apparently some sort of animal rights genius. Mental profile is that of a psychopath. FBI says when he was about thirteen-years-old he murdered his parents' while they slept. Defense lawyers talked a juvenile court judge into leaving it in kiddie court."

"No friggin' way!" Cole gasped, amazed that such a fact hadn't appeared in any of his databases or background research into Dr. Dell.

"Yep. Court records on the case were sealed, but Homeland Security doesn't let those little constitutional niceties stop them from prying. According to testimony from his trial, little Hadar waits until his parents are asleep, loads up a twenty-two rifle, then stands in the doorway and plunks Dad right in the temple. Mom wakes up, sits up in bed; he looks her in the eye and pops her in the neck and heart with a couple of rounds."

"Weird. Why?" Cole had always been fascinated with true crime and what motivated people to kill.

"Depends on who you ask," Nolan continued. "The defense team said it was self-preservation. They claimed Dad no longer found Mom attractive, so he forced Hadar to start sexually servicing her. Adopted kid anyway. Not real incest, right? Sick shit. Prosecutors say that never occurred. They say Hadar was motivated by anger after Mommy and Daddy told him he couldn't keep a puppy he had found wandering alone in the woods behind their house."

"Wow. Not that I don't enjoy a great story about an animal-loving teenager slaughtering his parents," Cole panned while driving illegally with the receiver up to his ear, "but you're holding back the good stuff—I can always tell."

Montana just sat quietly, taking it all in. The best talk radio couldn't touch one of Cole's phone conversations.

"I thought that was pretty good, but you're right. When he turned eighteen, the system sprang him. Homeland says he looked like he totally turned his life around. Mensa smart with a ton of college degrees. They knew he dabbled in animal rights causes, but didn't think he was CEO of anything.

"Come on. What else?" Cole asked patiently, taking mental notes so he could incorporate details into a future on-air piece.

Nolan loved knowing something the great Colton Wiley did not. It was a rare pleasure.

"Somebody in our government heavily funded Dr. Dell's research. They took a risk, and he went rogue. Now they have to find him and his strange army of loyalists to try and stuff it all back in the bottle.

Cole thought a moment. "I have an idea. Tell Homeland Security to open their ears."

The next exit didn't go anywhere except to a parking lot rest area filled with big rigs and beat-up RVs. A "Free Coffee" sign hung in a small office window. Cole had read in the paper that they added the office, along with a part-time Department of Transportation staffer, a few years ago, in an attempt to dissuade perverts from choosing the nearby woods for their casual encounters. The area behind the bathrooms had made an Internet top-ten list of best places to get a free hand job. Cole gave Montana a quick kiss and stepped outside the van, locking it behind him.

He dialed his Deep Throat animal rights source, mumbling under his breath a prayer to *please, please, pick up.* It rang strong twice before fading to a hollow-sounding flat tone; then Cole heard a small click. The static-filled silence let him know somebody was on the line.

"This is Colton Wiley. Can you talk?"

"You must have the wrong number," a deep voice answered.

Cole had no idea who was on the line, but he didn't care. His comments were for Big Brother to hear.

"You're a virus on society, as far as I can see. Four people, *at least,* are dead. You might think N-5-G is the bomb, but I'm not a passenger on that plane. Come out of your cave and tell me how this story ends."

* * *

Sitting inside a rustic café, sipping peppered tea in Khuzhir, Russia, Brian Zander was amazed that the phone had two bars of service. He was also thoroughly pleased with himself for retrieving his prey's cell phone from the cemetery grounds, reassembling it, and keeping it charged—all for this very moment. He and Oz had long suspected that Canyon was a traitor to the cause. Now he had definitive proof.

"You won't live long enough to find out, Mr. Wiley. You'll be sorry we didn't succeed in killing you and your forest-cop buddy the first time. Enjoy the suffering."

Zander hung up. He had finally confirmed what Dr. Dell long warned the group about: someone in their tiny group was having reservations. Wendell Canyon couldn't run his mouth off from the grave, and even if he had told some reporter a few juicy rumors, Dr. Dell said he had made sure Canyon was never in the loop on the bigger plan—especially the list of targets.

There was no stopping ALB's operation now. In less than forty-eight hours, half the planet would be in a mad dash to survive. On day one, thousands would die directly from drinking water tainted with Dr. Dell's chromosome manipulator. In three or four days, a quarter-million sick, frail, or elderly people would succumb to dehydration. In a week, three continents full of people would start battling for a dwindling supply of uncontaminated drinking water. The hoarding, looting, and armed thefts of supplies would shut down economies from New York to the flea markets of Ulaanbaatar. In a month or two, a billion humans would run out of bottles of pre-virus release dated sport drink, canned ice tea, jugs of generic super market water, and beer. Drinking tap water would be unthinkable, as would sipping from any stream, lake, pond, or farm-well. Zander overheard Dr. Dell tell Wynona the Russians would seize access to the polar ice cap in a desperate effort to melt it for drinking water. The Chinese would have a big problem with that. America would crank up its desalination plants, converting salt water from the ocean in San Francisco, Houston, and Miami. The Saudis would stop pumping oil and put all those resources into the Yanbu water plant. In the end, Dr. Dell told the group he hoped to reduce the planet's population back to what it was in the year 1790. Was it possible? Could ALB really wipe out billions of people? Wynona had told Zander she was certain the toxin worked. Now all the teams had to do was activate the most efficient delivery system ever conceived. He loved their plan and loved that he was going to have the key to living among the soon to be decimated world.

Chapter 25

Cole could tell that Montana was worn out from her stressful encounter with Big Vasil. He knew

what an adrenaline crash felt like and figured he better wrap up this adventure. Besides, he had

already mentally pulled out a different story file and needed to get to work on the ALB murders.

"You want a coffee before I drop you back at your condo?" Cole asked as he opened the

van door and leaned between the bucket seat and the fading gray steering wheel. "Based on how

much money the Department of Transportation collects in gas taxes, the complimentary Java

inside is probably Indonesian *kopi luwak.*"

Montana made a face. "No thanks. *Yuk.* Beans that've been swallowed and pooped out by

a weasel might be savory fair for Seattle coffee snobs, but I think I'll stick to generic drip."

Cole dropped Montana off in front of her building, kissed her, and slipped a twenty to the

longtime doorman to make sure he personally escorted her to the safety of her floor. In the

moment, he was less worried about Russian mobsters than about the self-medicating homeless

guy standing in the street with a 'help me' sign.

A warm opened can of Mountain Dew from the prior night sat on his desk at KZPR-TV.

Cole typed in his computer pass code, and there sat a flashing folder—results of his query

manipulating Dr. Dell's computer usage and history.

As fast as his mouse would double click, Cole began understanding for the first time what

Dell was up to. The scientist had recently spent an enormous amount of time studying not only

natural waterways but also how they flowed and connected. Two places stood out: Crater Lake

and the Ogallala Aquifer.

Cole started linking to the Web pages and speed-reading while taking furious shorthand

notes on a reporter's wire-topped flip pad. In the next hour, he struck the screen capture button forty times. He was awestruck that he knew so little about where drinking water came from. Like everybody else, he just mindlessly turned on the tap. He knew plenty about Crater Lake, having camped there a number of times. The stunning views and steep rock walls leading down to the cold surface were a favorite climbing spot for Montana. Even though it was supposed to be prohibited, rangers regularly looked the other way, as long as they could see that the climber had the proper safety gear. Montana adored a certain tiny cove that had a rock wall shielded from public view. Cole loved watching her muscles tense and stretch as she snaked her way up the blank-looking surface.

Cole had never even heard of the Ogallala Aquafer, so he delved into the subpage clues, left like breadcrumbs during the search. He was fascinated by the history of the massive underground lake, created during the Ice Age. Maps from the Department of Agriculture showed how the aquifer not only served as the main water source for crops but also provided fresh, pure drinking water to nearly everyone in eight states. The dark, fertile soils of Nebraska, South Dakota, and Kansas and the dryer plains of Colorado, Wyoming, New Mexico, Oklahoma, and Texas would be barren without the unseen thousand-foot-deep subterranean oasis. According to the U.S. Geological Survey, the aquifer was made of coarse sedimentary rock but developed in a way that didn't let it refill easily. "Paleowater," they called it. A layer of impermeable soil over the top kept rainwater from refilling its depths. Dr. Dell had reviewed a history of how humans had used the Ogallala. After discovering its riches in 1911, farmers immediately started using it for irrigation, cattle raising, and drinking water for towns. Now, with electric pumps, people on the Great Plains were pulling 160 million gallons of water from it every year. The Platte River ran right over the top of it before dumping into the Missouri, then the Mississippi River. The links included detailed hydrology research maps, complete with intricate earthen-layer

183

flowcharts. Dr. Dell had even spent time poring over a poem. Cole looked it over for clues but didn't see any except that, perhaps, it showed a sensitive side of Dr. Dell's personality.

So vast the plains, grassland seemed unending

Once home of the bison, wild pony and Sioux

Nomads each in eminent domain,

There beneath the sod they trod upon

In sediment, an aquifer lay

Shallow the sea, precious as gold.

Stretching from the Dakotas to the north Texas

Her sprawl as big as the Erie.

Cruel winters and summer drought held her coat,

But epitaphs of these prairies soon were written

For thirsty the well-digger and his spade

Waters found now gush from pipes of silver.

Now, "pivots" go 'round in slow carousel

Leave circles of green where raindrops fall

Man's food and fiber, newfound waters.

How sweet the smell of fresh-cut clover

Grazing cattle stand content

The aquifer, Ogallala, gives up her gold.

Beyond his screen, Cole noticed two female producers and the main anchor looking his way, eyebrows raised, sexy smiles on their faces. He knew that Nolan had just walked into the newsroom and was heading his direction. Cole swiveled around in his chair.

"Very clever, my esteemed muckraker," Nolan said as he raised his hand for a crisp high five. "The Echelon system at the National Security Agency flagged your last phone conversation with that unknown member of ALB. Seems like the words 'virus,' 'C-four,' 'dead,' 'N-5-G', 'bomb,' 'passenger,' 'plane,' and 'cave' triggered an alert or two! A satellite tracking station in Shoal Bay, Australia, picked up the signal. The cell phone isn't active any longer, but its last known location was on Olkhon Island. That's smack dab in the middle of the largest freshwater lake in the world, along the Russian-Mongolian border. Apparently, the Russians aren't too fond of the Echelon system, since we created it to monitor them during the Cold War. Despite that pissing match, the fur-hats are sending some KGB types to Lake Baikal to sniff around."

Cole spun back around toward his computer and typed in a simple query: "Lake Baikal." Enter.

"It's the world's oldest lake, sitting on the deepest continental rift on earth," Cole recited. "It contains twenty percent of the world's fresh water, drains in the Angara tributary of the Yeniseia, and is home to seventeen hundred species of plants and animals, two-thirds of which can be found nowhere else in the world."

"Wow, dude. You've got Wikipedia on speed dial," Nolan said while leaning down to view the screen.

Cole pointed. "I didn't do that search; Dell did. He was really into waterways: rivers, basins, bayous, coves, marshes, sounds, itty-bitty mountain tarns. Hell, it looks like he reviewed the making of puddles. He spent time researching Lake Baikal and this huge Arctic Ocean-size mass of water under eastern Only two other places topped that focus: Crater Lake and the Ogallala Aquifer."

Cole felt sure Nolan would catch on if he gave his synapses a few seconds to fire up.

"The Animal Liberation Brigade is going to try to fuck up our water?"

"You got it, pal. 'Try' is the keyword. What I don't understand is why they wouldn't bag an easier target, like the State Water Project or the Snake River. Destroy that and Los Angles is S.O.L. Maybe too much security? Might hurt wildlife? They don't really want to harm anyone? Just making a statement? Crap, man. Call your newfound buddies at Homeland and tell them to have the Russians do more than a casual drive-by at Lake Baikal. If they can scoop up one of our animal rights terrorists, maybe we could get a lot more intel. I'll even wear my 'I'd rather be waterboarding' T-shirt if that helps the Russians with any ideas."

Nolan waved at the eyes still gazing at him over the blare of scanners and audio from television feeds.

Cole pulled his friend's hand back down to his side.

"Earth to Nolan. Can you please ignore all that distracting pussy for a minute or two? This is real apocalyptic, end-of-the-world shit we're talking here. Dr. Dell didn't only love water; he loved genetics, too. And I mean weird, monkey-breeding genetics. All the articles were way, way, stratospherically over my head. While you're at it, ask your federal chums if they have a white-haired genius, like that professor in *Back to the Future,* who they can send these files to for a real analysis."

"I loved that movie—vintage Michael J. Fox, prejitters."

"Yup. Steady as a rock back in his *Teen Wolf* years," Cole agreed, pulling his thumb drive from the USB slot and dropping it into his pocket.

Nolan flipped open his notebook and tossed it on Cole's desk.

"Hey. I found out a thing or two as well. Your guess that Dr. Dell might own a pet was right on the money. He has two dogs. About three years ago, he had radio-frequency identification chips implanted in a pair of German shorthair puppies. The tiny silicon chips don't have satellite tracking capabilities, but if, say, an animal shelter wants to find the owner of a lost dog, they wave a paddle-shaped electronic wand over the chip, and the owner's address and name pops onto the screen. According to the Love Your Pet monitoring system, in the last week, a veterinarian in Keizer, Oregon, activated the chip. I sent a detective buddy of mine down there. The vet said she didn't know the man who came in. His dog had a high fever from an infection. It appeared someone else had stitched up a significant wound recently but accidently left some tiny bits of auto glass inside. The man was courteous but in a hurry. Paid in cash."

Keizer was in the heart of animal rights country. Cole knew it well. He had covered acid attacks on egg producers around Willamette, the torching of wild-horse corrals in Burns, smashing-up of science laboratories at Oregon State, and a mysterious fire at a meat-packing plant around Eugene. Cole had met many a fringe character along dark roadsides in Oregon. He never felt that he was in danger, despite typically being surrounded by a group of young adults all in black ski masks. He knew that the pale skin showing through the three holes belonged to avowed vegans or vegetarians, and it was hard to be too scared of a vegan. Cole was carefully chosen as the media contact for at least three different animal rights and environmental action groups. The activists understood that they needed publicity for their acts of sabotage, but trusting a reporter was unprecedented. Cole had earned their respect over years of testing and trial. The Animal Liberation Brigade first took notice when he did an investigative series on the illegal use of hunting dogs to chase coyotes, bobcats, and foxes at night. The public was shocked by his undercover video, but jaw-droppingly appalled at the audio. The sound of hunters cheering with glee as their baying mountain curs and Rhodesian ridgebacks tore a coyote to shreds on federal forest land was more than most people watching KZPR-TV could bear. The phones both at the TV station and in legislators' offices rang nonstop for weeks. Housewives, 90-year-old war veterans, Boeing union line workers, and Harvard-educated Microsoft multimillionaires all called demanding action. Some specified lynching; others wanted to temporarily legalize gladiator-style lions' dens to see how tough these hunters were without their guns and dogs. Some pleaded with the TV station to stop airing the stories, because they were upsetting children. Every voice was filled with emotion. ALB members noticed that Cole had an effective writing style, one that not only didn't feel preachy but also told a memorable story. He used the hunt scene to get viewers' attention, then educated the public on the history of animal rights without anyone's even noticing. He wove in analogies about a European children's club from the 1800s called the Bands of Hope, which taught kindness to animals. He showed how the Hunt Saboteurs Association blew horns to disrupt fox hunts in the 1960s. He drove home the point that such cruelty was once accepted sport but that Washington residents were starting to place limits on the use of dogs to track down game animals. Of course, ratings were through the roof. Cole learned quickly that animal abuse investigations drove the 25-to-54-year-old female demographic to stratospheric levels. Advertisers always paid top dollar to place a commercial in the vicinity of a Colton Wiley segment, but if they knew that an animal investigation was about to break, the ad bidding war made the pace of a Sotheby's art auction look like a church bingo game.

Nolan continued to dig through his messy notes made with differently colored pens.

"I drove by the house listed by the electronic dog-chip company as the owner's residence. It's a vacant rental. Looked like the landlord was in the middle of having the place repainted, recarpeted, and cleaned up for the next set of college kids. Neighbors provided some good descriptions. They remember two guys who rarely went outside during the day, and a weird woman. Several other men showed up a few evenings a week. Quiet group, no trouble. The neighbors sounded exactly like the sound bites you media folks get when you go interview neighbors of the latest serial killer. People are like, 'He seemed so normal! I never thought it odd that he liked to dig holes in his backyard in the middle of the night, but now that I think about it . . .' Jesus!"

Cole laughed despite the growing seriousness of the situation in front of them,

"Neighbors definitely described Dr. Dell as one of the men frequenting the house in Keizer. We're also looking for a muscular but wiry white guy with a military haircut and a beard. More on him in a second. The rest of the crew was described loosely as a Mexican dude, a chick with tree branches tattooed on her face, an Arnold-type with lots of piercings on his face, and a tall Iranian. I sent a sketch artist over there to draw up some faces."

"So now we know the general size of the Animal Liberation Brigade's wacky subgroup," Cole said, thinking hard. "It's a hodgepodge international bunch. Probably outcasts. I wonder if the tall Iranian is my anonymous caller. He had a subtle Middle Eastern accent. Terrorists aren't going to leave a forwarding address at the post office. Utilities will be in a fake name. Nobody will register their car there. Cops ever go to the address for any reason?" Cole inquired hopefully.

"Kind of. I couldn't find any nine-one-one calls originating from there or by someone else asking for a dispatch to that actual address. But a few days ago, police authorized their tow

189

truck service to haul away a car sitting in the street near the house. Some thieves had stolen the wheels off it and smashed the back side window to get to the stereo. The license plates were recently removed. The VIN number on the dashboard was filed off a long time ago. I went down to the impound lot to get a look and—"

Cole interrupted, "Older green sedan with a blue peace sticker in the back window?"

"Yep. Same one leaving the scene of a natural-gas explosion at Evergreen. I was pretty busy trying to save my eyebrows, but that car caught my attention."

"Nolan, my man. You're going to look really good to your bosses by tomorrow morning. Get a forensics team to CSI that car. I guarantee there will be dog hair all over the place. The dog DNA from that car will match hair found inside the abandoned SUV next to Trooper Fitzgerald's body. Once the state patrol ties Dr. Dell to the murder of a boy in blue, it's going to get harder than ever for him to hide. The national-security folks are snooping around trying to find our mad scientist, but they haven't put his rat face up on the news. Part of it is, they don't have any hard proof he committed a crime. But now it's a new ball game—a cop killer is a marked man."

Nolan gave Cole a thumbs-up and then did his best Columbo: "Oh, by the way, don't you want to see that last page inside my folder?"

"Holding out for dramatic effect," Cole said, pushing his chair back. "I love you, man. Do the reveal."

"Ta-dah!" Nolan boomed as he pulled two photos from the file and laid them out side by side. "Meet animal terrorist wanna-be Oscar "Oz" McKinsey. He tried to fry us at the Portland house."

Cole jumped in first. "He looks like Brad Pitt in *Fight Club*—tough, angular."

Nolan shook his head. "Nah. A lot uglier. Like, uh, Eminem in *Eight Mile*."

"Nailed it!" Cole shouted, offering a fist bump.

Nolan continued. "This other picture's a still frame from a Pho' restaurant parking lot videotape. They have a security camera right next to the veterinarian's office. It shows Dr. Dell standing with his back to the camera, looking out into the parking lot after he gets his dog fixed up. It's like he's waiting for a ride. I thought maybe a cab would come. Then this other guy comes walking up with a couple bags of groceries. There was a Super V in the same strip mall. He sets the bags down and has a smoke while chatting with the evil doctor. They are clearly friends. I ran facial recognition software on the mystery man and Oscar McKinsey matches. This is his old Army ID photo. Honorable discharge. Explosives expert. Fairly clean record. He's only been arrested and booked into jail once, for assaulting a neighbor. Come on, ask me why he assaulted his neighbor."

"Why did he assault his neighbor?" Cole played along.

"The neighbor chained his dog to a metal stake in the backyard, then left for the weekend. When the guy returned, Oscar met him in his driveway and pounded his face in. It appears Oscar has a soft spot for animals."

Chapter 26

Sitting on the rough marble shale overlooking Khoboy Cape on Olkhon Island, Siberia, Wynona Wanagi felt at peace for the first time in her adult life. She had long known that the thoughts of death, sadness, and despair that daily boiled from her soul were not normal.

"Brilliant and socially awkward" were traits the Russian military machine loved as no one else could. Hadar had taken her in, trusted her, given her a purpose. She was thankful for that, but she knew he didn't love her.

Wynona sat limp, with each thumb and forefinger together in the yogic *dhyana mudra,* feeling the water with her mind. She could see through the eyes of the freed seals: the marsh thistles at the water's horizon, the meandering silver coil of a passing sturgeon. She knew that her meditations were so vivid, so strong, because the world's energy was centered right here. Shamanism was born on Olkhon Island. The taiga forest's rich bounty of food plants had drawn mystics, Chukchi shamans, and devil worshippers to the shores of Lake Baikal since humans first walked onto the Asian continent. Area caves gave refuge from the snowy winters while the sheer mass of Lake Baikal kept it from freezing over. It was an abundance of life. If you could not hear your god in this setting, your god was dead or had abandoned you.

The sound of a far-off truck engine brought Wynona out of her trance. She rose slowly and, with two deep breaths, sucked back in all her rage and more. She was angry that the Russian government refused to keep its hands off the enormous resources the lake provided. The cool, free water was being polluted by a paper mill. Chlorine dioxide and lignin, created through the bleaching process, were deliberately pumped through an eighteen-inch pipe, straight into the lower layers of the lake. Wynona could see the effects on the biological oxygen demand by watching the fish gulp air at the surface. Some of her environmental activist acquaintances swore that the factory owner also had a carefully hidden valve in a generator shed near the shore. Every night, without a hint of regret, he released black liquor straight into the water. The especially deadly caramel-colored potion, left over from cooking and digesting pulpwood, killed everything in its path. Despite an outcry from the public that the pulp waste was destroying natural ecosystems, bribed politicians looked the other way. The government was even planning to place a uranium enrichment center at Angarsk, a few miles away. The storage of toxic and radioactive by-products in a historically active earthquake zone was stupid and shortsighted, and it would someday destroy every life form in every river, lake, and stream within a hundred miles. Wynona's mission in life was to stop such madness. Humans were weakened by greed, power, and feelings of superiority. They were incapable of learning equality with each other, let alone with the other creatures that shared their planet. She cupped her hands to drink from Lake Baikal one final time.

Brian Zander could see Wynona as he jogged up the gravel trail toting a large caliber rifle. He was sweating like a horse despite the forty-five-degree day.

"There's something happening in town," he said. "I don't speak Russian, but even a dope like me can tell there's a certain buzz in the air. Khuzhir is hopping with brown shirts and badges. I parked the truck way out of town, inside an abandoned barn, then pedaled on a bike to the Internet café to check for messages, like you told me to. There were plenty of European granola-head types roaming around, so my whiteness didn't stand out. Then, while I'm sipping tea, some military-looking young guys showed up. They spread out and started asking people on the street for their passports. You Russians always look miffed, but these boys were ultra serious. I snuck out the back of the café before they got there. I don't believe in coincidences."

Wynona looked as though she was fighting every urge in her body not to kill Zander right there on the spot; collapse his trachea with a punch to the throat, suffocate him, starve his brain for blood with a carotid hold just under the jawline, beat his face into unrecognizable street pizza with a fist-size rock.

"Your 'whiteness' certainly did stand out. The soldiers were looking for Americans, I'm sure of it. Back to our campsite," she said. "Although three coordinated strikes are essential for full impact, Dr. Dell and I talked about a secondary operation in the event we get discovered before the others are in place. We've always been the ones taking the biggest risk. So if this witch hunt in town is going to bring us some unwanted attention—or, worse, an unwanted visit—let's make sure our Sugar doesn't fall into enemy hands."

"Sugar? What's sugar?" Zander stuttered.

"The reason we're here. It's a formula perfected by Dr. Dell and I. It's a deadly toxin – a genetic manipulator which kills humans and allows animals to live. Those bombs we have are going to help us blow a hole in the bottom of the Lake. The Sugar will seep into one of the largest fresh water drinking supplies in the world."

Zander was flabbergasted, unsure if such a plan was only in Dr. Wanagi's confused mind, but he reacted with an assuring 'Okay.'

The two of them jogged back to the barn where the truck was stashed. They drove a few miles, past the outskirts of a rundown yurt village, to an isolated area overlooking a strait between the island and the mainland. A wide bridge connected the two pieces of land, which lay only a few hundred yards apart.

Wynona and Zander had chosen the spot because the two narrow ruts of mud that led to the camp space were heavily covered in a canopy of trees. The truck was camouflaged from drones and spy satellites, and the dense forest masked the sound of a generator. The loud clatter of Japanese tree frogs drowned out the rest of the noise. The camp was modeled after the jungle guerrilla hideaways of the Abu Sayyaf. There was no open-pit fire. Wynona built a small oven from rocks. Coals burned low beneath the ashes during the day; then, when the sun set, she would add wood for cooking. A pan set on top of the rocks was hot enough to boil water. If any smoke did curl up into the open, a stiff breeze flowing from the lake inland dispersed it sideways, not up. Four months earlier, Dr. Dell had started setting up and supplying camps for the select group of N5G ALB members. Each station had enough fresh water to last at least a year. It sat in fifty-five-gallon barrels, stacked like a supermarket end display. Dehydrated fruits and vegetables held all the vitamins two people needed to lie low until the time came to seek out additional targets. A stockpile of weapons was boxed under a forest-painted tarp: grenade launchers, Russian-made SKS assault rifles with hundred-round drums, bricks of C-4 explosive, and OZM-3 and Claymore antipersonnel mines. A small petroleum tank was sunk partway into the ground in case they needed to run the all-terrain vehicles. Zander knew Wynona was upset about this particular supply. Not only was gasoline the source of so much environmental destruction, but she could run twenty miles without stopping—she didn't need or want a redneck taxi.

Dr. Dell had apparently convinced her that sacrifices for the cause must be made. Zander knew if they needed to transport all their weapons or water, they couldn't very well haul it in a backpack. Besides, Zander argued with Wynona, she was an animal-rights advocate, not necessarily an environmental one. If the personnel aboard the *Sea Shepherd* had the same objections against using diesel fuel, they would never be able to track down whaling ships.

About twenty yards from the fuel tank sat two jet-black solar panels, staged along an outcropping of similarly black rock. They pooled the sun's power down a thick cable into a series of batteries covered by an open-fronted Amish-style wooden-pegged shelter. Wynona and Zander could sleep out of the rain and near the batteries for warmth. The batteries charged everything from the GPS to an MP3 player.

***

Wynona watched as the hired gun took a position in a tree stand he had built near the camp's entrance. In his camouflage gear, Zander was nearly invisible. Wynona told him she had a disturbing vision during the previous night, so he agreed to ready for worst case scenario. She stroked the smooth side of a grenade clipped on the top of her boot, clearly engaged in deep thought. The right mindset could mean everything.

Wynona suddenly remembered she had a dead airport manager in the back of the truck. She threw open the back and dragged the frozen corpse across the campground. She eased the body into Lake Baikal after stuffing the pockets, mouth, and a backpack with rocks. The near-freezing water wouldn't allow the flesh to decompose, bloat up with gas, and rise to the surface before the fish had their way with it. She swept the drag marks away with some branches, though she couldn't do much to hide the survivalist supplies. She could get away with the "just campers" pretense if hikers should stumble onto their location, but if the Russian military caught a glimpse, the operation would be compromised in seconds.

Wynona didn't have time to wait for her eyes to adjust to the dim light inside the back of the truck's massive cooler. Using a flashlight and a screwdriver, she pried open a small hatch that led to the false sidewall. The three-foot hollowed-out section ran the entire length of the truck. The fins of the bunker-busting bomb inside were hinged, folded flat against the tail.

Arming the device into ready mode was as easy as flipping on a light switch. The quiet hum of a small motor told her all she needed to know. The remote detonating box, no bigger than an oyster cracker, suddenly felt like an anvil hanging around her neck. If she had to explode the truck and its contents here, her mission would have to shift targets, but at least, the other two units wouldn't be compromised. There was not much space to maneuver inside the icebox. The interior was at most eight feet wide and eighteen feet long. Aside from a few wooden crates of salmon and halibut placed there as props, the rest of the truck was full of solid ice cylinders. They closely resembled scuba tanks because that was what Oz and Dr. Dell had used as a form. Light-blue shrink-wrap enveloped each bullet of ice; then a larger, taut piece of clear shrink-wrap tied forty-eight of them to each pallet. Once melted, the liquid would be enough to wipe out the human populations of most of Asia. If the Animal Liberation Brigade got *really* lucky, it could flow beneath Lake Baikal through Mongolia and China, then perhaps as far as the densely populated coastal areas of the Indian and Pacific Oceans. The "Sugar" would make some of the water deadly even if desalinated. The key was proper distribution. Dr. Dell had created dilution charts showing that just five parts per billion, once ingested, would start a deadly chain reaction at the cellular level, but he openly hoped lesser amounts could build up over time to create the same effect. Regardless, nobody would dare try to find that threshold, since each trial and error would cost a human life. And Dr. Dell had made bloody-well sure that every animal was immune from the deadly manipulator's effects. Wynona was pleased that the trashy, dirty, inaccurate medical studies done for years on primates, rabbits, cats, and rats would not be part of trying to solve the mysteries of the Sugar. She found a certain poetic beauty in the fact that animal studies would provide nothing useful. *As if any of those other primate studies had!*

She once had a colleague from Minsk working on his doctorate in genetics. His goal was to solve the mystery of men's hair loss. The subject of his research was so lame, so unutterably stupid; she couldn't believe that a university would fund it. That was before the billions of dollars made with the introduction of Rogaine. Her colleague had killed so many spider monkeys during the testing phase that he finally lost his government funding. Even the Russian government had a limit to foolishness and waste.

But instead of giving up, the researcher had obtained private funds. Old World monkeys started arriving at the back door of the lab in mesh bags, caught fresh from the jungles of Cambodia. The juveniles and babies were killed with a crowbar whack to the head and tossed into the incinerator barrel, like aborted fetuses from the vacuum canisters at a Georgia clinic. The man's ongoing slaughter was eventually rewarded with a fat paycheck and a French work visa sponsored by a European company.

She closed her eyes and daydreamed his death. It was hard to conceive of hoping to kill a billion people, but when she made it personal it became so much more satisfying. In one vision, that balding ghoul of a monkey mutilator would spurt blood from his ears, eyes, and anus, falling in convulsions onto a concrete floor. In another, he would be too scared to drink any liquid at all. She could see his chapped lips, cracked and caked with dried spittle like Clint Eastwood's character lying in the desert in *The Good, the Bad, and the Ugly* . . .

Her happy trance shattered suddenly when Zander sounded an alarm: the loud chatter of an angry squirrel, projected down toward the camp.

* * *

The dark-windowed sedan was so out of place on this serene island, Zander knew that it was trouble well before it veered off the road and parked on the narrow shoulder. Spotting human targets was second nature. Zander spent three years as a security officer for a brutal diamond mining operation in Sierra Leone.

He could see the driver's thick hands, two gold rings on his fingers resting on the steering wheel. Another person sat on the passenger side with a stack of manila papers in his lap. The two sat unmoving for long enough that Zander wondered whether they were waiting for some sort of backup team. He was relieved when they got out of the vehicle, looking more like auditors with the Russian Migration Control office than trained assassins. Neither carried a tactical weapon, though by the looks of their long coats, they were likely armed with some kind of handgun. Their cell phones might not work in this forest, so Zander wanted to make sure that if things went south, he could cut them down before they made it back to the car. A long two-way antenna rose from the rear bumper.

As he expected, the men didn't look up, oblivious both of their surroundings and that this was to be their last moment on earth. Their demeanor was that of two officials simply trying to get items checked off a to-do list. In fact, even without the high-powered scope on the 30.06, Zander could see that one of the bureaucrats was more concerned with keeping mud off his leather shoes than investigating the campsite in front of him.

* * *

Wynona could hear them coming but chose not to bother looking in their direction, as if she were unconcerned. She stood with her shirt off, B-cup breasts and erect nipples reflecting back off a crude mirror nailed into a decrepit larch tree. She slowly dipped a small paintbrush into a pot of henna ink, then swept it over the fading branches on her face. She could feel the men stop dead in their tracks to watch her—exactly what she expected from the filthy, weakened hearts of men. She knew that as long as they were staring at a half-naked woman they were not paying attention to anything else in camp.

"Excuse me ma'am" one of the young men finally announced in Russian.

Wynona looked his way, then back to the mirror to apply another black streak of plant tar across her cheekbone.

"I am not a 'miss' or a 'ma'am,' and you are not excused. You're interrupting my preparation for the Spirit Horse ceremony. Please leave," she continued in perfect Russian.

"We are looking for this American," the shorter of the two said while holding out a faxed copy of an Interpol mug shot. "Have you seen him?"

Although surprised they had a picture of her beloved, Wynona held her shirt in her hand and walked close to the men. She pressed her body into the personal space that, when violated by a stranger, makes almost anyone uncomfortable. She pretended to study the photo of Dr. Dell.

"No. *I have seen* another American though. A jarhead with ugly tattoos. He's hiding in that tree," Wynona sang as she pointed straight toward Zander. She stepped back and laughed.

The two interlopers looked at each other, one rolling his eyes, the other blowing a low whistle through his lips in disbelief. *This is one crazy chick,* was no doubt the last thought either of them had.

Zander fired a gumball-size high-velocity round through both temples of the man standing nearest him. The other watched his colleague weave sideways and fall, and then might have for a split second seen his own lung tissue, bright red, sprayed across the patch of yellow mushrooms growing out of a rotting birch stump.

Wynona spat on the two bodies as their hearts decelerated and stopped.

"I told you he was in the tree, you dumb motherfuckers!"

She paced furiously around the bodies for a few moments, but by the time she slipped her shirt back on she had calmed herself down.

"May you find rebirth as creatures of peace. Amen," Wynona chanted while tossing soil onto the dead men's cheeks.

Zander jumped down from his perch and jogged across the road. Wynona watched as he drove the agents' car into some heavy underbrush so it wouldn't be visible on a routine drive-by. He didn't have time to hide it completely, not that it would matter. The men had certainly called in their position. The unknown factor was how long a nonresponsive field op team would go unnoticed. By the time Zander reentered camp, Wynona could see the fax picture of "Wanted Terrorist" Dr. Hadar O'Dell, starting to wrinkle and go soft on the damp ground next to the whitening hand of victim two.

"Hey, psychopomp. You helping them transcend to a happy place, or sending them to shaman hell?" Zander quipped.

Wynona appeared as clearheaded as she had ever been. "Good instincts putting these two down," she said. "They were starting to pay attention to their surroundings. One was eyeing the generator. The other was wondering what's inside the boxes under the tarps. I assume a platoon will come looking for them when they don't radio in their hourly status check. Our mission's been compromised. We're not done yet, not by a long shot. However, it's our primary responsibility to make certain Dr. Dell's team and our lone Billy Goat, Chivas, can still succeed. We are simply not going to be able to distribute the Sugar according to plan. The formula must not fall into enemy hands."

"I like the sound of that," Zander agreed. "Destruction is my favorite verb."

"It's a *noun,* moron. And English isn't even my first language. Christ! It's taking everything I have left inside my head not to crush your skull with that iron pry bar right now. Gather a few supplies in a backpack and get a Quad runner. Although I would prefer a suicide mission so I could find death and return, we're going to try to get away. Those are my orders. The N-5-G project cannot fail. We're following plan B. The animals need us. We must make sure that the world does not yet understand the nature of our genocide. It will be clear to everyone tomorrow. I know H_2O and Chi will create the kind of destruction that will make ALB the most famous organization in world history."

Zander shrugged. "Then let's blow the camp and get out of here now. We'll have a huge head start. With your Russian skills and contacts, I expect to be on the first plane to Amsterdam or Paris or New York."

Wynona smiled. "And miss all the fun of watching men burn? I don't think so."

For the first time since leaving Oregon, the faded yellow refrigeration truck's generator went silent. Wynona shut it off, then punched a small hole in the vehicle's fuel tank with her trusty ice pick. A pinhole stream of putrid-smelling Novo Ufa-refined gasoline arced through the air. Meanwhile, Zander grabbed a minimal load of supplies—stuff related to traveling in the darkness: headlamps, thick waterproof clothing, and light firearms. Wynona helped him carry the dead Russian agents to the back of the truck and stack them in a grotesque pile of intertwined arms and legs. A trail of blood led from where they fell. Wynona thought it an exquisite attention getter—a painting as lovely as any by John Wayne Gacy.

As the minutes passed, Zander was starting to get nervous. He clearly wasn't sure what kind of dire plague they had in their innocuous-looking truck, but he was no fool. He knew that the process of melting was a bad thing.

"The stage is set, Weird Spirit. Let's find a line-of-sight hiding spot. I say we wait another hour at most. If nobody cares enough to come check on these boys, let's light 'em up."

Wynona ignored him. Zander waited only a second or two before moving.

"I'm taking our gear about five hundred and fifty yards north at eleven o'clock. Come find me or not."

He pressed the automatic starter on the ATV and zipped off south, then back in the direction of the road, in a long Z-shaped pattern. When he hit pavement he roared as fast as the machine would go, past the rutted mud driveway that led to their camp, north more than a mile. He zigzagged his way through the pines until he could barely see the top of the battery shed.

***

At Dr. Dell's urging, Wynona had been taking her medications for months. His advice rang through her mind three times a day. This was the first moment that the Risperdal was failing to help keep her multiple personalities in their separate cages. She wondered how Noah knew that God was really talking to him. She had been hearing voices her entire life. Those voices had never told her to build an ark, but they had told her to butcher a butcher. Was there any difference? Was one animal-saving command any more heroic than the other?

She could feel natural chemicals pumping inside her veins. Her impressive array of molecular biology, chemistry, and neuroscience knowledge told her that was a normal internal body reaction in this circumstance. She should run. Hide. There would be other days to save mice and turtles and mountain gorillas from the onslaught of human greed and shortsightedness. Her Chukchi heritage and vast knowledge of shamanism, here on the sacred ancestral grounds of her religion, instructed her to breathe slowly. Relax. Penetrate her inner fears with peace. Yet here she stood, arms held out straight, parallel to the forest floor, feeling the crazed condor within her. She wanted so badly to slide the long, slightly curved fillet knife from her hip and pluck the eyes out of the men who had seen her naked. *Breathe. Relax . . .*

With her bare feet gripping the loose soil covered in pine needles, she could feel the vibration of an old diesel engine even before she could hear it. The earth was giving her a chance to find a path back to reality. It was time to move fast to the end of the game or be lost forever. The muscle on the outside of her calf flexed first as she sprang to her left. She sprinted over the soft tissues of life strewn on the taiga forest floor. She ran at a five-minute-mile pace straight at eleven o'clock. Her pale legs were a blur as she dodged miniature muskeg bogs and lichen-covered rocks. The ground was cold enough to feel hot, like lava. The aromatic plants and grasses gave off a sweet perfume as her feet crushed open the oils in the leaves. She held the pendant dangling around her neck between her lips, breathing through her nostrils only. A large tattoo of a crescent moon with "N5G" in the center glistened with sweat over a hard six-pack of abdominal muscles. She nearly stepped on Zander, not seeing him until the last moment. He tossed her a set of green-and-brown fatigues and boots and motioned for her to get them on fast. The time for playing forest fairy was over.

From her slightly elevated perch, Wynona expected to see a Russian BTR-80 armored personnel carrier come rolling up with soldiers fanning out in all directions. To her, this was the beginning of a brutal war over animal rights—one that ALB was ready and willing to eliminate the earth's population to win.

History was full of small armies defeating bigger enemies with far greater resources. All it took was innovation, commitment, and the willingness to use the most cold-blooded, terrifying, effective killing techniques one could dream up. She had studied the Mongol invasions of Europe and Russia, started by Batu Khan and the Tatar warlord Dyuden, in middle school. They drew up a pair of the most successful killing plans ever assembled. The Khan's takeover bid led to the slaughter of as many as sixty million people, or 17 percent of Europe's population. The Tatars used massive stone clubs, adorned with human skulls, to bash their way through a dozen of Russia's largest cities. Their reputation for the treatment of slaves, from places like Vladimir, was so gruesome that instead of being captured, Russian men would stay inside their burning homes. In the years to follow, tens of millions more died from disease and intentionally inflicted plague. The Mongol invaders hated it when villagers started encircling their homes and hamlets with stone-walled fortresses. Everyone wanted to save themselves from capture, slavery, and death, but the Mongols figured out how to make those efforts fail. Waiting until the people inside ran out of food and water became a tedious, time-consuming game. Thinking outside the box, the Mongols came up with the first known use of biological weapons: catapulting disease-infected corpses over the walls. The black death killed many of the holdouts, but guards also allowed a few people to escape in the middle of the night. Those who fled thought they had found freedom when, in fact, they were merely carrying the disease to other towns. In two short years, around 1348, a good portion of Europe's population had been wiped out. Wynona felt secure history was on her side. She hoped the few Russian children left living would read about her instead of Batu Khan. History would see her as the most successful mass-murdering female ever.

Instead of an army, Wynona was disappointed when her binoculars spotted only four heavyset men in suits and ties. They did seem serious about their orders, fanning out with weapons drawn. *Older Soviet handguns—unimpressive.* She considered sneaking back to camp and cutting their throats, but the time had come to cover one's tracks and move on.

As long as they could get away, Dr. Dell had many more targets planned after the first wave of attacks. Even in the best-case scenario there would be pockets of fresh water supplies, which everyone would flock to. Just when all those lucky families thought they were going to survive, ALB would sneak back in with its "Sugar" toxin and taint the source. One day, little Tommy would be enjoying his sippy cup of lifesaving water: the next, he would be bleeding from his baby blues. Wynona hated kids, anyway—they always grew up into adults.

Wynona whispered, "The moment they open the truck door, I'm igniting the load. When the rocks stop raining down, we've got less than an hour to get off Olkhon Island. Russian military helicopters will be in the air fast and won't let us move unless we make it to the mainland. These dicks are useless, but loud explosions always bring in the military. They'll suspect Chechen rebels for a while . . . It's our nature."

"Whatever. Blow it already," Zander said without a care in the world.

Wynona's brain started whirring as fast as a Terra 100 supercomputer's hard drive. Calculations of the Jones-Wilkins-Lee Equation of State streamed through her mind. *"V" for volume of explosive product, over volume of the undetonated explosive. "E" equals internal energy per unit. "Z," "A," "B," "R1," and "R2" are constants. Heat expansion rate . . . shock force . . . eight-meter air buffer . . . vaporization temperature of aluminum . . .*

"What's the hang-up?" Zander hissed. "They've already opened the door!"

"Density equals mass over volume. Four hydrogen molecules linked together compared to a more typical three-point-four. Density of ice eight percent less than water." Wynona was mouthing the words.

"Blow the fucking thing!"

Scientists liked to be certain. They tested and retested. They underwent peer reviews. They measured with precision, kept meticulous control samples, recorded every change, alteration, and condition. Wynona was suddenly second-guessing the assumption that Oz's massive bombs were hot enough to vaporize their evidence. Every drop of chromosome-altering poison would definitely disappear into thin air if it were in liquid form, but ice held together with different properties, temperature points, and shock-wave carry weights. Did it matter?

She wrapped her hand gently around the detonator pendant hanging at her throat. She stroked the edges while praying for the well-being of the bluebirds in the surrounding trees, the termites in the decaying, blood-spattered stump, and the wolverines hiding in their underground den only fifty yards from the truck . . .

Zander couldn't help but let out an exuberant whoop when the bomb blew soil five hundred feet into the air. The depth of the hole created was impressive, though not up to bunker-busting standards. Its free-falling weight could not be used to penetrate the rock-hard surface of the ground, as it could have in the soft lake bottom. Its purpose, however, was served. Four live men, two corpses, a truckload of "Sugar", a cache of weapons, a crude hut filled with batteries, and a fishing pole Zander had hidden under a nearby tarp—all gone in a flash. The only things left intact were two terrorists and a thermos full of toxic ice strapped to an ATV.

Chapter 27

Driving across the Rocky Mountains and through Yellowstone National Park reminded Chivas Riviera why he so loved Mother Earth. Snow feathered the jagged formations, hiding imperfections in the fortresses of stone. Some crags resembled the Bororo-Boe arrowheads Chivas had found as a boy while digging for fish bait. Other peaks appeared to sag under their own weight, as if the burden, after so many eons, had finally become too much to bear.

Chivas had hiked all over Amazonia and the Andes, loving every step. Hence Dr. Dell's nickname for him: "Billy Goat." He felt his leader's affection, but he wasn't hanging out with ALB because he needed a gang as a family. He was 25 years old and needed no one.

Elk trooped along the tree line, grazing on the blue grama and fescue grasses. He even saw a black bear foraging through a huckleberry thicket. He was glad none of the tourists driving by had spotted the beautiful creature. If anyone had, a throng of wildlife paparazzi would be pulling over and hounding the bear away from the food it needed to pack in for the winter. The best part of the trip was imagining all the animal life that nature was hiding out of sight. Earthworms and wood lice tunneling through the leaf mold, Great Plains toads burping out their love songs, brown-capped rosy finches bringing home beetles and damselflies to their hungry nesting mates.

The trip was almost uneventful. The brakes on the refrigerated truck had started smoking on the backside of Homestake Pass, near Butte, but Chivas didn't fret. He just pulled over at a scenic overlook to take a nap and let the wheels cool.

Later in the day, down from the mountains and being a Brazilian in Middle America for the first time, he was excited to see the "fruited plains." But the flat, monotone landscape proved to be a bit of a letdown. Perhaps for those who grew up in the tiny towns dotting the rural

209

landscape, the scenery held some special magic, but he would need a thick set of beer goggles to see what they saw in the rusty windmills and endless furrowed fields.

"Ugly" was the only description that popped into Chivas's head as he pulled off the interstate to his final destination. A hand-painted wooden billboard stood tall in the ditch, proclaiming the "Cowboy Capital of Nebraska." He had done research on Ogallala before he rolled into town. The first statistic he looked up was the percentage of Hispanics from the latest census data. If he were black or Asian, he would have been screwed, because there were none. Latinos, on the other hand, at 6 percent of the population, were fairly well represented. He reasoned that somebody had to do the killing and butchering at the capon factory. Happily, it meant that he wouldn't draw any special attention as a visitor, despite the town's small size. Ogallala had only five thousand people, but it had a solid reputation as a quirky tourist destination. Front Street, with its barn-colored Old West facades on all the storefronts, looked like a low-budget movie set: saloon, barber shop, general store, jail.

In the late 1800s, Ogallala was considered one of the wildest, most sinful towns in the United States. The drovers loved the smorgasbord of liquor, gambling, and prostitutes so much that the town leaders decided it was probably best they not even build a church. No sense in asking God to come anywhere near such a Gomorrah.

Chivas pulled the white box truck onto the edge of the high school parking lot, under the stern gaze of the Indian warrior in full headdress adorning the side of the gymnasium. *So much for political correctness,* he mused.

A small group of tourists, new cowboy hats tilted back on their heads, were taking each other's picture along the boardwalk several blocks away. They joined another set of parents and kids walking up toward the town's biggest attraction: Boot Hill Cemetery. During the cattle-driving days, when men tended to settle their disputes with a Sam Colt's .45, the undertaker must have been one of the busiest men around. Their tombstones at Boot Hill were gray and worn, the names barely legible—all the better for a family vacation photo. The weather was warm for October.

Chivas repeatedly hit "Search" on the radio dial until a country station locked in. Along with the next weather report came the mosquito forecast and hog future prices. Thinking of those poor pigs being confined, sold, slaughtered, and eaten snapped Chivas's mental state back to the mission at hand: kill as many humans as possible; then escape so he could kill even more in the future. He took a map of Nebraska out of the glove box, unfolded it across the steering wheel, and traced upward with his finger to the junction of Highways 26 and 61.

The locals called the manmade lake north of town "Big Mac." On hot summer days, the sandy shorelines were filled with sunbathers and picnickers. Catamarans, sailboards, and kayaks floated about in a noiseless display of color. Lake McConaughy had once been corn fields, but construction of one of the world's largest earthen dams had changed all that, blocking the mighty Platte River's ancient pathway to make a fifty-five-square-mile lake.

Chivas studied the detailed structural plans of the Kingsley Dam on line. Built during the Great Depression, the dam was no high-tech engineering wonder. Powerful dredges had sucked gravel and sand from the river bottom and piled it on the shores. Once the dredges made the water's path narrow enough, workers drove walls of interlocking steel plates deep into the riverbed. Some of the steel pilings had to be sunk 160 feet down, until the dam's creators were certain they had reached the impervious layer of Brule clay. Without that clay, they could pile dirt as high as Everest to stop surface water from flowing, but the river would eventually break through it by tunneling beneath. Chivas had to laugh at the irony how simple it was to see the detailed design plans. The Central Nebraska Public Power and Irrigation District filed them with the Nebraska Emergency Action Plan District, which reported to the Federal Emergency Management Agency. They all wanted to make sure the plans were available to review in case something went wrong with the dam during a disaster. *Talk about handing a terrorist the keys to the candy store!*

"Hello? Anyone here?" Chivas shouted over the faux-oak countertop in the lobby of A. J.'s Sun and Fun Resort. He couldn't help but think what a nightmare this would be for a family getaway.

Horseflies caromed drunkenly off the window next to the cash register, as if intent on doing the job of the stained plastic fly swatter that hung from a nail nearby. From the back wall, a stuffed "jackelope" with three-point horns stared out at Chivas with strangely blue glass eyes. A rack of tourist activity brochures implied, as if he didn't know it, that visitors would do well to temper their expectations of fun things to do. He had missed the Keith County rodeo by a month. Apparently, Glen Campbell performed, though Chivas thought he probably had a hard time remembering all his own lyrics. From there, the choices went quickly downhill: tour a Victorian mansion, see an art gallery of carved petrified wood, or attend the Little Church in Keystone, where Catholics and Protestants shared the same space.

Chivas dinged the attendant's bell five times. "Hello?"

"Hold your shorts," came a loud reply from behind a flimsy plywood door. "Mama ain't as fast as she used to be."

The clerk emerged in rollers, pink lipstick, and a short cotton housecoat, carrying a cat in one hand and a tumbler of what looked like iced tea in the other. A tiny terrier yapped in staccato from a cramped kennel tucked next to the washer and dryer. The smell of feces drifted into the office with the help of the clerk's body circulating the air.

"Ma'am, I'm looking to rent a small cabin for a few days," Chivas said. "I'm driving this truck full of frozen seafood. The generator on top is pretty quiet, but it does have to keep running, and I don't want to be any trouble to the other guests. Do you have a room available that's out of the way?"

"Sweetie, I have the perfect spot for you. One time I had a big-city writer come here to finish a book. Said it was so quiet back there, she thought she was on Mars. Holed up in that cabin for a week—came out only a couple of times to eat some of my famous Sloppy Joes. Ever heard of *Dewey the Cat*?

"No. I'm afraid not, ma'am."

"Two nights? Three?"

"Just two."

"I need a credit card. Sixty dollars a night."

"I'll pay cash."

"Hm-m-m. I understand. Those banks won't give you fellas a break. "

Chivas wasn't exactly sure what she meant, but replacing "fellas" with "Mexican" seemed to help. He laid six twenties on the chipped gray Formica countertop.

Chivas pulled around to cabin number 8. There was plenty of parking. He crawled up onto the top of the truck and plugged a thick yellow power cable into the side of the cooling engine, then ran it through the cabin door. The freon-filled coils would continue to flow with far less racket, and he felt a bit better finally being able to cut back on using gasoline to keep his poison safe. Not that electricity was completely clean, but this close to the dam, the power in the

213

cabin would at least be generated by a renewable resource. His colleagues would argue otherwise. They would pretend they hated to see the valley landscape turned into a lake. They would talk about salmon spawning, snail habitat, and farmlands lost. But the truth was, to join the real environmentalists' pious clique, all your activism had to be aimed at punishing consumers and business profits. A poor world meant a better world.

Chivas looked around the yard to make sure nobody could see him, then opened up the truck's back door. A spooky fog whipped up near the floor. He knew the purported properties of the pile of frozen capsules—the theory that one droplet of melted ice could directly kill 18,158 people. The key was quiet distribution. With no way to detect the lethal agent, panic would kill far more humans once drinking water was identified as the vector. There would be no canary that people could send into the mine to die in their stead. Although Chivas trusted the science behind the DNA manipulator, he was compelled to test it himself. He was the member taking the biggest risk. Everyone left alive in this little burg would remember his face. The KC's gas station probably had a black-and-white security camera. He might not stick out in this crowd as long as things stayed all nice and Mayberry. But when his truck axle turned up in a cottonwood tree a mile from the biggest explosion since the Trinity test sent nuclear fallout across the Jornada del Muerto, Chivas was sure someone would remember him.

His orders were to sit tight, wait for word from Oz or Dr. Dell, then execute ALB's world-changing mission. But it was just too tempting. Chivas dug deep into his jeans pocket for the old two-bladed pocket knife he carried for good luck, then pulled on a pair of latex gloves. He tore a tiny hole in the shrink wrap, then paused—chipping the ice might send a few particles airborne. With a cigarette lighter, he heated the dull tip of the knife, and touched it to the frozen weapon of mass destruction. The blade turned cold immediately, but Chivas could see a gleam of moisture. He tossed the gloves on the floor, swung the door, put the padlock through the hasp, then walked around the side yard to the office. He stepped inside the empty room and dipped the blade into a sweating glass of ice tea on the counter. Then he grabbed a couple of tourism brochures in case anyone should wonder why he was in and out of the room so quickly. The top pamphlet pictured a growling stuffed polar bear and proclaimed "Big Game Steakhouse—largest collection of wild game trophies in the Midwest."

By the time Chivas walked to the far end of Kingsley Dam, his rage had simmered back down. With sunset approaching, he joined a dozen other nature lovers hanging over a thin railing near the hydroelectric plant. The ugliness of the massive human-built, nature-destroying plant was tempered by the sight of thirty-five bald eagles. It was proof that nature could make fertilizer out of shit. Bald eagles for hundreds of miles had migrated to the dam after it was built. Subzero temperatures in winter froze over every lake in the region, except one. A football field-size piece of Big Mac stayed open year-round, thanks to the generators inside the dam, which pumped out warm water around the clock. The eagles learned quickly that they could feast on fish here. Chivas watched them swoop, talons stretched wide. The grab-and-lift of a five-pound walleye was one of the most beautiful sights he had seen in years.

When the natural light faded and the plant's outdoor fluorescent lights clicked on, Chivas wandered back toward A. J.'s Fun and Sun, with a family of four nattering away behind him as they walked along the shoulder of the road. He had been gone only an hour, and the red and blue flashing lights caught him by surprise. A cop who looked about 19 years old sat in his car, writing a report. There was no sense of urgency at the scene. The ambulance door was open. A small crowd had gathered, keeping a respectable distance from the action, even though there was no yellow crime scene tape to hold them back.

"Oh, my gosh!" the mom walking with her husband and two kids blurted out, as if seeing emergency lights flash for the first time ever. Chivas kept strolling until he reached the gawkers. He stayed close to the family, pretending to be part of their group.

"What happened?" the mom finally asked a stranger taking pictures with her cell phone.

"Looks like Bonnie had some sort of seizure. Her mom died from a brain aneurism, ya know. Those things can be genetic, ya know. Poor woman. Husband says she went down like a sack of potatoes. Blood everywhere. Must've hit her nose on the way down. Morgan's funeral home is coming soon."

Chivas held in a gut laugh, covering the funny noises by feigning allergies. He moved away from the crowd, back toward his isolated cabin. By the time he stepped onto the sagging front porch his shoes and socks were soaked from the thick dew hanging on every blade of grass. Back inside, he dropped to his knees and prayed, creasing the dingy tan bedspread with his elbows.

"Dear Lord Almighty," he prayed. "They say you listen to us all. I am not asking for a thing. In fact, it might be unusual for you to hear: I have a direct message for you. You fucked up the sixth day. Hear me. The waters teemed with fish. You let the birds fly. You filled this earth with sunlight, oceans, sky, and thousands of species of living creatures. Then, you decide to have man rule over the fish. The seas. The birds and the sky. Over livestock. Over all wild animals. You fucked that part up, dear God. Now I am going to undo that little bit of your handiwork. Amen."

Chapter 28

"I have it on good authority that Colton Wiley was nearly killed in an explosion down in Portland a few days ago. How is that *not* news!" Rachelle Fredette barked in Chuck Reynolds's direction. "We can't hold that kind of thing from the public!"

"When Cole *nearly* gets killed, it's hardly news, Rachelle." Reynolds had to grit his teeth when saying her name. He wanted to say "sweetie" but knew she would correctly see it as talking down to her.

"Last year, Cole received fifteen death threats and two real attempts at deep-sixing him. Remember that pest-control company owner? Wow, was he pissed! And, Rachelle"—again he took extra care with his words, censoring out the "dear"—"the Portland stations all covered the fire. Are you saying you'd like to do a follow-up story on a gas line explosion that killed nobody, injured nobody, and is in somebody else's TV market?"

Rachelle's powerful turquoise eyes bored parallel holes through the assistant news director. "You're covering for him. I can tell. I haven't figured out why yet. It's not happenstance that Golden Boy was at the Portland arson and the Evergreen State College arson. And it's certainly newsworthy that the vast portion of this nation's domestic terrorism unit is in town. How could I *not* notice? Jarheads on a government expense account can't stay out of the bars. If I had a little less integrity, I could have pillow-talked this story already. ATF, FBI, NSA, USDA—all here, all chasing whatever Cole is chasing. I'm not really asking. I'm *telling* you that I'm jumping in!"

Reynolds nodded in agreement. "You're right. This could turn into a story that needs two reporters. I'll call Cole and get a status check. You can tackle it first thing Monday morning. I'd let you start right away, but I need a fill-in anchor for the weekend." He didn't really want her anchoring, but at least it would throw her into a résumé-enhancing, self-serving coma for the next forty-eight hours.

"Oh . . . That'd be great! All four main shows?" Rachelle instinctively bargained.

"Yes. And there's still seven or eight hundred bucks in the wardrobe kitty. Go out and find something in solid, bright colors. No prints." Reynolds was proud of himself for diverting her off track for the additional few days, knowing she would nearly sprint to Nordstrom the second she left his office. She said she cared about the serious journalism—they *all* said that. But when it came right down to it, in his long television news lifetime, Reynolds had met only a handful of reporters who would rather dig, uncover, and expose than anchor a newscast. Chuck Reynolds was old, but he wasn't dead. He stared at Rachelle's body as she high-heeled it back toward her desk. Sliding his glass door shut, he felt a little like a zoo animal. There wasn't really any way to have privacy in a newsroom, but he could at least get a small break from the blaring noise. He punched the large blue icon at the bottom of his computer screen. The Skype account sounded like a water drip while it tried to connect with Cole.

"What up, boss man?" Cole said as he stared into his mobile phone's camera.

"November ratings meetings are haunting my sleep. Brenda's big idea is to test the calorie count of all the doughnuts in town. Frank wants me to send him to Paris to do a feature on Airbus. Ed thinks an interview with Ichiro will get him an Emmy. Jodie might actually pull off a piece that we can promote: some tax-waste thing concerning travel expenses and the governor's daughter."

"I don't think Ichiro speaks English, does he?" Cole added unhelpfully.

"Jesus, I don't know. He's an Asian icon, which is our demographic, but the Mariners are fifteen games below five hundred again, so nobody's going to give a shit. Feels like a dud."

218

Cole panned his phone to Nolan driving. "I can prove to you I am working, not golfing. This guy is an official U.S. Forest Service arson investigator. Want to see his badge? It's cool looking. Dude, let Chuck see the badge.

Nolan kept driving. "Go screw yourself. Hi, Chuck. That wasn't aimed at you."

"He hasn't had his chai tea latte yet. Why you calling me, boss?"

"I don't doubt you're working. You're always working. Where are you heading?"

"Keizer, Oregon, then maybe Crater Lake. Lots of animal fanatics around. I might have to actually do some reporting. I've been shooting video, but I am woefully short on interviews. I haven't gotten them, because I'm only now starting to figure out what the hell is going on."

"And?"

"At least four murders and three arson fires are tied to a fringe element of the Animal Liberation Brigade. That's a no-brainer and a huge story, but the obvious carnage is tangential to a bigger plan. I'm thinking you should stock up on a couple of cases of water. Nolan got a text from Homeland Security that they're upping the security level at utilities. Vegas odds are they're going to try to hit a water tower or a dam that supplies drinking water to some city on the West Coast."

"You have three days to figure it out before Rachelle inserts herself into your investigation."

"Really? You think I need an assistant?" Cole affected a look of hurt and pain, then used his hand to wipe it away, like a mime. His demeanor switched to serious in an instant. "I can help with that unwanted intrusion into our lives. She can stay on the sidelines, where she belongs until I break this thing. *Why would she do that?* you ask. I'm sending you an encrypted file. You can't and don't need to open it. I'll give you the password later if necessary. When she sees the label

"RF GM," that alone should stop her in her tracks. If Rachelle wants to get bitchy and try to force her way into this, tell her Cole would appreciate the opportunity to keep his reporting exclusive, and he'd be glad to take it up with Alan if necessary."

"I look forward to offering her such an option. In the meantime, you need anything?"

"Yes, please. Put Jess on standby over the weekend. I might need the chopper."

"You got it. Stay safe." Reynolds clicked the computer closed.

At the top of the hour, Cole cranked up the radio, like a teenager catching a snippet of his favorite pop song playing in the background. The twelve-second snapshots of local, state, and national news held nothing special, but the international news grabbed his attention. The message was almost lost because the radio announcer read the wire story and then started making lighthearted comments about fat people. A bomb, fashioned by Chechen separatists, had exploded in an unpopulated area of Siberia near the Mongolian border. Officials figured they had gotten a break when the rebels accidentally blew themselves up before they could get the bomb to a city. The blast was so powerful, it registered 4.0 on Richter scale. He turned the sound back down and jumped onto his laptop. CNN had a few more details. *Russian military out of Irkutsk investigating . . . bomb hidden in truck . . . Several young government workers died.* Cole opened a new tab and went to RT.com, the best English version of breaking news in Russia. They had less information than CNN. The headline of another article, however, raised the hair on the back of Cole's neck. "CULT'S TEA CEREMONY A SUICIDE PACT? 35 DEAD." The subhead read, "Shaman followers drink poison at Harmony Yurt Camp on Lake Baikal." Cole didn't believe in coincidences—ever.

Montana picked up his call right away, but only to tell him she would call him right back. She was finishing up at a fund-raising luncheon. Cole spent the wait time multitasking with every electronic tool in his quiver. He surfed the Internet on a wireless laptop, texted messages to contacts with a station-issued phone, and used his personal cell to leave messages with animal rights sources. Having fifteen applications open all at once didn't feel hectic or overwhelming. He reviewed video on a small digital player in the middle of the biggest tangled-cord mess ever beheld. To Cole, the array of notebooks, pens, pieces of scrap paper, cords, files, audio recording devices, mini cameras, tapes, phones, and a few bullets spilling out of a backpack onto the floor of the truck held the comforting feeling of efficiency. The "Hot Blooded" ring tone notified Cole that Montana was free to talk. He let the song play as long as possible so he and Nolan could sing along while playing air guitar.

"Are you rested up from our latest action adventure?" Cole asked in all sincerity.

"Are you making fun? That meeting in B.C. was the scariest thing I've ever done! I had to sleep for, like, twelve hours to rid my body of all the adrenaline. An hour of Bikram hot yoga this morning finally got me back somewhere near normal. I suppose you're about to undo the balance."

"I am—sorry. I need you to go down to the Seattle office of the FBI. They abhor walk-in customers, but hold your ground. Office staff is trained to screen out frivolous complaints and crazies. Ask for a guy named Sid. Tell them you have information about Big Vasil. Sid will show up, I promise."

"And what should I tell Sid?"

"Everything."

Montana hesitated. "Everything?"

"Yep. Start with goon number one smashing your hand. Tell Sid about the extortion plot. Murder threats, etcetera, etcetera. End with 'Colton Wiley has video and audio of Big Vasil

221

saying "I vill kill your father, then vill kill you."' Do the best impression of his accent you can. 'I vill kill you.' Come on, let me hear you try it."

Montana was getting used to Cole's merrymaking on serious topics, so she wasn't offended by his use of "etcetera, etcetera" in place of terms such as "torture" and "throat cutting."

He continued, "Also, ask the feds to provide you with some big, bad gun-toting bodyguards. You won't need protection for long, I promise. The timing of this is fairly important. I'll signal you when to drop into the FBI, by sending a text with the address of their building. Oh! One more thing. Before you leave Sid, ask to fill out a written criminal complaint and take a copy with you. It's a cheap way for me to get a public record and a case tracking number. Make sure they time-stamp it. My lawyers love public records."

"Cole, you're nuts. Big Vasil is going to be furious when he finds out from the feds that you were videotaping his extortion and death threats. Don't you figure *you're* the one who needs some protection? He'll come at you with everything he's got."

"He can get in line. Just trust me. Wait for my text. Go see the FBI."

Nolan was a bit puzzled and annoyed after hearing one side of this conversation that had nothing to do with the animal terrorism case. It provoked a rare rant from the normally easygoing firefighter.

"WTF! You still working on *other* investigations? We are in the middle of the most serious criminal case I've ever even heard of. You're toying with *Anchov?* Have you lost your marbles?"

Cole glanced at Nolan, then punched in Big Vasil's personal cell phone number, which Montana had given him days earlier.

"Yes?" came a beautifully monotone Russian voice.

"This is Colton Wiley. I'm the investigative reporter for KZPR-TV. I need to speak with Mr. Anchov."

Even though whoever answered was covering the receiver, Cole could hear Russian voices speaking with growing ferocity. He didn't understand a single word, but it was clear that Big Vasil's kill squad was arguing about whether they should bother the boss immediately or take a message. After a minute, the monotone man drifted away from the phone, and Big Vasil's booming voice filled Cole's earpiece.

"Mr. Wiley. TV superstar calling me is an honor. To what I owe this pleasure?"

Cole motioned for Nolan to pull off the interstate and stop. This was one conversation that needed 100 percent concentration.

"I hope you appreciate honesty," Cole started. "I pride myself on being up front."

"I do, Mr. Wiley. That is how I run business."

"Then I've got one hell of a deal for you today! Just so you know the rules up front, it's not going to get any better than my first offer, and you don't get to negotiate. Again, I apologize for the blunt approach. I know you would normally have some kind of leverage to improve your position in most business transactions. You don't have any leverage with me."

"I see." Big Vasil chuckled with vast amusement. He had probably never in his adult life had anyone speak to him that way. "You are a brave, foolish man. I respect that, but do not forget, every man has weakness. Many of my former business associates thought they, too, were tough and fearless. None outlasted me."

"You are correct. I have one weakness. Her name is Montana Harms." Cole let that hang in the air.

Big Vasil stuck to his guns, despite a small moment of concern.

"Aw-w, that's sweet. You are puffing up chest to protect love. Now I *know* you are a very foolish man."

Cole fired right to the meat of the conversation. "Here's the deal, big man. Good news is, I am going to make you a hero back in Russia. TV interviews, political functions. Business deals. All the stuff that makes a clown like you the star of the circus. You'll be able to figure out how to make this deal immensely profitable for yourself. Bad news is, you won't ever do business here in the States again. You are going to get on a jet within the coming hour and leave this country. One-way ticket."

Big Vasil was bellowing with laughter by now. He couldn't even speak. His security staff no doubt thought he had finally gone mad. He had been on the edge for a long time. Cole waited patiently. It was not an odd reaction to hear. In two decades of manipulating the emotions of powerful people, Colton Wiley had seen it all. He was used to making men crumble, fall apart, and stand openmouthed in disbelief. Laughter was no more than a loud nervous tic.

After a long minute, Big Vasil flipped the switch to angry. "Nobody tells me what to do! I do not do business on telephone. How about I send a car for you? We chat face to face."

Cole didn't even pause. "No time. I videotaped your meeting with Ms. Harms. *Two* cameras, actually. I will say that the side angle makes you look a tad overweight. You should think vertical stripes. Might want to hit the gym, too, but I digress. The audio quality was top notch, too. I won't go over the list of crimes documented. I know you are a stubborn son of a bitch. I can tell you're already going over, inside your head, a long list of ways to get out of this big mess. The crimes occurred in Canada. The U.S. might not have jurisdiction, even though the threats were connected to gambling operations in America. Maybe the feds can't use the tape.

Slick lawyers can get the evidence thrown out. As a last resort, you're also thinking you can start killing witnesses so nobody will be there to testify. Kill me. Kill Montana. Kill the Special Forces guy who helped record the shakedown in the park. Oh. Just a side note on that last part: slim chance surprising him. In fact, suicide mission, in my opinion. Anyway, within the hour, the FBI will find out that a certain Seattle reporter holds videotape that will finally help them nail their biggest Russian mobster to date. The FBI *loves* that kind of publicity. Ever since Ruby Ridge, they really cling to the shit they get right. A midlevel organized-crime agent named Sid will be itching to hunt you down, because he has his sights set on being the special agent in charge. KZPR-TV won't have to wait for a subpoena to arrive, because—and this is my favorite part of the story—I am going to start airing a heavily promoted series of investigative stories about the Anchov empire. All the video and audio the feds want will already have been seen by a couple of million people. We'll post it unedited on our Web site. The feds can download it. That lets my bosses at the TV station pretend they are keeping to their journalistic ethics by not caving in to a court order for raw tape. I know, I've put your back against the wall. You're a bear. You want to come out, claws swinging. You want to save face and manhood, and damn the consequences. I get it, Big Vasil. I really do. That is why I have sweetened the pot. I don't want you to make the wrong choices."

Nolan wanted to step out of the truck, but he knew it was too late. Whatever he was witnessing was going to jam him up. Good-bye, badge. Hello, bartending.

Big Vasil took a deep breath so he could yell and threaten, but Cole remained in command. "Shut up and listen. I'm not even close to done. What I'm about to tell you is top secret. It's the kind of secret that will make you rich and famous but, more importantly, popular.

225

That's not an easy feat, given that you are a murdering, kiddie-prostitute-trafficking old-school gangster."

"You are fucking dead man! Got it? You will not last the day. I hope you are recording me right now. I will smile when they play at the murder trial!" Big Vasil was coming unhinged.

Cole ignored him. "I said listen. This is the most important part. An extremist animal rights group had plans to poison a massive freshwater supply originating at Lake Baikal. They've concocted some potion that is a real threat to the entire planet. I can't quite figure out why they're in Russia, but maybe it was a test run for a bigger plan. Might be a diversion. I know your brother is some sort of general in the Russian army. I couldn't care less if you love him or hate him, but it's time for a family reconnection. Tell him that the so-called Chechen rebel truck that exploded is more likely the work of an American terrorist group. They are trying to kill as many Russians as possible. Not with the explosion, but with something that was inside that truck. I figure the plan went haywire, so they sabotaged their work. I guarantee there is something at the explosion site that a few smart forensic scientists should at least be able to identify as unknown. The water in that lake could be messed up. I'm guessing that a couple dozen shaman followers were the first casualties. Russia will look like it's ahead of America on a global disaster. Cut a deal with your brother. Make sure he gives you credit in the media. He scores a few more stars and gets a new office, complete with a pretty young assistant. You get a hero's welcome, minimum. However, if you want to spend some of your own hard-earned money and really look good, start buying information from your long list of criminal cronies. Find out how some America-based animal rights terrorists got into your country. Catching American spies looks great on the résumé. Heck, they might make you mayor of Leninville!"

Cole stopped and listened to static fade in and out as an overhead power line at the rest stop surged its voltage through the air. *No wonder Tesla's power towers never caught on,* he mused.

Cole could hear Big Vasil sipping what sounded like the top off a glass of ice-cold vodka. He imagined the man sitting on an intricately carved barstool that had cost him more than most people's cars, with five more just like it lined up at his private bar. A shame, really, that he must leave such works of art behind for some realtor to steal.

"I do not know what kind of deal is this?" Vasil said at last. "I need to think. Make some calls."

Cole could hear the defeat in his voice. "The FBI will be revoking your visa and putting you on the no-fly list within a couple of hours. Get out while you can. Go enjoy your life, Big Vasil. Enjoy a life free of Colton Wiley." Cole hit "End."

"Am I now a witness to a host of federal crimes?" Nolan spoke softly toward the late-morning sun still rising over the Cascade Mountains.

Cole put his hand on Nolan's shoulder and squinted into the sun along with his friend. He felt almost like a father pulling his son close for a serious talk about hard life lessons.

"You never have to lie for me," he said. "If anyone asks, tell them what you heard. The FBI might claim I interfered with their investigation, but the truth is, they don't even know about Big Vasil's gambling threats yet. Once Montana has her complaint time-stamped then they pull my cell phone records and see that I spoke with the Russian an hour *before* Sid cracked his case file, and they'll have to back off. How can I interfere with an investigation that wasn't even open yet? Half the time when they go after some guy like me for some piddly reason, they must get the U.S. attorney to sign off on perjury or lying to an FBI agent or some other bullshit offense

227

like that. If we simply tell the truth, I'm certain everything will be cool. Now, let's go figure out why these animal rights groupies want to end the world. I promise, I'll focus."

Nolan nodded. "Cool."

Before Nolan even got back up to speed on the interstate on-ramp, Cole had sent a text to Montana: *"NW corner Pike and 2nd. Red brick bldg. Say hi to Sid for me."*

Chapter 29

The Kaman helicopter, fueled up and ready to go, was a gorgeous sight to behold. It could fly at 185 miles per hour with a choker load of harvested logs. Oz had learned to fly HH-3F Pelicans from a buddy in the Coast Guard reserves, but nothing could touch the sheer power and lifting force of the K-Max.

"It doesn't have a tail rotor. That helps us in the trees," Oz bragged to Dr. Dell as they drove onto the dirt parking patch near Bennie's Airfield outside Medford. How Bennie managed to keep an active Federal Aviation Administration license to operate an airport with rutted runways and a wind sock full of holes was a mystery to Oz, but Oz had spent months scouting airports within flying distance of Crater Lake, and this crop-duster graveyard was the perfect location.

When Bennie appeared out the side door of the rusting Morton building, he was yelling something in another language. Polish? Czech? Oz didn't much care. The crotchety old fart was a walking mummy who looked as if he had been around since the days of hand-cranked wooden props.

Dr. Dell rolled down his window to try to make out what Bennie was angry about.

"Can't park here without a permit!" Bennie shouted, peering at them through heavy-rimmed glasses that made his eyes look huge. "Gotta have a permit!"

Oz opened his door and looked around. Fields of orchard grass lay in every direction. "I'm glad to buy a permit, old man. Relax. Is that the K-Max chopper reserved for Mr. Jones?"

"You him? Bennie responded.

"Sure am. It's ready to fly?"

"Of course. Said it would be. I need a copy of your current aviation certification and thirty dollars for the parking permit."

Oz swung the tire iron, splitting Bennie's skull just above the temple. Blood and goo spattered the ground in a pattern reminiscent of a Jackson Pollock painting, and the 88-year-old decorated World War II vet was no doubt shooting the breeze with St. Peter before he hit the dirt.

Oz left him in a heap on the ground, like refuse, while he backed the used food-delivery truck onto two dirt parking spaces. Oz could still see "Schwann's" on the side—though the decals had been peeled off long ago, the sun had baked the yellow paint a shade lighter everywhere on the vehicle except under the old letters. He got out and tossed Bennie into the cooler.

"Sorry, old man. Thirty bucks might be worth it for front-row parking butted up to the pillars of Lambeau Field, but not for this hole."

* * *

Dr. Dell wandered inside the airport office building while Oz stayed out in the parking lot, rubbing droplets of blood into the dry dirt with his boot to cover any obvious signs of violence. Dr. Dell was glad to see a computer with an Internet connection. Minimizing the map of a regenerating Doppler weather radar, he brought up the secret flower pages so he could check for possible messages. He was relieved to see the first coded update appear in light-green Gothic lettering: *"ENJOYING THE MIDWEST. WAITING FOR YOU. BILLY GOAT."*

The second message had Dr. Dell mumbling under his breath as Oz made his way into the tiny office.

"Any news?"

For the moment, Dr. Dell ignored Oz, hovering over his shoulder.

"What's '*TRAVELING WITH THERMOS—FULL COOLER TOO HEAVY TO TAKE CAMPING*'?"

Dr. Dell started typing a response. "Sh-h-h! It means Wynona and that meathead of a mercenary likely destroyed the truck and its contents due to risk of getting caught but are on the run with a smaller amount of the toxin. I always considered the Lake Baikal operation a bonus, anyway. God it would have been fantastic to pollute waters from Russia to Mongolia to China. I never trusted my guesstimates of the density of the lake substrate anyway. The lithosphere is razor thin, but I could never properly calculate the P-wave impacts from the sloppy Russian data available. They can make thermonuclear missiles and pinpoint their impact on top of the goddamn Washington Monument, but they can't properly calculate Snell's law. The good news is that our terror partners are alive and free. With a little help from Mother Earth, Wynona can still kill a couple of million people using riverways as the back-up plan. Creating panic is key, and they can still do that."

"P-waves? Density? I just like to blow shit up—the more TNT, the better," Oz muttered as walked away.

Dr. Dell typed in "PLAN B." He wished he had brought his CyberCide binary program to wipe the computer clean, but a simple reformatting would have to do the trick. He set the system to restore all programs to its original purchase date, then headed back outside to inspect the K-Max helicopter. Oz was already there, connecting an adjustable lifting beam to a flange clamp on the underside of the aircraft. A bundle of cables lay carefully grouped and tie-wrapped on the ground, with a massive finned bomb attached to the wires by small shackle-shaped bolts.

"It will be dark in a little over an hour," Dr. Dell said. "I'm heading back to the lake. I have my eye on a research boat that's the perfect size. It's anchored fifty yards offshore on the north end. Getting cold up there, so I don't expect anyone will be around at the beach. If they are, I guess it's their unlucky day. He released the clip of his gun, checked that it was full, and slapped it back into the grip. "I'll direct this laser pointer on my Glock at the helicopter, so you'll be able to spot me."

Oz kept working. "Fine. Break a couple of green chem sticks, too, so I can clearly see the boundaries of the boat floor. I have night-vision goggles, so I can fly covert. Be patient. The timing must be perfect. I've been studying the Oregon active flight logs all afternoon. I found a way to stay off radar. Not only that, but the noise of the K-Max won't even draw a look up from anyone below. For the past eight hours, the Forest Service has been flying choppers between Crater Lake and a brush fire to the east of the Umpquah National Forest. They're scooping water to douse the flames. There's one guy going back and forth—takes him fifty-two minutes. I'm going to fly into the Crater Lake basin twenty-six minutes after he fills up with water. The federal rangers will probably think the fire crews called for a second air unit. The FAA control tower night-shifter won't even see a shadow of my bird. I'm flying barely over the tree line, so I'll look like electrical interference on the green screen. This beam I'm installing has a bail adjust, so our gorgeous bunker-busters will be cradled safe as a newborn baby in a stork's sling. I'll lay it down on the deck of any boat you care to steal as long as there are at least twenty-one feet of open space. All you have to do is unscrew this nut and pinch this clip, times three. If there are a few waves, no big deal—the torpedo fins will keep it from rolling around. I stabilized the Tovex explosives, so without a heat source, they won't go boom."

"I'm not worried in the least, my friend. Tomorrow, ALB will go down in the history books, not as terrorists but as heroes—martyrs who understood how man's vile actions toward this planet's creatures were going to make all life extinct. Of this, I am sure."

Oz didn't say a thing. He was touchy-feely about saving animals, so he couldn't really add to Dr. Dell's syrupy prose. He just wanted to murder as many humans as possible. That would have to be incentive enough.

After Dr. Dell left in the truck, heading back toward Crater Lake, Oz looked at the long preflight checklist. This was a combat mission, and he intended for it to succeed. Before starting the preflight, he taped a picture of his bomb-sniffing dog, Sparks, to the dash of the chopper. The image filled him with a volatile mixture of feelings: love, betrayal, rage. He removed a small screw in the bottom of the fuel tank outside, let a few ounces of blue-tinted aviation fuel pour into an old Mason jar, and swished it around, studying the bottom of the glass for contaminants before tossing the mixture into the grass. He checked the transmission area for oil leaks, made sure the air induction cowling was secure, studied the wear and tear on the main driveshaft aft coupling, and made sure the cooler blower was free of any obstructions. *Check. Check. Check.* Then he knelt and gently rubbed the surface of the bunker-busting bomb that he had fashioned from used parts. If the toxic hodgepodge was going to be successfully driven into the crust of the earth, this was the perfect tool to do it. It truly was his finest work. At first, Oz had thought a nuclear tip on the device would be most effective, but that was back when he thought he might be dropping it into the middle of a San Diego Chargers football game. *That really would have been fun.* But once Dr. Dell started planning to use the devices underwater, Oz abandoned the idea. He had studied naval history enough to know that underwater thermonuclear blasts were normally a dud.

A deepwater test in 1955, dubbed Operation Wigwam, had killed a bunch of fish, made some steam, and polluted the stratosphere with invisible poison, but it didn't have any great effects on the ocean or its floor. Another test, closer to the surface, was supposed to gauge how a nuclear device might affect ships at sea. It was an unmitigated public relations disaster. Oz never understood why Admiral H. P. Blandy wanted to test the effects of radiation on navy crews by tethering animals on the deck of the USS *Nevada*. Two days after a twenty-three-kiloton bomb, nicknamed "Able," wiped out all life on a small atoll called Bikini Island, all the goats, cattle, pigs, and chickens on the ships had died from radiation exposure. Animal rights activists were furious. From that moment forward, they set their sights on the U.S. military. No one could stop the lunacy of using minesweeping dolphins, conducting sonar frequency tests that interfered with an orca's directional guidance abilities, or shooting monkeys into outer space, but the military at least had to temper its goals to appease a now watchful public. Oz seethed at the animal abuse that still secretly went on. He had watched Ranger snipers practice shooting a scrambling, green-painted pig in the head at a thousand yards. He had watched the weapons sellers kill cats while showing the brass how blast patterns differentiated between pineapple- and baseball-style grenades. He had witnessed Marines slaughtering Assyrian village dogs in Northern Iraq, luring them to close range with scraps of sandwich. The men's laughter still rang in his ears. If those in charge of protecting and spreading the American way of life couldn't figure out a way to be compassionate toward helpless creatures, then they would get what they deserved: an agonizing, panic-filled, confusing death.

For a split second, Oz thought about his ex-wife and son. Neither had understood him after he returned from war. Did they deserve to die, too? There was no choice now. He couldn't warn them. *Causalities of war.* Was it hypocritical for him to have stocked a survival camp for himself and Dr. Dell? Perhaps this should be a suicide mission. Dr. Dell had said N5G project members had to live so they could keep moving its work forward—to make sure the animals thrived. Oz felt a twinge of guilt, wondering whether he was doing the right thing.

He walked over to a dusty payphone near the office, plunked in some coins, and punched in a Los Angeles area code.

A woman's voice answered immediately.

"Hello?"

Oz could hear a TV commercial and a little boy in the background making "va-room" sounds, like he was playing with a toy truck.

"Tell little Oscar I love him. I know you and I never saw eye to eye, but, um... Don't drink the water. Any water. Go to the superstore and buy as much as you can. You'll understand why soon. Goodbye."

It was time. Even though there was not a living soul within ten miles, after Oz jumped into the cockpit, he still verbally called out his preflight routine.

"Door secured! Clear! Engine power: on! Transmission pressure: full! Throttle: fifteen percent . . . twenty . . . twenty-five . . . thirty!"

A split second before he was ready to lift off the ground, out of the corner of his eye, Oz caught sight of a dark-haired figure and instinctively drew his sidearm. Before he could get it out over the passenger seat, the door was open and Wendell Canyon was inside the cockpit, attacking with all his might. Oz got off a shot, but it just pinholed the windshield and raised a poof of dust in the dirt fifty feet out.

Canyon smashed his forehead into Oz's nose, and the blood spattered the glass bubble that made up the flight box. Oz kicked, trying to break Canyon's arm against the instrument panel.

The ferocious fight for control of the chopper went on for a full minute; then Oz realized that if he could get enough of a gap between himself and his attacker, he could get to his boot knife. He popped the panel handle and fell out onto the tarmac. Canyon was on him like a leopard springing out of a tree. They rolled to a stop, with Oz on top. He pounded down with his elbows, trying to catch Canyon's throat or temple. The lanky, much younger outcast managed to break free and stand up. Oz came bulling into Canyon, trying to tackle him, but Canyon lowered his center of gravity and lifted Oz with all his might, like a linebacker in a goal-line defense.

The slowly rotating blade slammed against Oz's head. Gray brain-matter stippled Canyon's cheek as Oz went limp and spilled a good third of his blood into a pothole on the runway.

Canyon stood over the body and chastised the all but decapitated form beneath him.

***

"H_2O suspected you were weak! He could read your mind. You wondered if killing humans was the right thing. Well, now you can join the rest of the stinking filth turning into compost this week!" Canyon shouted at the corpse. Oz had been a valuable asset, but his inordinate love for just one animal was not enough.

Canyon took a rag out of the toolbox in the backseat of the K-max and wiped away enough blood to clear a round spot on the interior of the windshield. He left the headset on the floor. He wouldn't have to speak with flight control or Dr. Dell. The leader of the new world was waiting for him. Canyon watched the cables grow taut as the chopper rose into the air, as if the bomb were straining to stay on earth. But the helicopter appeared to understand the importance of the load, rising and falling slightly to help shift the suspended cargo into a more aerodynamic horizontal line. Canyon pulled hard to the east, toward the Cascade Mountains.

The dressing on his arrow wound showed fresh bleeding, but the pain didn't bother him. Dr. Dell had done such a solid job of convincing some other members of ALB that Canyon

236

couldn't be fully trusted, Oz and Brian Zander came up with the bright idea on their own to take Canyon out—eliminate any loose ends. It was a cowboy decision that had put H_2O into a frothing rage. He masked the reason for his anger, telling Oz he had put the entire plan at risk of a local police investigation if Canyon should show up at a hospital or morgue.

But Oz could never have suspected that Wendell Canyon was Dr. Hadar O'Dell's most trusted adviser and friend. The two of them, along with Wynona, had dreamed up the elimination of humans as a "wouldn't it be great if . . ." fantasy, then spent thousands of combined hours in the lab, successfully creating the Sugar. It was so simple, so innocuous looking, so beautiful in its design, if they had marketed it as a low-calorie breakfast-cereal additive, Kellogg's would probably have made a few factory-runs before figuring out that it crippled DNA structures. Canyon laughed to himself, thinking about all those dead kids, their faces in their cereal bowls, their moms running and screaming in terror around their mega homes. *Too funny* . . .

Chapter 30

A moment before Nolan got to the Highway 4 exit Cole motioned wildly to the left.

"Crap! Almost forgot you don't know where we're going. Left! One more stop. I need a serious computer whiz to look at this jump stick of data from Dr. Animal Love. And, dude, if Mary Lee Kissinger can't help, at least I can hook you up with a date. Next time you have to stamp out one of those scary brush fires that threaten a logging road near Glide, you won't be lonely at the local bar."

Nolan wasn't biting. "Smart chicks aren't my thing. Besides, no way a computer geek pings a nine or ten on the Nolan scale."

"She's really sweet. You're too picky."

They took a winding road along the North Umpqua River, stopping every few miles at the entrance of bridges too narrow for two cars. Cole pressed his finger into the window from the passenger seat.

"Okay. This is the coolest thing. Look. Look! Stop the car and look! Coming up is the only place in the world where two rivers collide head-on. The Umpqua smashes into the Little River. They start on different mountain ridges and, by the Lord's whimsical hand, end in exactly the same place. *Pow.* Makes a huge mess of whitewater. The force is amazing."

Nolan slowed to a crawl on the empty highway and stared at the tumult of foam and mist.

"I agree. That is spectacular. How much farther?"

"Jeez! That's all I get for showing you the ninth wonder of the world? Close. Take a right up at the end of that fence." Cole pointed to a small log cabin.

As they slowed to a stop on the lawn, a pair of Weimaraners bounded toward them, exuberant at the prospect of someone new to roughhouse with. Cole didn't disappoint them. He bear-hugged them both off the ground, then scratched them from ear to tail. The pair dashed over a low hill, yelping with glee, as Cole threw an old tennis ball that was lying in tall rye grass.

Nolan froze when he saw Mary Lee smiling from the porch.

"Colton Wiley, you certainly have made a name for yourself given where you came from." Mary Lee spoke as though her oldest friend in the world had just come back from the war.

The two hugged tight while both dogs tried to trip them up.

"M. L., this is my friend Nolan Burke. He's an arson investigator with the U.S. Forest Service. We need your expertise." Cole held up the thumb drive. "We have an animal terrorist who might have left us a clue as to his future actions."

"Right to business, huh? I know you won't say no to a beer. Come on in. I'll fire up the satellite."

The cabin's rustic look ended at the threshold to a modern-art museum inside. Sheets of stainless steel, bent in a shallow parabola, rose from floor to ceiling, creating a tunnel effect. A series of bolts sticking at various lengths out of the walls drew the visitor's eye along a curved path to a series of twisted metal statues. Mary Lee played docent, spouting a few interesting details about each piece as she walked by.

"Michelangelo's *Pietà* inspired this. Henri de Toulouse-Lautrec's brothels gave me the idea for her pose. Sexy, huh? I used an electric current to oxidize the top layer on Claude Monet's water lilies to get that blue color. I think I broke fifteen flowers before I got it right."

A short flight of stairs led the three of them into an alcove off the main room. A fifty-inch television hung on the wall, its asteroid screen saver emitting intermittent bursts of light. Mary Lee plopped down cross-legged into a swivel chair and started typing furiously on a wireless keyboard.

"Rainier, Bud, or Rogue Dead Guy ale? Pick your poison," Mary Lee barked while pointing with her chin to a mini fridge in the corner of the room.

"I'm going to use Stanford's computer servers—they have fantastic data-mining programs, bought for them by the Pentagon a few years back. Peace-loving students don't know the funding source. Even the most radically liberal profs get shy about asking too many questions when their department gets a fifty-million-dollar grant to study artificial intelligence. NSA watches in real time how the best and brightest students—many of them Chinese citizens— brainstorm new ways to get the computers to write their own improvement codes. I'm going to piggyback through the same secret back door."

"*It doesn't feel pity or remorse or fear, and it absolutely will not stop. Ever. Until you are dead!*" Nolan yelled into Cole's face, doing his best impression of John Connor in *The Terminator.*

Cole laughed. Mary Lee gave Nolan a look that said, *I so see why Cole hangs out with you. God help me.*

"How sensitive is this, Cole?" she continued. "Classified or not?"

Mary Lee paused as the screen waited for her to punch in a code after the words "Signal Sight Coordinates."

"It's not officially anything, but spooks all over the world would die to get a look at this: FBI, CIA, Russian FSB, et al., are just a tad behind me. I don't want you to get jammed up when they do catch on. Let's use quite a bit of caution."

"Then Oscar, Three, Echo, Echo, fifteen it is. I'm encrypting everything, anyway. That's my own special program. There is no key on the market. I just need to sneak my path into the server. After that, when I upload your files, they'll get spread out into tiny bits and bytes all over the western United States. The data-mining programs will link to each piece, but there won't be an analytical summary sent anywhere except to that screen right there. Unless I choose to install a recordable backup on the screen, when I shut down the system everything we do just evaporates into a nonsensical stream of ones and zeros. So what kind of mystery are we solving?"

Nolan, seizing the opportunity to get closer to Mary Lee, took charge.

"I was combing through what I thought was a routine arson fire near Mount St. Helens. Instead, I found a pair of dead college girls. Their necklaces linked them to an animal rights terror group. Cole agreed to help me track down some leads. I figured he'd get a pretty good story and I'd get the satisfaction of at least letting the victims' families know who killed them and why."

Cole saw what he was doing. Nolan hoped that last part would score him some sensitivity points with Mary Lee. Cole gave him the "good try" look and a tiny nod, and he continued.

"We think we identified the leader of the pack—some scientist. But now we're getting more than a little worried that he has grander plans than just offing three students, a cop, Cole, and me."

Mary Lee stopped typing. "Good God, Cole! Your death wish makes Freud's obsession with genitalia look normal!"

"Nolan loves dirty talk. Take that mom-son sexual tension chatter a bit further, and you'll have him hooked," Cole bantered back.

With a final tap on the "Enter" key, Mary Lee told Cole to insert his thumb drive into the USB port.

"We're in. Let's let the computer do its thing. Give it an hour."

With a mesmerizing sway in her walk, Mary Lee led Nolan and Cole to the outside porch. The noise of the river flowing around three-ton granite boulders created a relaxed mood, and for the next few minutes anyway, there was nothing either man could do to further the investigation. So, the three of them sipped cold beer from nearly frosted bottles and chatted about anything unrelated to work. Nolan worked hard to impress Mary Lee with his intelligence and storytelling skills, although, from the look of things, this was probably unnecessary.

"Okay, boys," she said a few minutes later. "Let's see if my MIT computer science degree and a decade crafting codes for NORAD inside the Cheyenne Mountain Station gives you some answers."

On the way back to the computer room, Nolan said, "I have to ask. How does a gorgeous, brilliant woman like you know such a narrow-minded, insane cupcake as Cole?"

"He didn't *tell* you? My, my, Colton Wiley! Always so full of secrets, even to the few people you allow to get close," Mary Lee said aloud to the room. "He is my brother and protector. I can't count the number of times he stood between me and our foster dad. That man was a vicious son of Satan. If you don't yet instinctively know it, your friend there will kill for you. Never doubt it."

Nolan was shocked into silence. He had always assumed that Cole was raised clutching a silver spoon. But before he could start hammering away at the pair of them with personal questions, Mary Lee gave a victorious crow.

"I am so good! Data mining works by grabbing obscure bits of information from seemingly irrelevant tangential information. Grocery stores use it all the time. For example, every time Nolan goes to the store and uses his Safeway card to get a discount, a computer logs his purchases. He buys a case of Coke every month for years; then, suddenly, he starts buying

242

Diet Coke. Safeway's computer notices and starts mailing coupons to Nolan's house for half-price Weight Watchers frozen dinners and Slim-Fast, guessing he's on a diet. The feds run a huge data-mining operation called MATRIX. It's far more sophisticated. They tap into *everything.* That computer system can read your frickin' mind. Say Cole buys a sweet strip of land along the Naches River. He files for all the right permits and asks to cut down ten trees so he can build a fishing cabin. The county screws him and says no because the shadow of the roofline might scare the bull trout. Two months later, Cole goes to Ace Hardware and buys a chainsaw, then fills up with gas at the AM-PM across the street. On a beautiful fall weekend, he drives to his peaceful piece of ground by the river, and two U.S. Fish and Game enforcement officers just happen to stop by about five minutes after he gets there. MATRIX pulled records from the county assessor's office on the land buy, the logging permit denial from the Bureau of Land Management, the chainsaw purchase from Cole's Ace Rewards card, then traced his movements to the Naches River using the GPS device on his cell phone. The computer determined that Cole could be about to break the law and cut down some trees anyway. MATRIX sends a text alert to the game officers. Scary, huh?"

Mary Lee took a long draw, downing the last of her beer, and continued.

"Social networking sites use that basic principle, too. The site gives you a list of people that have some connection to you because it filters through your work history, alumni association, and other people you've already chosen to accept. Then the computer program starts ranking the likelihood you might want to use some other person for a business contact. So, Cole was doing some rudimentary mining work when he reviewed how long this scientist stayed on a particular area of interest. He was eyeballing it. Stanford's system evaluated every word on every page of every site Dr. Animal visited. It took that information and searched every other spider engine in the world, looking for commonalities. What's this oddball's name?"

Cole rattled off the basics: "Dr. Hadar O'Dell. He was a prof at Evergreen. It appears, he leads a small group of animal rights extremists called the Animal Liberation Brigade. They are connected together by the moniker N-5-G, but we still have no idea what the hell that is."

"Shit. Hold on. Hold on!" Mary Lee typed furiously on two keyboards. "That's another piece of information the computer can use. The more the better. Wait. Wait . . . Voila! Streamed back to me already."

"And?" Nolan and Cole said in unison.

"It's not quite *that* simple, boys. You still must use what you know about this case to see if the data pointers give you new clues. Since you've wisely told me almost nothing, I'll go over what I see as a pattern. If you hear something you didn't know, stop me. We'll dig deeper into the system."

Everyone's eyes were glued to the monitor, which Mary Lee manipulated into a quadrant of images.

"Okay. Guy loves water. I assume we all know that. He also has a substantial fascination with both human and other primate DNA structures. So how about this? The computer says there is a high likelihood that the animal rights terrorists derived their N-5-G name from a mammalian sialic acid called N-glycolylneuraminic acid—Neu-five-Gc for short. Does that mean anything?"

"No. Sialic acid a poison?" Cole wondered aloud while looking at Nolan, as if his old pal's six quarters at Central Washington University would help answer that question.

Mary Lee took over. "It's not poison. It's just a simple sugar. There's a ton of technical papers Dr. O'Dell studied about a gene that codes the hydroxylase enzymes in apes. A German

244

molecular biologist basically discovered a 'hole' in the cell structure of humans. An oxygen atom is supposed to go in the hole—or, at least, it does in all other mammals. Some other scientists in China and Japan took that tidbit of info a step further and started inserting pathogens, viruses, the flu, cancer drugs—all sorts of molecular messengers—into the missing oxygen peg. The flu took to the hole, so they started researching the crap out of that to look for a cure. Sialic acid is rich in oligosaccharides, which conjugate glycogen on the cell surfaces of membranes to help keep water outside the cell. Like wax paper. The sugar has this overall negative charge. Water is positive because of the hydrogen atom, so water is naturally attracted to the sugar cell. Strip off the protective layer or send a signal to the body to allow some a deadly pathogen to be accepted into a cell, and a human could get sick while any other mammal would not. I'd say that is what Dr. Dell was trying to figure out."

After a long moment, Mary Lee looked them both dead in the eyes and exhaled. "God, I hope he didn't."

Nolan picked up his phone, stepped onto the porch, and dialed the assistant director of Homeland Security to pass on the information. Cole could hear only the end of the call as Nolan came back through the sliding glass door.

"Holding out? Are you *nuts*? Two days ago, I handed you all the information from the professor's computer. Just because you threw it in a drawer, thinking it was more exciting to dig through burned college campus rubble and do live interviews with Nancy Grace, doesn't mean *I* wasn't doing *my* job. Dedicate some people to it—like *now*! The potential here is catastrophic!"

In the blue haze of light thrown off by the monitor, Nolan's eyes watched Mary Lee's eyes dart from screen to keyboard to her notes. Over the next hour, the three of them dived into a heavy discussion of the murder investigations. A table full of empty beer bottles piled up as

Mary Lee listened to stories about April Slade's taunting clue to her parents, Cole's theory about a group of dead shamanists in Russia, and the scary potential contained in Oscar McKinsey's résumé. For another hour, they brainstormed about water: rain, Puget Sound, flowing taps in all the world's households with indoor plumbing, dammed-up rivers, bottled water on shelves at the gas station. Nothing made perfect sense. Mary Lee pouted as she again pored over the data-mining results.

"Water, water, everywhere, nor any drop to drink," she said under her breath.

Cole finished the next stanza of *The Rime of the Ancient Mariner* for her—a poem they had memorized together one long weekend long ago because she insisted it was the only way to get the twenty points extra credit in freshman honor's English.

"The very deep did rot: O Christ! That ever this should be! Yea, slimy things did crawl with legs upon the slimy sea," Cole pulled out of the deepest recesses of his memory.

"That's it!" Mary Lee shrieked, jumping out of her chair. "You always got that wrong. Not *upon* the sea. *Beneath* the sea! *Beneath* the lake! *Beneath* the river! *Beneath* the ground! Your nutty professor was studying how surface water flows into subterranean water networks. And if they weren't connected, he was trying to find ways to merge them! Force the connection! The data program pointed me right directly frickin' to it, but I let my biases trump the computer. Look at this!" Mary Lee ran the mouse over a large block of information on the screen, grayed it out, and then pulled it into another table to paste.

"Santiago, Chile. Two thousand seven. Geologists enjoy a long hike up into the southern Andes, where they plan to finish their rock formation research near this glacier lake in the Bernardo O'Higgins National Park. They'd just been there two months earlier. They round the corner of the trail and stand there, stunned. The caldera's lake is *gone.* A hundred-thirty-foot-deep, five-acre lake—bone dry! A warm summer melted more mountain snow than usual. They theorized that either an earthquake or the increased water pressure of the high runoff volumes punched a hole in this ice shelf on the bottom of the lake. The hole is no bigger than a community pool drain, but the force of the water tears it open. The whole lake goes down a tunnel into a subterranean river. That's a billion gallons of water—*poof*!"

Cole started scribbling notes onto the flattened inside of a used waffle box sitting in the recycling bin.

"Crater Lake sits on top of a volcano, just like the one in Chile. Does it have a network of underground water tributaries, too?"

Mary Lee was firing up multiple computer monitors and creating screen grabs to her personal laptop.

"There's scant documentation. Crater Lake is perched on an active volcano, so scientists assume the magma is too close to the surface to allow significant water flows underground. It would turn into vapor. However, Dr. Dell did extensive research on something called the Western Subsurface Drainage Network. It's mostly creepy UFO-type conspiracy crap, but let's assume for a moment there is a shred of truth there. In the late 1800s, gold miners were crawling through every cave from here to Arizona, looking for the mother of all treasures. Several journals documented extensive underground tunnels full of deep-flowing rivers. The lore says Hades' tributaries ran like the five fingers of a hand under the Mojave Desert, the Grand Canyon, Zion Canyon, the Carson sinkholes, and far below the Columbia River. They flowed through all the major aquifers on the West Coast, creating a churning movement through the larger bodies of subterranean lakes. All the water eventually ends up in the Pacific Ocean."

Before Mary Lee could finish the next sentence, a piercing audible alarm and a fast-blinking dazzling light had Nolan and Cole covering their ears and eyes.

"What the heck is that!" Cole shouted at the top of his lungs.

Mary Lee walked over and punched off the alert.

"Sorry, guys. That has nothing to do with our project. That's my curtain call—a little reminder how I earn my obscenely high salary. It's that loud so I can hear it when I'm out fishing or gardening. The Chinese keep trying to get into Microsoft's developing design cloud. Persistent suckers. My cyber security contract with Mr. Gates has me working at all hours, twenty-four seven. I have about sixty seconds to counter their wormhole or they start stealing some of the most profitable coding innovations on the planet. When I've defeated the enemy of our free-market system, I'll log more of the data mining on N-5-G. Give me a couple hours, will ya?"

Cole kissed her on the cheek and headed for the door, Nolan on his heels. Seconds later, they were tearing down the river road, the GPS set to Crater Lake.

Chapter 31

The chop-chop of firefighting helicopter blades echoed off the rock walls surrounding Crater Lake, beating the foggy air like meringue before whipping it to nothingness. The air temperature had dropped about thirty-five degrees as the sun sank behind the rock rim around the ultramarine waters, but Dr. Dell ignored the cold and remained on the deck of his pilfered research vessel wearing only a T-shirt and jeans. He couldn't remember the last time he felt cold or hot, or anything at all.

The *Elliot Bay* was easy to steal. Seventy feet long, with twin CAT 700-horsepower engines and about 600 square feet of open work area, she was a perfect fit for the mission. All summer, local colleges had used the boat to collect samples of algae. It was a popular excursion for the older male professors. Life on the lake could get awfully warm, and the young female biology students generally wore short shorts or bikinis.

Dr. Dell didn't have to wait for the ranger station attendant to provide him a research boat. Once she said there were still some available, he knew that the boats hadn't yet been put in storage for the winter. He had watched the dock from the nearby woods, looking for any movement on the *Elliot Bay* before he boarded. As it bobbed up and down, all appeared quiet. Anyone sleeping aboard would have fast become fish food. Dr. Dell had found the perfect—and, he thought, ironic—weapon for pummeling a victim to death. Sticking out of his hip pocket was a Northern club he had bought at a Medford bait-and-tackle-shop sale bin. Five bucks—a hell of a deal. The short stick was wooden on the outside but hollowed out in the center and filled with lead. Fishermen used it to crush the hard skulls of Pike or Muskie after they hooked them trolling with treble-hooked spinner lures. The needle-toothed, long-bodied freshwater fish were ferocious on the bottom of the boat, slashing about and whipping up carnage at the anglers' feet till the

249

club ended the fight. Dr. Dell was disappointed that vacancy on the boat meant his would remain unstained with the protein of human blood. He looked at his watch. Twenty-four minutes of silence. He pulled the glow sticks from the mountaineering backpack lying on the pilot's seat. Snapping the brittle plastic tubes that separated the chemicals inside the baton, he threw four of them along the baseboards of the boat. He kept one and waved it slowly over his head.

Canyon hovered over the *Elliot Bay*'s deck, inch by inch bringing Oz's bunker-busting artwork closer to the deck. The bomb was so much more massive than Dr. Dell had remembered. He shimmied around the behemoths, at times straddling the metal framework to unclip the cables.

* * *

Canyon peered out his door to see Dr. Dell's signal to pull away, then eased the bird leftward so he was no longer over the top of the boat.

The K-max twisted sideways so Canyon could look straight down from his seat into the water. He powered to full and raced across the surface, skimming close to the lake, frothing up a white foam path in a sweeping semicircle before flattening out the rotors and moving back southeast. Canyon watched the Terrain Awareness Warning System monitor as it turned an invisible radar ping into a computer-generated mountain, fast approaching and rising. He aimed the nose toward Applegate Peak and started climbing, for the first time staring up into the Milky Way. The ground proximity alarm beeped at him. Canyon ignored the reminder and enjoyed the thrill of controlling such a powerful machine. He throttled back and leveled out around 8,200 feet—barely a hundred yards above the precipice known as Dutton Cliff. The moon's reflection lit up Crater Lake. Canyon could see a rock formation sticking up out of the water like the ghost ship of some long-dead pirate. The masts were made of volcanic ejecta, the billowing sails of breccia sculpted by an angry Mother Earth four hundred thousand years ago.

Canyon followed the preset coordinates in his handheld GPS and lowered the helicopter into a small clearing near a place the locals called Sun Notch. A long-abandoned hunting cabin sat in the corner of the property. It was no doubt once filled with manly men seeking to kill a grizzly or bag a rack of moose antlers to hang above their Irish whiskey-stocked bar. A Depression-era castle now reclaimed by water and wind and termites. Canyon had chosen it because it no longer had a road connecting it to civilization. Thick patches of blackberry and nettles isolated the property from all but the hardiest or nimblest animals. Just inside the tree line, red eyes scattered as the Kmax engines thwacked to a halt. The forest was dead quiet as every creature for miles listened and assessed the threat potential of the strange whirling thing.

Canyon stepped outside and listened back, watching his breath intrude into the chilly night, until coyotes, toads, crickets, and possums resumed their movements. He made a quick visual check of the contents of his backpack while tightening the straps of a small LED headlamp around the black watch cap on his head. He felt for the indented "On" button and clicked through the cycle of lighting options: full power, flashing beacon, low-intensity red. He slid a machete into a long canvas sleeve and secured it where the pack normally held a rolled-up tent. It was about thirteen miles to the rendezvous site, with a steep climb and descent over Anderson Bluffs and around Mount Scott. Canyon could do it in his sleep. His last ultramarathon had taken him 135 miles through Death Valley in July, running on the white stripe painted on the right edge of the highway just to keep his shoes from melting. For twenty-three straight hours, he had kept pounding along, sucking down water and power gel and eating oatmeal.

Now he ran with easy grace, off road, over logs, across sharp rocks, through boggy ravines, all the while paying attention to that sixth sense in case a hungry mountain lion should start silently keeping pace. In full stride, he jumped onto a narrow animal path. Mother Earth drew blood after his first few steps as a spiked holly leaf lashed his leg. He had never felt so alive. He pushed the pace, not wanting to leave the ice truck and its precious apocalyptic contents unattended near the boat launch any longer than necessary.

* * *

Dr. Dell stared at his watch. Sunrise was in six hours. He walked over and punched up some preset codes into the boat's navigation system and brought the *Elliot Bay* out of idle. The glow of the depth finder served as his flashlight as he reviewed a small topographical map. He could hear his dogs inside the cabin, pleading for his attention. Their cries reminded him of his own painful whimpers while in juvenile lockdown at 13 years old. He had felt so helpless—just a boy, thrown into an unsupervised cell with near men. Beatings, rape, laughing. Beatings, rape, laughing. They were so strong, and he so weak. *Not today.*

The boat sliced along at three knots until Dr. Dell could see the bottom of the lake grow shallow as he approached the Merriam Cone, an underwater hill created by a bubble of lava. He steered eastward, staying in a deep channel off Palisade Point for forty-five more minutes. The boat moved at about the correct speed for trolling for salmon—a vicious sport that he would rather he had never seen. He couldn't shake the sound of his father's voice, chastising him for reading books when he should be making sure the herring on his line was floundering at the perfect depth to attract the eye of a chinook or a pink. Dr. Dell did feel a pang of remorse over the certain death of millions of fish and other tiny creatures that lived in or around Crater Lake.

They were carpetbaggers anyway, brought here by humans, never supposed to be here. The purity of earth was going to be restored.

Dr. Dell knelt and cracked open the tiny cabin near his feet. His canine companions raced onto the deck, then stopped in mid stride to press their noses to the metal of the bomb. They recognized the combination of smells: Oz and nitrates, from the warehouse. The hair on the scruff of their necks rose as they backed up, awaiting the next command. Dr. Dell shuffle-stepped along the starboard edge of the hull until he could reach the gray metal box hanging from a triangular hydraulic hoist. He pressed the lever down to slowly lower the ship's rigid-hulled Zodiac inflatable boat into Crater Lake. His sleeve got wet while he tied it to an eyebolt off the stern diver's deck.

"You two aren't going to be much help," he said.

Both dogs wagged their tails and inched near the dark, cold water lapping between their paws and the bouncing edge of the small boat. Dr. Dell French-kissed them both and scratched their ears.

"Don't be chicken. Jump!"

In a leap of faith, they landed safely and dry, skidding to a stop just short of the twin 200-horsepower engines hanging off the stern. They grinned toothy grins back toward their master.

"Good boys. Stay put until I join you. Okay, no turning back now," he said softly to himself as he swung the now empty Zodiac netting over the center of the torpedo shell.

Dropping one side of the cradle off the frame, he tucked it under the bomb's belly, careful to avoid tearing the limp nylon ropes by keeping them in front of the sharp homemade metal fins. He pulled a long-written checklist from his pocket. Oz had embedded a touch-screen laptop into the center tail section, sealing the edges with clear silicone. A twenty-key alphanumeric launch code fired up the bombs, batteries, and electronic functions. It hummed like a cranky streetlight.

Dr. Dell shivered, though he couldn't be sure the cold night air was to blame. He methodically marked off items one through seventeen, then got to work. *Input water depth. Lock navigation system. Solder shut cavity door. Push zero, zero, eight—wait for the yellow light— then hold down "Enter" on the remote control for ten seconds. Extend the reception antenna. Twist fuel cells on the belly two full rotations . . .*

With each step, he felt more like a soldier going to war. The pride and passion and sense of danger welling up inside made his heart race. The motorized pulley and the sling snugged against the underside of the bomb creaked under the strain of the enormous weight, but the underpowered hoist engine managed to raise the heavy device without failing. Inch by inch, it rose high enough to clear the gunwale.

After turning off the research craft's lights, engine, and navigational beacons, Dr. Dell grabbed everything he could find and slid it starboard. Gas cans, iron skillets, anchor, boxes of maps, television, refrigerator—anything that would start the *Elliot Bay* listing to that side. When the boat looked like an America's Cup sailing yacht cutting across a thirty-knot wind, he untied the Zodiac, with his dogs aboard it, and pushed it a safe distance away. They whined and howled, confused. Dr. Dell pushed the button on the cradle control to swing the bunker buster out over the water, and as it reached its outward limit, he released the tension on the lines. The explosive device plunged into the water, pulling the *Elliot Bay* onto its side as the cables paid out and caught. The boat flipped with violent force.

Dr. Dell jumped and swam to the drifting Zodiac to join his barking, whining dogs. The *Elliot Bay* belched air as the rudder surfaced and pointed toward Deneb, the tail star of Cygnus, the Swan.

By the time Dr. Dell pulled himself aboard the Zodiac and changed into loose-fitting military-style dungarees and a hooded sweatshirt, the research vessel was silent and still, floating bottom-up. Its brace of homemade bombs dangled in the net just below the surface, waiting to be cut loose for their free fall into the seventh-deepest freshwater abyss on the planet.

Dr. Dell raced the Zodiac back to the Cleetwood Trail boat ramp. As he approached the dock, he could tell that the tall, lanky shadow waiting at the end was his ever-faithful acolyte. He stepped out of the Zodiac and hugged Canyon for an uncomfortably long time before speaking.

"It is so good to hold you, my friend. I am truly sorry Oz and that idiot Zander tried to kill you. Oz thought it was the right thing for the group's survival and success, so I cannot fault him for his loyalty. Apparently, you didn't have too much trouble killing him?"

"Surprise has always been the best advantage in battle. Oz hesitated a fraction of a second—I think because his mind was telling him I was just an apparition. How did the torpedo setup go?"

"Fantastic. The ship is serving as a bobber, and with its low profile, there is no way anyone can see it from shore. As soon as the sun comes up and you can get your TV pal Colton Wiley down here with a camera, we can burn the name Animal Liberation Brigade into the minds of everyone on this planet for the short remainder of their existence."

Canyon beamed with pride. "Biomechanics was my best subject in school, but I also got an "A" in theater production."

He checked his new burner cell phone; it had one bar. Perfect. He dialed.

Cole picked up right away. "Blocked numbers always intrigue me," he said. "Friend or foe? Cop or crook? I can't resist letting them go to voice mail."

Canyon spoke quietly and quickly, hoping the poor signal would throw in some static for dramatic effect.

"I've been trying to warn you about N-5-G and H_2O, but now it's too late. I haven't seen anything on the news about these animal terrorists. Now they're going to do something really bad. You can't stop this disaster now."

Cole no doubt perked up, instantly recognizing the voice. "For the record, I'm not responsible for stopping disasters. I report on them. Calm down. Lay out what you know. Stop being so secretive and maybe I can help."

Canyon didn't want to be questioned. "Meet me at Crater Lake at the picnic tables on Pumice Point in five hours. Unless you're a moron, you're already somewhere in western Oregon following leads. Bring a camera. Can you make it by seven a.m.?"

"If I don't sleep again, yeah. It's the middle of the night. You know this, right?"

Canyon started to answer, almost falling for Cole's smooth, subtle attempts to personalize and extend the conversation.

"Please, Mr. Wiley. Hurry. There's a lot at stake." Canyon hung up.

He looked at Dr. Dell. "He doesn't have a clue he's been used."

Dr. Dell gave an approving nod. "In 1934, Hitler and the Nazi Party needed Leni Riefenstahl to document their powerful message. Today, Colton Wiley will shoot the final scene of our *Triumph des Willens*.

Despite having run more than a half marathon through the mountains, Canyon felt energized. Waiting for Dr. Dell, he had eaten two protein bars and downed a large bottle of

Gatorade left for him on the front seat of the old grocery store truck. He studied Dr. Dell's journal. It was filled with chemical formulas, math equations, and testing observations. Canyon didn't see any mistakes. The Sugar looked like the perfect bioweapon. Still, one issue was nagging at him, and he had no fear of sharing his only concern with Dr. Dell.

"H_2O, my friend, we reviewed Oz's bomb-making résumé together. He was a pro. He was the perfect choice to create our wormhole into the subterranean water system. Every explosive mixture looks right. The force perspectives are spot-on. And yet . . ."

Canyon let Dr. Dell finish the sentence.

". . . and yet, *if,* for any reason, Oz's bomb doesn't cause the right amount of destruction to the bottom of the lake, and *if* it doesn't fully crack a hole through to the next layer of earth, and *if* it doesn't flush every drop of our poison down a whirlpool drain into the underground series of rivers, our plan will be exposed before it kills anyone. I know. I don't like ifs, either. I have the same concern, albeit small."

Canyon stood quietly while Dr. Dell continued.

"The bunker-buster concept should work even better underwater than if it were dropped from the air. We're going to guide the torpedo down to the deepest part of the lake's bottom. When it explodes downward with all that force, it will disintegrate the thin layer of soft lava rock and create deep fissures. For a split second, thousands of tons of water pressure will move away from the spot in a series of compression waves. A steam void will make a bubble—hot gases expanding outward. Then it will reverse direction with disproportionally high force, like turning on a giant vacuum pump. The pressure of the bomb alone should break a significant hole through to the underground voids and waterways beneath Crater Lake but add the heavy weight of water at that depth, as well as all that rock, and you have catastrophic failure of the caldera. The entire mass displaced by the explosion will come streaming back to a tiny area, all of it pressing hard to escape. The hole should grow proportionally. What may start at the size of my fist will expand to the size of a bus as the layers crumble."

Canyon waited a moment, then added his two cents.

"I think it would be safer to wait and see if the bomb cuts through the lake's shell before floating our DNA-manipulator ice capsules in the water. Your calculations show that the draining could take several hours. If the explosion works and we see the vortex start the lake water rotating counterclockwise, then we can release all the Sugar into the lake. I did some reconnaissance. There's a big flat area near the top of Sun Notch, to the side. I think twenty-five or thirty miles an hour will send the truck through the barrier, off Dutton cliff, and clear into the water a couple of thousand feet below. There's also a workable spot on the west side of the lake, at Devil's Backbone. A thousand-foot rock chute there looks like a slide at a water park. Our scuba-shaped ice packs would slide down from the top and right into the water. So would the entire truck, for that matter.

Dr. Dell jumped back into the conversation.

"The impact would fillet the vehicle's tin shell wide open. The ice blocks float, then get sucked down the drain almost intact from that point, still frozen. Less melting means more dispersion of high concentrations of the Sugar over a wider area underground. Some of those capsules might make it damn near to the Pacific Ocean before they melt. Then we have to extra surprise inside too, eh my friend?"

"Oh yeah. We do," said Canyon with a mischievous smile. "But, worst case, if the explosion is a failure, we can still slip out of here, hopefully with our bioweapons intact, and try another entry point. Below the Amazon River flows the longest underground waterway in the world. That'd be a pretty cool backup plan. If the bomb fails and we've already put all our Sugar in one place, this isolated lake will just hold it all in. There are no humans up here, and nobody pulls water from this lake to drink. It would only serve as a giant testing lab for the government to figure out our formulas and come up with an antidote. And that, my friend, would be the end of ALB and our human-free utopia."

Dr. Dell didn't love the idea of separating the catastrophic events, but his closest adviser and colleague had a good point.

"I hear you. Let me think. It's time to send the 'go' signal to Spirit in Russia and Billy Goat in Ogallala. It will be the most glorious sunrise ever!"

Chapter 32

"Jess! Get up! Out of bed! I need you, man. Put on that funny hat with the leather earflaps and fire up that big metal bird you have on your back lawn!"

Jess Teeter was used to having Cole ask for chopper time at odd hours, but this was ridiculous.

"Cole. I've been to court ten times with my neighbors over the noise ordinance. The judge finally ruled in my favor, saying I could fly the station helicopter home, but I can't operate it after midnight or before six a.m. I love not commuting in a car. Having all that traffic hell below me instead of in front of me is dreamy. Please don't make me lose such an awesome privilege!"

"Come on, bro! That neighbor on the right is a crooked contractor. He takes fifteen grand promising to renovate a kitchen, then spends the money on a new bobcat and leaves the kitchen in shambles. He has no shame. One call from me, and he's not going to complain. And that couple below you run a fake pharmacy without permits. Nolan here is a federal agent—not a real cop, but kind of. He flashes his badge and they piss themselves. And the angry retired guy two doors down is one signature away from an involuntary seventy-two-hour psych evaluation. (The medical director at Western States Mental Hospital owes me one.) Come on, Jess. Time to fly. I really, *really* need you!"

"Okay, okay. Where'm I going?" Jess asked as he turned on his bedside table lamp and shoved a pair of drugstore glasses over his nose.

"Crater Lake. I need beauty shots but keep your eye out for anything strange. I've finally figured out what these animal terrorists want to do. Nolan called Homeland Security with our theory. They didn't laugh out loud, but they didn't exactly put it on the top of their to-do list.

Said they'd check into our theory right after the two tips they'd received about Bigfoot. I have the power to make them listen by warning the public."

"And what do I need to be warned about?" Jess asked out of obligation.

"Don't drink the water, man. If it's not in a bottle in your fridge right now, don't drink it."

Jess was wide awake. "And you're going to tell everyone on the West Coast that tonight on the news?"

"Yep."

"Holy shit, Cole. The panic that will create is beyond comprehension. Are you sure?"

"There are still some missing puzzle pieces, including the precise stage this plan is in, but if I'm scared to drink from the tap, how can I not share that with my audience? Get to the Crater Lake area. I'll be nearby, so just hit me up when you're close. We'll shoot some video. I'm going to need a ride back to Seattle to start putting together the biggest story ever—not just of my career, but maybe in history. It's big, man. Really big. Every second is critical."

Cole shifted his attention to Nolan.

"Okay, Mad Max, drive like the wind! It's time to wake up a couple of television newsrooms, too. There's a twenty-four-hour cable station in Medford we have a video partnership with. It's only about two hours to Crater Lake from there. It's three in the morning now. That gives me almost two hours to start slamming elements of tonight's investigation into a decent video editor before going to meet Mr. Charming at the picnic area. I know that look. This isn't just for me, dude. You need a shower and some of that eye-popping coffee those overnighters drink. Then you gotta get on the horn to those pinheads in D.C. Push them to finish analyzing Dr. Dell's computer data. Push them to get you the toxicology results for the two initial arson victims. Push them to do more than just sending a frickin' e-mail to each of the fifty states' emergency management division, asking them to be extra alert for suspicious people around dams and water towers. Are you kidding me? An *e-mail*? Every time I go to Grand Coolie Dam, there are, like, two dozen fishermen standing on top of it and another seventy-five people taking a tour inside the walls of the thing! An alert isn't going to stop the Animal Liberation Brigade."

Nolan pulled into the Cable 53 parking lot. Cole stopped ranting and went right back to lightening the mood.

"Medford-Klamath Falls is what they call this market in the TV world. It's bigger than Lubbock, Texas, and smaller than Duluth, Minnesota. If you work here, you're either right out of college or a demoted journalist who got caught jacking off in a state park undercover sting with his pants around his ankles."

"I'll make sure to avoid eye contact with anyone older than twenty-three."

"You got the right idea, Smokey."

Cole launched through an employee-only door as if he owned the place. Following the sound of police scanner radios, he quickly found the assignment desk editor and introduced himself.

"Sorry to bug you. My name is Colton Wiley. I'm the investigative reporter at your affiliate station up in Seattle. Mind if I take up some space in an empty edit bay for a while?"

"I know who you are." The editor was a bit grumpy, but overnight desk duty did that to everyone. "I've seen some of your stories on the satellite feed. Make yourself at home. I only have one reporter here and she's out on a bridge closure. The place is yours."

"You got a shower?" Cole added, remembering Nolan was standing behind him.

262

"Down that hall and to the right, through the makeup room." The assignment editor pointed while cradling a receiver to his ear.

Cole didn't waste any time. He loaded pictures of Dr. Dell, Oscar McKinsey, and police artist renditions of several other suspected ALB members seen around Willow House in Keizer. He lightened the veterinarian's security camera photos, added a circular border to resemble a lens, then created a fake camera pan and push to enlarge Dr. Dell's image. He didn't know the names of the Russian woman or the Hispanic man who were part of the Willow House group, but letting the public know their general descriptions might help jog a viewer's memory. Cole figured that even if ALB members didn't have the means to pull off their grand poisoning scheme, simply *talking* about such an attack on civilization was enough to send them all to prison forever. And having a few million TV viewers on the lookout for them would certainly limit their movements and opportunities. At a minimum, Cole could craft his investigation into a story about the international manhunt under way for members of an active terror cell. He could hit a higher profile by tossing in the group's ties to a couple of murders. In order to hit a grand slam, he had to confirm that the Animal Liberation Brigade had crafted a weapon of mass destruction and was ready to use it. He knew he didn't quite have those facts yet, so organizing and prepping the material he had gathered so far was the best use of his limited time.

He stuck three sixteen-megabyte memory cards into three separate editing-suite readers and started downloading all his raw video. The system would regenerate HD-quality pictures in a tenth the time it took to shoot the video, then store them in little snippets. Every time he pushed the record button on the camera while recording in the field, the computer read it as the length of the clip. He electronically grabbed every file, then, over a series of network hard drives, pulled them all into one place.

Cole created five different sequences from the raw video, trimming extraneous material and selecting a few choice interview sound bites. He labeled the first sequence "CABIN_ARSON." It was only a minute's worth of material, containing images of a dirty, moon-shaped N5G necklace, a pair of bright yellow body bags, a photo from murder victim April Slade's high school yearbook, five shots of the burned cabin, a broken glass beaker, and a portion of Nolan's interview. Nolan looked rugged but professional. He was framed in a medium shot, kneeling next to some still-smoldering rubble. You could see the soot-covered latex gloves on his hands as he pointed to the crime scene.

Nolan looked straight into the camera on his taped interview, getting right to the point. "The days of 'do no harm' are over. Some members of the animal rights movement earned their terrorist designation today. The United States Forest Service will commit every resource at its disposal to make sure the persons behind this atrocious act are caught and punished."

Nolan, who had been quietly watching from the edit room doorway, stepped closer, smelling like Irish Spring soap. He patted Cole on the shoulders.

"I seriously appreciate you picking the one sound bite in which I didn't sound like a stammering idiot. Thanks."

"Not hard to do. It's a kick-ass clip," Cole replied, glancing at the dwindling time. "Grab a chair and watch the master."

He labeled the next sequence "OZ_HOUSEFIRE."

"So close to getting killed. Pretty cool," was all Nolan said as Cole electronically bookmarked two additional pieces of video. The first was a longer uncut clip from Cole's handheld camera as the two of them knocked on the rental house door and entered the kitchen. The microphone picked up the sound of dripping liquid, some swearing, then a loud explosion.

The video between "Shit!" and the big boom, looked like something from *The Blair Witch Project* as Cole ran for his life. The lens picked up the image of Nolan rolling over on the lawn to look at the flames, then stringing together an impressive line of swearing worthy of a long-haul truck dispatcher.

"Not quite as eloquent on that interview. I'll bleep out that those swear words later."

The only other image Cole placed in the sequence was a long wide shot of the house fire roaring into the sky as Portland's finest scrambled to contain it with torrents of hydrant water.

The third sequence, "EVERGREEN_SWAT," started with SWAT guys hammering holes in a building. The video clip ended with a still shot of an ash-colored bone.

"Hey!" Nolan stopped Cole. "I thought that went to Homeland Security on the raw tape I shot and then handed over to them."

"It did. I grabbed a screen capture from the live feed when I saw the clip of the girl's partially burned remains. My computer automatically saved it as a JPEG file. The moving video is too grotesque, anyway. For God's sake, do her parents know yet?"

"Good question. I'll call the Thurston County medical examiner and ask before you go beaming the information to the world. I can just picture Dad and Mom watching the news with friends, expecting to see some fluff package on college friends handing out 'missing' flyers. I'm sure they're still hoping that any second, their kid'll come stumbling home from an unscheduled long weekend getting wasted at a Dave Mathews Band concert at the Gorge Amphitheater. Then old Colton Wiley comes on TV with an exclusive: SWAT team finds incinerated human bones ten feet from where little Betty Boops' backpack and broken glasses were found. Hm-m-m. Who might the bones belong to? Let's try to avoid that."

Cole ignored his pal. He had only ten minutes left before they had to hightail it to Crater Lake for a meeting with Mystery Man. He jammed a thumb drive into the port—his own personal stash of archived footage of animal rights actions: spray-painted barns, WTO protesters kicking in bank windows, smashed condo lights near turtle hatchery sand beds, a couple of arson fires, and a logging road sit-in. He deftly manipulated two shots of an anonymous pair of hands flipping the pages of an underground newspaper, the *Final Nail*. Finally, he linked up an audio file from Rammstein, a heavy-metal band popular with young anarchists. Cole set aside the hidden camera footage of Big Vasil but created a "Misc" file and threw in a couple of other things he didn't expect to use in the first series of investigative stories. It was always smart to keep the video organized in case the rest of the week really went to hell. The final sequence contained grainy file video of Lake Baikal in Russia, the trooper's murder scene and funeral, random clips of water towers, drinking water running out of a kitchen tap, and a sign that read "Department of Homeland Security." Using a FireWire, he dumped the entire load back into his laptop and headed toward the door with a quick thank you wave to the assignment desk.

While driving toward Crater Lake, Cole strategized with Nolan on how best to physically approach the subject who had been calling Cole with obscure tips. The informant obviously knew more than he was saying. Nolan thought it best to take the guy into custody and let the FBI sort out the truth. Cole argued that if the source was indeed a guilt-ridden member of the N5G plot, he'd probably lawyer up immediately. His silence could cost more lives. Cole thought he could get the guy to tell him details of the operation if the guy knew he could walk away and disappear into the woods.

The brainstorming session threw every scenario onto the table. Could Nolan pretend to be a station producer and walk up with Cole? Should he hide behind a rock? Would an undercover camera be discovered? If Nolan decided to arrest him, did he have to read a terrorist his Miranda rights? What if the source was acting under duress—say, knew that if he got caught passing on secrets, they would kill his kids? Ideas went around and back and around again. In the end, the investigative reporter and the federal arson investigator decided that the simple truth was going to have to do the trick, no matter the consequences.

Cole texted Montana. He knew that to mark his messages, she had downloaded a special alert ring tone of a lion roaring.

The text read: *"FILL YOUR SUV WITH CASES OF WATER. BUY ME SOME AMMO. ANIMAL TERROR MISSION IS TO TAINT SUPPLY. LOVE YOU. NEWS AT 5."*

Chapter 33

Nolan couldn't help but gawk in awe at the sight of Crater Lake as they got on Rim Drive. The lake's glassy surface glimmered in the dawn light. Despite its twenty square miles of surface, the surrounding canyon walls' crimson reflection near shore gave it a quaint, puddle-like appearance. Cole thought it would be fun to see how many times a flat stone would skip toward the center before it sank.

A heavy layer of frost covered the tops of the trees and softened the pink of the phlox growing along the road. The sun had inched up but wasn't actually going to shine—just radiate enough to remind everyone that it existed and would be back sometime in May. Nolan slowed down for a hiker walking her pet husky past a "no pets" sign at the entrance to Watchman Tower. Ivory-colored dacite boulders the size of hay barns framed the trail that led to a popular overlook. Out of good habit and training, Cole slid the clip out of his Kahr nine-millimeter even though he knew that it was still full, then slapped it back in and strapped the weapon to his ankle. Neither spoke as they drove past Hillman Peak and Marriam Point and into the nearly empty parking lot next to the meeting place.

"Cell phones don't work here," Nolan cautioned Cole. "I'm assuming that's not random."

"Probably not. You ready?"

"Yep. No worries. We're only going to have a casual chat with a dedicated animal lover, right?"

"Well, maybe. Ted Bundy was an animal lover, so I'm not sure how you want me to answer that."

* * *

Wendell Canyon lay on his belly under a small lava outcropping, watching with binoculars as his prey prepped for their encounter. He hadn't expected Cole to arrive alone. Chivas had rigged up an elaborate series of tracking devices, phone bugs, and computer keystroke-capturing devices on all Cole's electronics months earlier. Chivas and other ALB members had gathered video of Cole working and dining with his girlfriend. They grabbed up every scrap of information, court record, and Internet rumor to be found concerning Colton Wiley and tracked every one of them to its source. None of the stuff that looked bad on the surface was true. He was so squeaky clean, Dr. Dell had made them go back and double-check. The state politician's suit against Cole for defamation came unraveled during depositions, when the politician admitted to a special fondness for teenage boys.

Accusations that Cole was a sleazebag and a criminal trespasser for secretly videotaping rats at a popular steakhouse turned out to be false when the restaurant's assistant manager later admitted to shooting the video and leaking it to Cole. "Liar," "manipulator," "bastard," "user," "lowlife"—all these terms were used to describe Cole, but none matched reality. It appeared that all the rumor and innuendo against him was hatched by slick lawyers and public relations companies merely attempting to defend the indefensible by attacking the messenger. In the end, of all the reporters that ALB had secretly tested for this job, Colton Wiley was the hands-down winner. His award-winning reporting on animal issues and abuses made him credible to the movement. If he said it on TV, the public would believe it. Few would think he faked a story. If he said aliens had landed, the public would likely believe it. He was well spoken and ruggedly attractive, and he came with a built-in loyal audience matched only by a few talking heads at the network level. Nobody could possibly deny the Animal Liberation Brigade credit for creating the planet's greatest single moment—not if they had Colton Wiley telling the story of the day animals inherited the earth from the humans.

Cole and Nolan walked through the empty park to a green picnic table by a cold fire pit with an open rusty grill. Canyon let them wait several minutes before he walked out of the trees. He created some intentional noise by breaking a thumb-size stick between his foot and a rock. Pretending to be nervous, he looked around in every direction, aware that Cole and Nolan were judging him every step of the next fifty yards.

"I thought you'd come alone. Who is this?" Canyon asked, expecting some bullshit story or other. None came.

"This is a federal arson investigator," Cole replied.

Nolan flipped open a black leather case, revealing an embossed eagle flying through flames.

Cole continued. "Don't run off. If he was going to arrest you, he'd have already done it. I'm not going to lie. He wants to know if ALB killed a couple of college kids near Mount St. Helens earlier this month. I want to know if Dr. Hadar O'Dell is some psycho with delusions of grandeur. And we both want to know if this animal terror group can really sink poison into the center of the earth."

"Yes, yes, and yes."

Canyon overenunciated the words, and with the last "yes," he slid a four-inch skeletonized dagger out of his coat sleeve and drove it deep between Nolan's bottom two ribs, nicking the left lung after slipping through the diaphragm. With his other hand, he aimed the barrel of a "Baby Glock" at Cole's chest to freeze any attempt to intervene. Nolan doubled over in pain but kept his wits about him. He slid his holster snap back with his thumb, but before he could draw, Canyon sliced through the tendon attached to Nolan's elbow. The entire arm fell limp. Nolan had plenty of fight left in him and threw a roundhouse kick at his attacker's ribs. Canyon blocked it, turned, and fired a single shot at near point-blank range into Nolan's ankle.

"Fight's over!" Canyon declared. "Colton, put your piece on the table; then tie this around his lower leg. He's not supposed to bleed to death for some time. That's not to imply I actually give a shit about Mr. Burke's life—I don't."

* * *

Cole watched for a momentary lapse of concentration from his source. He so badly wanted to fire the Kahr into the middle of the guy's forehead, but he had no chance. He set his gun on the picnic table and tied a tourniquet just above the swell of Nolan's calf.

Cole stood back up, palms up. "What the fuck was that? And, by the way, how do you know *his* name?"

"Always the reporter, asking questions," said a raspy, high-pitched voice behind Cole. "I guess I'd have been disappointed with anything less."

Cole turned to see a short, thin man with wild, long black hair and a flattish nose. He looked intelligent. Given the setting, and the grainy pictures from the vet's office, he had to be the man known as H_2O.

"We know an awful lot about you, Mr. Wiley. I remember the first time I saw you on TV. Purple tie and dark gray suit. I'm sure you'd been on the air many times before, but I never cared to watch the news—too much violence. But on this particular night, I'd seen a promotion for one of your investigations. You made me cry. Not just a little, either. I bawled for hours. You showed home video of some men—state lawmakers on a hunting trip to Canada, I think—killing a mama bear. They then kicked her two confused young cubs to death as they tried to come lie by her dying side. A thud, followed by some agonized animal whimpering, followed by a thud, repeated until the only audio that remained was the laughter of those drunken pricks."

Cole looked down into the brown eyes staring into his from less than a yard away.

"I did what I could to make it right. After I aired that footage, a judge didn't have any choice but to give them the maximum jail term: three hundred sixty-three days each. Though I suppose a lifetime of public ridicule, joblessness, and not getting laid is punishment, too. You must be H_2O."

"I am. Your friend there is going to bleed to death. I'd say you have about two hours to get him to the hospital. Canyon here is fairly proficient at finding internal organs. The good news is that Mr. Burke can't walk. That might prolong the time you have to accomplish your task, but still, I wouldn't dawdle. You never know."

"'*Dawdle*'? Who says that? Let me see your teeth. You British?" Cole pushed, looking for a way to control the conversation and get into the mind of his nemesis. "If you're going to pretend to be the human version of Bagheera, ruling over the animal jungle, you'd better toughen up the vocabulary. How do you know Nolan's name?"

Dr. Dell sat down calmly at the picnic table, elbows on the lacquered top, fingertips steepled at his lips. Canyon remained standing, arm straight out, the handgun still trained on Cole's temple.

"Mr. Wiley. It's time for you to set up your camera and conduct the most important interview of your life. I will answer any question. You ask, I will provide. There is only one caveat. You have twenty minutes. I'm sure you can appreciate that I have some important matters to attend to. Canyon will make sure you make good choices as you go back to your truck for the gear. Time has started. The twenty minutes includes setup, so I suggest you move with some alacrity."

Cole turned and sprinted to the parking lot. He had no idea where the keys were, so he picked up a rock and smashed the back window and unlocked the doors. He stuffed a microphone, video chip, headphones, and two fully charged batteries into a bag and picked it up in his left hand. He slung the tripod over the right shoulder while carrying the video camera in his right hand. In a rapid series of clicks, Cole had the camera set up level with Dr. Dell's face. He propped a directional microphone over his backpack, aimed at his subject's mouth, and plugged the cord into the audio 1 jack. Slipping on the headphones, he snapped his fingers.

"Check, check. We're set."

Cole looked at Nolan and gave him a reassuring nod. Nolan grimaced as he did his best to slow the bleeding from the torso wound with his own palm. Cole hit the record button and looked into the viewfinder to make sure the red light was blinking, and the dual sound meter was moving up and down with the breeze.

"Name and title?" were the first questions Cole asked every interview subject.

"Dr. Hadar Orin O'Dell. Microbiologist and cofounder of an extreme animal rights organization known to many as the Animal Liberation Brigade"

"What's N-5-G?"

"It's a project nickname. Like a military operation. ALB is a small, dedicated group of activists who believe the time has come for animals to inherit the earth once again. The top-of-the-food-chain mentality of humans has created so much suffering, death, and humiliation for other creatures that the only solution is the extinction of *Homo sapiens.*"

"Sounds like a lot of crap. There are many other solutions. You're talking genocide? Really? How many people would you like to kill?"

"All of them."

"Including yourself?"

"I don't mind dying for this cause."

"You didn't answer the question. Are you on a suicide mission?"

"No. Project members will survive so we can make sure humans don't make the same mistakes in the future."

"So, you aren't too sure that your plan to kill *all* of them will work?"

"You asked how many I would like to kill. I said all. The truth is, we've done the math and applied the proper science, and our calculations are that we can kill at most several billion people over the course of about two years. Those left will be worried about basic survival, not which zoo to visit on the weekends."

"Two or three billion people? Dead? You sound nuts. How are you going to pull that off?"

Dr. Dell gritted his teeth at the "nuts" editorial but continued.

"In the coming hour, ALB members, positioned in strategic locations, are going to unleash a . . . I'll say '*toxin,*' for lack of a better term. It's really a DNA manipulator. A bio weapon of unimaginable magnitude. Fresh water will be undrinkable. There is no antidote. No medicine. No cure. And no way to detect the presence of the substance. Upon ingestion, death is almost immediate. I have nicknamed it 'the Sugar,' or '*El azúcar*' for its many Spanish-speaking victims-to-be. The only way to stay alive is not to drink liquids. Dehydration is a slow and painful death—one of the worst, in fact—but within a couple of weeks, that is what will kill more people than the toxin itself."

Cole shook his head, ready for an argument about common sense.

"It's impossible to contaminate every water tower, river, lake, and freshwater aquifer on this planet with such a small group of people. It's impossible to contaminate the oceans. Even if it were possible, I can think of ways to get drinking water. Collect rain in a barrel. Melt some ice from glaciers or the polar cap. Evaporate seawater and collect the condensation."

"You might be one of the few who survive, then, Mr. Wiley. You mention things that take time and reasoned thought. When a planet full of people realize, all at once, that there might not be any safe water to drink tomorrow, I guarantee, the results will be apocalyptic. I am counting on the selfishness of people and their governments to kill with far greater efficiency than my formula alone. If you think *oil* is precious, just wait."

"*How?* How are you going to pull this off?"

"Simple. By blowing holes in the surface of the earth and dropping our special poison into a vast network of underground waterways. It will ebb and flow, polluting at different rates, depending on the conditions. That's the most beautiful part of our plan. One day, a drinking water source appears safe. The next, it might kill you within a minute. Only humans are affected, so who is going to be the guinea pig? There are only so many people brave enough or foolish enough to be the king's food tester."

"So, the formula doesn't hurt animals? Are you sure? You tested the bioweapon on every single living species?"

Dr. Dell paused. He glanced at Canyon who silently reassured his leader that the interview was going exactly as they expected it would.

"You are very good at this, Mr. Wiley. At questioning people, yes, I already knew that. But I mean at trying to get me to doubt my plan. Your question isn't so much a question as much as an attempt to create uncertainty. Yes, I am positive animals will thrive. Fruit bats can lick the liquid like nectar. Your lovely cat, Mr. Wiley, can drink all the water it wants. Oh! You have made me think of something! Can you please tell your audience to free all their pets? With the owners dead, the poor things might end up trapped in some awful apartment. That would be an easily preventable crime."

"You know I have a cat. You know Nolan's name. What color underwear do I have on?"

"We needed a messenger. That is you. We've known it for a long time. I know deep down that you understand why we're taking such drastic action. We don't want money. There is no ransom. We don't want peace, nor are we looking for compromise. What we're about to do is a final act of desperation."

"For the record, I'm not interested in becoming an honorary member of your satanic cult. I can't fathom any of this. Crater Lake must be one of your targets. What are the others?"

Cole peered through his viewfinder: three minutes left.

"Good question, but I'm afraid an element of surprise is essential to the success of those missions. I can directly control only what's about to happen right here and now."

"And that is . . . ?"

"I am going to fracture the deepest crevice of Crater Lake with a bunker-busting bomb, then pour the lake's contents—and our magical toxin—into the freshwater supply of the entire western United States.

"You have someone in position to ruin the water supply for the rest of America? Okay. I know you also have that crew in Asia. Sounds like they already screwed that one up, though."

"I can assure you, the death toll in Asia and Europe will be immense." Dr. Dell looked at Cole, then straight into the camera lens.

"I need you to make sure that the future leaders of the new world know that we will always be watching. You labeled us terrorists. Now we have become what you say we are. Because of us, the mountain gorillas will be able to safely reclaim their foraging grounds from encroaching farmers. The Matschie's tree kangaroo can again roam freely in New Guinea. I'm telling everyone listening to my voice, N-5-G has a potion that will make sure humans and animals live as equals or humans won't live at all."

Cole got up from his seated position and paced a few steps behind the tripod. Nolan had stopped writhing in pain, which Cole knew was not a good thing. Dr. Dell's eyes shifted back and forth across the camera lens as he watched Cole.

"I'm not sure I want to be used to spread your message of pixie dust and animal happiness!" Cole finally shot back. "What happens if I decide to shit-can this interview; toss it in the lake? Nobody will ever know who was behind this attempt to pollute the most important resource we have."

"Time's up, Mr. Wiley. That's your last question. You will broadcast every detail of what you've uncovered here, because if you don't, the world will blame Colton Wiley for the deaths of millions of additional people. They'll whine, 'If only I had known, then I wouldn't have let my kids drink from that stream! That son-of-a-bitch TV guy *knew* but kept it a secret! Funny, huh? Those same kids will die of dehydration because their parents will prevent them from drinking water, but at least they can't blame *you*. Your information sharing will make ALB infamous, but it will also buy many people time before they die. Families can bond, as they do around a loved one with cancer. Don't they call those last days a 'celebration of life'? I believe that is the euphemism. Tell them about our plan, and they can also pray to their gods and keep hope alive. Hope that some scientist will crack the DNA coding. Hope that all their money can buy up a truckload of Gatorade and an armed security staff to protect it so they can live for a month or two instead of a few days. Hope that it rains and rains. People want to know stuff, Mr. Wiley. That's why they watch the news, right? You might as well do your job. Who knows? It really might save a few lives."

"Let's start with my friend there," Cole said. "He needs to get to the hospital. Is there something I can do to make sure that happens?"

"I have it all worked out," Dr. Dell replied as he stood and started walking back toward the parking lot. He tossed Cole a small pen. "I'm guessing your helicopter will be here any minute. Get the pilot's attention with that green laser pointer. Have him land here in the park. Load up and climb to one thousand feet. Videotape the lake for one hour; then you may leave. Don't lose focus on your rather simple mission. I don't want to see any big elevation changes or fast maneuvers. I would have already killed Mr. Burke, but that might sap your will to finish the task in front of you. And as we were just speaking about hope, I'm telling you he probably won't die within the next hour."

"And what if I decide I don't want to accept your mission?"

"Simple. Canyon here will turn the news chopper into a fiery ball of falling debris. He's as good with a rocket-propelled grenade launcher as he is with his knife."

Cole shot back, "I guess your message to the world would be toast, too. You wouldn't want that."

"Don't flatter yourself too much. My backup plan would be to use YouTube. Not the same cachet as using Colton Wiley, but effective. Good luck surviving our new world. You won't see me again."

With the push of a button, Dr. Dell rather dramatically let Cole know that the mission was a go. Dr. Dell peered out toward the middle of the lake to see a small puff of black smoke rising from the capsized *Elliot Bay*. The vessel started sinking.

"That's the first step," Dr Dell crowed. "Now I drive the bunker buster to the right depth."

From his cell phone, Dr. Dell opened an app and studied the screen while he moved his shoulders side to side, like a teen trying to jiggle a pinball machine. He was manipulating the most realistic video game Cole had ever witnessed.

Unseen, hanging underwater below the *Elliot Bay,* an engine strapped to the torpedo tubes, whined into action. As the propeller started spinning slowly the blades cut through the netting that had previously secured the Zodiac to the deck. As the boat burned, tilted, and started sinking the homemade bomb broke free from its cradle. The lopsided weight of the nose pointed the explosive downward. The props started turning at full speed, pushing the explosive payload toward the bottom of Crater Lake's deepest trench. One thousand nine hundred fifty feet to go.

Chapter 34

The noise of the KZPR helicopter was muffled by the thick foliage and damp ground. It was almost past Cole before he had a chance to pinpoint Jess's windshield with the laser. Jess felt a surge of anger, wondering who would be so careless as to tag him. For decades, only the military had access to powerful lasers; then suddenly, every drunk kid partying around a campfire in the woods by the airport had one in his pocket. Jess eased the throttle down and swung around fast so he could spot the jerk who had put him in danger of going blind. He used his thumb to trigger the record function on the gyroscope-mounted high-definition camera hanging from the bottom of the *Robinson Eurocopter.* What he saw instead reminded him of 1971. There was rarely a day when he didn't fly over a small group of embattled U.S. soldiers, waving for help in a jungle clearing. Sometimes Jess could drop in to rescue. Other times, ground fire made it impossible. Now he tried to concentrate on all the men he had saved, but what he couldn't forget were the scared faces of those he had to leave behind. Jess wondered for a second if the blood-soaked body lying in the field in front of him was an image from back then returned to haunt him, or reality. But Colton Wiley, waving a green KZPR-TV sweatshirt wildly over his head, answered that question. There was plenty of room to land.

As soon as the blades slowed enough for Cole to jump into the cockpit, he pulled up Jess's headphones and started filling him in. Jess listened to the briefing, taking mental notes. Parts of the story seemed so far-fetched, it crossed his mind that Cole was on something or had hit his head on a low tree limb. One look at Nolan's slumped and bleeding form disabused him of any such notion. There was no room in the backseat for Nolan to lie down, so the two men strapped him sideways with his leg propped up awkwardly on top of a metal bracket. Nolan was semiconscious, trying to stay awake despite the overpowering urge to sleep.

Jess watched Cole run as hard as he could back to the truck and grab the first-aid kit, two road flares, and Nolan's backup gun, tucked into a homemade holster under the driver's seat. By the time he returned to the helicopter Jess could see that Nolan was fading.

"Hey, buddy, you're in luck," he said. "Cole grabbed fifteen of those tiny Band-Aids, a pair of latex gloves, and an ounce of iodine. We don't even need to go to the hospital now!"

"Yes, we do," Nolan muttered. "If I'm ever going to pitch for the Tacoma Rainiers, I need a tune-up on this throwing arm."

Jess gave Cole some quick instructions on how to plug one side of the lung wound with a semi-inclusion dressing—a trick he had learned in Vietnam to keep a soldier breathing for a short while even if blood was filling the lung. Cole kneaded a chemical ice pack and put it on the knife wound, pressing harder on the spot than he should, thinking that pain might be the best way to keep Nolan awake.

Suddenly, the ground moved. The earth under the helicopter's footprint rose a foot, then sank, then rose and fell again. Through the noise of the idling helicopter engine, Jess felt more than heard a muffled, long-drawn-out boom. He turned to see a series of towering waves spring from the center of Crater Lake, rolling shoreward. It would be hard put to tell the difference between an earthquake and this. Cliffs of pumice, andesite, and dacite cracked and calved off into the water. Avalanches of glasslike porphyry and gray basalt ground into dark clouds as boulders and dust slid down Llao Rock, Grouse Hill, and Skell Head. The soft lava ash that had helped mold Wizard Island had managed to keep its hat shape for more than seven thousand years. Now the work of one madman and his demented disciples was undoing in mere seconds what countless volcanic eruptions, forest fires, and meteors had failed to do over millennia.

"Time to go, Cole! Cole! Get in! We are thirty seconds from needing gills!" Jess shouted over the ramped-up whine of his turbo engine. "Water's coming fast!"

Cole took a quick look around. Dr. Dell and his psycho sidekick were long gone. Hitting record on the camera, Cole jumped into the Robinson's passenger seat and hooked his leg around the seat belt strap without clipping in. He hung precariously out the open door, one foot on the landing skid, capturing the cataclysmic events unfolding around them. Grabbing his headset, he spoke, and a microphone automatically opened the internal communication line so he could speak with Jess.

"I need you to climb to a thousand feet and roll a wide shot with the mounted camera. Do a steady hover. Don't make any sudden moves, and whatever you do, don't leave this airspace and don't contact the FAA tower in Medford."

Jess was stunned. "You callous son of a bitch! I'm not hovering! I'm getting Nolan medical help, right now. No news story is worth a life. Come on, get some perspective, man!"

"I forgot to mention one teensy detail," Cole said, looking straight into Jess's eyes. "A terrorist has an RPG trained on us. You deviate from their plan, we all die. I feel like a dupe, but they set me up to carry their message to the world. I'm open to ideas."

"Crap. Heat-seeking or aim-and-shoot RPG? Did you see it?"

"No. You think the guy was bullshitting?"

"Probably not. They're easy to buy, easier to use. Here's what we do. Instead of staying in one place, I'm going to fly slowly around the rim of the lake, nose facing the center, tail toward the trees. Even though we're not staying in one spot, to the guy on the ground it will look like we're trying to get the best possible video, from all angles. I want you to use the digital zoom on that camera to scan for anything out of place on the roads or trails. Knowledge is power. Let's see if we can pinpoint that RPG's location."

The scene unfolding in front of Jess's eyes was like looking down at a hurricane forming. A whirlpool was taking shape in the middle of the lake, swirling in a counterclockwise rotation. Forty-foot waves of water from the initial blast were wiping the shoreline clean. Campsites, cars, tourist cabins, a hotel, and the main ranger station were whisked away as he watched. Visitors who came outside their tents or cabins to see what was going on were treated to one final, astonishing image just before they died. Dozens of bodies were being sucked toward what looked to Jess like the drain of a giant bathtub.

* * *

Seeing the destruction, Dr. Dell let out a rare impassioned whoop. He knew what was happening to the crumbling crust several thousand feet below Crater Lake. As he drove the ice truck at sixty miles per hour along the crest of a butte winding along the east side of the lake, he knew that Oz's explosive calculations had been perfect. The earth had cracked under the initial blast, and then the weight of water, combined with a pocket of empty space above the underground river, created inertia that was impossible to stop. The hole would grow until all the water drained from Crater Lake.

From the passenger seat, Canyon monitored the news helicopter the best he could as the truck barreled toward Dutton Cliff. Most of the road ran above the tsunami destruction zone. Occasionally, Canyon bumped into the side window as his mentor maneuvered around washed-out sections where the initial burst of water had slammed into the hills and then sucked back toward the caldera core. Dr. Dell could hardly keep his hands on the wheel as he pumped his fists with glee. His vision was becoming reality.

"Looks like our reporter-puppet is following instructions. We are going to be the most famous two people in history! Let's finish this plan and get the Sugar into the lake ASAP!"

Canyon encouraged Dr. Dell to drive even faster. "Fucking *go*! We can launch the load off the cliff right next to where I parked Oz's helicopter . . . *my* helicopter, whatever. We can be at our hidden camp before anyone even knows what hit them!"

* * *

Even through the canopy of trees that intermittently blocked his view, it wasn't hard for Cole to see flashes of yellow from a large truck speeding south on the east side of the lake.

"Hey, Jess, look to your left. Crazy guy said he was going to fracture the earth, then unleash his toxin. I have no idea how, but let's assume they haven't yet dropped that shit into the hole. That truck is the only thing out of place. Even if we're too late, we can't let these maniacs escape. Time to pucker up and see if these creeps really have a rocket! You in the mood for some combat flying?"

Jess gave a dark grin. "I'm a tad rusty on escape-and-evasion tactics for fast-moving missiles, but I'm with you on this one. We have to try something."

He pushed the engines to full throttle and veered the helicopter toward Grotto Cove. The ground beyond the lake rose fast, so Jess started climbing: two thousand . . . three thousand . . . four thousand feet. Cole had always said he wasn't afraid to die, and he was at peace with the moment, but he did feel a twinge of guilt that his thrill seeking might lead to the death of his friends. He looked over at Jess, racing ahead to find a spot in the road where they could make a stand. If they were going to break one commandment of the animal terrorists, they may as well break them all.

284

"If we're going to let them see us make a maneuver, I'm not keeping radio silence any longer," Jess growled. "We need some big guns here fast. Maybe Homeland can scramble four F-Sixteens out of McChord."

Cole gave a thumbs-up, and Jess spun his radio frequency to 121.5.

"Mayday. Mayday. Mayday. Attention McChord. Attention Kingsley Field One-seventy-third Fighter Wing. This is a KZPR-TV Robinson helicopter, located over Crater Lake, Oregon. Mayday. We have reason to believe a terrorist attack is under way. Flight crew and two passengers aboard, one injured badly by suspected terrorists. RPG suspected in area. Mayday. Contact Homeland Security. Over"

Cole continued to scan the horizon, expecting to see the orange rocket flash from the end of a shoulder-fired tube at any second. The radio was silent for a moment, then sputtered into action as a monotone voice cut through the light static.

"This is Joint Base Lewis McChord, ordering all other air traffic to maintain emergency radio silence. All channels are clear for KZPR chopper pilot."

"What's your name, pilot?" a controller drawled in a casual-sounding West Texas twang.

"Jess Teeter, sir."

"This is Airman First Class Jenkins. JBLM has a report of significant earthquake activity in the Crater Lake area. Attempts by the University of Washington team to confirm have failed. Rangers are not communicating. What are you seeing, pilot?"

Jess took a deep breath. "Sir, it might look like an earthquake, but the seismic incident was actually an explosion set off by a terror group. Crater Lake is draining fast. The bottom appears to have been cracked."

"For what purpose?" the controller responded with increasing curiosity, still unsure whether the civilian pilot might be hallucinating. Flying too high caused an oxygen shortage in the brain, which often spawned hallucinations.

"To poison as much of our fresh drinking-water supply as possible. We believe that at least two men associated with an animal rights group have some sort of bioweapon and have set off a bomb to disperse it underwater. They are still in the area. We are trying to track them but are in danger of being shot out of the sky by them. Can you send help?"

When he got back on the microphone, his calm voice gave no hint of emotion to Jess and Cole.

"Let me work on it. We don't have authorization for military intervention. It's a civilian police action until I get other orders. Calls are going out as we speak. Hang in there, chopper. You be our eyes until we can figure this out. Over."

* * *

Dr. Dell wasn't monitoring the mayday frequency, but he had an 800-megahertz police scanner clipped to the sun visor. His mind raced as he started hearing chatter between sheriff's deputies about an "explosion." All conversation to that point had been about reports of an earthquake. And then, when he heard KZPR-TV mentioned, he knew it wouldn't be long before an official emergency response headed their way. No matter. One more mile, and it would be impossible to reverse the cataclysmic chain reaction of events underground. The ice cylinders would soon deliver their deadly load to the heart of the planet. As a bonus, Colton Wiley and his friends were all going to be blown to bits. Dr. Dell could feel Canyon seething with anger to his right as they both watched the helicopter veer from its course. Canyon screamed, throwing spittle on the dashboard between the air vents in front of him.

286

"Those motherfuckers are so dead!"

* * *

As Cole watched from above, the speeding truck jerked to a stop in the middle of the roughly paved road, smoke drifting into the wheel wells. The passenger door flew open, and the tall, dark-haired young man in military fatigue pants and black jacket who had nearly killed Nolan sprinted toward the rear of the vehicle and disappeared. Jess guided the nose of the helicopter— and the mounted camera—straight at the refrigerated truck. The driver was leaning down, eyes even with his steering wheel, to get a better look at the action above.

"Cole!" Jess screamed. "Grab those road flares out of your pack. When I say 'Pop and throw,' don't hesitate. And for God's sake, get your ass strapped in. We're going roller coaster!"

From the helicopter, it wasn't hard to see what the man Dr. Dell had called Canyon was doing. He dropped a short, stubby missile into the tube and pulled back hard on a thick metal lever to seal the chamber, then stepped to the edge of a field of small lava rocks. Canyon mounted the weapon on his shoulder, pressed his finger lightly on the trigger to activate the laser scope, then seemingly took aim at the KZPR chopper's engine. The recoil pushed the tube back against him as the projectile started slow out of the barrel, then picked up speed.

"Now!" Jess screamed. There was no room for a Cy Young Award-winning Felix Hernández kind of windup. There wasn't even room to throw the flare overhand. Cole felt as if he were 10 again, holding on to a lit Roman candle at a Fourth of July picnic. He flicked it sideways, Frisbee style, spinning the fire and smoke in a rapid circle—a dog chasing its tail. He knew that Jess had no idea what kind of missile was coming at them. If it was heat seeking, the flare might buy them some time. If it was point-and-shoot, Jess had plenty of experience with avoidance maneuvers, dodging Viet Cong that jumped up from the elephant grass or paddy rice with an RPG.

Jess dived hard to the left at full speed, toward the rock rim of the lake. Cole felt momentarily weightless as his seat dropped out from beneath him. A painful reality followed the weightlessness as the seat harness straps dug deep into his flesh. Nolan's body came up and down with a loud thud but stayed in place. The Robinson's engine whined. Cole kept his head on a swivel, giving Jess play-by-play on the rocket's progress. He could see the orange trail through the glass bubble bottom between his feet.

"It's arcing away . . . it's following the flare!"

An explosion sent shockwaves beneath the rotor blades, causing a stutter but not a stall. Jess leveled out and kept to the left, flying in a wide circle over the water, then back toward the truck. Out of the corner of his eye, he could see waterfalls sluicing down giant boulders that, until this moment, had been underwater for thousands of years. Crater Lake was half empty already. By the time the news chopper was facing Dr. Dell again, The RPG had already been reloaded. Jess was guessing he had five or ten seconds before the second heat-seeking missile turned them into the *Hindenburg*. He headed straight at the truck, shortening the distance between the RPG launcher and his hot engine exhaust. He knew that the missile's computer ran a simple program to find its target, based on a heat signature, but that program didn't ramp up until the rocket reached 75 percent of its optimal speed. Military defense programmers did that so the weapon wouldn't immediately turn around and follow its own heat trail back to the operator. The rocket whizzed past Cole's door, headed out near the middle of the lake, then swooped around once it found its heat source target again.

"Incoming. Six o'clock blind!" Cole yelled. He thought he should pray, then debated the authenticity of such an act. God knew what he was. No sense lying to the Big Man this late in the game.

* * *

To Dr. Dell, it looked as though the helicopter pilot was intent on suicide. He threw the bulky truck into reverse, leaving Canyon standing alongside the road. He picked up speed. Ten, twenty, thirty miles per hour backward, using the mirror to avoid crashing. The helicopter closed in and caught the vehicle. As soon as it got over the truck the pilot opened up the aviation fuel spigots, bounced the skid rails off the top of the truck's box, then accelerated slightly and dropped his tail behind the rear fender, flying only feet above the road and inches ahead of Dr. Dell's backward escape route.

Dr. Dell looked away from the side mirror in time to see the fins of the rocket go past the top of the windshield. It found the false target the news helicopter pilot had intended: the Briggs and Stratton cooling-generator engine bolted above Dr. Dell's head.

The sound from inside the cab was deafening—literally. Dr. Dell felt his eardrums pop. Blood spattered on the windows, and it took him a second or two to realize that it was his own. He looked down at the speedometer and saw that the truck's engine was still propelling him, still running. He jammed on the brakes and threw the transmission into drive. Flames, roaring out the top of the truck, lit trees on fire while trying to consume what was left of the paint and rubber and insulation of the refrigerated truck box.

The faster Dr. Dell drove, the less he felt the heat. He knew his route: *a quarter mile to the bend in the road, an eighth of a mile to the bend in the road, and just a few more yards to the end of man.* The fire was starting to melt the capsules. They sweated away liquid, each little dewdrop potent enough to kill thousands. Dr. Dell fought hard to stay conscious long enough to achieve his goal: to drive the truck and its poison off Rim Road and down a four-thousand-foot cliff, straight into Crater Lake. He could see the spot where Canyon had removed the guard-rail and barreled toward it. Time seemed to stand still.

Dr. Dell wondered whether he had, in fact, died before plunging off the edge. He knew he should be feeling pain, but there was instead a warm calm inside. In a flash of light, he found himself staring at a vast green pasture. A kingdom of animals was communing quietly, staring at him. They sat in rows, as if at a revival, waiting for the preacher to speak. Giant loggerhead turtles grazed on long grass between the raised stage and a line of antelope. Animals of every kind had gathered here as far as he could see. This was his thanks. In his final seconds as a demonic human, Mother Nature was showing him what a martyr's paradise would look like for eternity.

A sharp crack of gunfire and the searing pain of molten lead tearing through his chest brought his eyes back into focus. In front of him was Colton Wiley, hanging out the door of a helicopter, pulling the trigger on a Glock as fast as the slide would throw a new round into the chamber. That warm feeling evaporated, and everything went black.

The truck veered off course by a few feet. The front-left fender caught a thick wooden post set in concrete, spinning the burning truck sideways, then tipping it upside down. The deceleration caused by the collision sent the truck tumbling and slamming down a rugged old lava flow before skidding off a sort of natural ski jump. The flaming mass arced downward like a big, slow meteor into what used to be Crater Lake, but there was no splash. The rapid outflow of water had left behind only a rough patch of flat, wet granite and a hundred flopping trout. From the cliff top, four-foot-long cylinders of ice slid in a glistening trail down to a pile of smoldering truck debris.

* * *

Jess opened every frequency. "Mayday. Mayday. Mayday. This is the KZPR news helicopter. I know you're listening, McChord. We have stopped the immediate terror threat, but you need to skip protocol and send every biohazard containment unit you got! I swear on the graves of my fallen friends in the Twenty-first Squadron, you do not want to be late to this game!"

"I have not yet received all the necessary clearances, pilot," the air traffic controller responded, "but I believe these may be what qualify as extenuating circumstances. You had just better be right, or my Colonel says he will make it a point to *find* you. I can't wait to hear what the hell happened out there. Ten-four. Help is en route."

Jess patched Cole through to a landline inside Homeland Security while the Air Force listened in. He gave them the bullet points of his ALB investigation. At some point, Cole heard someone say the vice president had joined the conference call. The news helicopter raced toward Medford Tricare Hospital as a small squadron of military helicopters and fighter jets screamed past them in the opposite direction. Nolan was ghost white but shivering uncontrollably, which meant he was still alive.

"Looking good, Fireboy!" Cole yelled, reaching back to pound on Nolan's good arm. "I see you're all dressed up for Halloween already. Zombie! Nice! Hang in there. Ten minutes till you get some happy drugs."

* * *

Wendell Canyon watched the F-16 fighters pass overhead. Then came a rumbling wave of CH-47 Chinooks and, soon after, droves of Humvees along the road below. Men in full combat gear began cordoning off swaths of land with yellow tape, vehicles, and sandbags. From the safety of a narrow lava cave hidden by a clump of serviceberry bushes, Canyon could see dozens of soldiers change from fatigues to all-white suits equipped with air tanks. Aides secured every arm and leg hole with thick wraps of duct tape. Less than ninety minutes after the detonation, Crater Lake was empty of water. The only liquid left was a few small pockets caught in natural rock.

"I'll be goddamned," Canyon said aloud, looking at the dry volcanic indentation, then toward the heavens. "H_2O, my friend, you didn't die in vain. Your vision was true and pure. I won't let you down."

The damp path in front of him led southeast and straight over a mountain ridge. At this point, taking the helicopter out would be suicide. There was unfinished business: *Sugar* to make and deploy. Canyon started jogging. Only a marathon away was the ghost town of Kirk, Oregon. He felt empowered knowing that Billy Goat and Spirit would follow their irrevocable orders and destroy their targets. As part of the backup plan, if Dr. Dell should fail to change the coded message hidden inside the group's secret-flower Web site, every other mission would know that was the "go" sign. It meant "Destroy. Kill at will. *We have nothing else to lose.*" In an hour, all the drinking water in the Midwest would be a deadly cocktail from Chi's work, and the population of Asia would be too terrified to take so much as a sip. And as a bonus, Colton Wiley was going to scare the living shit out of the rest of the planet by planting a seed: no one could ever again feel safe consuming a drop of liquid.

Chapter 35

The soothing *pah-toomp, pah-toomp* of steel wheels over rail joints had long since lulled Zander to sleep. Wynona watched him snoring softly, his stocking cap resting on the cold window. She was glad his beard had grown thick and dark. Very Russian-looking. A military-inspired canvas duffel bag sat snuggly between his feet.

There were only five stops on the Trans-Siberian Railway between Irkutsk and Novosibirsk, and five times, brusque security men had stopped by each set of seats in the business-class section. One had done nothing but glare. The others had stared at passports, brown cards, tickets, and driver's licenses, eyes darting between faces and the pictures pasted on the documents. Wynona shared the same story every time. Her name was Vivi Gorgon, and her husband's name was Benjamin. They were going to Moscow to meet her parents. She was Russian. He was Greek. She had met the love of her life through an ad in the back of a magazine. Wynona always smiled coyly when describing the most amazing part of their relationship: that her husband didn't speak Russian, and she didn't speak Greek. They communicated through conversational sign language. He was deaf and mute, as was her father. A perfect fit! Zander would watch her hands as she pretended to explain why the security men were asking questions. Zander responded by bellowing out nonsensical sounds. More often than not, the combination of humming and mouthing simple words brought comments of "cnaboymhbln," or "idiot," but the official always moved on to the next group of passengers, and that was all that really mattered.

A thousand eight hundred forty-three miles of gazing out at birch trees, Norway Spruce, roaming reindeer, and the occasional curious polecat allowed Wynona to maintain a state of calm equilibrium. She was a scientist, an activist, and an animal lover. Ten miles from now, who could say which personality would get credit? She knew only that "international terrorist" was about to be added to her résumé.

The Ob River, running through the outskirts of Novosibirsk, had long been Siberia's lifeline for transportation of goods, electrical power, and drinking water. A thousand grim and shabby cities dotted the landscape downstream all the way to the Kara Sea. Wynona fondly remembered, decades earlier, living in a small apartment along the Ob with several molecular chemists. The work environment at the Akademgorodok Center for Science complex was thrilling. Whether in science or gymnastics, the Russian way was always to bring together the brightest talents and tailor them for greatness, from childhood on. Abnormally intelligent college students like Wynona were often recruited with money, housing, and promises of travel visas for the entire family. To resist was worse than pointless, since the added risk included trumped-up criminal charges of subversion or plotting against the good of the state.

She jabbed her seatmate and whispered into his ear.

"Hey, hubby."

Brian Zander clearly could never quite get used to the oddity of the woman he was paired with. So brilliant, so dangerous. He opened his eyes and looked at his diver's watch. They were getting close to the new target.

Wynona slipped on a cheap pair of headphones and tuned an old Walkman to Voice of Russia. She bobbed her head up and down as if music were playing, though she was listening for warning signs. At some point, authorities would surely start figuring out what had happened at the campground. No one left alive had seen her face, but how long would the military stick with the "angry Chechens" theory? She needed only another hour.

Every Siberian knew that Novosibirsk sat at the hub of a series of shortwave relay communications set up early in the Cold War. The invention of cell phones had done little for people in the sticks. Most couldn't afford one, and those who could had to spend hours tramping around on every hawthorn-thicketed knoll, trying to find a signal. Most days, the ham radio chatter on Voice of Russia consisted only of local news and gossip, recipe tips, the location of hot fishing spots, and weather forecasts. It was technically unregulated, but to live in Novosibirsk and truly believe in freedom of speech was not just foolish but downright dangerous. Everything was monitored by the wolf ears and heavy hand of Big Brother. Still, much as with all-access cable channels in the States, any topic was fair game if it didn't offend anyone with clout. Wynona listened to a local politician haranguing anyone bored enough to stay tuned. She had hoped to hear the soothing sounds of two older women chatting in Chukchi about too much rain causing rot on their beets, but instead found long gaps of dead air. She spun the frequency dial back and forth with her thumb. Still quiet.

"Get up and follow me," Wynona said casually to her muscular sidekick. "Something's not right."

She rose, backpack in one gloved hand and a large stainless-steel double-insulated thermos bottle shrink-wrapped in blue, in the other. They moved quickly through the cabin and forward through four cars, toward the conductor's booth.

A few feet outside the engineer's tiny window, three armed guards were flipping cards onto a wooden crate, playing *durak*. Their heavy coats, gloves, and hats lay piled up on another table. The leather straps of shoulder holsters were cinched tight over their T-shirts.

Strangers who failed to stop at the "Halt – Employees Only" sign taped to the heavy sliding door weren't all that unusual to the security men. Wynona had seen it happen every day.

Plump moms with plump kids often stuck their head into the car to ask if they could meet the train conductor and maybe get a picture or two. For most, traveling on the Trans-Siberian Railway was a big event, something to remember for a lifetime.

Only one of the card-playing guards glanced up from his all-hearts trump hand as Wynona snapped the latch open. His eyes didn't stay on her long. They instead followed the trajectory of what looked like a small fire extinguisher, tumbling up the aisle in their direction. As it rolled forward and clanked to a stop against the flimsy metal bulkhead the nearest soldier frowned, as if his brain were racing through thousands of hours of boot camp, military training, and field experience to identify the canister.

The explosion blew bits of window glass and human flesh out to the deep, weed-filled ditches at the edge of the tracks. Wynona could hear many voices screaming from the rear of the train, but from the locomotive ahead came only the sounds of electronic equipment melting and fusing in the fire. As expected, the train's emergency stop procedures kicked in. The whine of a brake was followed by a jerky lurch, over and over, until the train parked itself in the middle of an empty stretch of countryside. Frightened passengers poured out the narrow exit doorways dragging suitcases, boxes of fruit, grandmothers in wheelchairs, and neon laptops down the steps to the gravel. Shouting guards moved hurriedly against the stream of people. Wynona and Zander shuffled into the pack, moving away, blending into the confusion.

* * *

Five miles away, from inside his high-tech mobile command center, General Anton Anchov's team knew that something was wrong, before the first radio transmission of trouble came across.

"Sir," a private began in crisp Russian, "the train has stopped. Fifty-five-point-zero-one degrees north, eighty-three degrees east. Redirecting Predator drone. We should have a visual from that camera in less than one minute."

"I need two special-ops units heading in that direction," General Anchov screamed. "Reiterate the no-kill order. Have a regular army unit seal off the area!"

Vasilyev shifted his weight back and forth nervously as a TV monitor aired footage from the unmanned aircraft moving beyond the outskirts of Novosibirsk.

So, the rest of the military team wouldn't fully understand the next conversation, General Anchov switched the conversation to English. "Very good, baby brother. It appears information you provide me about the two American terrorists is accurate indeed. We now both become famous, yes?" He smiled broadly at Big Vasil. "Perhaps these animal lovers are a bit smarter than I gave them credit for, but nonetheless, we will catch them in the coming hour. The noose tightens."

"I hope so," Vasil replied. "The intel cost me a fortune."

While still on a jet bound for Russia, Vasil had put the word out to every crime syndicate in Asia that he was offering a $288,000 gold brick as a reward for information about two animal rights activists who had apparently slipped into their beloved country. A town cop from Irkutsk, who protected the local mob boss's sports gambling racket, overhearing a couple of thugs talking about the bounty, had headed straight back to the police station to play out a hunch. To avoid sharing the reward, he had snatched the entire evidence bag from the theft investigation locker labeled *Performing Seals.* At home, he reviewed surveillance videotape taken from the performing arts aquarium parking lot. To ID the pair, he called an airport security buddy and pretended he was in command of the seal abduction case. His friend remembered seeing the refrigerator truck and pulled the customs clearance paperwork. The cop, mining for the reward, went to the airport and saw that the exit signature was illegible, but he had a local lab run the forms for fingerprints. A positive match came back to Wynona Wanagi, a military-grade scientist wanted for treason. The cop took a big risk and put out a service memo for police to be on the lookout for Wanagi, saying that she was wanted in connection with a simple vandalism. He made sure to note that she was not dangerous and that police were not to arrest her—she was just wanted for questioning. All very low key. An eager-to-please train security agent who was angling for a real job at the Irkutsk police department tipped the cop, who passed the information on to Big Vasil.

"General! Drone cameras are picking up the heat signature of two humans, moving away from the stalled train. Everyone else is staying in a pack, near a highway crossing a half mile out. Video is coming in now!"

Everyone squinted at the screen.

"That's got to be them!" Big Vasil crowed in the semidarkness of the command trailer. "American terrorist and traitorous Russian spy girlfriend! I see headline now. Anchov brothers save the world!"

* * *

Since the moment he joined ALB, Brian Zander had never questioned a single order, never challenged an idea, and certainly never doubted that the cell would succeed in its ever-evolving mission. This moment was not the right time for reconsideration. Mercenary, rather than activist, was the role he cherished most. He simply liked the idea of being a criminal. He had grown up a misfit—a slacker hanging out with piercers and tattoo freaks and cutters and huffers. The animal rights movement had changed that. Dr. Dell introduced him to intellectuals, freethinkers—real activists who had not only a vision but also the courage to do what was necessary. Zander had soon found himself ready to lay down his life for the entire group: Dr. Dell, Wynona, Chivas, and Oz. No degree of risk or personal danger mattered, if he was helping the cause. And getting paid. At this second, however, Zander had a realization that made him question his purpose. He was willing to kill or be killed in defense of his comrades in terror, but was he truly willing to kill and die to save the life of an animal? As he ran, Zander started breaking it down in his mind. *Die so an animal can live.* Would he jump in front of a bus to save the life of a gray squirrel? Not a chance. How about stepping in front of a napalm torch to save a colony of Burmese ferret badgers? Nope. Drown in a trawler's net to free a sea turtle or a dolphin? No and no. As he trudged ahead, out of breath, a few feet behind Wynona, he suddenly realized that his personal survival was more important to him than anything else.

"Hey, Spirit," he gasped, his lungs and legs burning. "We're not going to outrun this . . . You have a plan?"

Wynona had her eye on a farmhouse and barn, barely visible through a windbreak of ash trees. She broke to her left, planted her foot, grabbed the top of a barbed-wire fence, and leaped over to the other side. Blood welled out of a puncture near her ring finger and ran under her nails.

Zander stopped, pulled the rusty wires apart, and crawled through. Exhausted, he stayed on his knee for what was surely less than a minute. By the time he looked up, he was alone. He hoped Wynona had found some transportation on the farm. With the lactic acid burn gone from his legs now, Zander sprinted out of the clearing to head across the chicken-spotted lawn. He hadn't traveled more than a few strides before a distinctive string of dust puffs ran across in front of him, close enough to throw soil onto his boots. The stream of bullets was clearly aimed in front of him, not directly at him. He slowed to a jog, then a walk, then stood still, while putting his hands on his head and dropping to his knees. He didn't speak Russian, but he figured it was a universal sign of surrender.

He felt his cheekbone break as the first rifle butt hit. It didn't drop him, and he decided that if his captors were going to beat him even though he was surrendering, he would see how much pain he could give back. If they wanted to kill him, they would already have done so. Pretending to be gravely injured, Zander knelt low, folding and twisting his torso so that all his weight was on one leg. Then he sprang, kicking his heel into the throat of a young and very surprised soldier. The sickening gasp of a man dying from a crushed trachea caused two others to take their eyes off the target. Snatching a heavy two-way radio from a belt in the scrum, Zander caught one of them openmouthed, knocking teeth onto the ground.

A wooden baton bounced off the back of his head. It didn't hurt, but Zander felt his eyelids close. A rush of colored lights filled his mind and scrambled his thoughts. In that final second of consciousness, he thought he was in Wisconsin, setting a thousand dairy cows free.

Within moments, General Anton Anchov's convoy of H-3 Hummers—ironically, built in Shreveport, Louisiana—raised a cloud of dust that drifted over the farmhouse. He put on his hat and stepped out into the early afternoon sun. Big Vasil followed him, making sure to stand always slightly behind his brother, in deference to his powerful position.

"Wake him up!" Anton shouted. A medic rifled through his bag for a stick of ammonia-soaked cotton, broke it, and waved it under Zander's nose.

"American!" the general said in perfect English, "You are on Russian soil with the intent of doing this country harm. Do you understand the seriousness of this charge?"

Zander nodded his head. One eye had swollen shut.

"We will make sure you get proper medical attention." Then, to the soldiers around him (even though few knew more than a dozen words of English), he said, "This man might be our enemy, but we must make sure we treat his injuries, which must have occurred in the train explosion. He might be trying to kill Russians, but we will let our courts sort out his fate. Let's make sure we follow the rules set up by the Geneva Convention. Take good care of him."

Big Vasil could feel the presence of the six-person film crew rolling two cameras behind his ear. A microphone hung from a ten-foot boom over the heads of the downed American terrorist and the general. A new high-definition camera zoomed slowly from a wide shot of the general grabbing Zanders' shoulder, tight into his face as he spoke. The Anchov brothers had thought that the footage, soon to be provided to Channel One Russian Worldwide for its nightly newscast in Moscow, would be a nice documentation of their heroic deed. Vasil loved that his sibling was making sure NATO and the Red Cross couldn't complain, while creating a future propaganda tool against the United States government. The State Department would be sweating as a worldwide audience learned that the very first of the terrorists to be captured had gotten his ideas while in an American university. Vasil found it all the funnier that his brother had made general, not by his compassion for suspects, but because he was willing to line up a thousand Slovakian dissidents, shoot them in the head, and bury them with a bulldozer. Making him a sympathetic humanist, worried about his fellow man, for the nightly news was hilariously ironic.

"And, comrades, I need your attention. I want you all to thank my youngest sibling, Vasilyev, for identifying this American's location and for exposing an enemy plan to poison our drinking water. Vasilyev is a loyal hero and a credit to Mother Russia."

The soldiers clapped while the general gave Big Vasil a bear hug. Both smiled broadly for the camera and did a slow pageant wave. The video crew gave thumbs-up and started breaking down their equipment, hurrying so they could get back to the studio. They still had to edit, get approval from censors, then uplink the precut package to TV stations before the nightly newscast. CNN Asia would get it an hour, after all the Russian-owned networks had a chance to air it. Big Vasil leaned down and snapped a picture of Brian Zander with his cell phone. With the propaganda portion of the day over, General Anchov gave the real orders.

"Take him to the Minusinsk Prison for interrogation. Use any means to find out all he knows. Then kill him."

Chapter 36

The hallway outside the Medford hospital operating room was dingy. The extra-wide space was normally left empty so that crash carts and dying patients on gurneys could be whisked through without interruption. Colton found a folding chair crammed into a closet and plunked it next to an electrical outlet. Various staff members repeatedly tried to usher him into the visitors' waiting room, but he wasn't budging.

They finally stopped herding him after eliciting this crisp warning: "Tax money paid for this space. I pay taxes. Go away."

As a friend, Cole wanted to make sure that if Nolan died or needed more surgery or his sister showed up sobbing, he would be right here. Just being here on the scene made him feel slightly less guilty about having to devote 98 percent of his attention to work. Still, all the concern in the world wasn't going to heal Nolan's wounds any faster. A powerfully crafted news script, however, might save millions of lives. That it could also kill just as many—as Dr. Dell had envisioned—was also in the forefront of his mind. Choosing the right words, with the proper inflection, while adding relevant video images, was second nature to Colton Wiley. He buried the enormous pressure of needing to get this piece perfect and typed furiously on his laptop. Realistically, he would be able to make only one or two prepackaged stories look slick. The rest of the live news segment was going to be improvised. He had a plan. He just hadn't shared it with KZPR-TV yet. He dialed up Chuck Reynolds.

"Wiley! You can't ignore fifteen calls from your boss. I don't care how big a hotshot you think you are!" Reynolds screamed loud enough to make him pull the phone away from his ear. "The FBI has put out an all-points bulletin on you. Agents showed up with a search warrant an hour ago. They're crawling all over the station looking for videotape of some Russian mobster!

Judges *never* sign warrants for TV stations. It's political suicide. I don't even know what they're talking about! They are going to arrest your ass the second they find you. I've got two top attorneys on standby. It's not safe for me even to ask where you're at!"

"Chuck, I need you to trust me more than you've ever trusted anyone in your life. There's no time to go over this twice. I need you to go to the news desk, put me on speakerphone, then punch up our station's building intercom. Call in every single reporter, producer, anchor, editor, photog, graphics geek, and intern to help us get a story on the air ASAP. This makes my Russian mob exposé look like a Charles Kuralt *On the Road* feature story. Do it now, Chuck. I'm not kidding. I'll call you back on the main line in ten seconds." Cole hung up.

***

The hair rose on the back of the assistant news director's neck as a crazy warmth surged through his body. He stepped out of his small office and started frantically weaving his way around desks and stacks of files, through the newsroom and toward the massive assignment desk, yelling instructions along the way.

"Get off the phone. Pay attention. Mandatory meeting. Now! Drop everything you thought was worth doing and listen up!"

Reporters hung up their phones and stopped typing, grabbed notebooks, and gathered in a bunch near the front of the newsroom.

Chuck Reynolds turned the volume down on the scanners and pushed buttons in rapid fire, clearing every call in progress or on hold. Two FBI agents, digging through metal file drawers, paused to see what was going on. When the main line rang, Chuck hit the speaker image stuck on the phone with Scotch tape, and propped the receiver of another line on top of a phone book so that Cole's voice retransmitted to the in-house speaker system and to field crews through FaceTime connections.

"Cole, you're on," Reynolds's voice boomed through the five floors of the station.

The first sound that came across was some background noise of the hospital paging system, asking for a Dr. So-and-so to report to the surgery floor. Cole waited for that to stop but didn't mess around getting to the point.

"For several weeks, I've been investigating an animal rights terrorist organization that calls itself the Animal Liberation Brigade, or the N-5-G project. Its stated mission is to kill every human on earth. I know that sounds impossible, but a former Evergreen State scientist by the name of Dr. Hadar O'Dell formulated an evolving DNA manipulator that, if placed in our drinking water supplies, will do exactly that. Less than an hour ago, ALB successfully blew a hole in the bottom of Crater Lake, draining the water into an underground system of tunnels and aquifers. Those aquifers run beneath the water supplies of at least eight states. Homeland Security and the military have sealed off the area around the lake. I could not see if the toxin made its way into the system, but we can't take any chances. We have to warn everyone on the West Coast about the plot. There is strong evidence that other terror cells are active and ready to launch similar operations. The Russians are tracking members there, and I'm sure a lone wolf is prepared to spring up somewhere in the Midwest or on the East Coast. I'm shipping the station a bunch of video files, sound bites, partially edited stories, and mug shots via the server. I put our KZPR-TV logo as a shadow graphic over the top of all of it so, when the other stations and networks start ripping off our video in the name of 'fair use,' viewers will at least know where it *really* came from. You all go through the material for some background; then start doing what you do best. Hit every source over the head—hard. I'm in Medford with Jess. The helicopter has a microwave transmitter, so we'll use that as a stand-in for a live truck. I'll get in front of a camera and simply take our viewers through what I know. I'm going to pace it backwards. Start with the crazy shit that happened at Crater Lake, and the drinking water threat. When I need a piece of tape to roll, I'll call for it. The director in the control room will have to wing it. It might be a bit rough technically, but within the hour, KZPR will be the most watched TV station in the world. Let's not blow it. A lot of lives depend on how we do this."

Chuck Reynolds didn't ask a single question before flying into a crisis news mode— usually reserved for jetliner crash-landings on rush-hour traffic-filled freeways.

"Anchors. Get on set! If you don't have your paint on, you have five minutes! Strike that—three! Assignment desk. Grab a marker and start writing on that board. I want a crew to head to Seattle's main water supply. It's the Cedar Creek Watershed, right? By the time we get there I bet Homeland Security will have armed guards. That will be a good sign we're on the right track locally. Call Becky what's-her-name. She used to prosecute these animal rights nuts. I want her fat butt in that side-set chair doing analysis. Holy shit! What's *that*?"

Everyone turned to a series of monitors relaying images from the feed room. Cole was sending in his raw video of a missile racing behind their helicopter, then exploding into the top of a truck.

Chuck shook his head in disbelief and kept shouting. "Holy Christ! Send a reporter back down to Evergreen State College. Get a crew to the biggest beverage warehouse in town. You better call first and tell them to start hiring some serious security. Let's assume, even as polite as Seattleites are, that riots for bottled water will at least be as bad as WTO. Call SPD. See if they're ready for that. I also want five teams—reporter, photog, and editor—heading to the feed room. Each of them can start researching names, places, organizations—any tiny bit of information Cole sends here. I want it flushed out. And, you, FBI. Get the hell out of my way!"

* * *

A nurse approached Cole as he reentered the hospital from his impromptu rooftop TV studio.

"Surgeons are done fixing up your friend's arm and ankle. His lung might need more attention tomorrow, but we've got him stabilized. He was hitting on one of the student nurses when I left the room, so I wouldn't worry too much about him."

Cole was so relieved, he wanted to kiss her. "You . . . are . . . awesome," he said while sprinting back out through the heavy fire door.

When he got back outside to the roof, Jess was fiddling with a long cable but had already set up two bright lights, a camera on a tripod, and a TV monitor on a milk crate.

"You're the man, Jess. Highest paid set-construction monkey in the biz! Our live shot tuned in?"

"Yep. Throw that IFB in your ear and grab that mike on the ground. The station is ready to roll. They want an audio test, and if you've got a lead line for the anchors to read as soon as they break into programming, they'd be appreciative.

"Mike check . . . one . . . two . . . check. Producer? Director? Anyone? If you're listening, keep the lead simple. How about 'An international plot to poison drinking water from Washington State to Siberia is unfolding as we speak. *Blah, blah, blah.* Investigative reporter in Medford. *Blah, blah, blah.*' How's that?" Cole inquired, staring into his own reflection from the lens positioned four feet in front of him. Reynolds's voice suddenly chirped into his earpiece.

"Cole. You've got blood all over your shirt. You all right?"

Cole looked down.

307

"I'm fine. That is distracting. No time to change. I'll address it."

Cole took two deep breaths and waited patiently as he heard KZPR roll its "Breaking News" logo and music in the middle of *Judge Judy*. The anchors read Cole's suggested lead line, then improvised another line or two to set up a piece of video. Cole could hear the whir of the helicopter, the fizz of a missile, shouting, swearing, then an ear-shattering explosion. He looked down to his small television monitor, thinking, *That should probably get everyone's attention.*

The anchors continued: "Those images were taken from a camera mounted on a KZPR-TV helicopter chasing a group of animal rights terrorists near Crater Lake, Oregon, a few hours ago. Our investigative reporter, Colton Wiley, was not only aboard but, we are told, was the target of the missile attack."

In his earpiece, Cole heard a quiet cue from the control room: "You're hot, Cole. Take it away."

"Folks," Cole began, "I'm not going to sugarcoat this. This is real blood, from a real battle. An animal rights terror cell, led by a professor from Evergreen State College in Olympia, not only tried to kill me today but has plans to kill every single one of *you*. They are fervently dedicated to the idea that animals should roam the earth in a human-free environment. In an effort to make their utopia come true, they developed a DNA manipulator—a toxin, for lack of a better term—that destroys our cells. Before I say another word, I need you all to understand this: our drinking water may not be safe right now. It's possible that a toxic substance could make its way into every lake, river, ocean, aquifer, and well on the West Coast—and, in coming weeks, into many freshwater sources around the world. You don't have to believe me; you can hear it from the leader of the Animal Liberation Brigade himself, Dr. Hadar O'Dell. With a gun pointed at my head, I sat down and interviewed him earlier today. Roll."

The interview was mesmerizing. As it progressed Cole understood every network, cable channel, and local station was pirating KZPR's signal off the satellite and began broadcasting it. The AP wire reporter, sitting in a cramped office along Eastlake Drive, would likely soon started typing a synopsis of Cole's broadcast, then hit "Send" every minute or so. Within ten minutes, the KZPR-TV logo would be on fifty channels. Web-site traffic could reach critical melt-down levels. The station's Webmasters would have to scramble to reroute servers.

Cole had a few minutes to prep his next segment while Dr. Dell talked. As he jotted down notes and slipped large segments of video together, the fat, jowly face of Big Vasil jumped onto his cell phone screen. He slid the arrow at the bottom of the phone and tapped "Speaker." There was no hello, just business.

"Mr. Wiley, I am sending you two pictures. I want you to know I have captured an American who has a driver's license in his pocket that reads Brian Zander. Put that on TV. I want to be famous there and here. Greedy, yes, but I know no other way. The other woman you seek is named Wynona Wanagi. She was brilliant Russian scientist long time ago. We haven't caught her yet, but assure you that my brother, the general, will. No hard feelings, Mr. Wiley. You kept up your end of promise. I am glad I do not have to kill you. Good-bye."

The phone binged twice. Cole looked briefly at the pictures and forwarded them to the graphics department with a message to put them in the hopper. It was an important reminder that he needed to get all the faces of the animal rights army on TV as soon as he went back live on the air. He scribbled furiously, revamping the segment. As the interview with Dr. Dell wrapped up, Jess pointed at Cole that he was back on live TV.

"I wish what you just heard were the ravings of a lunatic, but based on my findings, his colleagues are more than capable of carrying out the plan. I'll take you through all the reasons in a moment, but everyone who can hear my voice, I want you to look up at your TV right now. These are the faces of the Animal Liberation Brigade. Several of them are no longer a threat, but others are free and, most assuredly, plotting to do great harm to our water supplies.

First up, the leader. You saw his interview. The group called him H_2O, or Dr. Dell. He's dead. I know this because I shot him a few hours ago as he was attempting to drop a truckload of his bioengineered poison into Crater Lake."

Cole hoped Montana wasn't watching. She'd be worried, but he continued without a hitch.

"Next, look at this image of an olive-skinned twenty-something named Canyon. This is a fuzzy freeze-frame of him I took at the very end of my interview with Dr. O'Dell. Canyon's combat skills are impressive, so he may have a military background. He was last seen in the Crater Lake, Oregon, area escaping on foot. If you know his real name or see him, call nine-one-one immediately. He is extremely dangerous. Do not approach him."

The graphics department was rolling with the punches the best they could, but didn't know who was supposed to be next, so they put a split screen of JPEG files labeled "Brian Zander" and "Wynona."

"Thanks, Mark. You're doing a great job with the graphics. Keep it up," Cole coolly complimented the station's behind-the-scenes people while watching the tiny monitor.

"I'm glad to report that the Russians have caught the guy on the left of your screen. His name is Brian Zander. A man fitting his description frequented a house in Keizer, Oregon. My law enforcement sources tell me Zander is a criminal suspect in a number of animal rights actions up and down the West Coast."

The audience was growing. Life in homes, businesses, and government offices ground to a halt as the nation stopped to stare at the television. Super Bowl ratings were going to have nothing on this news segment.

"I have it on good authority that Zander was captured a short while ago in Siberia by General Anton Anchov, with the help of his brother, Vasil. I have been working on a report about Big Vasil's criminal activities as a major organized-crime boss in the Seattle area, but he recently fled the United States to avoid an FBI probe. The bigger issue is the woman on the right. Wynona Wanagi remains a threat and free somewhere in Russia, near a city called Novosibirsk. You'll notice she has a few dramatic features: tree branch tattoos across her face, and large almond eyes. Wanagi and Zander were in the area of Lake Baikal, near the Mongolian border, when thirty shamanist nature worshipers died of a mysterious illness in the past week. I can't say if the two are connected, but if they were testing their poison or DNA manipulator—whatever you want to call it—it appears to have worked, at least on a small scale."

* * *

The governors' offices in both Washington State and Oregon were screaming into the phone simultaneously at the assistant head of the Department of Homeland Security.

"We will mobilize the National Guard, but it's a sad day when we have to tune into a fucking local TV broadcast to find out how our citizens are all going to die. And the news has to come from that prick Colton Wiley? We hate him. He's the only reporter we know that doesn't ever play by the rules. Fuck. Is he right? He *is*? Jesus!"

Cole would have been proud had he been listening in on the conversation.

* * *

The control room didn't know what to do next, so they put Cole back on the air live. Seeing his own image out of the corner of his eye, he immediately dug into his file folder and pulled out the surveillance photo earlier provided by Nolan.

"And this is former Army Sergeant Oscar "Oz" McKinsey." Cole held it right up to the camera lens. "This photo shows him with Dr. Dell less than a week ago in Oregon. McKinsey's résumé includes military training in explosives."

The connection between an explosives expert with a bad temper, and the leader of the terror group seemed obvious, but playing by journalistic rules was often inconvenient. Cole wanted to make the leap that Oscar had made the bomb that emptied Crater Lake, but it was only a guess. Maybe the guy was just a consultant. Maybe he and the nutty professor were buddies from the Army. He decided to move on to the most important piece of intel he had.

"Before I send our team coverage back to Seattle, where our reporters are fanned out in every direction gathering important details to help you survive this threat . . ."

Cole knew that when Chuck heard that sly warning, he would jump up in the production booth and started dialing up other reporters on their earpieces, telling them to get in front of their cameras.

Jess slowly zoomed the lens tight onto Cole's face.

"I have to ask for your help," Cole said to the camera. "Despite all my connections, I have failed to identify one member who wants to carry out the N-5-G project. Right now, he is the most dangerous person on the planet. I apologize up front for the broad character description I'm about to give, but I think we can all agree, this is no time to worry about political correctness. Be on the lookout for a Hispanic male with a likeness of this police artist's rendition. Late twenties. Probably alone. Likely driving a truck with a refrigerator-freezer unit. You heard the interview with Dr. Dell that we played a few moments ago. From that, I got the feeling this person was sent to pollute a major water supply somewhere east of the Rockies. Let's use some common sense, folks. The last thing police and Homeland Security need is to be wasting time chasing down thousands of false leads. Before you accuse the guy, who delivers flowers to your workplace, think about it first. Let's head back to the studio now for more exclusive coverage of this fast-developing international terror plot."

Cole saw the screen go to another reporter, standing in front of a hydroelectric dam with military guards scrambling in the background. He dropped the microphone onto the rooftop and headed back indoors. Despite all that was going on, he felt the immediate need to make sure Nolan was okay. He knew his pal's survival might be the only feel good moment of his day.

Chapter 37

Reggie Von Holt loved harvest time in western Nebraska. The hum of his grain elevator's enormous dryers never stopped for anything when the combines were wheeling in their gold. Ogallala's air hung thick with light bits of husk and corn dust swirling skyward, before gravity pulled the grit back onto rusty pickup truck hoods and cracked windshields lining the downtown streets. Somewhere else—say, in Europe or Japan—they would be breaking out the surgical masks and calling it a pollution crisis, but to folks around here it was just the sweet smell of fall. The Ogallala elevator was paying six dollars and fifty-five cents a bushel for corn, twelve dollars for soybeans. Below the faded black plastic numbers on the marquee, in letters twice as big, were the words "Congrats Lady Indians Volleyball! State Champions." Fox News quietly played on an old analog TV in the corner of the elevator's waiting room. A Dubble Bubble vending machine offered either a handful of Boston Baked Beans, or mint-flavored Chicklets for a quarter. Black coffee sat, thick as tar, in a glass pot next to the cash register. Nobody minded the faint whiff of hog manure tracked in on nearly everyone's boot insteps.

"Hey, Reggie! You got the clicker back there? We can't hear worth a damn!"

Reggie knew everyone within a fifty-mile radius by name. He had cut checks to farmers from North Platte to Bridgeport. He helped his brother coach the high school football team, his dad was the Methodist preacher, and his wife was the only licensed real estate agent in the county.

"Yeah, yeah, hold on!" Reggie bellowed from behind a pair of swinging saloon doors that separated his tidy office from the main counter. "It ran out of batteries yesterday. Give me a second to change 'em out." When he emerged, he was surprised by the size of the group pressed close to the television. The only time that ever happened was on some Saturdays, when the Cornhuskers were playing football. Reggie pointed at the TV and pumped up the volume on Shepard Smith.

"What's going on, boys? Must be big if you're watching the news in the middle of the day."

Everybody started talking at once. Reggie let it go until things quieted down some; then he pointed at Mike Travis, who had at least done two years at community college.

"Mike, I'm an old man. Make it simple for me."

"Yes sir, Mr. Von Holt. Some TV station out on the left coast is reporting that animal rights activists are trying to poison underground water supplies by blowing holes in the ground and dumping in stuff that kills everyone. This reporter says to be on the lookout for some José driving a refrigerated truck."

Reggie rubbed the stubble on his double chin. "Well, that's certainly a worthy piece of news," he said. "You boys won't do much good sitting in here, though. Keep your eyes open while you're on the road. Look for anything weird on side roads and around the streams and ponds. Now, best get back to those fields—set that ass back down on a combine seat where it b'longs."

The group dispersed, and Reggie turned off the TV. He didn't like bad news. He tried to go back to penciling in farm credits and debits on his ledger, but he couldn't shake a nagging feeling about a stranger he'd seen eating breakfast downtown at his regular coffee shop for the past few days.

* * *

315

At the same moment, less than a mile away, Chivas Riviera was turning off his television, too. Suddenly, his cabin hideaway at A. J.'s Sun and Fun seemed like the most dangerous place on the planet. Chivas grabbed an emergency cell phone off the kitchen table, threw his green military duffel over his shoulder, and headed out the cabin door. The cedar steps leading to the lawn felt mushy under the weight of his boots. Walking around the side of the truck, he unplugged the orange electrical cord snaking its way up to the generator. It was quiet for only a moment as he jumped in on the passenger side, slid across the bench seat, and started the engine with a loud, cranky rumble.

He looked in every direction to see if anyone was staring at him, but nobody seemed to be paying attention. Chivas texted both Wynona and Dr. Dell, as specified by backup plan B.

"Still planned 2 go swimming at 6. Hot today. Should we go now instead?"

H_2O had shared with Chi his dreams of pummeling the Midwest with its worst disaster ever. The Ogallala Aquifer represented a certain purity which, once ruined, would force every American to think 'nothing is safe'.

Chivas stared at the phone for the longest three minutes of his life, then slammed it shut and threw it on the floor. He pulled a moss-green hand grenade from the glove box and tucked it partially under his leg so it wouldn't roll around while he drove.

"Plan C it is," Chivas said under his breath while pulling the lever on his COBRAY 9-millimeter submachine gun with a Titan muzzle brake screwed onto the barrel. Chivas was disappointed that he might not get to pollute as much of the water in eight or nine Midwestern states as he had hoped, but killing most of the people in Omaha, Kansas City, and St. Louis would have to do. With a little luck on the dilution rate of the Sugar, it would also be nice to wipe out New Orleans once and for all. To punch a hole in the Ogallala Aquifer, Oz's bomb

316

would have to work perfectly, but there was no more time for perfection. Taking down the dam was a no-brainer, however, even without the explosives. Chivas could see the destruction play out like a dream.

As the dam caved in under its own weight, the entire volume of Lake McConaughy would envelop town after town. Two million acre-feet of water, slowly gaining speed, would wipe out day-care centers, suburban McMansions, churches, burger joints. The city of North Platte would have less than forty-five minutes to evacuate. Clueless kids and old people in nursing homes would drown first. Housewives and guys sitting in their insurance sales offices would get brained by door frames as they got sucked and swirled outside. Chivas enjoyed envisioning how the bodies would get stuck beneath the torrent, wedged into nooks and under porches. SUVs carrying daddies home to save their families would get picked up by fast, shallow waves streaming over a road, then dumped and sunk in deeper waters. Thinking about all the bloated bodies floating downstream and clogging up the Platte River gave Chivas a happy feeling inside. The immediate death of a bunch of small-town hicks caught in Big Mac's wash was icing on the cake. N5G's potion, making its way down the Platte to the Missouri, to the Mississippi, to the Gulf of Mexico was truly the perfect silent killing machine. The Mississippi River Basin alone provided drinking water to eighteen million people. More than fifty cities sucked the life-sustaining fluid out of its channel, through giant metal pipes and into treatment plants. Membranes filtered out the muck, algae, and cow manure. Then they added chlorine, fluoride, bromide, and iron to purify it, telling everyone it was crystal clean. *Right. Real pure.* The chloride treatments often reacted with organic materials in the river and made cancer-causing trihalomethanes and haloacetic acids. And no city even cared to test the level of radiation and arsenic, for fear the public would find out the results. And they didn't even *have* a test for the Sugar's toxic formula.

Dr. Dell had created some colorful maps that showed the team the kill rate of plan C: a surface flow release in the Midwest. The reds and purples spread like seven-year locusts on a Kansas plain, month after month. A quarter million dead the first hour. A half million the first day. Two million by the end of the next day. The Department of Homeland Security created its response on the false assumption that if drinking water in a city was targeted by terrorists, it was a local attack. They would spend precious time trying to identify known chemical agents and waste even more time securing water supply access. But all the guns on the planet couldn't stop the Sugar. When they tested the water treatment plant and water towers, everything would appear fine. With each passing second, a higher and higher concentration of household pipes would be filling with the DNA manipulator. The toxin's molecules would bind with the metal, get caught in the porous PVC plastics, fill school water fountain filters, get pumped into the Budweiser bottling plant. Infrastructures dug deep into the ground to pull water to the masses would be ruined forever. The cost to fix them would be beyond imagination. The best the federal government could do was say, "Don't drink any water." The animal instincts of human nature would kick in about three seconds later. The rule of law would evaporate, but N5G's killing formula would not. Chivas hoped that was already beginning to happen on the West Coast and in Russia, but he had to push that joyous thought out of his head for the moment so he could focus on his assignment. Dr. Dell had put a lot of trust and faith in him, and he wasn't going to let his beloved mentor down. Even if those other missions were somehow compromised, Chivas didn't want to forget their oft-recited motto: "Kill as many as possible; then escape to do it again."

Careful to use his blinker, he eased the truck and its frozen cargo out of the Sun and Fun parking lot. Traffic out to the Kingsley Dam was light. It was cool and overcast, with dark clouds building. Before nightfall, the first snow of the year was a definite possibility.

As he approached the south end of Big Mac, Chivas could see an enormous tower. It had stood watch for decades over the six-pointed jackstones, perfectly fitted together like a set of Lincoln Logs to build the dam. Today, Chivas's first move would be to relieve the sentry of his duties. He pulled the truck into a maintenance vehicle stall between the tower and a morning glory-shaped emergency spillway. He sat and waited. The importance of his surveillance and observation earlier in the week became clear to him at once when a round-faced county utility employee opened the tower door and stepped onto the thin metal platform at the top of the 185-foot stairway.

"Hey! You gotta put that truck somewhere else, buddy! Hey! I know you can hear me! No fishin' here, no stoppin', no *nothin'*! Can't you see the sign?"

Chivas didn't move—just stared straight ahead, listening to the clank of the stairs under the man's feet. *Ting. Ting. Ting. Ting. Shuffle. Shuffle. Ting. Ting. Ting. Ting.*

When his prey reached the asphalt, Chivas looked to his left. The man was struggling to zip his coat up over an ample belly. The wind chill along the lake made it even more difficult because his hands were shaking with cold. Seeing that the poor bastard didn't have so much as a baton to defend himself with, Chivas threw open his door and moved fast. Oh, well, if his family lived upstream, maybe they would at least live long enough to learn that Daddy died like a hero, trying to protect America from some bad men.

The fight really couldn't be called that. One punch to the thorax stopped the watchman's heart and collapsed the lungs. A utility worker isn't usually much of a match for a Brazilian jiu-jitsu coral belt holder. In a flash, the look of shock turned into a blank, dead stare. The back of the man's skull hit the pavement so hard, it bounced his torso up nearly to a seated position before slamming down again. Chivas wished the guy weren't so fat. Dragging the body back to the truck seemed like a lot of work, so instead, he rolled the warm corpse down the sloping embankment and into the chilly water. It made a loud splash.

Chivas sprinted up the stairs to the open tower operating center. The gauges and buttons were easy to understand, with tiny engraved signs labeling every item. An instruction manual sat on a cheap particleboard shelf between a shriveled potted plant and a lava lamp. Chivas thumbed through it. *Inflow design flood . . . maximum flood specs*. He stopped on the one that read "Emergency Shutdown of Overflow."

It was common knowledge that earthen dams couldn't tolerate overtopping, so that was the first thing that needed to happen. Water was heavy—the more of it that pounded up against the dam, the easier it would be for Oz's homemade bomb sitting inside Chi's truck to blow the dam to bits.

Chivas turned off the automatic controls so the system couldn't correct itself. Then he flipped three switches to shut down the alarms and eliminate outside monitoring. Ironic that the operation had recently been hardwired to eliminate the possibility of a cyberattack from foreign mercenaries and military snoops working for entities such as the Chinese Red Army. The public laughed out loud at the ridiculous waste of tax money. They called in to talk radio shows and railed about the impossibility that anyone, anywhere in the world, should find a strategic advantage to screwing with the drinking water in Boondock, Nebraska. Chivas loved that Americans were so damn trusting. A bunch of government workers presented a facade of security at airports, inside train tunnels, and at natural gas pipeline epicenters, but nobody was

320

really expecting anything to happen. It was just a way for more workers to get a paycheck. And if anything did happen, there wasn't much any of them could do to stop it. Chivas thought of the Israelis—they would never allow a terrorist of any kind anywhere near a place like the Kingsley Dam. Their crack security teams would have stopped the truck and searched it miles away, scanning and cross-matching the license plate with any suspicious person or organization before it ever got close. If anyone cared at all about the dam, it would have been covered with several hundred cameras while sets of trained eyes watched for the slightest hint of pattern deviation. Real security profiled who needed to be profiled. Mossad agents checked out travelers, businesspeople, and rabbis alike. A guy like Chivas would be caught in a matter of moments, thrown in handcuffs, interrogated, found guilty, and hanged faster than you could say "Adolph Eichmann." Not in Nebraska. Folks wouldn't want to accuse a Latino like Chivas of anything, lest someone think they might be racist.

In the middle of the control panel was a thick, black dial that told the pump how much water to release. Chivas gave it a hard turn to the left to stop the turbines. That should test the fault tolerance. The dam's massive irrigation regulators and gated chutes went from gushing 420,000 gallons a minute to nothing.

A thick parka with a name patch that read "Mr. Gibbs Supervisor," hung on a peg near the door. Chivas grabbed the government-issued jacket and wore it back out to the truck.

A few cars whizzed by on the highway, but nobody noticed a thing. In this moment, Chivas envied the other team leaders, who had muscle to help them. He turned the truck around and opened the back doors.

Man, I wish I could sink this thing! he said to himself, staring at the bomb tucked along the side. But to effectively utilize the blast, the explosion had to be on the dry side of the dam.

He punched a series of codes into the side of Oz's bunker buster and listened. A high-pitched whine from the tail told him he had got the alphanumeric sequence right.

Chivas pulled on long rubber surgical gloves and donned a mask and goggles. He could have cared less if the substance broke through the barriers and killed him, but Dr. Dell's orders were to try to live. Then, with the mentality of a dock worker, he dug into the task at hand: throwing long cylinders of ice over the edge of the dam and into the lake. Each rock-solid sculpture bounced end over end down the slope and *kar-plooshed* into Big Mac. It was like uploading bales of hay. *Pick it, lift it, throw it. Pick it, lift it, throw it.* Chivas felt sweat beginning to soak through his clothes, but he pushed on. He had no idea when a cop might come around the corner and ask what he was doing. His back and arm muscles burned. *Pick it, lift it, throw it.* He could see the eighty-pound chunks of poison forming a little flotilla, bobbing up and down in the light waves. The ice was clear except at the center.

A dark gray, elongated balloon ran down the middle, encased in the ice. Dr. Dell had inserted toxin into a secondary membrane, much like a time-release medication. Long after the poison had melted and dispersed, the balloon would still be floating along, bobbing and waiting to spring a leak. Maybe a bird would pick it open, or the sun's hot rays would weaken it, or a sharp twig along the outer curve of a riverbank would snag the latex. Chivas loved the design. Drinking water wouldn't be safe for ages. He loved even more that he was one of three people on earth who knew how to spot the tainted water. Given the radio silence from the other ALB teams, it occurred to him that perhaps he was *the* only one left alive with such knowledge. He pushed the thoughts of profit and greed out of his mind, knowing the value of such a monopoly. *Pick it, lift it, throw it.*

When the flash-bang went off inside the ice truck, Chivas immediately bent over and began vomiting on his boots. The concussion of the explosion rattled his eardrums, telling his brain that he had vertigo. He stumbled toward the light, barely visible through the thick smoke. Glowing red dots pierced the fog, hovering like frenzied hornets around his heart.

"Get down! Get down!" a voice bellowed. "I'd rather shoot you, so get the fuck down now or you will be eliminated!"

Chivas was desperately trying to remember how to set off Oz's bomb manually. He tore off his rubberized slaughter house apron, gloves, mask, and goggles. It was just one big button? No, he had to push a couple of numbers, then a button? Dr Wanagi had the only fob, or did he have one on his neck too? His mind moved slowly, as if he were in a deep sleep, dreaming. He was so discombobulated as he moved toward the bomb, he fell onto his side. As soon as he hit the freezing stainless-steel floor, two beefy pairs of arms yanked him outside onto the concrete dam parking lot, chipping his front tooth and sending blood pouring from his lips. A knee pressed into his neck. His wrists seared with pain as someone crimped a zip tie, stacking his arms in a cross behind his back. His feet were similarly bound. There was plenty of shouting, but Chivas distinctively heard, "Samsonite the son of a bitch!" a moment before being picked up like a piece of luggage and tossed hard into the back of a Humvee with a sticker on the side that read "MP."

Chivas watched a stream of red cascade down the fake leather and into the seatbelt crevice. A pretty color, it reminded him of the molten lava he had seen, as a boy, running down rock crevices in the Cerro Hudson volcano in southern Chile.

As he started to regain his bearings, Chivas began to wonder how easy it might be for a military tech to disarm Oz's bunker-busting bomb. He doubted that it was possible. It would be a glorious moment if it went off right now.

The door in front of him opened. Chivas tilted his head, so it rested on his chin, and stared into the face of a muscular black man with a bald head and a short beard. How odd to see someone black in Nebraska! He tried to think whether he had seen anyone of color since he arrived here, except for the Honduran maids who cleaned the cabins.

"My name is Brigadier General Terrell Ryan of the Nebraska National Guard. Son, you are in my custody. You don't have the right to a lawyer. You don't get to call anyone. I'm not much for chitchat, so I'll get to the point. That ice of yours is pretty nasty stuff. I ordered four of my men to fish it out, and as soon as they touched the capsules, the men started convulsing. Those boys were dead in less than a minute. I witnessed mustard gas do that in Iraq. I saw a friend of mine die inside a silo after the nitrogen dioxide sucked all the air out of his lungs. I saw a murdering rapist in the army ingest a cyanide pill to get out of doing life in prison. Compared to what I just saw, all those deaths were as peaceful as dying in your sleep. And I see you're smiling now. Thank you. You've told me all I need to know."

***

General Ryan closed the car door and placed his cap back on his head, then strode with purpose straight to the ice truck, ignoring a dozen concerned men asking him to stop. He jumped into the front seat and shifted the manual transmission to center, then left and up toward the dash, starting slowly so that the men in the back end who were studying the newfound bomb could jump. He rolled down the driver's window.

"Close this place down. I want every road blocked. Every dock, boat ramp, and old man fishing for carp off a shoreline rock needs to be cleared. Use air support, armed troops, and tanks if need be. Martial law is in effect. Tell the governor I'll call her in seven minutes. And for God's sake, get a biohazard team here—yesterday, soldier! Someone who knows what the hell to do with that ice."

Ryan ran an internal stopwatch in his head. Men scrambled and yelled as he drove the truck up the highway that passed over the dam. Once he had cleared the structure, he parked about a half mile beyond what he figured was the danger zone. A red clay lot, used in the summer for ATV trailers, looked like the perfect spot. He set the brake, made sure the cooling generator was running, then slammed the doors and triple-timed it on foot back to the dam tower.

When Ryan arrived, his aide handed him a secure satellite phone.

"Governor, this is beyond red alert, ma'am. My teams are securing the area, but I could use all the hydro engineering help you can offer. Until we know what we're dealing with, we should not resume flow through this dam. There is some sort of chemical or deadly poison in Lake Mac. At some point, I understand the water volume entering the lake will force water right over the top of the spillway. That is something we need to avoid at all costs. What I don't know is whether we have three hours, three days, or three weeks to figure out how to stop that . . . Yes, ma'am, I do believe this is part of that animal terror plot they are talking about on the West Coast."

While the governor barked orders to people on her end, Ryan did the same on his. "Get that suspect to Offutt Air Force Base. Full quarantine. Nobody talks to him until I say so!"

He watched as a large, black panel van belonging to the bomb squad of Keith County's Emergency Response Team sped past.

"And for God's sake, stop those knuckleheads. We're not losing any more men on my watch! Yes, Governor, you do have my full attention. Yes ma'am. We will talk again in fifteen."

Chapter 38

Nolan could hear a series of clinking sounds on the table next to his hospital bed, but the dreamy drift from the painkillers slowed his ability to identify them right away. He pried his eyes open and peered through the metal side railing.

"*Cole*? I figured you'd be on TV nonstop."

"Hey, buddy. I've been on the air all over the world for hours. Just taking a short break while our other reporters cover fun stuff like the looting of local grocery stores. It's pretty chaotic, but not *War of the Worlds* crazy just yet."

"I got lots of guns and ammo. Stick close to me," Nolan replied half seriously.

"Yeah. You look like quite the warrior in your flowered nightgown."

"These are *not* flowers. They're, uh . . . Jesus!" Nolan stared down at the cotton gown across his chest. "They *are* flowers . . . How the manly have fallen!"

Cole patted him gently on the knee. "Relaxing time is up, Bro. Doc says you need to get up and move around. Some circulation or blood clot thing. That sounds pretty sucky to me, so I decided to provide you with an incentive. You get over to that chair, and I'll hand you cold beer I have in my pocket."

Nolan wrapped the thin gown around him and hopped a few feet over to a chair in the corner. He couldn't move fast or far while leashed to a plastic tube and a rolling IV drip bag. The 60 stitches didn't help, either. Cole handed him a plastic cup and poured a foamy drink. He threw back the bottom remnants of the can, while he allowed Nolan to sip in silence.

Nolan closed his eyes and laid his head back. "Man, that is good! I was so damn thirsty in that helicopter, I would've drunk out of a cow track. Now I know what Del Gue felt like in *Jeremiah Johnson*."

Grimacing, he repositioned himself in the chair.

"Thanks for digging me out, man."

"Anytime, pal. I gotta get back to the roof and cut a few more stories. Flip on any channel and you'll get up to speed on what's happening. Your head clear enough to call back the Lewis County Medical Examiner? He's freaking out. Called, like, fifteen times."

A nurse stuck her head in the room, smelled the alcohol, and scowled with a disbelieving look on her face. Nolan hugged his glass tight to his chest, shooing her away, then slid back into bed and speed-dialed "Lewis ME" on his cell phone.

"Nolan Burke from the U.S. Forest Service. You got cause of death on those two girls from the cabin arson?"

"Kind of. They didn't die in the fire. They were poisoned, for lack of a better term—with what, I don't know. The symptoms mirror those I see in chemical asphyxiation cases. Cyanogen chloride, for example, prevents cells from using oxygen. People unlucky enough to get a whiff go into anaerobic shock, start gasping for air, have seizures, and die. These girls didn't have anything like that in their lungs, but every molecule in their bodies had a foreign object attached to the oxygen void in their sialic acid piping. Sometimes, pathogens like cholera or malaria get a foothold there, but this looks almost synthetic. I'm going to send a sample of tissue over to the University of Washington tomorrow. Weird deal for sure. I'm pretty sure it regenerated, split, and multiplied postmortem."

"Don't do that," Nolan warned. "I suspected for a while these girls were guinea pigs for this animal-terror outfit. Now I know for sure. I need to call my friend at Homeland. No doubt, some armed soldiers will be there shortly. Give them everything you got. The military will fly it to the Centers for Disease Control, in Atlanta, for analysis. Nice work, Doc. Maybe you've given us a jump start on figuring out what to do next."

"You got it, the ME replied. "And, Nolan, sorry to say, the femur from the incinerator was from that missing college girl, Anna Dipler. You want me to tell the family?"

"I guess you should. Do it right away. If they're watching TV, there's no telling when her face will show up as a casualty of this demented plot. Might have already?"

The television hanging from the far wall was on but muted. Nolan turned it up. Cole, who had just been in his room a few moments ago, filled the screen.

"The entire Crater Lake area has been sealed off by the military, including airspace, so I can only read to you this statement just released from the Department of Homeland Security. I can't personally verify the accuracy, so please take it with a grain of salt."

Cole felt the color of light from the TV monitor change, telling him he was off the screen and a graphics department written statement replaced his image. He read the statement.

"Earlier today, at approximately o-nine-hundred hours, a U.S.-based animal rights organization attempted to place an unknown substance into a major West Coast underground water supply. We believe that the attempt failed; however, we are asking the public in the states of California, Oregon, Washington, Nevada, New Mexico, Utah, Colorado, and Idaho to avoid consuming tap water."

Viewers at home saw Cole on their screens once again. He stopped and looked into the camera lens, pausing to let the information sink in. He knew that the next words out of his mouth were going to cause an all-out panic but withholding information might do even more harm.

"In the past few minutes, I have also confirmed that members of the same terrorist group have poisoned a major water supply in the Midwest. As I say these words, troops are securing a large area surrounding the Kingsley Dam in Ogallala, Nebraska. My sources tell me everyone downstream is at risk. Troops with heavy earthmoving equipment are digging furiously to create a relief canal near the dam before the poisonous contents breach into the North Platte River. If they don't stop it, it pollutes the Missouri, then the Mississippi and right on down to the Gulf."

* * *

General Anchov watched the news on a CNN satellite feed from a spacious custom-designed suite aboard his private Boeing 747. A large, green stainless-steel thermos sat securely clamped near the cabin door in place of the fire extinguisher. He sipped ice-cold orange-flavored vodka from a tumbler, then raised it in a toast.

"Like in the race to outer space, our motherland will be victorious. As the world cowers in fear, wondering where their next drop of clean drinking water will come from, I will provide. Isn't that right, my dear?"

Wynona Wanagi raised her glass in front of her eyes, staring at Anchov's distorted image through the array of clear ice cubes.

"Only to the highest bidder, my General. Considering that three billion people in this world live on less than two and a half dollars a day, we both get what we want. You get rich. I secure my place in history as the most prolific mass murderer who ever lived."

"And don't forget, you're helping the animals, my darling."

"I have not forgotten. We have a Sinaitic covenant, binding us with each other and with God's command. The animals will flourish, and man will have to start over just as the Overseer wanted all along. Pray with me.

General Anchov bowed his head in feigned reverence while Wynona chanted a verse from Genesis: *"Then the LORD saw that the wickedness of man was great in the land, and that every intent of the thoughts of his heart was only evil continually. And the LORD was sorry that He had made man in the land, and He was grieved in His heart."*

"What would you like me to do with your friend Mr. Zander?"

"I figured you'd already killed him. Whatever. He knows nothing. Only I have the knowledge of how to mass-produce our special potion."

"And is there an antidote?" General Anchov probed, hoping for an affirmative answer. He didn't want to have to trust the crazy woman sitting across from him. An antidote would be even more profitable than access to fresh water.

"Dr. Dell is brilliant . . . was brilliant," Wynona said. "A warrior of true passion and conviction. He didn't want any one person to bear the burden of knowing all. I am the creator of destruction and hold its key inside my mind. Canyon carries the formula's antidote that would be humankind's salvation, but he will never share it—only use it to make sure The Animal Liberation Brigade survives to keep killing. Chivas is all seeing, harboring the secret of premonition . . . of detection."

General Anchov didn't like the idea that two people on the planet could potentially interfere with his monopoly, but he set those emotions aside. It was time to celebrate. He finally had a tool of war more powerful than his nuclear arsenal.

Chapter 39

The KZPR-TV newsroom looked like the front entrance of Macy's the day after Thanksgiving. Panicked staffers ran hither and thither, scripts instead of coupons in hand, as the scanners tucked behind the assignment desk gave out shrill whistles interspersed with the squawking voices of panicked law enforcement officers.

"Can I *please* get a crew out to Woodinville?" Chuck Reynolds yelled. "Hordes of people are looting every winemaker in the valley, and I don't think the private security guards are going to hold off that crowd outside the brewery much longer!"

A managing editor threw up his hands. "We're out of reporters, but . . . hold on. Yes, I can divert that photog that was heading to Starbucks headquarters. I already have the written press release that they're immediately closing all their stores."

"Talk about causing a meltdown in public confidence," Chuck retorted. "Do it. Divert. We'll pull the file of Starbucks and let the anchors read the statement."

The basement of the TV station was a place where only the weekly janitor and the furnace repairman had ever ventured, but it was Chuck's favorite hideout. It required a special key just to get onto the floor, then another key to open the various rooms. An old spin-dial phone, from back when no one knew it was even possible to drop a call, was the only thing in the storage room not covered in dust. Over the years, Chuck had crafted a secondary office here, out of displaced anchor sets and morning show props. From here, he would call his daughter on her birthday—the only day she would take his call. It was where he could grab a nap on a lime green shag-looped couch when a new overnight crew needed babysitting during May ratings.

Reaching inside the back of a plastic palm tree used for a Survivor Island promotion, Reynolds pulled out a bottle of Captain Morgan spiced rum. He drew a sip and held it in his mouth, gently sucking air over the top of his tongue and between his teeth as if judging a Petrus Pomerol merlot. He typed a short electronic note to his star reporter:

"Rumor: US Army Intelligence PSYOPS or Para-psychological team testing water samples using mentally ill and brain-damaged patients at Rainier School for the Disabled. Perfect subjects. Can't complain. Can't talk. If they die, nobody is the wiser. Any way to confirm?"

He poured a shot into a Dixie cup and waited.

"That is seriously awful," came the response from Cole. *"Makes sense. Hurts to say, but have Rachelle track it down. After the 11 news, Jess and I are flying to check on some very important new leads."*

"Fill me in when you can," Reynolds wrote.

* * *

After 8 hours on the hospital rooftop, airing live reports, it had recently dawned on Cole that he needed to check his tip line. The message center was set up to hold only an hour's worth of voice mail. It didn't normally need to be longer than that, because rarely did anyone leave him a message. Cole's sources liked to speak in person. He spent a few moments rapid-firing through the tips, deleting both the *"thank you for saving our lives"* drivel and the *"you're a sensationalizing yellow journalist trying to kill everyone on earth with your panicked monologue*" drivel while jotting down the few interesting leads on his notebook. The most intriguing one was from a woman who claimed she had found an odd stash of survival gear in the woods along Highway 97, north of Chiloquin, Oregon, while looking for American matsutake mushrooms a few months back. Cole hit "Replay" three times to get all the intricacies and specific location.

"*. . . It was almost impossible to see. Someone dug into the side of the hill to make a tiny cave, then mimicked the natural foliage to recreate a door of mesh. I stumbled into it when I slipped on a slimy rock. I went to brace myself for a fall into the hill, and it gave way like a sheet. I sneaked a peek inside the camouflaged tarp. There was a generator. Dried foods. A Quadrunner. Barrels of something. I suddenly realized I might be trespassing on private land, so I skedaddled out of there . . .*"

The caller went on to say she didn't think the supplies were that strange—that only a foolish, trusting person would leave them there unguarded, given that plenty of folks would steal from the pile if they discovered it. When she saw the destruction at Crater Lake and noticed the proximity, she thought of Cole's request for information on anything unusual. But it was her final words that sent Cole's internal news radar on high alert.

"*I thought it a little odd that the barrels were marked with black Sharpie: 'For H_2O'— not just labeled 'H_2O.' I mean, why write 'for'? Anyway, I hope that helps. Bye.*"

Chapter 40

Canyon had a tough time finding Kirk, Oregon, on the map. In fact, it didn't really exist except in historical lore. The only reason there was even a tiny black dot in its general location was because two generations of mapmakers had been too lazy to remove it. Tucked between the Sun Pass State Forest and the Winema National Forest, the town had no residents, no post office, and only one dilapidated, long-abandoned, raccoon-infested structure. It was once a busy stop on the Southern Pacific Railroad tracks; now its only visitors were a few dozen ghost hunters a year.

Canyon snapped open the valve and drew a long drink from his camelback. He loved the choice of this location as his hidden encampment. Dr. Dell had figured that once Crater Lake and the surrounding wells were contaminated in so gloriously public a fashion, everyone within hundreds of miles would flee in terror, assuming that the concentration of toxin was most dangerous nearest its release point. As Canyon stood on the termite-riddled remnants of the railroad passenger platform, he could see that the flight had happened fifty years ago and had nothing to do with ALB. Had the implosion of the lake bottom and the release of the ice capsules gone as planned, it really wouldn't have mattered where anyone drew their water supply from—every drop in ten western states would have been lethal. Since he was still unsure whether the operation had fully succeeded, it was more important than ever to hunker down, lie low, and plot new targets. The salvation of the world's animals had never been based on a single event. The blueprints were a rolling avalanche of terror—sparks of action to plant seeds of death and doubt that would last longer than humans could survive without water. The Animal Liberation Brigade wanted to sap the will to live from billions of people. The utopia that followed could restart Earth's clock, allowing species near populated areas to do as those in the Galapagos Islands had done when left free to evolve and adapt without human intervention. Like the magnificent frigate bird's unique downhill run before takeoff, ALB had finally picked up enough speed for a successful flight.

Canyon hadn't been to the campsite in more than three months. Looking across a rushing ford in the Williamson River, there was no way to spot the edge of the camouflage netting he had set up to protect supplies from the elements and prying eyes. Of course, the chances of never being seen by anyone while at the campsite were virtually zero. A non-news-watching clueless hiker, camper, canoeist, birdwatcher, deer hunter, poacher, or angler might walk by at any moment. The key to staying undetected was to blend into the environment—be so normal that the human mind wouldn't even register the sight of him. Canyon kept his supplies under a tarp but made a small, circular fire pit in the open with cantaloupe-size rocks. He put a wood-and-canvas folding chair near the flames. An arrangement of marshmallows, graham crackers, and Hershey bars sat on a flat section of log nearby, along with a carefully sharpened stick. Canyon pulled his ball cap low over his face, threw the hood on his sweatshirt up, and became part of the landscape.

* * *

"That's the guy—the one that sliced and diced Nolan," Cole murmured softly to Jess Teeter while they both lay partially sunk into the boggy forest floor. Both wore waterproof rain jackets and pants in fall-color camouflage. Streaks of green, black, and brown greasepaint adorned their faces.

"Man, I don't know, Cole. I can't remember. I was pretty focused on that hot missile trying to part my butt cheeks."

"Trust me, it's him," Cole said, focusing his binoculars down the ridge and through the trees.

"Okay. We should call in the big boys to pick him up."

"Not yet. We've been lying here on alert all night and half the day. What's another hour or two? I want to see if someone else shows up to join him. Plus, a clip of video wouldn't hurt a thing, would it?"

"Earth to Cole!" Jess hissed. "That guy might have the key to ending life on this planet! It's the most serious threat since the Chicxulub meteor wiped out *T. rex* and his pals. We have to call in the military!"

"I have a feeling it'll be worth waiting. You know I've got fantastic instincts. Besides, if they catch him, you think he's going to talk? Not a chance in hell."

Cole scooted to the right a few feet, put his handheld Sony camera on top of some soggy leaves, and gently pressed the silver and black record button. He used a digital zoom to push into the Canyon's face. It was grainy at this distance, but it was a safety shot. Cole planned on getting much closer before the sun set. There were no bugs to speak of, so the afternoon was pleasant enough. Jess would never complain about the conditions unless the whole place was ablaze. Compared to hiding in a mangrove swamp in the Mekong Delta, this was like lying on a fluffy bed at a five-star resort.

* * *

As the day wore into evening, Canyon was surprised how often he thought about taking a drink of water. He felt constantly dehydrated. His throat got so dry, it was hard to swallow his own saliva. *Psychosomatic. Relax, man. You have plenty of water*, he said to himself over and over. As the shadows lengthened Canyon enjoyed the loud *hoo-hoo-hoo* of the great horned owls conversing in the trees above his small campfire. The noise signaled not only that they had accepted him as a part of their environment for the night, but also that there were no other strangers within earshot.

He couldn't help but wonder if the stream flowing along the bank near his boots had been contaminated with the Sugar yet. He would have to flee before he knew for certain whether Dr. Dell had managed to inject the ice beneath Crater Lake. It was best to assume success. Considering that his risk of being affected by the Sugar was zero, Canyon decided it was time to sip from the ice-cold river. He wanted to feel like a god. Indestructible. All-powerful. The masses would someday be in awe of his wizardry. An opiatelike rush filled his veins with warmth as he dipped the mouth of a one-liter plastic water bottle into the river.

* * *

Cole took thirty seconds to flip a switch that would normally take a fraction of a second. Although the rumbling noise of the stream would surely drown out the sound of the night-scope assembly, this was a critical moment when absolutely no risk was acceptable. He felt the raised ridges on the button at the left front end of the camera, slightly worn from the repeated sliding of his finger over the years. He kept his eye pressed tight to the viewfinder so the glowing green backlight would not escape. The stark color contrasts would give him temporary blindness unless he shut down the left side of his brain. He wanted to focus all his energy onto a single point in the distance. He watched as Canyon drew water into a container, set it on a large, flat rock jutting out over the stream, and then disappeared. Cole waited patiently and kept recording. After a long minute, Canyon reappeared from inside the hill, looking like the Pied Piper of Hamelin. Cole was firing through the dictionary in his head, trying to place a name on the device. All he could come up with were the words "flute," "fife," and "piccolo." The shiny chrome wand had a series of valves along one side, and the guy cradled it like a father carrying his newborn infant. Stranger still, he was talking softly to himself.

***

"How beautiful you are. I know what Alexander Graham Bell felt like the moment before he rang Mr. Watson. I know what Captain Nemo felt like the first time he raced beneath the sea at fifty knots. I know the exact thoughts that were running through the Wright brothers' minds as they took flight."

He raised the short pipe skyward, pointing it east, then straight toward the ground.

"From knowledge springs wisdom and goodness. Let the waters be pure. Our Mother Earth wakes refreshed."

Canyon instinctively paused and studied the dark woods around him before punching a series of security keys. A mesmerizing glow of indigo light leaped from the end of the wand. He focused the beam on the bottle of water, scanning it slowly from top to bottom and back.

It was gorgeous. *So pure.* Only he could drink, while the rest of the world suffered. He opened the lid and poured the slightly warm liquid down his throat, letting it spill out the top of his mouth and down his cheeks. He laughed aloud while gurgling the sweetest drink he had ever tasted. Dr. Dell had truly given him the greatest gift since Prometheus handed fire to mankind. While working side by side all those years, dreaming of a way to kill humans while preventing any harm to animals, they had been so focused on creating the deadly elixir, they rarely thought through the end result. ALB members had to have a way to survive. The survival of God's small creatures on the weaker side of the evolution chain depended on the fear their little group could continue to spark in humans. As soon as they held the Sugar, they must also think of a novel and

338

undetectable way to kill it. A secret like that of the Ark. A solution that humans would seek until the end of time.

The human body had the innate ability to kill viruses that invaded. The NK, or natural killer, cells hid in every person's body by the billions, just waiting to attack the foreigners. When cells in stress called for help the NK cells released small cytoplasmic granules of proteins perforins and granzymes. The beauty of the Sugar was that it not only invaded quickly but also replicated far faster than the NK cells could do battle by reprogramming the cells to commit suicide. The research found that viruses couldn't be killed until they attached to a healthy human cell, so once a human ingested the Sugar there was no way to reverse the process. But Dr. Dell had engineered a way to kill the deadly DNA manipulator *outside* the body—a therapy so specific that it was almost impossible for anyone without direct knowledge of the Sugar's formula to discover it. It involved *shaking* the cell-morphing toxin to death with an extremely high sound frequency. Canyon had spent years testing every frequency between 60 and 302 gigs. Microwaves, TSA body scanners, satellite communications, and Predator drone weapons tracking systems all used extremely-high frequency, or EHF, but none of those killed the Sugar. Then, late one night just a month before their plans were set, Dr. Dell found that a laser with a frequency of 301.24 gigahertz shattered their DNA manipulator like an opera singer breaking a wineglass. After figuring out how to reduce the heat emitted from the wave while keeping the frequency steady, they crafted the most important tool in the history of the world.

Canyon finished quenching his thirst, gave a guttural shout to the stars, and vanished into the side of the hill for a long-overdue night's sleep.

339

* * *

Cole recorded every detail of what looked to him like a medieval madman celebrating the death of the king by drinking his blood.

After the target disappeared from view, he put down the camera and slowly let his eyes readjust to the dark forest floor. When he looked to his left, Jess was gone. Before Cole could think about slowly working his way back up the hill to see if his helicopter pilot friend was waiting out of sight, an eruption of gunfire lit up the far riverbank. The crack of a pistol drew return fire from a machine gun.

Jumping to his feet, Cole drew his borrowed Glock and ran toward the camp. The embers of the fire pit glowed enough for him to see where he needed to end up. Dodging trees along the way, he positioned himself low along the trunk of a massive oak. It occurred to him that if he had any sense at all, he should be running in the opposite direction, but he had a gut feeling that after today, life was just as dangerous everywhere else. The orange flashes of gunfire sparking off the end of a barrel stopped. Cole held his breath and aimed around the side of the tree, ready to fire at any movement. The sound of Jess Teeter's footsteps broke the tension. Cole lowered his gun to his side and took his finger off the trigger.

"Jess? You all right?"

Jess didn't say a word as he sat down on the very rock where, fifteen minutes prior, Nolan's would-be killer had set a liter bottle of river water.

"What happened? You were like a phantom next to me for the past five hours; then suddenly you go all Rambo?"

Jess motioned for Cole to come sit next to him while giving him the "okay" sign.

"I just murdered a man. Gimme a moment."

The pair sat in silence, staring out over a rapid formed by the force of glacial melt running over a giant stone sitting just beneath the surface. Flecks of foam swirled into the slower-running eddy beside the chamber before popping and dissolving back into the mass.

"I'm not one of those veterans who, perhaps deservedly, bitch and moan and complain about posttraumatic stress. I liked Nam—loved it, actually. The best part was that I got to kill people without really getting a good look at their faces. We'd lay down heavy rounds from those big guns right into the jungle, cutting down trees and anything else that was hiding in there. One day, I was ordered to land the chopper a couple clicks away from an encampment that supposedly held some of our boys. I snuck up there with a small crew. We could see the Cong throwing rocks down some pits. It was clear they were torturing prisoners. There were only a few of them. We each picked a target and decided on a silent three that we'd kill them where they stood. I focused too much on the face of my guy. He was only about sixteen years old. On three, my team jumped up, and *pop, pop, pop*. Everyone fell dead. I froze for just a moment, wondering if God was going to judge me. That kid had enough time to pull a grenade from his belt and drop it into the hole. He just smiled as the prisoner I was supposed to rescue disintegrated into a pile of body parts. The other guys mowed him down. I said my gun jammed, but it didn't."

Cole didn't look at Jess—just nodded and added some verbal filler that seemed appropriate.

"That sucks."

Jess chuckled. "Sucks indeed. Anyway, when I saw this clown today, I knew it was a chance at redemption. I snuck up to that false tent flap and peered inside. It was pitch black. I knew the terrorist was in there. I stayed low and fired a round inside, then used the light from him firing his gun as a beacon to zero in on him. I'm not sure I feel any better, but I do know he won't be able to hurt anyone else now."

"Your secret's safe with me. I think I heard that machine-gun fire first, then the crack of a pistol," Cole said without a hint of sarcasm. "Yep, that's exactly what I heard."

"You heard what you heard. Don't go making shit up after all these years of telling the truth. You got me?" Jess pulled a strange-looking wand from the inside pocket of his jacket.

Cole nodded emphatically.

"All right, then. Let's get airborne and back to the city. I'd like to see what the hell this thing does that makes water taste so good."

Chapter 41

Brigadier General Ryan yelled out to a middle-aged accountant type who had just dared slip under the caution tape strung across the dam's main road. "You in the suit! Stop or be shot!"

Three of Ryan's heavily armed bodyguards swung their M-16 rifles straight at the man, fingers on their triggers, awaiting the next word.

Kevin Lewis, the governor's top adviser, froze, with a sudden insight into how Gary Gilmore felt at 8:06 a.m., the minute before being executed by firing squad inside a Utah prison.

"Please don't . . . ," Lewis started in a quiet voice.

"I don't take requests, so don't start your sentence with 'please,'" Ryan growled, closing the physical distance between himself and the unknown invader in fifteen rapid strides. "State your business or forever hold your peace."

"The governor sent me. She asked that I give her updates from the field. Tough to really know what's going on from the capitol."

Ryan took the man's credentials and handed them off to his men to be scanned, checked for imposture, and then entered on the contamination-area log sheet.

"You're in mortal danger here. You get that, right?"

Lewis nodded.

"All right, then." Ryan relaxed as his crew gave the thumbs-up on Lewis's identity and position. "I don't need a babysitter, but make all the calls you want. I hope you didn't just come to watch, though. You got some good news for me from all those meetings going on in Lincoln? Those politicians think differently from the rest of us, so I gave up guessing. What's the contingency plan on the table right now?"

Lewis dug into his shoulder bag and pulled out a clipboard thick with notes. "Engineers say you've got about three days before the dam breaches water—less if it warms up and we get more rain than expected. Mayors from Kansas City to New Orleans would like to start storing as much untainted water as possible. Not tomorrow. Right now! They know they might have to shut everything down. The big question is, how sure are you that that poison has been contained in Big Mac? If a drop of it escaped downriver, that extra-storage plan actually contaminates their current water supply."

"I'm not a goddamn virologist, but I wouldn't risk it," Ryan snorted. "What I do suggest is that we immediately start a plan to buy as much time as possible to stall that breach. Every hour I can keep this bad water in this particular lake is another hour someone with an IQ above a hundred and sixty-one might be able to figure out how to detect this molecule or find a way to neutralize it."

"And you've . . . got a plan?" Lewis stammered.

"The governor isn't going to like it, because I'm just playing out a hunch. People who run for office are usually reluctant to take risks—which, if you know anything about military history, usually spells disaster."

Lewis jumped in. "I'm on your side, General. Maybe we can learn from history. What's the plan?"

"I've been talking to my explosives team. They got a good look at the bomb in the cooler truck. If this knucklehead animal rights ice thrower had wanted to blow the dam, he could have done it with a lot less firepower. A good fertilizer-jet-fuel mixture would have done the trick a lot cheaper. My boys think he had other plans. The torpedo design was created to go into the water. That video we saw from Crater Lake draining into the earth was the most likely scenario for this lake, too. The Ogallala Aquifer is a far more important water source than the North Platte River. It sits right beneath our feet. But—and this is a Mount McKinley-size 'but'—if we detonate that bomb on land in just the right spot, it might make a hole big enough to store millions of gallons of extra water. Kind of like how a golf course developer uses those ponds to capture runoff from building homes. If we blow too deep, we've just done the terrorists' work for them. If we get it just right, it buys us more time, especially if we use it just as a starting point. Get fifty bulldozers in here tonight, and we can make a mighty big outlet in three weeks."

Lewis turned paler. "I'll round up every geo engineer in the world to run some calculations to see if the soil and clay east of the lake can stand the blast without caving. In the meantime, the *President of the United States* has granted the legal authority of extraordinary rendition on your terror suspect. He is no longer going to Offutt Air Force Base. That's all you really need to know. If he provides us with intel that's useful, I will relay it to you."

He handed General Ryan an embossed letter with a presidential seal.

"You've kidnapped my prisoner?" the general sputtered. "I thought you were just an aide to Nebraska's governor?"

"You don't think we trust the states to run themselves, do you, General? Get that truck bomb in your best-guess position. I'll let you know if and when you can pull the pin. Good day, and thank you for your service."

A pair of black Escalades pulled close to the perimeter, and Lewis waved a perfunctory good-bye. Just before he slipped into the passenger seat, Ryan shouted one last thought.

"Hey! Have you reached out to that reporter in Seattle? He seems to know more than the rest of us combined."

"By the time Homeland Security got to the Medford Hospital where he was broadcasting, he was gone," Lewis yelled back. "In the wind now. We're searching. Odd, huh? Makes me wonder if he's more than an independent observer. We'll be in touch, General."

Chapter 42

Long before the trio of shady federal agents, wearing ridiculous sunglasses on a rainy day, arrived at Mary Lee's cabin door, she had known they were coming, right down to the exact time and reason for their visit. She had invented a forward-search program that constantly traced worldwide communications that included her name, former and current addresses, and social security number. She figured she could find out if old boyfriends or classmates were trying to track her down. Maybe even surprise a credit card hacker who thought her account would be an easy steal. When eight text messages between the Justice Department, NSA, the Pentagon, and the field agent director in the FBI's Portland office included all her personal information, an animated red flag on Mary Lee's laptop chirped to attention and started waving. She programmed it to unfurl a banner that read "Snooping Alert."

"Sorry, guys. Not converting to Jehovah's Witnesses today," Mary Lee deadpanned through the screen. Her dogs stood on each side of her, snarling a warning that the visitors had come close enough.

"Ms. Kissinger, I'm sure you can understand that we need to speak with Colton Wiley," the lead suit said. "Is he here, or have you heard from him in the past twenty-four hours?"

Mary Lee laughed. "Don't you clowns watch TV? He's been on air nonstop with this big animal-terrorist thing."

The men's irritation didn't show. So maybe the Ray-Bans had a utilitarian function after all, she mused.

"He hasn't been live on the air since eleven last night. You and I both know his insight would be really helpful toward solving this tainted-water crisis."

Mary Lee flicked on a video monitor on the wall behind her and allowed the men to see themselves, captured on the security camera mounted just above her door.

"Get lost, guys. This feed is being broadcast to a secure location, to friends I can trust. I wasn't too keen on the message you got from your bosses. Let me see . . . This exchange was particularly enlightening: *'Need Wiley at all costs. Terror ties unknown. Permission to detain sister Mary Lee if needed.'*

"Really. *You think I'm some sort of bargaining chip?* Pathetic. You think Cole might be a member of the Animal Liberation Brigade? How else could he know all that shit about them while you drooling simians are left in the dark. No way all your special software and hordes of informants can miss such a huge, world-ending plot while a TV reporter digs up all the facts. Chasing a hero so you don't look like the villains. Classic. You'll never understand that the key to knowledge is to *listen to people.* Follow their breadcrumbs to the end of the trail. I know that's a lot of work, and being that you're a government worker, that's a foreign concept. Cole, however, being a classic private entrepreneur, is very good at that. You should consider him an asset, not an enemy. He knows you're looking for him by now for sure. Wave 'hi' to the camera! It's being fed right into the KZPR-TV servers. They might even be broadcasting it. By the way, just so this exchange is all legal, Cole said I should tell you that your voices are being recorded—two-party consent states require such a notification."

Chapter 43

The University of Washington campus buildings sprang from the banks of Lake Washington like willow reeds beside a country pond. Jess came in fast and low, just clearing the Highway 520 floating bridge before roaring above I-5 north to the Tulalip Indian reservation.

Cole could see a group of Native American men, dressed to the nines, as Jess set down the banged-up Robinson helicopter in a grassy field next to the casino. Cole jumped out and kissed Montana before warmly shaking her father's hand.

Chief Harms was in his 70's, sporting a long black and gray ponytail and an expensive, turquoise bolo tie. Cole handed him the two-foot-long laser light mechanism that Jess had pulled off the body of Canyon.

"Chief Harms. Protect this with your life," Cole said as he gazed seriously into the man's weathered face.

Chief Harms looked over the rather dainty object with some doubt.

"It does not look that important."

"We'll know soon. A University of Washington PhD will be here shortly. He's an expert in electronic speckle pattern interferometry. Christopher is his name. Nobody else sees this. Got it?"

The Chief nodded yes.

"This land, like the Cherokee nation, is sovereign ground – a separate nation within this great nation. I and my brethren will protect it. Your federal government has no jurisdiction here."

Cole smiled. "But they are sure gonna try. You sure you're up for that kind of trouble?"

"For you, for Montana, and for Mother Earth. You have my word."

349

"Thank you. I needed someone I could trust, and that's getting hard to come by. I was a hero to Homeland Security for about an hour before they started getting public heat for failing so miserably to head off this attack. Now they'd like to throw me in the slammer for a few years for making them look bad. No way they really think I'm hooked up with this crazy N-5-G hit squad, but powerful people like to get even when they can't be competent. I also got some solid intel that the U.S. military thinks this deadly toxin might be a pretty cool weapon if they could control it."

Cole slapped the old man on the arm and gave him a thumbs-up before jogging back to the helicopter, head dipped low.

Just before he boarded, he heard Chief Harms yelling a question at him. Cole turned, cupping a hand to his ear.

"Mr. Wiley? Is it really so bad that these terrorists want man to stop harming animals?"

Cole shouted back, "Maybe not, but just remember: animals can't lose a fortune playing blackjack and craps!"

Chief Harms smiled and spoke softly to himself, "Very good point."

Cole thought it quaint that Jess still scrupulously followed all the safety procedures before he took off again. Funny, considering that just yesterday they were hanging out the side door, firing flares and weapons at a truck. Ingrained habits died hard.

The KZPR helicopter did a tight nose rotation a few feet off the ground, then pitched hard straight up, causing raindrops to pound into the windshield with tremendous force. Cole shook his head at the traffic jam below, stared longingly toward Montana's condo building, and peered through the windows of the Space Needle's restaurant. Instead of the usual diners staring back at him, he saw armed military police patrolling inside. As they approached the station's rooftop helipad, Cole dialed up Chuck Reynolds one last time.

"Hey, Bossman! The First Amendment still holding up, or did the big boys with the guns make us the Homeland Security Shopping Network?"

"We're still broadcasting original content, but, *Jesus,* I've never seen so much heat. Special-ops soldiers are wandering around the editing rooms. They say it's for our own safety. The FBI has, like, fifteen people here. Our teams of lawyers are keeping them at bay for now. I think there's a jail on wheels in the parking lot with your name on it. Don't come in."

"Where's your sense of adventure?" Cole shouted above the chopper's noisy cabin clatter. "I'm coming in with Jess. I need a two-camera, wireless live operation to meet me on the roof. Those backpack transmitters'll work great. In fact, they should probably start shooting live images of me in the chopper even before I land. That should help keep the cuffs off me until I get to do my shtick. Have the anchors toss to me while I'm still in the air, coming in to land. The lead should be something like *'We've just confirmed that a wanted animal rights terrorist has been shot dead. Among his possessions was a device that appears to purify contaminated drinking water. The discovery, by KZPR's very own Colton Wiley, is so monumental, he is personally going to brief the Department of Homeland Security live—right now.'*

* * *

A collective *Holy Shit* went through the minds of the Washington, D.C., briefing room, set up as a central command for decisions on the terror plot. Ribbons and stars adorned the chests of the men and women in the room. The secretary of defense had the final say on all matters. For two days now, the noise level inside had rivaled a Who concert at Charlton Athletic, but now the nervous click of a ballpoint pen was the only sound louder than breathing.

A few questions and comments went out to the crowd as they all watched Cole descend in a helicopter toward a live camera. *"What's the legal consequence of cutting telecommunications links? Did anyone get a field confirmation that we killed a member of ALB? God. Please don't tell the public that it was the U.S. military that really funded Dr. Dell's research."* All eyes were on the giant monitors as Cole stepped out onto the station's rooftop, grabbed a wireless mike, and started his impromptu show. *"What the hell is he doing?"*

The secretary of defense yelled an order: "Get me a line to that newsroom. Now!"

* * *

This was the kind of limelight Cole had dreamed of since he sat in his bedroom closet with a soupspoon, pretending to call play-by-play at a Minnesota North Stars hockey game. He was ready to enjoy every second. Millions of viewers were pulling up a chair and stopping whatever they were doing to listen.

"Before I begin, let's pan the camera over to those guys standing over there." Cole pointed at the armed agents glaring at him. "Those men waiting for me here at KZPR-TV are patriots—soldiers following orders. Their orders are to take me into custody, throw me on a jet, and take me to an interrogation room at Quantico, Virginia. The U.S. government wants to know what I know. I understand that. You, as viewers, understand, too. My investigation into the Animal Liberation Brigade has been groundbreaking, and although I have shared most everything I know about the organization with you over the past few days, there are those in our government who believe I might know even more—that I might be so caught up in this story that I have turned against the best interests of America. To put that notion to rest, for the first time in history, you, the viewer, are going to get to see them question me. I'm up for any question. As they ask, you are going to get to hear the answers and, along the way, get the most comprehensive insight into the newsgathering secrets of investigative reporting."

Chuck Reynolds watched as Cole came down the stairs into the main newsroom with two live cameras rolling, one photog in front walking backward, the other behind.

"An FBI agent named Sid—Hey, Sid! How you doing today?—is going to conduct the interrogation right here and now. You folks in Langley and at the Pentagon can join the party, too. Sid can verify the codes and make sure whoever is asking the questions is the real deal. While they get that lined up, let me give you some of the best news I can provide. Early this morning, I used a hidden camera to record a terrorist I know only as Canyon. Roll that tape, will you, boys."

The control room hit a blue button on the board, and Cole's grainy video, shot with the night scope from the forest floor, lit up the screen.

"He is using some sort of laser to apparently purify river water near Crater Lake. I don't know if the water was contaminated with the N-5-G virus that the Animal Liberation Brigade created to kill humans, but apparently, neither did Canyon. You can see from the video, he is scanning the water with some sort of light frequency. After a heavy firefight, my partner and I obtained that laser. A moment ago, I received word from one of the world's most renowned experts in electronic frequency that the laser was designed to shatter a very specific deadly virus. Scientists promise to run further tests, but it appears that we have the first bit of hope that this nightmare will soon end. A cure, so to speak, could be possible."

The live cameras came back to Cole, sitting at a large conference table with Sid. A triangular speakerphone sat on the table in front of him.

"Go ahead, Sid. Where should we begin?"

The questioning went on for hours. Cole started from the beginning: the cabin arson fire near Mount St. Helens, the crescent-shaped images on the N5G necklaces, the explosion that nearly killed him at Oscar McKinsey's rental house. Sid got off the plot a couple of times, trying to find out more about the undercover operation of Big Vasil, but a crisp command from the phone warned him to keep to the details about the animal rights terror plot. Cole never felt so free. He always had to hold something back from his viewers—some bit of information that his gut told him was true but that he hadn't yet verified. Not today. Every suspicion he had was laid out for all to see. If nothing else, no one in the newsroom would ever again question what the hell he did with all his time.

After seven hours, the feds were satisfied. Cole, his tie long since thrown over a chair in the corner, sat silent. Chuck Reynolds ordered the camera crew to stay put. Some silent reflection on the enormity of what had just happened seemed appropriate. After a minute, the control room faded to black, then rolled a Ford truck commercial. After all, November ratings had begun.

Chapter 44

The rain finally stopped. The misery of enduring eight months of round-the-clock cold, misty fog and spit evaporated along with the realization that the next four months were destined for nearly continuous sunshine. Cole knew the cycle well and was thankful that his skin could trade its greenish winter glow for a new, healthier tone.

"Go home, Wiley." Chuck Reynolds's voice broke Cole's trance as he stared out the window. "Human resources called downstairs to the newsroom this morning and ripped me a new asshole when they saw how many comp days you've acquired."

Cole spun his swivel chair toward his boss and smirked his famous smirk. "And I totally lied, trying to stay off the radar up there. Should be fifteen or twenty more days than I turned in. I wasn't sure when the N-5-G stories would start drying up and didn't want to miss out on anything."

"No doubt you owned it. Congrats. Now, go home. Bye! Get your shit right now. Out of here. I don't want to see you for a month." Reynolds made shooing motions with his hands as if Cole were a housecat with muddy feet.

His truck badly needed washing, but that task was about one hundredth on his growing list of long-delayed errands. Cole left it and decided to walk to Montana's condo. The puke of colors on the Experience Music Project museum temporarily blinded him as he strolled past. *New sunglasses—put that on the list.* A pair of Japanese tourists, three children in tow, stopped him. Cole took their picture and smiled back at the kids. He couldn't help but notice, even after being on the international airwaves every day since November, that nobody recognized him. Autographs were apparently for entertainers, never news people. At least, the concierge didn't ask for identification before allowing Cole through the secure door to Montana's loft.

355

"I hear you're taking a vacation," Montana cooed as soon as he stepped onto her travertine entryway floor.

"Chuck called?"

"He cares about you in his own odd way. I've already pulled the Daddy's-little-girl card and nabbed the casino's private jet. We're heading to Maui. I hope that's okay?"

Cole pulled Montana close and kissed her softly.

"Anywhere as long as you're by my side. The past eight months have been brutal. I've aged in dog years. That's not to say a streak or two of gray on the temples hurts a guy's TV career, but I'm not going to miss hanging out of helicopters and running away from fiery explosions."

"Who says you're any safer with me? I haven't had sex since forever. I plan to wear you out."

"That's my kind of danger," Cole laughed, scooping her up for another, longer kiss.

Within the hour, the Gulfstream G200 lifted off from Boeing Field. Cole could feel the tension fall away with the ascending aircraft. Montana poured him a scotch and draped her legs over his lap from the adjacent leather seat. He enjoyed the quiet—normally not his strong suit. Since he broke the story about the terror plot, the world had fallen apart and restored itself back to a new normal. The United Nations updated Resolution 687, placing the Sugar on its list of weapons of mass destruction, right between Sarin and VX nerve agents. Rumors continued that the Russians were selling their version of the DNA manipulator to warlords in Africa and the Middle East. Every cholera outbreak brought a new wave of panic, and companies like REI were selling consumer versions of Canyon's laser purifier under the names "Shatterproof" and "Pure

One." The Food and Drug Administration created an entire division dedicated to enforcing its strict rules on bottling distributors, ice makers, and municipal water suppliers.

Cole's phone binged with a message from Mary Lee, marked "Urgent." He ignored it.

"By the time we hit that sandy beach I hope I can entice you into forgetting about the news," Montana whispered into his ear. "I bought a new string bikini."

"That will definitely do the trick," Cole said. "I promise. No phone. No computer. No watching CNN or reading the *San Francisco Chronicle.* I really do need a break. In fact, I've been thinking, I'm not sure I can go back and do it any longer."

"*It?* You mean investigative reporting? Come on, Cole. It's who you are."

"I know but chasing down some crooked contractor who didn't finish a kitchen remodel just isn't going to have the same thrill. The bar is set too high."

"It matters to the poor old lady who might get her money back," Montana replied with a perspective befitting Socrates.

"That it does, my Cherokee princess. That it does." Cole nodded sagely.

As he looked down over the vast Pacific Ocean below, he couldn't help but think, *Water, water everywhere. Nor any drop to drink.* The hidden depths teemed with life: marlin and blue whales and tiny seahorses dancing on thermal undercurrents. The creatures thrived in an environment that would kill Cole in the time it took him to suck in one breath.

Epilogue

Such a beautiful sky.

By lying on the concrete table in the middle of the day room and looking straight up, Chivas Riviera could see just the barest slit of azure. The silhouette of a bird—a raptor—soared through his narrow glimpse of the outside world.

Terra Haute, Indiana? Florence, Colorado? Both places had red-tailed hawks, and both had supermax prisons.

Wherever he was, conventional windows had not figured in the architect's plan.

"Your hour of free time is up. Back to the cell." He had heard the same words, every day at exactly the same time, for eight months.

Two guards moved close and once again linked his wrist and ankle restraints. Chivas shuffled as slowly as he could—the inside of his five-by-seven-foot living space was nothing to hurry home to. He stopped and stood with his face just inches from the thick steel door, so close he could smell the lubricant. A series of echoey clicks and buzzes preceded its opening, then two more shuffles, and another door loomed in his face. It would stay closed until the one behind them shut. The security box was a tight fit for three, but rules were rules.

Out of the corner of his eye, Chivas could see other guards inside the Plexiglas control room booth, watching monitors and doing paperwork. He turned to stare into the room.

A barrel-chested man in a razor-creased gray uniform pressed a button.

After a momentary delay, a tiny intercom speaker chirped, "Eyes forward."

Chivas whispered under his breath in Spanish, and the guard to his left leaned in.

"He speaks!" the guard chided. "Since last fall, every interrogator in the U.S. military has been in here to question you and got zip. I'd love a promotion. I'm all ears."

Chivas switched to English. "Don't drink that water," pointing with his eyes at the drinking fountain inside the control booth.

Both his handlers broke out in laughter.

"Haven't you heard?" said the one who spoke earlier. "You and your animal-hugging cult didn't get the job done. Water's safe now."

The other guard reached past Chivas and punched the intercom button.

"Hey, guys! He says don't drink that water!"

The collective laughter was loud enough that Chivas could hear it through the security window. A young guard inside stopped laughing and mockingly mouthed, *You mean this water?* while pointing to the sparkling-clean fountain by the fax machine.

Chivas stared blankly as the guard played the clown for his colleagues, lapping the fountain's stream like a dog and letting some of the liquid flow down his face and neck and across his starched collar. He finished the childish comedy routine by rubbing his stomach in theatrical fashion and mouthing *Yum!* right up against the Plexiglas, inches from Chivas's face.

Chivas shrugged. "Okay, boss. Just trying to help."

The guard had not yet noticed that the capillaries in his eyes were starting to burst and pool blood. Chivas fought back a grin. The next fifty-six seconds were going to be a lot of fun.

#

www.ingramcontent.com/pod-product-compliance
Lightning Source LLC
Chambersburg PA
CBHW032136190626
46814CB00005BA/1712